Book One

THE GATEWAY TRILOGY

NIGHT GATE

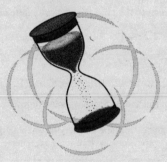

ISOBELLE CARMODY

A YEARLING BOOK

Published by Yearling, an imprint of Random House Children's Books
a division of Random House, Inc., New York

Originally published in Australia as *Billy Thunder and the Night Gate* by
Penguin Books Australia, Camberwell, in 2000

Visit us on the Web! www.randomhouse.com/kids

Educators and librarians, for a variety of teaching tools, visit us at
www.randomhouse.com/teachers

ISBN-13: 978-0-375-83017-4
ISBN-10: 0-375-83017-0

Reprinted by arrangement with Random House Books for Young Readers

Printed in the United States of America

May 2006

10 9 8 7 6 5 4 3 2 1

*This book is for my mother,
because all children, out of love,
try to save their mothers.*

*If human lives be,
for their very brevity, sweet,
then beast lives are sweeter still. . . .*

1

Rage Winnoway sat under the big, untidy shrub that grew beneath the window of the next-door neighbor's kitchen. Mr. Walker was curled on her lap, asleep, and Bear lay alongside her. From time to time Rage caught sight of Elle and Billy through the leaves as they romped together. The shrub was a round shape, with gaps where she could hide. Sometimes she pretended that it was a giant tree in the depths of a dark, greenish forest filled with wet, mossy smells. She imagined the whisper of raindrops falling around her, blotting out the babble of thoughts in her mind.

Today, however, she did not imagine rain. Instead, Rage felt so tense and heavy that a storm might have been gathering in the sky overhead, all boiling gray and churning purple fury.

Bear gave a snuffling sigh, lifted her misshapen head, and rested the weight of it on Rage's leg. The huge, loose mouth and pushed-in nose gave the old dog a ferociously ugly appearance, but to Rage she always looked wise and sad, as if she knew too much.

Elle pushed the branches aside and dropped a soggy

1

green tennis ball at Rage's feet. Rage reached over Bear to pat the bull terrier. "Poor wooden dog. You don't think enough about anything to be sad, do you?" That was what her mother had called the sleek tan-and-white dog when she brought her home from the pound: the wooden dog. Elle was so stiff-legged that it seemed she must be made of wood. Sometimes Rage wondered if Elle's head were made of wood, too. She was terribly brave but not very smart. Most people were afraid of her because bull terriers had been bred to fight one another in pits while men watched and made bets on the winner. Mam always said the men who trained the dogs to fight were the real beasts.

Rage threw the ball and watched Elle hurtle after it. There was nothing vicious in her nature, despite her long, sharp teeth and hoarse cough of a bark. She wasn't even the boss of the dogs. Bear was. For all Mr. Walker's yapping and nipping, Bear had only to look his way to silence him.

On summer nights Rage and her mother often sat on the back step and watched the dogs, the way other people watched television. They didn't have a television set. Mam said it was chewing gum for the eyes. She wasn't like other mothers. She was much younger than most of them and, being very small, looked even younger. Her black hair was short and spiky like a schoolboy's. She never used makeup, wore her own homemade perfume, and only dressed in black, moss green, and purplish crimson. People seeing Rage and her mam together couldn't believe they were mother and daughter. "Night and day," Mam always laughed, and told people that Rage took after her grandmother Reny, who had also been a cream-skinned blonde. The only thing Rage and Mam had in common was their amber eyes. Mam said all the Winnoways had eyes that color, even Grandmother Reny, because she had been a distant cousin to Grandfather. Not that anyone saw Mam's eyes much, since she always wore dark glasses.

Rage thought of her mother lying still in a hospital bed, her soul hidden behind her closed eyes all these weeks. But it was only an imaginary picture. Everyone agreed it was better that she didn't see Mam.

Water gurgled down the pipe behind the shrub, which meant the tap at the kitchen sink had been turned on.

At the same instant, down at the far end of the yard, Rage saw a flash of color—orange and molten red, like the embers that glow underneath burning wood in a campfire. Rage squinted and saw it again, this time in the orchard, flying over the ground. Not fire after all, but some kind of animal. Maybe a fox?

Now it was streaking up the side of a tree. A cat?

Mr. Walker woke as Rage leaned forward to see better, and gave a suspicious growl. That was enough to set Elle off. She abandoned the ball and began barking wildly, racing down to the end of the yard. Above Rage the kitchen window slid open with a protesting rasp.

"Now you quiet down, you dogs," Mrs. Johnson cried in a tremulous voice. "I can't hear myself think in all that noise!"

Elle was earnestly sniffing the wind, lifting her head up high to catch hold of any smells that might try to slip by her. She turned toward the orchard, shivering with excitement. Mrs. Johnson's goat had scaled the brick wall and was trying to reach the upper branches of a fruit tree. Elle put her front paws up on the wall and barked at the goat.

"Oh, those dogs," Mrs. Johnson sighed through the window.

Rage patted the tan Chihuahua in her lap until Mr. Walker settled back to sleep, tucking his little dark snout under his feathery tail.

"You're too old for all of this, Rose," said a younger, sharper voice.

Rage grimaced. It was Mrs. Somersby from the town. Mrs. Busybody, Rage's mother called her.

"We're neighbors," Mrs. Johnson was saying.

Mrs. Somersby made a snorting noise. "Where is the girl now?"

"Out somewhere by herself, sitting and brooding, I suppose," Mrs. Johnson answered with another sigh. "She's been like this ever since the accident, poor little mite."

"You mustn't indulge her. Youngsters should not be allowed to wallow."

"Surely it's natural for her to be upset," Mrs. Johnson said reproachfully.

"That girl is slow. I always said so."

"Not slow . . ."

"But what else can you expect, with the upbringing she's had? A flighty, irresponsible mother and no father to speak of."

"A lot of children have only one parent. I read in a newspaper article that it's far better to be the child of one good single parent than of two parents who hate one another."

"What a child needs is a strong parent. You can

hardly call Mary Winnoway that. Look at the way she ran off when she was just fifteen and came crawling back with a child."

"Hardly crawling. She came back to nurse her sick father, which is a credit to her, given what he was like. If you ask me, Mary ran away as much to find her brother as to escape her father."

"Well, she found *someone*," Mrs. Somersby said nastily. "A girl has no business running away like that. It's different for boys. And what did she have to run away from, anyway? A bit of discipline never hurt anyone. It wasn't as though her father hit her."

"He did worse than hit. He crushed her and everyone around him, though I don't like to speak ill of the dead. I knew Mary's mother when she was a girl, and she was like a bright little bird. Adam Winnoway married her, and she lived in his shadow for the rest of her short life. I always feel as though she faded rather than died. After I married my Henry I came to live here, and I just watched her get paler and quieter every year."

Rage shivered. She had no memory of Grandmother Reny, who had died before she was born, but it was a cold thing to imagine a person fading like a blot of disappearing ink.

"Fanciful rubbish!" Mrs. Somersby snapped. "Reny Winnoway was weak-minded, and so were her children. Rage is the same. She has no idea how to fit in with people. Do you know that she has no friends at school? Not a single one!"

I do have friends, Rage thought. *I have old Bear and Elle and Mr. Walker. I have Billy Thunder. It's not friends I want. It's Mam.* Her eyes filled with tears.

"She's right, Rose." Mr. Johnson's crackly voice broke

in. "All she has are those damn dogs. Four of them, for heaven's sake. It's ridiculous. It was mad, bringing home abandoned strays the way she did. They could turn on you at any time."

"Now Henry, you know those dogs are as sweet as pie with Rage."

"That mean old dog of her granddaddy's growls at me every time I walk in my own yard!"

"I don't suppose the poor thing had much kindness in its life, with him keeping it chained from daylight till dark. Besides, Bear's old, and that makes some folk mighty cranky," Mrs. Johnson said pointedly. "There's no harm in the dog except for someone who would hurt Rage. All of them are devoted to her, especially that pup of Bear's. That Billy Thunder."

When Mrs. Somersby spoke again, her voice was sulky. "All I'm saying is that the child might just as well be told that her mother is unlikely to wake up and come home. Knowing a hard truth is better than bearing false hope."

"Where there is life, there is hope," Mrs. Johnson said firmly.

"My sister's a nurse at the hospital. She said Mary Winnoway will die if she doesn't snap out of this state and exert some will to heal."

Snap, Rage thought, turning the word around in her mind and feeling sick with dreaminess. *Snap, crackle, and pop.*

"We've done our neighborly best," Mr. Johnson said piously.

Rage looked down the yard to where Elle and Billy Thunder were playing. They were barking, but the wind was carrying the noise away from the house now. It was like watching the television with the sound turned down.

"They'll have to go, of course," Mrs. Somersby said.

"It will break her heart," Mrs. Johnson sighed.

"If you ask me, we might as well get rid of them right now and be done with it," Mr. Johnson said briskly.

"Maybe we could advertise them in the paper, but I don't know what good it will do. Someone might take the little dog, and maybe even Billy. For all his size, he's not much more than a pup, and I never saw a sweeter-natured animal in all my born days. But I don't know about Bear or Elle. Bear's too bad-tempered for anyone to want, and Elle is so strong and so aggressively friendly."

"If the police find that brother of Mary's, he can take them," Mr. Johnson said.

Rage took a deep, shaking breath. What she had overheard told her what she had already sensed. If they were talking about getting rid of the dogs, time must be running out for her mother. Rage was sure Mam would get better, if only she could find a way to see her. But when she had asked, her words had been brushed aside as if they were a bit of spilled flour.

Don't ask, whispered an urgent little voice into Rage's ear. *Just go.*

Rage shook her head automatically. She couldn't just sneak away without telling anyone and make her way alone through the hills to the hospital in Hopeton. It would take days, and she'd certainly be caught before she got there. She would get into terrible strife. Mam always said to make sure she didn't cause anyone any trouble.

But she can't say anything, the little voice urged. *She needs you.*

The thought that her mother could need her scared Rage—that was not how it was supposed to be. But she could not get the urgent voice out of her mind. *She needs you.* A picture of Mam smiling flashed into her mind, and something in Rage's chest twisted hard and seemed to tear free.

She gave a gasp and suddenly felt half suffocated by the shrub, the dogs, the voices inside and outside of her. She pushed Mr. Walker to make him get up and crawled out from under the branches.

Rage found herself heading for the gate in the fence that led to Winnoway Farm. Mr. Walker ran down the yard to join the other dogs, but Bear followed Rage as she went into her own front yard and up the back step. Fortunately, the homesteads on both properties were close to the fence line that divided them, so it was a short walk. Her hands shook as she used the spare key under the mat to get inside, and they shook harder as she opened the hall cupboard to get her good long coat and her hiking shoes with the rippled soles. She dared not think about what she was doing. It was too frightening. Who would have thought that being bad would feel so dangerous?

Once she had changed, she went to her bedroom and took her mother's pink-gold locket out of her jewelry box. She hardly knew why, except Mam cherished it above everything they owned. It had been the last present given to her by her own mother.

Opening the locket, Rage gazed at the photographs inside. There was one of Grandmother Reny looking sweet and vague, and one of Uncle Samuel, taken not long before he had run away. He had been only a few years older than Rage was now. He had dark, unruly hair like Mam's and a wild, hurt look on his unsmiling face. Had he been thinking of leaving when the picture was taken? Everyone always said it was different for boys. Perhaps that was why Mam had come back to Winnoway, while Uncle Samuel had never returned. He had written a single letter to Mam, which she kept in her handbag.

Rage wondered if the precious letter had been burned up in the car crash or if it had been rescued along with the locket. Pushing the locket deep into her coat pocket for safety, she went out the front door and closed it quietly behind her.

"Maybe they'll let her keep one of the dogs, though how she'll choose which, I don't know." Mrs. Johnson's voice floated on the air as Rage and Bear walked down to where the other dogs were playing.

The dogs stopped when they saw her, wagging their tails and crowding at her, making themselves into a warm, furry barrier. She bit her lip hard. "I have to go and see Mam," she told them, but saying the words out loud made her feel as if she were too close to a high cliff edge.

She hesitated and thought about putting the locket back. Billy licked her hand and whined a little. Rage looked into his warm brown eyes and felt like crying. Worry for the dogs was mixed up with fear for Mam. If only there were someone to tell her what to do.

At that moment the goat stopped eating the fruit

tree and jumped down from the brick wall and into Mr. Johnson's backyard. Seeing the poor, bedraggled thing climb so easily over the barrier seemed like a sign to Rage. After all, she wouldn't be running away. She was just going to visit her mother in the hospital, and no one had actually forbidden it.

She pushed through the dogs to the gate, shooing them away. But when she slipped through, they surged past her as if they had been waiting for the chance to escape. Rage stared after them, horrified.

Opening her mouth to cry out, she realized that she couldn't, because then Mr. Johnson would come out and the moment for going would be lost. She closed her mouth and the gate, heart beating fast. The dogs would have to come with her. She did not know what she would do with them once they reached Hopeton, but the fact that she would not be making the journey alone lightened her heart.

They cut across the property alongside Winnoway Farm and kept away from the roads, because that was where the police would go when Mr. Johnson rang them. He would not call the police until he was certain she was gone, and it would take time for him to be certain. Maybe he would even wait until morning.

"We have to get as far as we can before that," Rage told the dogs.

She could see the water glimmering ahead and wondered if the reservoir behind the dam really was bottomless, the way some of the boys at school said. It was important to keep in sight of the shoreline, because it would bring her to the little gorge leading into the next valley. It would save hours of climbing, and it led to a track that cross-country skiers used in winter. That would take her all the way to the outskirts of Hopeton, and there were huts along the way where she could sleep.

The dead trees looked more and more like claws sticking up out of the flat water as the sun fell toward the horizon, and Rage walked faster, spurred by the thought of what the dam would look like at night, under the moon.

Rage had a sudden vivid memory of Grandfather Adam standing at the fence bordering Winnoway Farm and staring over at the dam with a blank expression that had frightened her with its emptiness. She knew the whole valley had once been Winnoway land. It had been divided between Grandfather Adam and Great-Uncle Peter when their father died.

"What happened to Great-Uncle Peter?" Rage had asked Mam once, imagining another cold, hard man like Grandfather. Mam had shrugged, saying he had left after the government forced him to sell his land for the dam project. Grandfather Adam had pleaded with his brother to use the government money to buy land in the next valley, but he had refused.

"Did Grandfather want him to stay?" Rage asked, surprised.

"I think he wanted him to stay very much," Mam had answered.

"Why did Great-Uncle Peter go, then?" Rage was old enough now to know that had been a bad question, because it reminded Mam of her brother running away.

"He had to do what was right for him," Mam had answered in a low, sad voice.

Remembering this, Rage decided that she did not

believe people should do what was right for themselves without thinking about what was right for other people as well. No doubt Uncle Samuel had left Winnoway because that was right for him, but his going had not been right for Mam.

Rage realized she must have missed the opening to the gorge because she was still climbing and she had long passed the end of the reservoir. Now she would have to go to the top of the ridge to get her bearings. It would be a hard climb, but she knew she would be able to see the bleary arc of light given off by Hopeton.

It was slow going over the uneven, brambly ground. Every time they came to a rusted barbed-wire fence left from the days when this was farmers' land, she propped open the strands with the stick she had picked up to smack at the grass and frighten snakes away. The darker it got, the harder it was to walk, and she kept tripping over blackberry runners.

She began to worry about what she was going to do with the dogs when she got to Hopeton. They would stay if she told them to wait just outside the town, but after a while they would come looking for her. It wasn't disobedience. It was just that their minds weren't made to hold orders for very long.

She felt like crying again. It was too much, having to worry about the dogs as well as about how she was going to find the hospital and convince the nurses to let her visit Mam. She knew from listening to Mr. and Mrs. Johnson talk that the nurses were very strict about visiting times and about how many people could visit. They were sure to make a fuss about Rage being there without an adult.

You must get in, Rage told herself fiercely. She found herself remembering the awful night when no one had come to pick her up from school. She had sat in the headmaster's office and listened to him phoning the police. From the way his shoulders hunched she knew that it was bad news.

She made herself concentrate on watching the dogs. No matter how bad she felt, that always made her feel better. Elle was rushing ahead and coming back every once in a while to walk a few steps beside her. Mr. Walker ran round and round her in circles, covering double the distance of the others. Billy Thunder trotted at her side, behind his mother. Mrs. Johnson was right about him being the sweetest dog that ever lived. Billy was pure honey and sunlight, which was a wonder when you thought how near he'd come to dying almost as soon as he was born.

He was the only one of the dogs born on Winnoway Farm. Mam had been amazed to discover that Bear was pregnant because Bear was so old. When her puppies were born too soon, Grandfather said they were too small to feed and ought to be drowned. He might even have done it if he hadn't been so ill by then. Mam called the vet, who said he could not come until the following evening and that they must milk Bear and feed the puppies all through the night. Mam only managed to get a small cup of milk from Bear.

"It is not enough for all of them," she said. "We have to choose one."

She stood looking at the five puppies for the longest time, until Rage knew that she could not bring herself to choose. But if a choice was not made, then all of the puppies would die. Sometimes Rage thought that was the worst moment in her life: looking at those puppies and knowing that she must choose, and that whichever puppy she chose meant choosing that the others would die. Billy had begun to wriggle then, and she had picked him up because she had thought he might be stronger than the others and have a better chance to survive.

They had carried him inside, leaving Bear nuzzling and worrying at the other puppies. Mam heated Bear's milk and watered it down, then she told Rage to put her finger into the mouth of the puppy so it would suck, and she would dribble the milk into its mouth with an eyedropper. Rage obeyed and was horrified to feel that the inside of its mouth was cold. She had not wanted to touch him after that because she thought death had already got into him, but Mam said death did not always win.

Billy had lasted the night, but the other puppies died. Bear had moved them out of the garage and under the house, and that was where they found her with the poor things in the morning. Mr. Johnson came and took the bodies away, but Bear kept scratching under the house as if she thought the ground had swallowed her puppies up. Then quite suddenly she seemed to realize that Billy was inside. She howled and sniffed at the door, but they couldn't give him to her because he was too small and sickly.

It took them a long time to make him well, and when they did let him outside as a gangling, floppy boy dog, Bear had sniffed at him with disinterest.

"Perhaps she doesn't know Billy is her son," Rage said.

But Grandfather had said Bear knew all right but that she didn't care. "Love can end," he had added malevolently.

Rage tripped over a furrow. Picking herself up, she was startled to notice how dark it had become while she was daydreaming.

Now that she and the dogs were all still, she could hear something rustling through the grass behind them. Fear poured through her veins, but Elle seemed not to scent whatever was making those soft noises. Rage told herself she must be imagining things. But still she could hear twigs snapping, the sound of creeping movements through the grass. A rabbit, then, or birds?

What sort of animal would creep after a human and four dogs? she wondered with a shiver. *Wouldn't a wild creature run away as fast as it could from such a strange procession?*

She remembered the dazzling flash of orange in the orchard and wondered if a cat or another dog was following them. But if so, why wasn't Elle barking?

A branch cracked as loudly as a gunshot, and she whirled, catching Elle by the collar.

It must be a person, Rage thought. Someone following and hoping she had money or something valuable to steal.

There was another rustle, and this time something big and white emerged from the dark tangle of foliage. Rage gave a little sobbing laugh of relief when she found herself looking into the strange, square-pupiled eyes of Mrs. Johnson's goat. It shook its curls and gave a loud, plaintive bleat. Of course none of the dogs had barked. They had recognized the strong smell of the goat's wool. Elle, who liked the goat especially, trotted over to it and snuffled at its long white ringlets.

It occurred to Rage that the goat could only have

followed them if the Johnsons' gate was open. Except she distinctly remembered closing it. Shutting gates was one of the important rules on Winnoway Farm. That meant someone else had opened it.

"Don't be silly," she told herself, fighting panic. "Why would anyone deliberately let the goat out?"

There was a snicker of sound somewhere behind her, and Elle leaped up, barking frantically.

"Elle!" Rage cried, but it was too late. The bull terrier had plunged away with Mr. Walker at her heels. Bear stayed by Rage, growling softly, while Billy sniffed the air in a puzzled sort of way.

Rage stood there stupidly, indecisive, until Billy gave an urgent bark.

Spurred by the thought that Elle and Mr. Walker would head back to the farm, Rage began to run and stumble after them, pushing brambles aside and ignoring the jagged thorns scratching and tearing at her bare skin.

It was full dark now, and Mrs. Johnson would have begun to worry. Bear and Billy trotted at her heels, the goat skittering along behind them, but the others were too far away to see. "Elle," Rage yelled. "Mr. Walker!"

Rage completely lost her sense of direction as the ground began to slope suddenly down into a fold where the undergrowth was even thicker and more tangled. She could hear Elle and Mr. Walker barking ahead, but it sounded as if they had stopped running. Maybe they had treed a cat or bailed up a fox in its hole. She was scratched to pieces, even through her jeans, when at last she broke through a wall of blackberry bushes and into a small clearing.

Right then the bright crescent moon that had risen

behind a cloud bank slid out into the open, bathing the world in a silvery light.

Rage stopped dead in astonishment. Right in front of her, looming far above her head, was a high, wild wall of brambles, and in the midst of the tangled branches was a perfect archway, like the gate in the hedge at home. Spiders had spun their webs, tying all of the leaves together with a silvery lace that glimmered in the moonlight, but not a single cobweb stretched across the opening.

2

Elle and Mr. Walker growled at the strange gate. The goat trotted up to stand behind them. Beside Rage, Billy Thunder whined. When she dropped a hand to his head, she found that he was trembling all over.

"What is it, Billy? What do you smell?" Rage asked, trying to understand who had created such a thing in the middle of the wilderness, and why. It was far too perfect to be an accident of nature.

Then came another of the snickering chitters. Elle began to bark again, inching closer to the bramble gate.

"Elle!" Rage said sharply. To her relief the bull terrier came to heel, Mr. Walker following. She ran her hand along Elle's back and found all the hair standing up on her spine, stiff as bristles on a toothbrush. What was it about the strange gate that had got the animals so upset?

Studying it, Rage saw that it offered a clear path out of the brambles. But why would someone make a gateway here? Nothing could be kept in or out by it.

"Who made you? I wonder," Rage murmured aloud.

"Wizard making bramble gate," answered a purring

voice out of nowhere. "Is enchanted gateway."

Rage froze in shock. "Who said that?" she whispered.

"Am being firecat, Ragewinnoway," the voice responded, soft and rough as a cat's tongue licking the evening air.

Rage's heart gave a nervous jump as she looked around, but she could see no one. "Wh . . . who is that?"

"Am firecat," the voice repeated.

Rage licked her lips. "How do you know my name?"

"Am knowing many things," the firecat responded, its voice beguiling, but with a hint of teeth in it. "Am knowing Ragewinnoway is thinking about sleeping mother."

Rage gasped in fright.

"Not hurting Ragewinnoway," the voice said hastily.

"What do you want?" Rage wondered if someone was using ventriloquism to play a nasty trick on her. Except who could know so much about her?

"Firecat helping Ragewinnoway wake mother," the voice said.

"I . . . I don't need any help," Rage quavered.

There was a hissing laugh. "Mother of Rage being far away . . . and even if finding her, daughter-calling not powerful enough for waking mother from such deep and dangerous sleeping. Ragewinnoway needs waking magic."

Even through her fear, the sneering words cut Rage. She had been a fool to think she could wake Mam when the doctors had failed.

"Come through bramble gate, Ragewinnoway," the voice invited. "Wizard will conjure waking magic."

"How do you know about Mam?" she asked, blinking hard to stop herself from crying.

The firecat ignored her question. "Ragewinnoway must forget being careful if wanting to save mother.

Must become Ragewinnoway whose name is Courage and enter bramble gate. All questions being answered on other side."

"I don't understand what you mean," Rage stammered. "My name isn't Courage. It's Rebecca Jane Winnoway. Rage for short."

"Naming something hidden can bringing it out of its hiding place. Firecat can smell boldness hidden in Rage Winnoway. Firecat smells that Rage Winnoway can become Courage Winnoway," the firecat said slyly. "If wanting to helping mother."

"Of course I want to help her," Rage said.

"Then coming through bramble gate," the firecat said eagerly. "Wizard helping."

Rage shivered and wondered if she could be dreaming. But when she pinched the inside of her wrist, she did not wake. "How do you know the wizard will help Mam?" she called out.

"Waking magic being payment for service to wizard," the voice said briskly.

"What service?"

"Wizard needing something delivered to him. Something small. Very, very small."

"Why don't you take it to him?" Rage called. There must be a microphone somewhere because she was sure no one was concealed in the brambles. The voice appeared to be coming from the bramble gate itself.

Again the speaker ignored her question. It said, "Come through, Ragewinnoway, before too late for sleeping mother."

"Who are you?" Rage called again. "What has this to do with you?"

There was no answer.

Rage stared through the bramble gate. Who would play such a trick on her, and why? And most of all, how?

She thought of Mam lying in the hospital bed, and a tear trickled down her cheek. She had left Winnoway Farm to help Mam. The slinky voice had made her see that she had behaved as if she were in a fairy story about a girl going to save her mother, with happily ever after waiting around the corner.

But what if it really was an enchanted gateway? "Oh, don't be such an idiot," Rage cried, dashing away the tear. Of course there were no such things as magic gates and powerful wizards. Any more than daughters who could save their mothers.

Rage drew closer to the gate, and the air fizzed against her skin. Startled, she looked down at her arms. All of the hair was sticking up. Rage told herself it was only static electricity. They had done experiments with torn-up bits of paper and combs in science class at school. She was determined to expose the trick. Entering the gateway, she found herself wishing that the animals were human so that she didn't have to face this alone.

But as she passed through the gateway, the air began to glow. A slit of darkness opened under her feet like a greedy mouth, and she screamed as she fell into it.

She fell and fell.

She was in the living room, a fire burning in the small, deep hearth. Mam was on the couch with her feet curled under her, reading a thick book. Rage was on the floor, making some plasticine dinner for her plasticine fairies. Grandfather Adam was in his chair, staring into the flames just as he always did. Outside, the wind whined and rattled the glass in its frame.

"Mam, could I have a sandwich?" Rage asked.

"The girl did not eat dinner when it was offered," Grandfather said, never taking his eyes from the flames. His words were like stones set in the center of the room. A fierce coldness came off them.

"We ate early tonight," Mam said.

"The girl is not to run wild under my roof," Grandfather answered. Then he began to cough. His whole body shook with the force of those coughs. Rage waited for them to shake him to pieces, but he closed his mouth and forced them back down his throat.

Then there was nothing but the sound of a heavy, raspy breathing full of sharp points and edges.

Rage woke to find herself lying on her back and staring up into the night sky. Only a few stars and a misty sliver of moon were visible. She sat up. There was no fire, no Grandfather (because, of course, he had died), no Mam (because she was in the hospital, lost in her dreams).

Rage's head hurt, and she guessed she had hit it. The last thing she remembered was running after the dogs in the darkness. Then there had been a dream about going through a magical gate. Fingering her head for the bump, she looked around. She was on a grassy slope hemmed on all sides by a dense forest. The faint moonlight made long shadows that striped a dark patch of brambles to one side of the clearing. There was no sign of a gateway, enchanted or otherwise.

"It was a dream after all," Rage said aloud. The animals were nowhere to be seen. Had she also dreamed of taking them away from Winnoway Farm? She heard something making its way through the trees toward her, and opened her mouth to call out. Then she closed it, because whatever was pushing its way through the trees was a whole lot bigger than any dog.

A huge, shaggy black bear pushed its way out into the open.

Rage froze. She had read that bears have weak eyesight, and she prayed it was true.

The trees rustled again, and a barefoot teenager with straight, toffee-colored hair stepped into the clearing. One lock of hair flopped untidily over his left eye. He brushed it aside with a dirty hand. His other hand rested on the bear's flank.

Rage almost laughed out loud. Seeing the bear, she had thought for one second that she really had gone through a magical gateway. But the bear must belong to a circus and the boy was its keeper. Before she could call out, the bushes rustled again and out stepped a man the height of a large cat. He looked quite human but for his size and two soft, furled elf ears sticking up out of his pale golden-colored hair, which perfectly matched a silky-looking tail.

"I can't find her," the little man told the boy.

Rage couldn't believe her eyes. "I must still be dreaming," she whispered.

"I suppose she'll smell her way to us." The boy sighed.

The bear creature gave a deep groan and sat back on its haunches in a weary way. Rage saw that it was not a bear after all. Or not exactly. It was the right size but the wrong shape. It was like a bearish dog, or a doggish bear. "I hurt!" it said huskily.

Rage gaped to hear it speak.

"I don't see what you have to complain about," the little man told it querulously. "You've hardly changed at all. Look at me! I'm completely misshapen. All my lovely fur is gone, my bones hurt, and my nose has shrunk."

"You don't *look* horrible," the boy said kindly.

"I think a person ought to be asked before they are changed," the little man said, casting an accusing sideways look at Rage.

She took a deep breath and made an effort to stop her mind from reeling. Dream or not, she had to say something. "Hello. I . . . I'm Rage Winnoway of Winnoway Farm."

The trio stared at her.

"Did you hear that?" the little man demanded of the other two in his sharp little voice. His ears twitched in agitation.

"She must have hit her head," the boy said. "A hit on the head can make you very confused. I remember once when a man threw a stone at me and I forgot my name for ages."

"Amnesia!" the little man said triumphantly, then he gave Rage a severe look. "Have you lost your memory?" he asked loudly, as if he thought loss of memory also caused deafness.

"I've not lost anything. I told you, I'm Rage Winnoway of Winnoway Farm," Rage said, thinking she might as well behave as if the dream were real until she managed to wake up. "What *is* this place?"

"You must know where we are. You brought us here!" the little creature said indignantly. "You even wished for us to be human."

"I . . . I what?" Rage asked faintly.

"She's not really to blame," the boy protested. "Not completely. After all, haven't we all wanted to be human from time to time? Haven't we secretly wished it? To be free? To be able to decide? To be masters of ourselves?"

"I never wished to be human," the bear creature said heavily. "I fought the gate magic and it hurt me."

A young woman with very short, sleek blond hair leaped into the clearing. She was dressed in a tan body-suit belted at the waist and looked like one of the warrior women in Rage's book of legends. She stretched and then stared alertly about out of deep-set, almond-shaped brown eyes.

"We were looking for you," the boy said.

"I was trying out this shape," she answered, turning her beautiful eyes on him. "It's fast, and it's strong, and it's not stiff like my old shape was. Is there anything to eat?"

Rage shook her head, for this last question appeared to be aimed at her.

The young woman appeared momentarily downcast. "That won't do at all." She brightened. "Shall I go and look for some food?"

Rage nodded in bemusement at being asked such a question by an adult. The Amazon immediately sprinted away into the trees, and Rage wondered if the denizens of this place were as mad as the White Rabbit in *Alice in Wonderland*.

"You should not have let her go," the bear creature told Rage.

"It's only right she should have to find us something to eat," the little man declared. "She started all of this by running off without thinking, as usual."

"She couldn't help it," the boy protested. "It was the smell. It caught hold of her. You ran after it, too," he added. "It was so interesting! Sly and slinky. Almost a cat smell, I thought. But not quite."

"It smelled hot," the little man said, ears twitching back and forth. "But I could have resisted if Elle hadn't run off like that."

Rage's mouth fell open. *Elle?*

She looked incredulously at the odd collection of beings. Was it possible that they were the dogs—her dogs—transformed into these *creatures*? The big bear-dog could be Bear, and Billy Thunder might be the barefoot boy in jeans and a bomber jacket; Mr. Walker was the little man in hooded pajamas, and Elle was the Amazon. But how could they have been so changed?

The little man had accused her of wishing for them to be human, and it was true she had wished that just as she stepped through the gate, but she hadn't really meant it. Besides, they hadn't become humans. Bear actually looked more wild than she had on the other side of the bramble gate, though she claimed to have resisted the transformation. What if each of the animals had reacted to the magic according to their nature? Mr. Walker might have resisted out of characteristic stubbornness, whereas Billy had admitted wanting to be human sometimes, and maybe Elle felt that way also.

"Bear?" Rage called softly.

The huge animal turned sad, dark eyes on her, and Billy Thunder beamed. "There now. You've remembered Mama's name. Maybe you didn't hit your head very hard after all."

"Oh dear," Rage said faintly, and sat down. Surely everything must be a dream—running away from Winnoway Farm to help Mam, the firecat and the bramble gate and the transformation of the animals. It was a dream. It must be, except that she had never had a dream that felt so true.

"It's a shock," Billy said kindly. "But at least you are yourself. I kept falling until I learned how to balance on two legs. It's easy once you get the trick of it, though. You've been asleep for *hours*."

"Look who I've found," said Elle, coming out from the trees and leading a skinny, depressed-looking young man by the hand. Only he wasn't a man because he had goat legs. He was, Rage marveled, a faun, like Mr. Tumnus out of *The Lion, the Witch and the Wardrobe*. He even had two elegant horns.

Goaty, Rage thought, feeling dazed. He would have followed the dogs through the gate. He must have resisted the gate magic, too, just as he always resisted everything.

"Look what has happened to me," he bleated. "I have become a terrible monster." He shivered violently.

Billy took off his jacket. "You're not a monster," he said gently, helping Goaty into the coat. "You've just changed a bit. Now you're partly human."

"What on earth are you doing here, anyway?" the little man demanded. "No one invited you."

Mr. Walker, Rage reminded herself. *Mr. Walker, as always scolding and worrying at Goaty.*

The faun plaited his bony fingers. "I'm sure I don't know. It's a wonder I know anything at all. Sleep in a puddle and your brains leak out. Everyone knows that. I'm dreadfully wet!"

"You shouldn't have followed," Mr. Walker said. "She never intended for you to come. She shut you in."

"She did," Goaty agreed, giving Rage a reproachful look. "She left me behind, the way everyone always leaves me." His pale eyes widened, and he shuddered. "On this occasion I might not have minded. But then that thing came and undid the gate, and I couldn't help following. It's in my nature," he added apologetically.

"What thing?" Rage asked.

"The hot thing," he answered, glancing over his

shoulder nervously. "I couldn't see what it looked like exactly. It was very bright and shifty. In the end it flew spitting at me, and I ran from it in terror."

The Amazon grabbed his arm and began sniffing his sleeve vigorously. She snuffled right along his arm and up to his shoulder. Then she stuck her nose into his armpit, sniffed intently, and gasped. "That's it! That's the smell that made me run out the farm gate." She held Goaty's arm out to Rage, inviting her to smell it.

Rage shook her head, but Mr. Walker and Billy sniffed.

"The same smell," Billy Thunder confirmed solemnly.

"Exactly," Mr. Walker said. "But what does it mean?"

"It's obvious," Bear said heavily. "Whatever let Goaty out, whatever lured Elle after it, it wants us here for a reason."

"No doubt it means to eat us," Goaty said gloomily, chewing absentmindedly at the end of his pale ringlets. "It had very sharp-looking teeth."

Rage licked her lips. "I think it was the firecat," she said.

"The *what* cat?" Mr. Walker asked.

"A . . . a voice spoke to me before we came through the bramble gate," Rage explained. "It said it was the fire-cat, and it told me that the gateway was magical, and on the other side of it was a wizard who could give me magic to wake Mam, if only I did an errand for him."

"Why would a wizard need your help?" Mr. Walker asked.

It was a good question and one that Rage now wished she had asked the firecat. But she had thought that the voice belonged to someone playing a trick on her.

"What errand?" Billy asked.

"I have to deliver some small thing to the wizard," Rage answered. But she was remembering how quickly and lightly this had been said, as though the firecat had been pretending that something important was unimportant. She thought of the ring in *Lord of the Rings*. That could be called a small thing, but Frodo had almost died in delivering it to Mount Doom.

"What small thing?" Mr. Walker demanded.

"I . . . I didn't ask," Rage admitted.

Billy and Mr. Walker exchanged a look. Then Billy shrugged. "She had to come if there was a way to help her mother."

Mr. Walker scowled. "Who says that the firecat was telling the truth about the wizard being able to help her mother? I've heard of magic to make people sleep, but not to wake them up."

"It all happened so fast," Rage cried. "I was running after you, and then I saw the gateway, and the next minute there was this voice telling me that the only way to save Mam was to go through to the other side! I was upset about Mam, and I thought it was some kind of mean trick. I only went through to prove it wasn't a magical gateway."

"Except it was," Mr. Walker said severely. "You ought to have thought it through more carefully, just in case."

Rage had the urge to shout that she was too young to think properly about things, but that was stupid. The dogs seemed a lot more judgmental now that they could talk, especially Mr. Walker.

"Where is this wizard, then?" Billy asked gently, sensing she was upset, just as he had done when he was a dog.

"I . . . I don't know. But the firecat said it would answer all my questions if I came to this side of the gate," Rage said, though that wasn't exactly what the voice had said. "Probably it will come in the morning," she added quickly, to forestall another pointed question from Mr. Walker.

Billy said they might as well try to sleep while they waited.

"Nice sort of creature this firecat must be, luring us here and then forcing us to sleep in the middle of a forest like this," Mr. Walker grumbled as they sat under a big tree and settled themselves for sleep.

Rage sat stiffly with her back against a tree, and the others took up sleeping positions similar to their usual animal ones, only instead of Billy trying to lie across her legs, he lay down beside her. Mr. Walker curled into Rage's lap, and Elle flung herself on the ground beside them. Goaty sat beside Elle and shyly invited her to rest her head on his fleecy lap. Only Bear moved apart, preferring to sleep under another tree.

In a remarkably short time the animals were all asleep, snuffling and snorting. Rage tried to stay awake to think, but before long she drifted off as well.

She was traveling on a train, and suddenly Mam said they must go back to Winnoway.

"Your grandfather is sick and he needs us," Mam said, but it was she who looked sick.

"What is the matter with him?" Rage asked.

"He is sad," Mam answered. "That is a sickness, too."

He is sad and sad and sad, *the train wheels whispered.*

3

The next day Rage woke to Goaty's volcanic sneezes and to the realization that what had happened was real!

It was raining, though the drops were so fine as to be more of a thick mist. Rage's coat was clammy with it. Goaty sneezed again and declared that he had a cold, only he said "code" because of his blocked nose.

Shaking and squeezing the ends of her coat, Rage tried to remember everything the firecat had said to her, but a picture of Mam lying still and silent in a hospital bed kept getting in the way.

Elle did not trouble herself with thinking. She sprang out into the rain and vigorously rubbed the tan bodysuit, which Rage could now see was part of her, like hair or fur. She was less human than she had appeared last night, which meant that she *had* resisted the gate magic. Only Billy seemed to be completely human.

Bear came out from under her tree and looked up into the drab sky. She sighed heavily and dropped her head to lick at her paw. Rage felt guilty, as if somehow the rain were her fault on top of everything else. In the cold light of day, going through the enchanted gate seemed madder than ever. Mr. Walker was right. She ought to have known no one could play such a terrible and complicated joke. She should have thrown a stick through the gateway instead of going herself.

Then a happier thought occurred to her. If the gateway was enchanted, maybe there really was a wizard with waking magic. Rage made up her mind. If the firecat was right and the wizard wanted something brought to him, she would do it, no matter what it was, just so long as he agreed to help Mam. The trouble was, like Dorothy in *The Wizard of Oz*, she had to find the wizard before she could learn what he wanted her to bring him.

In the misty daylight, she could see a sort of path through the trees on the slope above them. "I think we should go up there and have a proper look around," she said, pointing.

"What about the firecat?" Mr. Walker muttered, but Rage pretended not to hear him.

"We'll ged wed and all die of code," Goaty said. It took a minute for Rage to figure out what he had said.

"It's not really cold," Billy told him cheerfully. "And walking will keep us warmer than sitting still."

"Exercise will do us good," Elle said heartily.

Mr. Walker gave Rage his soulful look, and she automatically picked him up, just as she had when he was a little butterfly-eared Chihuahua, tucking his tail under her arm.

"No one ever carried be," Goaty sniffed sadly.

"No one ever stepped on you, either!" Mr. Walker said snappishly.

The break in the trees was not a path after all, only a natural thinning along a rocky seam, but it made walking easier. Although the rain was fine, Rage soon found she was very wet. Fortunately, Billy had been right in saying it was not cold. The rain began to ease as they reached the top of the hill, which was a cap of hard stone where nothing green could grow. They climbed down into a valley and began another hard climb, up the next hill.

Rage stopped to catch her breath and looked back. A dense, trackless forest spread away beneath them until it became a greenish haze that merged with the sky. There was not a single sign of life, just forest blanketing the hills and valleys. It was the way Rage imagined Winnoway might have looked before people arrived. It was beautiful to see a forest so untouched, but she hoped there would be something more than wilderness on the other side of the hill.

"Up," Goaty urged. He trotted ahead, and at first Rage was puzzled by his sudden enthusiasm. Then she remembered that it was the nature of a goat to climb, and for all his transformation, Goaty was still more goat than anything else. He had never climbed a hill in his life, let alone a mountain, but his wild ancestors had lived on steep-sided mountains, so perhaps this was buried in the deepest part of his mind.

Bear was making heavy work of the hill, and Billy hovered, looking worried. She stumbled slightly. When he caught at her she snarled and slashed the air in his direction with her claws extended. Rage heard the wheezing sound her breath made and felt anxious. It was how Grandfather Adam had sounded before he died.

"I'm sorry I got you into this," she told Bear, who gave her a weary look before going on climbing.

"She doesn't blame you," Billy said quietly, coming up beside Rage.

"She seems so unhappy," Rage murmured, slowing so that they could talk.

Billy sighed. "Life has been hard for her. Your grandfather was not a kind master. Mama never had a pat or soft word until you came. And then there were all of my brothers and sisters dying, and you keeping me from her. I remember hearing her calling to me when I was sick, like a voice in a dream. Calling and calling."

"But you would have died if we hadn't taken you. . . ."

"She knows. I know. But it doesn't make any difference to the hurting of it."

"She hates me, then," Rage said, devastated.

"Oh no," Billy said. "Hating's a human thing. She's just all filled with grieving, and sometimes when it gets too much, she lashes out. But she cares very much for you and your mam."

"And you? Doesn't she care for you?" Rage asked.

Billy Thunder looked up the hill after his mother. "I think it hurts her to look at me," he said, very softly.

Toiling up the last bit of the hill, Rage was weighed down with a sadness as heavy as her sodden coat. It seemed so unfair that Bear could care for her and Mam but not for her own son.

"Hey!" Elle yelled. Rage looked up to see that she and Goaty had reached the top of the hill. "I see a road and there's a river alongside it, and over there, in the forest, is a big house with pointy bits."

The top of the hill was a perfect vantage point. Before them an enormous valley opened like a seam between parallel ranges of towering, white-streaked mountains. Thick masses of clouds rested on their peaks, concealing what lay beyond. A river emerged from the farthest mountains and wound its silvery way the length of the valley. To the east of the river, the valley was densely forested but for a castle on a hill—Elle's big house with pointy bits. A faint track ran from the castle, through the forest, and around the foot of the hill they were standing on, before joining a road that ran beside the river.

Rage noticed a small settlement not far along the river road. "What do you see there?" she asked, pointing it out.

"Houses and gardens," Mr. Walker answered, wriggling to be put down.

"A stone well in the middle of a little square in the middle of houses and streets," Billy said.

"People," Elle said.

"*People* people?" Rage asked.

Elle squinted. "People of some sort," she said at last. "What difference does it make?"

"Oh, it makes a great deal of difference," Bear said thickly. "People only care about people who are exactly like them."

Rage was hurt by the scorn in Bear's voice, but she only said, "I was thinking we could go there and ask about the wizard."

"If there are people, they will want to send me to the abattoir," Goaty said. He sneezed, very wetly.

Mr. Walker looked at him in disgust. "Do you mind! You spat on me just now."

"No one will dare to send us anywhere!" Elle declared. She bounded into the trees and emerged with a dead branch. "I'll make a spear!" She waved the stick around so wildly that it poked Goaty in the eye.

He rubbed it and said mournfully that it didn't matter. "I have another eye, and I doubt three eyes would be enough to see all the trouble that we're bound to find if we go down into that valley. Going down is a bad thing."

"Why don't we go there instead?" Mr. Walker said, pointing to the castle on the hill.

"It's a castle," Billy said.

"Of course it is," Mr. Walker snapped. "And in it there will be a king or queen or a wise advisor who will be able to help us find the wizard. Perhaps even the wizard himself lives there."

Rage was startled to find that Mr. Walker and Billy knew what a castle was. Then she remembered that Billy and Mr. Walker had always sat with Rage when Mam read her stories.

"That track leading to the castle doesn't look very clear," Rage said.

She did not want to admit that she was afraid to go to the castle. In fairy tales there was always something dramatic and violent happening in a castle—somebody being stolen away or put to sleep for a hundred years, somebody getting his head chopped off or being usurped. She wasn't actually sure what being usurped was, but it sounded at least as bad as having her head chopped off.

"The village is closer," she argued. "They can tell us who the castle belongs to, and if the wizard owns it, we can still go there."

Mr. Walker looked mutinous.

"What if we vote?" Rage suggested, thinking it had been easier when they were dogs.

"I vote for the village," Billy said promptly.

"I vote for the castle," Mr. Walker said.

"I vote for the castle, too," Elle said enthusiastically.

"Oh dear, oh dear." Goaty sighed and wrung his hands. "I suppose each way will be as bad as the other. In fact, surely the most sensible thing is to stay right where we are. That's what I vote for."

"We can't just stay here forever," Rage protested. "We ought to try to find the wizard."

"I expect he will just want to eat us when we find him," Goaty said in a depressed voice.

"I think a wizard would have better ways of getting food than cooking his visitors," Mr. Walker said coldly.

"I would like to see what a castle smells like. Let's go there at once," Elle said impatiently.

"No use in going to castle," said a familiar slinky voice. "Nothing there but spiders scuttling. No food. No treasure. No sleeping princess."

"Who said that?" Mr. Walker demanded, his high-pitched voice barely audible over the ferocious rumbling growl of Bear. She looked much more like a bear than a dog now that she was curling back her lip and showing her teeth.

"It's the firecat," Rage whispered.

"It's the thing that unlocked the gate for me," Goaty observed gloomily.

"I don't like this one bit," Mr. Walker whispered loudly.

"Not liking hairy little man-dog, either," the firecat said.

"Where have you been?" Rage asked. "You said all of my questions would be answered when I came through the bramble gate!"

"Firecat is having many things to do. Many important things," the voice said sulkily.

Rage bit her lip to stop herself from saying that since it had convinced her to come through the bramble gate, it ought to regard *her* as important. Instead she said, "Where is the wizard and what does he want us to bring to him?"

In answer there was a lurid flash of purple smoke. A tiny hourglass full of pale, glittering sand appeared on a stone knoll. Rage bent down and gingerly pinched its waist between her finger and thumb. It was surprisingly heavy for such a small object because the bottom and top were capped in densely patterned silver. The glass felt thick and was faintly discolored. A few glimmering grains of sand fell through the neck of the hourglass as she watched.

She turned it upside down, but instead of the grains running in the other direction, a few more gleaming fragments floated up from the bottom chamber and into the top.

"A magic hourglass," she murmured, glad it was not a golden ring.

"Hourglass telling how to find wizard," the firecat said.

Rage examined the hourglass and found there were two lines of ornate lettering engraved into the silver:

BRING ME TO THE SHORE OF THE ENDLESS SEA

STEP THROUGH THE DOOR THAT WILL OPEN FOR THEE

"These are not proper directions!" she protested.

"Ragewinnoway clever. Figuring out riddle," the firecat said.

"No!" Rage said. "You send us back home at once."

"Home?" the firecat echoed with a tinge of mockery. "Home-going needing powerful enchantment. Only wizard having such magic."

Rage's anger turned inward once more. Why had she

chosen to go through the bramble gate? The worst thing was knowing that she had gone through it solely because she hadn't believed it was magic. Now they would not be able to get back home unless she could figure out the wizard's whereabouts from the riddle on the bottom of the hourglass.

If only she had not gone through the magic gate . . .

If only she had not run away from the Johnsons' . . .

If only her mother had not been in an accident . . .

"I wouldn't trust that cat thing one bit," Mr. Walker said.

Bear said shortly, "Any fool could tell it was a liar. It smelled like a liar, and it sounded like one."

Rage hung her head and said nothing.

Billy put his arm around her shoulders and said stoutly, "We should go into the village to see if anyone knows anything about the wizard. Maybe it won't be as hard to find the Endless Sea as it sounds."

Rage feared it would be every bit as difficult as it sounded, but before she could say so, Bear growled impatiently and began to descend the hill.

"We'll all be killed," Goaty sighed glumly as they set off after Bear.

It was midday before they reached the road. Going down had turned out to be a lot more difficult than going up, especially where the steep rock face was slippery from rain. At least the weather had warmed up, but Rage was beginning to feel dreadfully empty. The animals must be as hungry as she was, and she feared they would expect her to feed them, just as she always had. Maybe they would be able to get something in the village. In books, people always begged, or chopped wood for their supper. Sometimes they stole it. Rage had never stolen anything, but in stories it never seemed as awful to steal as it did in real life.

"We must be careful, though," she muttered to herself when they were in sight of the road. She had got them into enough trouble by failing to think things through. She could not make the same mistake again.

"I'll protect us!" Elle declared, brandishing her stick.

"Put that down before you do poke someone's eye out," Mr. Walker said crossly.

Rage peered along the road in both directions. It seemed to be deserted, but she looked to Elle, whose superb bull terrier eyesight seemed to have been carried over into her new form. "Do you see anyone coming?"

Elle looked along the road in the direction of the castle and shook her head, but when she looked toward the river, she frowned. "Something is coming. . . ."

"Someone, you mean," Mr. Walker corrected.

"It's not a people," Elle said slowly. "It's . . . something biggish and brownish and it has . . . a lot of legs."

"Probably a giant poisonous jumping spider," Goaty said.

Rage resisted the urge to smack him. She was not afraid of spiders exactly, but she preferred them to stay on the ceiling or on the other side of the room. It occurred to Rage, rather horribly, that whatever was coming might be something worse than a spider—some sort of monster. Unlike Goaty, she kept this terrifying possibility to herself. They agreed to stay hidden until whatever it was came nearer and they could judge if it was dangerous.

"Probably it will sniff us out," Goaty said.

"At least if it eats us, someone will have a full stomach," Mr. Walker said, giving Rage a sideways look.

She bit back a retort and shifted to a spot that

allowed her a clear view of the road. As she waited, Rage was surprised to find her eyes growing heavy despite her apprehension. Mr. Walker climbed into her lap and fell immediately asleep. Beside her, Billy was silent, lost in his thoughts. Only Elle seemed wide awake, standing and rubbing a stone along her stick to smooth it. Goaty, who was as fond of her in this shape as in the other, held the stick steady for her, from time to time looking back up the hill with dreamy longing.

Rage's eyelids grew leaden, and finally she could not resist letting them close. She drifted into a dream of her mother crying, only Mam was a little girl, younger than Rage.

"Sammy! Sam! Don't go!" *Mary wept.*

"Let him," *her grandfather said coldly, his hair black instead of silver. "He does not care that he is leaving you. People who go never care what they leave behind them."*

Rage woke with the queer, unhappy thought that by falling into a coma, Mam had gone away and left *her*.

Mr. Walker growled.

"It's nearly here," Billy whispered to Rage, and a thrill of terror ran through her veins.

She listened hard, but what she could hear did not sound the least bit spiderish. It sounded more like a horse clip-clopping lazily along. She pushed Mr. Walker off her lap and got up just as a woman on a horse came riding into view. It took a second more for Rage to realize that the woman and the horse were a single creature. The bottom half of her was a horse, but from the waist up she was human.

"It's sort of a horse," Goaty whispered.

"It's a centaur!" Rage breathed, enchanted.

"Is it really? I can't see," Mr. Walker complained, and Billy picked him up. "It *is* a centaur," he said, sounding delighted. "I wonder if they really do have a human stomach and a horse stomach."

"Stay here. I'm going down to talk to it," Rage said, determined to be Rage-Winnoway-whose-name-was-Courage, as the Firecat had advised. After all, if anyone would know about magic, it must surely be this legendary beast. In the stories she had read, centaurs were always noble and honorable creatures. She slithered down the last bit of the hill overlooking the road, meaning to stop herself at the edge and climb down with dignity, but it was steeper than she thought, and she flew out and landed hard on her bottom.

"What in the wild!" exclaimed the centaur, coming to an abrupt halt.

Rage could feel her face growing very hot. She got up with as much dignity as she could muster and brushed her clothes off. "Good afternoon, centaur," she said, noting that the fur from the creature's horse half grew up into a sort of shirt for her human half.

The centaur lifted beautifully arched brows. "Good afternoon to you, too, girl. What are you doing here without any sort of keeper?"

Rage felt this rather a rude thing to say. Somehow she would have imagined a centaur to have a high and poetic way of talking, with lots of *thee*-ing and *thou*-ing. "I am looking for the shore of the Endless Sea. Do you know the way?"

The centaur snorted in a very loud and horsy way. "I have never heard of it."

"What is this place called?"

"We are on the road that runs between Wildwood

and Deepwood and leads to the River of No Return." She tilted her head. "How is it that you know so little about where you are?"

"Because I don't belong here!" Rage burst out. "It's all a mistake. I came through an enchanted gateway that disappeared, so I couldn't get back."

"Ah yes, well, they do that. Many gates in but only one out," the centaur said absently. "Enchanted gate, you say? That means you used magic?"

"You said there is a gate out?" Rage asked eagerly.

"I was just repeating an old song my dam used to sing to me. But tell me, you used magic to come here?"

"I said the gate was magic," Rage said.

"But there is magic where you come from?"

"There are lots of *stories* about magic, but I didn't know it really existed." Rage hesitated. "I . . . I heard there was a great wizard this side of the gateway who could work powerful magic."

"Once, long before my creation, a wizard lived in the castle on the hill in the middle of Deepwood," the centaur answered. "He made Valley, they say, so he must have been very powerful."

So Valley was the name of the world they had come to, Rage thought. "Where does the wizard live now?"

The centaur shrugged. "No one knows. The witch women say he got sick of the keepers coming to the castle for advice all the time when he was trying to do his spells, so he magicked Deepwood into a thick tangle, to make it hard to get to the castle. Then one day he just wasn't there anymore."

Rage's heart sank. Witches! And who or what were keepers? And how on earth was she to find a wizard who had disappeared ages ago? More importantly, why had the firecat told her the wizard wanted something brought to him? She remembered uneasily that Bear had said it smelled like a liar.

She thought over all that the centaur had said. "If the witch women are magical . . . ," she began.

"They *work* magic," the centaur corrected her. "Only a wizard can make magic. Terrible curious the witch folk are about him. But the wizard became a recluse before they moved to Wildwood, so they never really had much to do with him. You would need to ask the keepers in Fork about him. Time was, there used to be a lot of coming and going between the castle and Fork."

"Fork?" Rage echoed in bewilderment.

"Fork City. Other side of the River of No Return. Just follow the road to the crossing place."

"Who lives in Fork?"

"Humans, of course. It and all of the villages along the road are keeper territory. It is the road that marks the land ruled by the keepers, not the river." She stopped and suddenly glowered at Rage. "You're not a keeper spy, are you?"

"Don't touch her!" Elle cried, and bounded onto the road between Rage and the centaur. Billy jumped down, too, and stood boldly beside Elle, who was brandishing her spear.

The centaur stared at them both, then all at once the stiffness went out of her bunched muscles and she chuckled. "You are clearly not from Valley, for here no one would be foolish enough to provoke a centaur." Without warning she reared up and drove lightning-fast hoofs into the earth between Elle and Billy.

Rage screamed in fright.

"Fear not, girl," the centaur told her. "You are lucky

that I am not one of my brothers, for they are far more warlike." She turned to Elle. "Put aside your weapon, little warrior, for I mean no harm to your friend. What sort of things are you?"

"I'm a dog." Elle was staring up at the centaur in admiration.

"Me too," Billy said.

The centaur frowned. "There are dogs in some of the villages, but they do not look like you."

"We were dogs before we came through the enchanted gateway that brought us here," Billy explained. "It changed us."

"There must have been a mighty magic in that gate," the centaur said.

"I was told that the wizard made it," Rage said.

The centaur shrugged her massive shoulders again. "Maybe he did. I don't suppose gate making can be much harder than the making of Valley." She gave a shiver, as if her skin were impatient to get moving. "Well, I must go. The witch women have summoned all wild things to a grand council at the heart lake in Wildwood. Would you like to come with me? I'm sure they'd be interested to hear about your world."

Rage shook her head firmly. "We will go to Fork."

"Be careful, then. Keepers rule their territories with hard hands and cold eyes. They don't like anything out of the ordinary," the centaur added, seeming to forget that it had been her idea to seek out the keepers. "Best not to call any attention to yourself. And obey all their rules." Her skin twitched again. "Now I will say goodbye, for I doubt we will meet again."

Rage watched the centaur vanish into the trees beside the road. A moment later she wished she had thought to ask about the firecat. She had no doubt now that it had deliberately lured them through the bramble gate with its promise of magical help from the wizard. The question was, *why?* It hadn't told them about the wizard disappearing, but it had given them the magical hourglass with its riddled directions, so maybe the wizard was hiding somewhere, waiting for someone to unravel the riddle. Rage saw that they had no choice but to look for the wizard since he was their only way home.

"What a lot of words saying nothing," Bear growled, lumbering out of the trees.

"I'm hungry," Mr. Walker said, jumping down.

"Me too," Goaty sighed, following him.

"Shall I go and look for food?" Elle volunteered.

"No!" Rage almost shouted. "I just need to think for a minute before we do anything."

"Thinking is very useful," Elle said doubtfully.

"I don't like the idea of witches," Billy said.

"Me neither," Mr. Walker agreed. "Witches fatten you and eat you, or poison you with apples."

"I don't think we'd better rely too much on what fairy tales say about them," Rage said, thinking that the centaur had not been much like centaurs in stories.

"There's no need for us to go near the witch women," Billy said. "After all, the centaur said that they didn't have much to do with the wizard. We need to talk to the keepers."

"What is a keeper?" Goaty asked.

Rage frowned. "I don't know. A human adult, I suppose, since the centaur asked why I was without one."

"They live in Fork, and the centaur said humans live in Fork, so they must be human," Billy pointed out.

"They *rule* Fork," Mr. Walker said. "Maybe the witch

women rule the wild parts of Valley."

Goaty looked around as if he expected a witch to leap out of a bush.

"She asked if we were keeper spies," Billy murmured. "The keepers wouldn't spy on the witch women unless they didn't like them. Maybe they're at war."

Rage sighed impatiently. "It doesn't matter whether keepers and witch women are at war! We're not on either side. We're only going to Fork to find out about the wizard."

"I still think we should go to the village first. We have to get some food, and we can ask about the keepers and the wizard at the same time," Billy said.

"I vote for food," Mr. Walker agreed promptly.

4

The village they had seen from the top of the hill was less than an hour's journey away. It lay in a place where the road curved inland from the bank of the river. As they approached, Rage could see that it consisted of about twenty houses and smaller outbuildings arranged into four twisty streets that radiated from a central square. A couple of men sat on a step smoking pipes, and another man was chopping wood. A group of old women went down a street carrying baskets and chattering. There were a lot more houses than people. Rage guessed that most of the villagers were inside or had gone off to work somewhere else.

"I'll go in. The rest of you wait here for me," she said.

"Not alone," Billy yelped.

"Mr. Walker can come with me, in my coat pocket. If anything goes wrong, I'll send him for help."

"No," Billy said. "I will come, too."

"Let him go," Bear growled before Rage could argue. "I don't want to hear his whining."

Rage and Billy entered the village, leaving the others

hidden in bushes behind them. "Why does Bear talk to you like that?" Rage asked.

"I don't mind," Billy said.

Rage bit her tongue to keep from saying *she* minded, because how could she when Billy didn't? She would have minded very much if Mam had been as cold and sharp with her. But Billy seemed to accept his mother's treatment and to love her anyway. Was that because he was a dog or because he was sweet-hearted?

Bear as a bear was both a lot angrier and sadder than she had been as a dog. Rage tried to imagine living her whole life with Grandfather Adam's stone eyes on her. She decided she would have run away like Uncle Samuel. Of course, being a dog, Bear couldn't run away. Animals didn't have the same freedom as humans. Then again, maybe humans didn't have much freedom, either, because if she had left, she would have had to leave Mam. She could never do that.

I would have taken Mam with me, Rage thought.

An approaching red setter regarded them expectantly. "Good day," it said cheerfully.

Both Billy and Rage stopped and stared.

"You can talk," Billy said.

"So can you. What of it?" the setter said, then it sniffed and tilted its head. "You look human but you smell like dog."

"I am—" Billy began, but Rage elbowed him in the stomach to remind him that they had agreed not to tell anyone else that they were strangers. "I mean, I—I have a dog as a friend," he stammered at last. "That's probably what you can smell."

The dog tilted its head at Rage.

"We're travelers," Rage said quickly. "We came to see

the wizard who lived in Deepwood, but we have learned that he has moved away."

"I wouldn't know anything about wizards," the dog said.

"We heard that he used to visit the keepers in Fork," Billy said.

"I wouldn't know about that," the setter repeated. It studied Rage for a time. "You smell like a human she-pup."

Rage gave up trying to get information about the wizard. "We were hoping we might be able to work for some food here." The dog flapped its long ear to dislodge a fly. "Do you . . . I mean, whom should we speak to about getting work?"

"I play with the baker when he smells in need of a bit of frisking," the setter said easily. "He feeds me for that. Maybe you could play with him and he'll feed you as well."

Rage blinked at the thought of getting fed for romping with a grown man. "Maybe he'll have something else for us to do. Where is he?"

"I'll show you." The dog rose and stretched enormously, then clawed violently at a spot behind an ear. Billy scratched the spot obligingly, whispering to Rage that he knew just how that felt. The dog gave Billy a lick on the feet, and Rage noticed that there were toffee-colored tufts of hair on Billy's bare toes. These seemed to be the only reminder that he really was a dog.

The setter led them down one of the streets to a small round dumpling of a cottage on the bank of a stream. A wooden waterwheel was turning slowly beside it. The dog bid them farewell and trotted lazily away.

"He had a nice smell," Billy said, looking after him wistfully. Rage couldn't help but smile. Sometimes Billy was so doggish.

They found the baker inside the round building. He turned out to be a thin man wrapped in a huge white apron, kneading bread on a marble counter.

"Excuse me, sir," Rage said hesitantly. "We are in need of food, and a dog told us you might have some work for us."

The baker stopped his kneading and stared at her. "Well, well. I suppose you have come a long way."

It sounded more like a statement than a question, and though it didn't seem to make much sense, Rage nodded politely. Then she said, "The dog . . ."

"Ah, that dog is a fine, playful beast," the baker said, returning to his kneading. He shot her a speculative look. "I've heard them as lives in the outer villages hold loose to keeper ways."

Rage smiled and shrugged, sensing danger. Given the centaur's question about her being without a keeper, she wondered if there was a rule in Valley about children traveling alone. It struck her that she had not seen a single child or young person in the village.

"You say you're prepared to work for food?" the baker asked, and Rage nodded. "Happen I do have something needing doing, but it's hard, dirty work." He gave her and Billy a searching look. "I need someone to clean out my ovens. It'll take a bit of muscle."

"I can work hard," Billy said eagerly.

The baker beamed. "I like to see a lad prepared to put his back into a job. Just let me finish this and I'll show you where the ovens are. They're all cool now because I don't bake until night. Too hot in this weather."

They watched him shape the dough into loaf tins. "They'll need a good few hours of rising now." He laid a damp cloth over them, then wiped his hands on his apron and looked at Rage. "You're too small to do this work, but you can pick your pay while the lad labors. There are berries all along the back of the hedgerow, and I've also got tomatoes and potatoes growing out back. And there are pots of jam and relish and some cheese and butter in the cellar store. And some bread, of course. As much food as the two of you can carry for the job."

Soon Billy was up to his waist in the enormous ovens, and black with soot from head to furry toes.

Rage went to a hedge on the pretext of picking berries and let Mr. Walker out so that he could tell the others what was happening. She began collecting berries, pleased to find they were firm as plums. It would have been impossible to carry real berries without squashing them. The berries tasted rather like vanilla custard, and Rage ate as many as she picked for her bucket. She had just finished digging up a small pile of potatoes and was wondering how they would manage to cook them when the baker called her to the porch. He had assembled several jars of jams and relish, a stone dish of butter, some small crusty loaves of bread, and two fat wheels of cheese wrapped in cloth. Beside them were two cloth bags to pack everything in.

Rage thanked him profusely for his generosity.

"You're a pair of workers, I'll say that," he said, showing Rage a pump where she could wash her hands. "My sister will bring a bite of supper before I start the evening's baking. You're welcome to share that if you like, and stay the night in our barn. It's nice to see a couple of young faces around the village."

Rage thanked him, but hearing him refer to the lack of children made her nervous. "We ought to get on," she said, trying to sound diffident.

The baker nodded. "I suppose it's best not to dawdle on the road. It's not often you see girls traveling without keeper guardians these days." He grinned. "To tell you the truth, I thought you were wild things when I first set eyes on you. Sprites do wander over the road from time to time, poor things. I'd feed them if I could, but as you know, they can't eat ordinary food."

Rage was thrilled at the idea of sprites. She would have liked to ask what they ate, but feared this might be something that was commonly known. "We saw a centaur," she said, thinking it safe to contribute.

The baker sighed. "Used to be a great herd of them hereabouts, but not anymore. What I say is, it's a shame."

"You'd best hold your tongue, brother," a sharp voice said.

Rage turned to see a thin, dark-eyed woman carrying a basket over one arm. Her clothing was gray and plain, her hair pulled into an enormous severe bun. She wore a pair of heavy silver bracelets, one on each wrist. They looked very strange with her workaday attire.

"It's not treason to have an opinion, Rue," the baker said mildly, rising to take the basket from her.

Rage felt the woman's eyes bore into her. She resisted the urge to fidget, since that always made adults think you were guilty of something.

"How do you know this girl will not report to the keepers on which villagers secretly support the witch women and their activities?" Rue asked.

"Activities? It's not like there can be more than a skerrick of magic left for them to work with. I daresay they think more of their dying pets than of intrigue."

Rage was startled. What did the baker mean by saying there was little magic left? Surely magic was not something that could be used up, but was a force to be summoned by spells and incantations.

The baker's sister spoke again. "The witch women

would do anything to feed those unnatural creatures they created."

The baker laughed at his sister. "Ah, Rue, the city has made you cold and hard. Have some compassion for the poor wild things. Is it their fault the witch women created them?"

"You are a fool," the woman said to her brother. "Your careless talk will see us both dragged up before the High Keeper and cast into the River of No Return when this girl tells what she has heard."

"The girl is not banded yet, so how could she be a keeper spy?"

Rage wished Billy would hurry up. She didn't like the talk of spies and being thrown into rivers. And what was banding?

"Who said anything of spies? She's bound for Fork, isn't she?" the woman snapped. "The keepers will question her. They always interrogate new girls to find out if the witch women have tried to recruit them."

There was a charged silence.

"Have you been to the city?" Rage asked the baker lamely, trying to change the subject.

"Never been, never wanted to." He gave his sister a pointed look. "I was born right here in this village, back when it was still common for children to be raised this side of the river. If you want to know about Fork, it's Rue you should ask."

"I do not take kindly to being discussed as if I were not here," the thin woman said. She turned one of the metal bracelets on her wrist and rubbed at the delicate patterning with her thumb. "Where do you come from?" she demanded of Rage.

The baker laughed and flapped a floury hand in his

sister's face. "Now, Rue. You're starting to sound like the keepers, worrying about everything being in its place."

"There is much to worry about," his sister said icily. "As you would see if you ever looked past the dust on the end of your nose, you bumpkin!" She flounced back into the cottage and slammed the door behind her.

The baker sighed. "Don't mind her," he advised. "'Tis her time in the city made her all sharp and nervy-like. She fought being taken to Fork, but she was a girl who might become a witch, so she had no choice. Rue talks proud of the city now, but all that stone and cold water in Fork left its mark on her."

Rage pretended to rearrange the food in the bags, but her mind churned with the knowledge that girls were forced to live in the city of Fork by the keepers, to stop them becoming witches. That must mean the witch women were humans who had learned to work magic. Rage willed Billy to hurry, and this time, to her relief, he appeared. When the baker went to check his ovens, she whispered that they must leave as soon as ever they could. The baker came back beaming and renewed his offer of supper and a bed. But they thanked him and took their leave. Only when they were out of earshot of the village did Rage tell Billy what the baker and his sister had said.

"So there are hardly any children this side of the river because keepers take all girls to Fork," Billy mused. "But I wonder how being in the city stops a girl becoming a witch. It must be because there are no witches there to teach them how." Seeing Rage's look of admiration, he flushed. "It's easier to think in this shape."

"You don't mind being turned into a human?"

"Sometimes it feels very strange," he admitted. "I

can't do some of the things I used to do as a dog. I can't run as fast, and my nose seems to be almost useless. That's the worst thing. But I can remember things better now. There is more space for keeping things inside my head. I'm not completely human, though. Humans can do more things with their minds than I can. But the longer I am this shape, the more my mind grows."

Rage tried to imagine what it would be like if she were transformed into a dog. She realized with shame that much as she loved the dogs, she wouldn't want to be one. Mostly because it meant she would belong to a human, who might be like Grandfather Adam or Mr. Johnson. And because dogs weren't allowed to decide things.

"I don't think I'd like to be completely human," Billy went on apologetically. "I thought I would, but now I can see that human minds are growing all the time, until they are like enormous houses with thousands of rooms and twisty passages and dark hallways all full of cobwebs and shadows and forgotten things. No wonder there is so much confusion in humans. Dog minds are like standing outside. There are no walls, the wind blows freshly, and light falls everywhere. The best thing about being human is that I can talk with you."

Rage wondered if her mind was full of twisty passages and dark shadows. She didn't feel like it was true, but maybe that was only because she was not grown up. Certainly she could imagine Grandfather Adam being full of dank, secret niches, and even Mam's mind must be full of hidden corners.

"How do the others feel about being changed?" she asked curiously.

"They don't talk about it much. Mama doesn't know

how to be happy, so being changed doesn't seem to have made much difference to her. Mr. Walker complains, but he likes complaining, and Goaty is just as scared as he was before. Elle likes being human-shaped because it's something new."

They lapsed into silence. It was hard work carrying the heavy bags. When they arrived, the others greeted them with hungry delight. Soon they were enjoying a hearty sunset picnic on the bank of the river. Rage told them what had happened, then she took out the hourglass and they all studied it.

"It's strange that the wizard would want such an old-fashioned way of telling time," Rage said, noting that the grains continued to float from one side of the hourglass to the other. But most of the grains had yet to fall.

"I suppose he needs it because it's magic, rather than because it tells the time," Billy mused.

"I wonder why the firecat wants to help the wizard, anyway," Rage murmured.

"Why *us*, is what I'd like to know," Goaty muttered.

"Maybe it wanted strangers," Billy said. "If it had tried to get someone from Valley to look for the wizard, they would just refuse or give up when it became too difficult, but we can't."

Rage couldn't help but be impressed by Billy's perception. He must be right, too. No one in Valley could possibly want to find the wizard as much as she did.

"Maybe the hourglass measures something other than time," Mr. Walker suggested.

"Whatever it measures is running out," Goaty murmured.

That made Rage think of Mam in her dangerous sleep, which might last forever. Whatever the risk, she must decipher the wizard's riddle and find him. She put the hourglass back in her pocket and looked around at the others.

"I think we must still go to Fork," she said. "One of the keepers must know where the wizard is. We should be safe enough as long as we obey the rules." She was confident she could do this. She was good at being obedient.

"But we don't know what those rules are. And they won't let you leave again, because you're a girl," Billy objected.

"I don't see how anyone can guard a whole city properly," Elle said. "I'm sure we could escape if we had to."

"Cities are no place for animals or even for half-animals," Bear pronounced grimly.

"That's true," Goaty said. "I vote for what Bear votes for."

"She didn't vote for anything, you nitwit," snapped Mr. Walker. His tail twitched in irritation.

"I don't see what else we can do but go there," Rage said, feeling more troubled than ever. "We have to find out where the wizard is if we ever want to get home. And I'm sure Elle is right and we can slip out of Fork again when we want to leave."

"Even if these keepers know all about the wizard and where he went, they might refuse to tell us," Mr. Walker said.

"What do you think we should do, then?" Rage asked.

The little man opened his mouth, then closed it, looking slightly self-conscious. "I suppose we have to go to Fork," he said at last.

"So let's go!" Elle said impatiently. When no one argued, she packed up the remaining food into two bundles, neatly tying this to that until she and Billy could sling them over their shoulders. Rage said she was amazed that Elle was so *hand*-y, given she had spent most of her life with paws. This seemed to her a very funny joke, though the animals stared at her in puzzlement when she laughed.

"I guess you have to be human," she muttered as they set off again. Even Billy looked bemused, and she supposed that his mind hadn't grown enough to make space for jokes. She had a painful longing for Mam, who had always laughed at her jokes, even when Rage messed them up and said the funny bit in the wrong place.

By the time they left the village behind, dusk was deepening into night. When Rage looked back at the village, she could make out lights in a few of the cottage windows, and little dribbles of smoke coming from the chimney stacks. They heard the setter barking—not in anger, but in a casual way. The barking faded as they went on. The road drew nearer the river until Rage could smell its dank odor and hear it slap and gurgle against the bank.

"I hope we don't walk off the edge into the river," Goaty fretted.

"Stay close to me," Elle said heartily. "If you fall in, I'll save you."

"Once upon a time there were rivers where one sip of the water was poison, or where falling in meant forgetting everything you ever knew," Mr. Walker said dreamily.

"That wasn't this river," Billy said.

"You never know with rivers," Mr. Walker said.

Rage was surprised once more at how much Mr. Walker's thoughts revolved around the stories and myths her mother had read to them.

The narrow moon was setting when they stopped for

the night, having decided it was too dangerous to go on in the darkness. Rage studied the moon curiously, wondering if it was a different moon from the one that shone over Winnoway Farm. It looked exactly the same, but how could that be?

Rage was very glad when Elle found a huge, hollow tree trunk with a dry, woody floor that was big enough for them all to take shelter in. Even Bear could fit in, and though it was a tight squeeze, they were glad to cuddle together. A chilly mist had risen off the river and drifted just above the ground, luminous in the darkness.

Sleep came almost at once. Rage dreamed that she was walking through a jungle looking for Uncle Samuel. Though he must be a grown man now and she had no idea what he looked like, it didn't seem to matter in the dream. After a bit she thought she could hear a man's voice in the distance, calling her name, but no matter how long she walked, she never seemed to get any closer.

Sunlight woke her, slanting through the leaves and into the hollow, insistently poking at her eyelids. Rage found herself cuddled warmly between Billy and Bear. It felt so safe and nice that she wished she could stay like that forever. Mr. Walker was asleep in Billy's lap, snoring.

None of them woke as she eased her way out from between them to go to the toilet. She found a place a short distance from the others and dug herself a shallow hole. It was a nasty, messy business. Covering it over, she thought it was much better in stories, where no one ever had to go to the toilet or eat or bathe. The need to wash her hands drew her to the river, and she was startled at how close it was to where they had slept. The bank was steep, but she found a flat stretch where the river had slopped over the bank to form a quiet lagoon. The river was wide and the current looked strong and swift, but the lagoon was calm and inviting.

She stood gazing at it for a time, remembering Mr. Walker's words about the dangers of unknown rivers. A poisonous river seemed unlikely, but where there was magic, anything might be possible, even if the magic was dying out. It would be truly awful if she found the wizard only to discover he had no magic to send them home or save Mam.

Sitting on the bank, Rage took out the hourglass again. As before, the grains floated from one end to the other without interruption, no matter which way she held the hourglass. Even when she shook it gently— thinking about Mr. Walker saying that the fall of sand might measure something other than time—it did not seem to affect the inner motion of the sand at all. If it was sand. She held the device close and peered into it, wondering if the grains of sand were magic and what would happen if the glass broke.

"Has Ragewinnoway guessed riddling of wizard yet?" a familiar smoky voice asked.

Rage started violently. "I wish you wouldn't creep up on me!" she snapped. "I'm not talking to you anymore unless you show yourself."

There was a faint sizzling noise, and the water in the lagoon began to boil. Rage stared warily into it as the bubbling subsided, but instead of seeing her own face peering back up at her, the water was stained red and orange and flecked with slivers of light that might have been eyes or sharp teeth.

"What does seeing say to Ragewinnoway?" the firecat asked, and the water seemed to shimmer mockingly.

"I can't see you properly," Rage complained.

"Ragewinnoway seeing only what is to be seen."

There was the suggestion of a shrug in the voice. "But does she see what wizard is telling in tricky words?"

"I haven't figured his riddle out yet. But there are some things I want to ask." Rage was determined to get some clear answers from the elusive creature.

"Maybe answering and maybe not answering," the firecat said contrarily.

Rage counted to ten. "Where is the Endless Sea? Is it beyond the mountains?"

"If firecat knows where is Endless Sea, firecat can bring hourglass to master," it sneered.

Rage blinked. The firecat had called the wizard its master! "How long has the wizard been missing?" she asked.

"Long time," the firecat said vaguely.

Rage guessed from this that it didn't understand how to count time. "They say here that he disappeared from his castle. Is that true?"

The firecat made no response.

"Did he ask you to bring the hourglass to him before he went, or did he send a message to you?"

"Hourglass belonging to wizard. But is dangerous. Be careful. Not breaking," the firecat warned, and for the first time there was nothing but seriousness in its tone. Perhaps it was even telling most of the truth for once.

"What does the hourglass do?"

There was a hesitation. "All wizard knows is in hourglass," it answered finally in a purring voice.

"Why didn't the wizard take it with him?"

"Firecat not knowing. Wizard saying obey words on hourglass and be rewarded with what you deserve."

Rage didn't like the sound of that at all. It almost sounded like a threat. She had intended to ask if the wizard was good or bad, but now that she knew he was the firecat's master, she doubted that it would answer truthfully—especially since it wanted them to deliver the hourglass. It was clear, though, that the wizard had instructed the firecat *before* disappearing, which meant he really must want the hourglass. But why hadn't he simply taken it with him, or given simple instructions, instead of creating a difficult and mysterious riddle?

"The wizard told *you* to bring the hourglass to him, didn't he?" Rage guessed. "He promised to give *you* a reward if you would bring it to him. So why do you need me?"

"Hurrying," the firecat hissed, then the water began to bubble and spit, and gradually the colors faded.

"I should have asked it if magic is really running out in Valley," Rage muttered aloud, although the firecat seemed to have no shortage of the magic necessary for appearing and disappearing. She thought over its answers and decided it really did not know where its master was or how to find him.

The urgency of its final, hissed word made her think of the sand in the hourglass. What did it measure? The firecat had warned her not to break it, saying it was dangerous. No doubt it had only said this to make her careful. The wizard would probably be furious at it if the hourglass was damaged. The biggest puzzle was why the wizard had asked the firecat to bring the hourglass to him at all.

Unless the riddle was a test for the firecat itself!

Rage bit her lip in excitement, certain she was right. It was the only explanation that made sense. It even explained the firecat's evasive manner—by getting Rage to try to figure out the riddle, it was obviously cheating.

Another thought occurred to her. If she was right about the quest for the hourglass being a test, maybe the sand in the hourglass represented the amount of time the firecat had been given to solve its master's riddle.

Rage wondered how the wizard would feel about *their* solving the riddle, if they managed it. Maybe he would be angry. He might turn them all into frogs or river slime. The firecat had said they would be rewarded, but it was clear the creature would say anything to get them to do what it wanted.

A drab little bird fluttered to the ground and tilted its head to drink from the tea-colored water. Flinging off her clothes, boots, and all thoughts of the firecat and the hourglass, Rage climbed gladly into the lagoon. The water was warm from the sun or maybe from the firecat, and she was still paddling in her underclothes when Billy appeared. He ran at the lagoon with a whoop of delight and plunged in with a great splash.

"You ought to have taken your clothes off," Rage spluttered, laughing.

He looked embarrassed. "I forgot." He climbed out and peeled off his T-shirt, jeans, and jacket and jumped in again in cotton shorts. Rage studied him curiously for signs that he was really a dog, but there were none, other than his hairy toes. His skin was creamy pale, and his shoulders were broad and muscular. There were little patches of toffee hair under his arms and a fuzz of hair down his legs, but grown men had those. In human years, Billy appeared to be about sixteen, but as he looked over the small sandbar that separated the lagoon from the river, his expression of longing seemed very young to Rage.

"It's dangerous," she said firmly, remembering how he had always been attracted to water as a dog. He sighed and came away from the edge. As they paddled, she told him about the firecat's appearance. He agreed that it was very likely that the riddle on the base of the hourglass was a test that had been set for it.

"But it doesn't make any difference to us if it is," Billy said. "We still have to solve it if we are to find the wizard, get home, and help your mam."

"The wizard might be mad that *we* solved the riddle," Rage pointed out.

Billy frowned. "I'm more worried about the keepers than the wizard, to tell you the truth. That centaur said we ought not to draw any attention to ourselves in Fork, but if we tell them how we came to be in Valley, it's sure to cause a fuss."

"I know," Rage agreed.

"I wonder if the wizard setting a test for the firecat could have anything to do with his disappearance," Billy murmured, now floating and staring at his hairy toes. "Maybe he made the riddle and went to the shore of the Endless Sea to wait for the firecat to solve it, and he's still there waiting because the firecat can't figure it out."

"Why would he wait so long? He'd use his magic to come back and see what had gone wrong," Rage said.

"What if he couldn't?" Billy countered, turning onto his stomach. "What if, instead of the hourglass containing a record of all he knew, it actually held all of his power!" His brown eyes glimmered with excitement.

"It doesn't make sense," Rage objected. "Why would the wizard risk his power to set a test for the firecat? Besides, like you said, maybe the firecat was lying about the hourglass. That riddle on it doesn't say anything about the wizard, after all."

"Then what on earth does the firecat want of us?" Billy dog-paddled neatly around the lagoon, looking glum. Coming back to Rage, he said, "That centaur said the keepers kept annoying the wizard for advice—advice about what?"

"Maybe about everything. I suppose it was because of him making Valley. He must have been like the king here," Rage said.

"Only he didn't like being the king, so he became a hermit and then he vanished."

"I wonder why he made Valley in the first place if he didn't want to live here," Rage pondered.

"I've just thought of something!" Billy pushed his hair out of his eyes. "What if he put the magic in Valley when he created it, and it's dying out because he has disappeared?"

They were distracted from this interesting idea by the arrival of Elle and Mr. Walker. Rage climbed out of the water because her underclothes needed time to dry out. Fortunately, the sun was shining brightly and the air was pleasantly warm.

Elle and Billy romped and splashed in the pool. Mr. Walker drank daintily and washed his hands and face but otherwise avoided the water with a shudder. Rage spread out her coat and laid out a breakfast of slightly squashed berries, bread, and cheese. Bear was nowhere to be seen, but Mr. Walker said he could smell her nearby.

After they ate, Rage dressed, checking to be sure the hourglass and Mam's locket were still safe. She went through the ideas that she and Billy had discussed, but there was no way of knowing which were right. Talking had got them no closer to unraveling the riddle of the wizard's whereabouts, and in the end that was really all that mattered.

The others were having a last romp on the bank

when Bear came out of the bushes. Rage offered her food, but the old dog shook her head and sat down to lick at her paw.

"Why do you keep doing that?" Rage asked.

Bear regarded her through tiny black eyes. "A thorn from the bramble gate got into me."

"Why didn't you say so?" Rage asked, undoing a pin she kept in the hem of her coat and taking the huge paw firmly in her hand.

"A dog's pain is a dog's pain. Dogs don't complain," Bear said with melancholic poetry as Rage probed the swollen flesh.

When she found the shiny black top of a thorn driven deep into the pad, she looked at Bear with concern. "I am afraid I will have to hurt you to get it out."

"It is in the nature of humans to hurt," Bear said, staring bleakly into her eyes.

Rage swallowed and stuck the pin into the paw, forcing it under the thorn and levering it out. The breath hissed through Bear's lips, but she did not growl or groan.

Rage drew out the long, sharp thorn with dismay.

5

The road wound along companionably with the river, sometimes going right along the edge of the bank, other times turning away to avoid a thick clump of trees. Late in the morning, they came upon a group of little stone houses between the road and the water, but they had clearly been abandoned long ago.

"We could stay a night here," Mr. Walker said. Rage could see he was attracted to the smallness of the houses.

"We don't want to stop again so soon," Elle said firmly, striding ahead.

"Probably those little houses are so old they would fall on our heads and squash us flat," Goaty said.

Rage glared at him, wondering if this was what came of being around Mr. Johnson, who always saw the worst side of things first. Mam used to say that you could show Mr. Johnson a pretty wisp of cloud and he would see the end of the world.

"Like Grandfather?" Rage had asked.

"Like Grandfather." Mam's eyes had grown sad.

Rage remembered that this conversation had happened on a train. Mam loved trains. "They're so much gentler than cars. They don't roar through cities; they wind politely around them. They stop to let people in and out. People exchange newspapers or talk or just sit together. People sleep in trains and walk in them. They drink cups of tea and eat scones in them. Trains are for sharing."

"I like trains," Rage had said earnestly.

Mam laughed. "Imagine a city where all of those roads were turned into green paths. People could stroll and eat their lunches. Imagine looking out of a high building and seeing paths with big trees growing along them, fruit trees with masses of blossoms and huge cedars. There'd be no car noise, no pollution from the engines. People could lie under trees or watch buskers or just read. You wouldn't feel like you were in the city at all."

Mam had been like that. She would have an idea about something, and suddenly it would turn into a much bigger idea. Everything would be sucked into her idea and turned into something better. After they came to Winnoway, they had taken few train trips. There were no more talks or sing-alongs, no more stories or laughing tumbles together. Mam had become silent and distracted. She went on long walks alone, or she sat for hours gazing out the window. Sometimes she had smiled at Rage without really seeming to see her.

Rage shivered, remembering what Mrs. Johnson had said about Grandmother Reny growing more and more silent until she had just faded away, and the cold seemed to go inside her bones.

She tried to think about something she and Mam had done together after they shifted to Winnoway, something that they had really enjoyed, but she could think of nothing except those wonderful train journeys before they had come to Winnoway. Rage was startled to discover that Winnoway Farm, and even her own bedroom with its lilac wallpaper, was hard to picture. The farm seemed as if it belonged in someone else's world, in a story.

Did people in stories feel themselves to be real? How would she know if somebody had made her up? Then she wondered if maybe all that had happened was a story she was telling herself.

Thinking like this made her feel dizzy, as if she were turning round and round on the spot. She grinned, remembering how she had done that while holding Billy when he was a puppy. He had sprawled and lurched and sat down hard when she put him on the ground.

She looked at Billy and found him watching her.

"You were smiling," he said.

"I was remembering how dizzy you were after I swung you round and round when you were a puppy."

He threw his head back and laughed. "I thought the ground was jumping under me. I felt so sick in the stomach."

It occurred to Rage that what she had done was cruel.

Seeing the look on her face, Billy said, "It was no worse than when a puppy bites his brother or sister too hard on the ear."

"You weren't angry at me?"

"I love you," Billy said simply.

Rage opened her mouth to tell him that she loved him, too, but Elle interrupted to warn them that she could smell someone coming along the road behind them. They hurriedly decided that Billy would stay on the road with Rage while the rest of them got out of sight behind some bushes a little back from the road.

Before long, a gray donkey appeared. It was harnessed to a small open carriage bearing several very little girls in spotless white tunics and stockings and three women in long, colorful tubelike dresses. The women carried elaborately painted parasols to shade them from the sun. At first Rage thought the women were all deathly pale, but when they came closer, she could see that their faces were painted white, like those of Japanese ceremonial dancers. Their dresses even looked a bit like kimonos. The children had been laughing and chattering gaily, but they fell silent when they noticed Rage and Billy.

"Wild things!" piped one.

"Stop," shouted another, and the donkey obeyed. "Ahoy there. Are you wild things?"

"I'm just a girl like you," Rage said.

"You are almost a woman, yet you *are* like us, for you wear no bands," the girl chirped, lifting both of her bare arms up for Rage's inspection.

"Why don't you come in the cart with us?" one of the other girls invited.

"Impossible!" the eldest of the women said sternly. She waved an arm in an imperious gesture, and Rage noticed that she was wearing heavy metal bracelets like the ones worn by the baker's sister, Rue. Being banded must mean having to wear such bracelets, which seemed to mark the wearers as loyal keeper subjects.

"Why shouldn't she come with us?" another of the children asked defiantly.

"Perhaps she does not go to be banded," hissed the plumpest of the women. "Perhaps she is a witch woman."

The children stared at Rage solemnly.

"Don't frighten them with foolish talk, Ramis," the older woman said in a no-nonsense voice. "Witch women do not venture from Wildwood. This girl is clearly from one of the outer villages and is traveling with her escort to Fork to be banded. They often come in somewhat older. It was so with you, was it not, Ania?" she asked the youngest of the women.

Ania nodded meekly, but when she spoke, it was to the children. "Even if the girl is a wild thing, you have nothing to fear. You will see many wild things in the city."

Rage heard this with puzzlement. Hadn't the baker said that wild things were not supposed to enter keeper territory? To her delight, one of the children voiced this very question.

"The High Keeper has given wild things leave to enter Fork," the plump woman said piously.

"But why? They're so strange," the girl complained.

"I do not know why, but they do no harm with their strangeness," Ania said. The other two women stared at her askance. She shrugged. "Well, it is not as if they can draw magic from the earth without a witch woman's help, and witch women are forbidden to cross the river."

"They cannot be permitted to drain the other side of the river of magic as well," said the older woman icily.

Rage blinked, wondering if she had heard correctly. The woman seemed to be saying that there was still magic on the other side of the river, although it had almost died on this side. Was it possible that magic could be in one part of a land and not another? Did it form in the ground like gold or silver? And how could the witch women have used it all up?

"I think wild things should be stopped from coming

over the river," said the plump woman. "It is so depressing to see them drifting about looking sick and starved."

"More depressing for them to be starving, don't you
think?" Ania asked.

"The wild things are only dreams the witch folk
brought into being. We should rather pity them than fear
them," said the little girl who had invited Rage to ride in
the cart.

"I should not voice such opinions when you are in
Fork," advised the severe woman dryly. "Now, let us
continue. I'm sorry we cannot take you and your friend,"
she added to Rage. "But you ought to go along as quickly
as possible."

"There really isn't room," Rage pointed out when the
little girl looked as if she might argue. Belatedly, it
occurred to her that she was wasting a perfectly good
chance to get more information. "Uh, before you go, we
met another traveler who spoke of the Endless Sea. Do
you know where that is?"

The plump woman snickered rather meanly. "She is
from the outermost village in Valley, surely, to ask about
a child's myth as if it were a real place."

"I heard that the wizard who made Valley had gone
to the shore of the Endless Sea," Rage persisted.

Ania opened her mouth as if to speak, then seemed
to think better of it.

"I do not know where the wizard has gone, but it is
said he will return when things are properly in Order
again." The severe woman spoke these words as a chant,
then bid the donkey continue.

"The wild things must eat magic," Billy said when the
cart had drawn out of sight. "They're starving because it
has run out on this side of the river."

"It's horrible being hungry," Elle said. "Why don't the keepers let the witch women give them some magic from the other side of the river?"

"They're probably afraid it will all be used up," Billy said.

"How do you eat magic?" Goaty asked.

"How do you get it out of the ground?" Mr. Walker muttered.

Billy's mind had been going along a different line. "I wonder what that woman meant by saying the wizard will come back when there is Order here. What is Order?"

Rage could see Billy was enjoying his new ability to think complex thoughts, but she was sick of questions with no answers. The women in the cart had laughed at her for asking about the Endless Sea, calling it a child's myth. Rage wondered if they were going to find the answers they needed, even in Fork. She was beginning to be afraid they would never get back home and that she would never see Mam again, asleep or awake. That thought made her throat ache.

"I wonder what is over the river besides the city of Fork," Mr. Walker said.

"A dangerous, wet land, probably," Goaty said.

Rage lost her temper and rounded on him. "Why do you always have to imagine the worst?"

Goaty hung his head and looked so pathetic that her anger drained away. After all, she was really angry at herself for getting them into such a mess. "I'm sorry I shouted at you, but all those bad things you keep saying are like stones we have to carry. They just make everything harder."

"I know," Goaty mumbled. "That's why no one wants me around. I make everyone feel bad and sad. It is because of the hole in me that comes from never having a name."

"But you have a name."

He looked up at her. "Would it be a name if you were called 'girly,' or Elle were called 'doggy'? Goaty is not a name. It is the name given to a thing no one cares about enough to name."

Rage swallowed hard, remembering that her grandfather had always called her "the girl."

"We will give you a name," Elle said enthusiastically. "What shall it be?" She looked at the rest of them.

"A name can't be decided just like that," Billy said admonishingly. "Naming is a serious business." He sounded so like Mam that Rage felt perilously near to tears again.

"We will think of the right name for you," she told Goaty thickly.

"What I want to know is how we are supposed to cross the river," Mr. Walker muttered, for they had reached a part of the road that ran right along the very edge of the swift-flowing water.

Rage was carrying him because his little legs could no longer keep up.

"I'm sure there will be a bridge," she said, and she was sure, for how else would the women and children in the cart get to the other side?

"There will be guards on it," Mr. Walker said. "Rulers always have soldiers to make people obey them. The more rules, the more soldiers are needed to keep them."

"Maybe the keepers keep their own rules," Rage said.

But Mr. Walker shook his head authoritatively. "In stories, the makers of rules are never the ones to force people to obey them."

"No one said anything about soldiers," Rage said.

"Where there are rules, there are soldiers," Mr. Walker insisted.

"I'm afraid Mr. Walker is probably right," Billy said. "Humans are fond of rules and even fonder of giving people the power to make sure they are obeyed. Besides, there are bound to be guards at the bridge, if only to stop witch women from going over."

Rage thought of something that one of the white-faced women had said. "How will they know *I'm* not a witch woman?"

Billy shrugged. "When we reach Fork, you must say you have come from one of the outer villages to be banded. I just wish we knew exactly what banding meant."

"It's getting metal things on your arms, like the bracelets those women in the cart wore," Mr. Walker said. "Like getting a dog collar."

"If that were all, what would stop witch women putting on the same sort of bands and coming to steal magic from Fork for the wild things?" Billy asked. "I think the keepers have some way of making sure magic can't be taken from the ground, and I think the bands are part of it."

A chill crept up Rage's spine as she understood what Billy was trying to say. "You think being banded is more than just getting those bracelets?"

"I don't know," he admitted.

"If banding stopped women from working magic, why would they be kept in Fork for so long?" Mr. Walker asked.

"So they can't have daughters who might be recruited by the witches?" Rage suggested.

"Maybe," Billy said. "Anyway, if we see anyone else on

the road, we must be sure to ask about banding. When we get to Fork, they will want to band you, and we need to understand what that means."

They did not meet anyone else until it was almost dusk, and by then Mr. Walker was asleep in Rage's oversized coat pocket and Bear had disappeared into the trees alongside the road.

A wild-looking girl came round a bend in the road in front of them. She was flanked on either side by two coppery red winged lions, only slightly bigger than Bear in her dog form. The lions could only be wild things. Rage's heart beat fast at the sheer wonder of them.

Goaty moaned in fright and stopped, trembling from head to cloven hoofs.

"Good dusk," the girl greeted them in a thin, high voice. Up close it was clear that she was a wild thing, too. Her eyes were an impossible hue of violet, and her great tangle of black hair rippled as if breezes blew through it. She wore a ragged bit of a shift that showed a lot of her skinny greenish limbs, and her wrists were unadorned.

The winged lions began sniffing Billy, who laughed. "It tickles," he said apologetically.

The sprite cocked her head at the lions. "They ask why you do not answer their greeting. And they ask what manner of thing you are."

"I'm a dog," Billy said.

One of the lions licked his toes, then looked at the sprite. "He says you smell like and not like a dog, as does your friend." She pointed to Elle, who was now being examined by the lions. Fearless as ever, Elle ran her hands through their manes. The sprite laughed and danced across to caress her golden hair. "Pretty. Strong. And what are you?" she asked, coming to Goaty and tugging at his ringlets. "Soft. Pale. Half human, half beast. Are you not a wild thing?"

Goaty tried to speak, but the winged lions converged on him, and he fell into a quaking silence.

"They say you stink of fear," the sprite said, tilting her head curiously. "You do not need to be afraid. We will not hurt you. Why don't you come with us to Wildwood? I will make a crown of living ivy for your hair, and you shall learn to dance and ride on my friends as I do, and you will forget fear." She threw her arms around his neck and kissed Goaty passionately on the cheek.

"Oh, please don't eat me!" he shrieked.

"Don't be a fool! She's trying to kiss you, not eat you," Mr. Walker said crossly, poking his head out of Rage's pocket.

The sprite stared at him in delight. Sighing, Rage let him out onto the ground. The lions sniffed at him, and the sprite knelt to look at him. "I thought you one of the little people, but my friends say you are like that one and that one." She pointed to Billy and Elle. "A not-dog." Her face grew puzzled. "The witch women ask us to tell them of things that smell of magic but are not wild things."

Rage felt even more wary of the witch women now that she knew they were responsible for draining magic from the land. "We are not magic, but magic has been worked against us," she said carefully, knowing the centaur would tell the same story if the witch women asked. Better not to speak of the firecat and the hourglass. "We are looking for the wizard, to see if he can undo what has been done to us," she added.

"The witch women also seek the wizard, for they say

only he can restore magic to Valley," the sprite said. She bent to pet Mr. Walker. "You are a pretty thing, with your soft ears and big eyes. Magic has made you into this shape, and whence comes the magic?"

"An enchanted gateway brought us here and changed us," Mr. Walker said, twitching his ears.

"Where is this gateway?" the sprite asked. Mr. Walker started back in alarm from the sudden hunger in her eyes. The sprite looked abashed. "I did not mean to frighten you. It is just that magic is so scarce here now, and we are hungry."

"You haven't come from Fork?" Billy asked.

The sprite nodded. "Wild things cannot eat unless food is magicked for us, and there are no witches there. My friends and I went to the High Keeper to ask if they would not allow the witch women to come to Fork and create food for us. We had to wait a long, hungry time. Then he looked down from his seat of dead willow and said it was best that we fade, since we were never natural things and upset the Order of the land."

"I'm sorry," Rage said. "I wish we could help, but we really don't have any magic."

The sprite nodded sadly. "My friends say your words smell of the truth." Then she stopped and listened to the lions again. "My friends say there is another. . . ."

Bear came lumbering out of the trees lining the road, and the lions turned as one to regard her with their flaring golden eyes. Rage suddenly felt frightened that they might hurt her. But before she could say anything, she saw that the lions were merely sniffing Bear, who strangely allowed it. They then withdrew and sank on their bellies before her, purring loudly and spreading their glowing scarlet wings.

"They humble themselves before your companion," the sprite told Rage. "They say your companion is . . . I do not know a word for it. Greater magic? My friends can see a little into the future, and what they see makes them honor this great dark beast. Can you not hear them?"

"I can," Mr. Walker said with uncustomary shyness.

The sprite touched his face, then drew a deep breath. "Well, we must go back to Wildwood." She turned to Bear and made a low, graceful curtsy. "Farewell, Great One. If I have done naught in my life but look on you, it is enough."

The lions rose, and all three of them went on down the road.

"Well!" Elle said, staring after them. "What was all that about?" But no one answered, for they were staring at Bear.

She growled at them to leave her be. "I don't know why those creatures acted like that. There's nothing special about me. Nothing at all." She turned away and went back into the trees. She disliked being in the open now, even more than when she had been a dog.

"Could you really hear those lion things talking?" Elle asked Mr. Walker, as they set off again.

"I said so, didn't I? But it wasn't exactly talking. It was sort of a deep, purring music. A bit like the firecat's voice, but not so sneering and sly."

"We should have asked that sprite about the firecat, and we forgot to ask about banding, too," Billy said, but his eyes were on the bushes where his mother had gone.

"I don't suppose she would have known much about banding," Rage said. "And I don't think we should tell anyone anything about our business anymore."

"Maybe the firecat is a wild thing," Elle said.

"It couldn't be," Billy said. "Wild things can't work magic to feed themselves, and the firecat uses magic every time it appears."

"Maybe it can work magic because the wizard made it, and he is more powerful than the witch women," Mr. Walker said.

Rage said nothing. The encounter only seemed to have produced more questions. The sole interesting thing they had learned was that the witch women believed the wizard could restore the lost magic to Valley and were searching for him.

"Dangerous wild beasts," Goaty said, looking down the road after the sprite and the winged lions.

"She was very small," Mr. Walker said, and he sighed.

Not long after, the sun sank. They were beginning to think about finding a place to sleep when Billy pointed out an arc of light on the horizon.

"I bet the bridge to Fork is just over this rise," Rage said, excited.

But she was wrong.

6

It wasn't a bridge but a river port. Rage and her companions looked down on it from a low mound beside the road. The gray donkey and cart were tethered to a wooden pier with a hut built at the end of it. Obviously the little girls and the women in kimono dresses had already gone across the river. Rage noticed a big metal winch with thick, twisted iron cables stretching out across the water, which pulled the ferry across the currents to the opposite bank.

The darkness and width of the river meant that she could not see the other side. "Elle?"

"I see nothing, but I smell water and stone on the other side," Elle reported.

"I have been thinking," Billy said when they had been standing there staring down silently for some minutes. "The High Keeper told the sprite that wild things ought to be allowed to die because they upset Order here, and the woman in the cart said the wizard would not return until Order had been restored. What if the keepers are letting the wild things die because they think that will bring the wizard back?"

Rage stared, beginning to feel just a little bit awed by the way Billy was able to figure things out. She did not know what to say to his grim idea, but it struck her that a lot of people in Valley were looking for the missing wizard.

"Let's go down," Elle said impatiently. "We have done enough thinking, and talking about thinking."

"Going down is always a bad idea," Goaty murmured.

"I don't think we should go down just yet," Rage said. "Let's wait until a boat comes."

The others agreed. Billy suggested they travel in two groups when the time came to cross the river. "Rage will go as a human girl I am escorting to Fork to be banded, and the rest of you can pretend to be wild things," he explained. "You can be going to plead your cause to the High Keeper, like the sprite and the winged lions."

"I don't want to see the High Keeper," Goaty protested. "He sounds horrible."

"He does," Billy admitted. "But remember how the sprite said they were made to wait a long time to see him? He won't see you at once, and that woman in the cart said there were lots of wild things in Fork, so they must be able to move around the town."

"What about the other wild things?" Mr. Walker protested. "They will smell that we are not wild things."

"You'll just have to avoid them," Billy said, sounding exasperated. "You have to go as wild things, otherwise we will have to explain about the bramble gate and admit to coming from another world."

"I don't understand," Elle said. "I thought we were going to see the keepers about the wizard. Surely we'll have to tell them everything."

Billy glanced at Rage, and she saw that, like her, he had come to the conclusion that they had better avoid the keepers. "I think we should learn a bit more about the keepers before we reveal ourselves to them," he said.

Elle cast herself down on the grass with an expression of utter boredom and said she might as well sleep if they were not going anywhere. Goaty lay neatly beside her, and Bear and Mr. Walker curled up to sleep, too. Billy stayed beside Rage, gazing down at the pier. Several people were moving around the hut and the winch. They looked like workers, not passengers.

"What do you suppose the lions smelled on Bear?" Rage asked Billy.

"I don't know," he said. "It was very strange. That sprite said they saw something in her future." He shivered. "I could not bear it if something bad happened to her, Rage. Her life has been so hard already."

Rage understood. She felt the same about Mam. But she was beginning to see that something had been wrong with Mam even before the accident. That was why they had moved so often, and why Mam never made any friends. Rage had thought they went back to Winnoway for Grandfather Adam's sake. Now she wondered if they had come back because Mam hoped to heal whatever had been hurt inside her.

But Grandfather Adam had been just as cold and hard as ever.

Strangely, instead of hating her grandfather for the way he had been, she found herself trying to imagine what had happened to make him so blind to joy and laughter, so stony to Rage and her mother. It couldn't be because of Mam and her brother running away, as she had always thought—Mrs. Johnson had said Grandfather Adam was like that even before he married Grandmother Reny. That meant something must have happened to him even before Mam was born.

Later, as Rage laid out a supper of what remained from the baker's supplies, Elle vanished for a time. Returning, she shook herself mischievously, showering Rage and Billy with water. She had been for a moonlight swim. Goaty woke from his nap with a shudder as Elle and Billy fell into a wild romp. They were scolded happily by Mr. Walker, whom they almost squashed. Remembering what Billy had said about the difference between being a dog and being human, Rage wished she had their ability to put aside cares and live in the moment. But she was too human. Billy had once said that to be human was to be free to make choices, but really, being free only meant you had to worry about everything your choosing might cause.

She leaned back against a tree and closed her eyes. Listening to their puffing and panting, she could almost pretend she was home with Mam.

She wondered what the kids at school had thought when she didn't come to classes. They knew her mother had been in an accident and had been awkwardly kind when Rage returned to school, but she hadn't wanted anything from anyone except to be left alone. One of the boys had asked why her father didn't come, and the teacher had shushed him, but Rage wasn't offended. There were lots of kids in the school who did not live with their fathers, and at least one other boy who didn't know his father. Unlike him, Rage never thought about who her father might be. She didn't know why, but his absence hadn't hurt her at all. She had Mam, and that was enough for her.

After they had eaten their fill, Rage suggested they all sleep. It was unlikely another boat would arrive before morning. There were some bushes on the side of the mound farthest from the road, where they would not be seen. The animals curled up readily enough, even Billy, but Rage found she could not sleep, despite being tired. She wrapped her coat around her shoulders and thought about Mam, wondering how she was.

She could hear Mrs. Somersby: *Mary Winnoway will die if she doesn't wake and exert some will to heal. . . .*

Rage found she was crying, but it didn't much matter because it was dark and all of the animals were asleep. Then she noticed Bear watching her with dark eyes that caught the light of the moon in twin points.

"You are thinking of your mother," Bear said in her soft, gruff voice. "I smell your remembering. Long ago, I cried for my son. It is hard when you call and no one comes."

Bear's words made Rage feel guilty, but they also reminded her of a time when she had wakened to a cry in the night and had gone into her mother's room to find her asleep and dreaming. "Sammy!" Mary had cried, turning to the window. Moonlight poured onto her wet cheeks. "Don't leave me. . . ."

"Life is full of calls that are not answered and people who go away and do not return," Bear went on.

Rage nodded, her thoughts jumping to Grandfather Adam and his brother, Great-Uncle Peter. Mam told her that Great-Uncle Peter had fought against the creation of the dam in their valley. He and a lot of other people had marched and chained themselves to bulldozers and written letters to politicians, but it had been useless. The day the river was dammed, the water flooding what had once been his property, he left Winnoway forever. Could Great-Uncle Peter's departure have hurt Grandfather, just as Mam's brother's leaving had hurt her?

Rage looked at Bear, blinking back tears. "I'm sorry we took Billy away from you, but at least he lives and he is with you now."

"Sometimes it is too late," Bear said, so softly that Rage thought she might have imagined it.

Rage shivered and thought with longing of Mam, and of the times she had crawled into bed beside her on cold nights and had been kissed and cuddled close to her. More than anything in the world, she wished that she were home and that Mam were sleeping an ordinary sleep, safe in her own bed.

"I have to find the wizard and get home," Rage whispered to herself. The whisper fled before her into a dream of boots crunching along the river road.

She heard a voice calling her name and thought it was Mam's voice, faint because it had to travel from one dream to another in all the confusions of sleep.

"Help me. . . ."

"I'm coming, Mam," Rage muttered.

"Beware . . . dangerous . . . magic . . ."

Rage frowned and came closer to waking. The voice was not her mother's after all, but that of a man.

She opened her eyes to find Billy kneeling in front of her. Behind him the sky was still pitch-black.

"You were calling out," he said softly.

"I was dreaming." Rage rubbed her eyes and looked around to see Elle, Mr. Walker, and Goaty all cuddled up together, still asleep.

Billy helped her up. "Sometimes I used to dream I was chasing a ball. I would wake and find myself biting my own tail."

"Do you miss being a dog at all?" Rage asked, putting

her coat on properly.

He sighed. "Life was very vivid and simple. I didn't think so much. Once you start thinking, it is hard to stop." He shook his head as if that was not quite what he had meant. "The world you make in your thoughts is brighter than the real world." Again he shook his head.

Rage stuck her hands in her coat pockets to keep them warm and turned to look down at the pier. She was surprised to find a square, flat-topped boat tethered there. A cabin in the middle of its deck had an enormous wheel on each side, where the iron cables that stretched across the river were attached. The water was barely visible, for a thick, impenetrable mist lay over it like a ghostly eiderdown. There were torches lit around the pier and on the ferry, the mist smearing their brightness.

From the activities of the crew on deck, it looked as if departure was imminent, though there did not seem to be any passengers.

"We ought to go," Billy prompted her gently.

Rage hesitated. The centaur had called the water the River of No Return. Now that the moment of crossing was upon them, she hoped that the name would not prove to be an ill omen. *Maybe I should go over alone,* she thought.

"We must stay together."

She turned to find that Bear had spoken, and wondered if it was possible that the old dog could read her mind. She knew better than to ask. Since they had come to Valley, Bear had communicated almost as little as when she was a dog, though she had given up bossing the other dogs.

Rage drew a deep breath. "Billy and I will go first. Remember, you three must convince them that you are wild things wanting an audience with the High Keeper."

"What about me?" Mr. Walker asked sleepily.

"You can go in my pocket."

"What I want to know is, how are we going to find out about the wizard if we don't ask the keepers?" Elle demanded.

"We have to go to an inn, of course," Mr. Walker said. "Then we'll find a keeper who doesn't like the other keepers, or one of their servants, and they'll tell us what we need to know."

Rage looked at Mr. Walker and wondered if he was ever going to realize that life was never as easy as stories made it out to be. She did not voice her fears about the nature of banding or of keepers. She glanced over Billy's shoulder and saw that there was an increase in activity around the winch. She wondered if they ought to wait and catch a later boat. But if there were more passengers, it would be more dangerous. Better to use the cover of darkness while they could.

"We'd better go before we miss the boat," she said.

Mr. Walker climbed into Rage's pocket. Then she and Billy set off, having instructed the others to wait a little before following.

A big-bellied man, wearing a white cap and a thick black jumper that matched his wooly beard, watched them come down the hill.

"We would like to cross," Billy announced.

The man jerked his head at a small ramp running from the shore to the deck of the ferry. "Get aboard, then. Ferry casts off in ten minutes."

The ferryman's eyes slid down to Rage's wrists, but she had deliberately let her coat sleeves fall down over her hands. Then he looked up and past her, his eyes narrowing a fraction, and she knew the others must have arrived already.

"You together?" he asked Rage.

She turned and made a play of looking behind her vaguely, then shook her head. "Of course not," she said, and went aboard, followed by Billy.

"We three wild things wish to see the High Keeper," Elle announced to the ferryman, exactly as Rage had bidden her.

"Three, you say?" Rage turned in time to see the ferryman's eyes harden as they settled on Bear. "What is a true animal doing this side of the river?"

"What is the matter?" Rage asked, trying to sound like a curious bystander.

He slanted her a look. "Surely even folk from the outer villages know that keeper laws allow only cats and dogs and domestic true beasts this side of the river. A bear belongs in the provinces. The stone mountains, maybe, or the greenland. The keepers are bound to want to know how it got out of Order and into the hands of the wild things."

Rage swallowed. "I heard its friend say it was a wild thing."

"It's a bear, or my life on it."

Bear lumbered forward and gave a rumbling gurgle that was almost a growl. The man paled and held up his hands. "Take no offense, bear! It's keeper business, keeping Order. I'm a riverman, and river folk go with the flow. I'll take you, for there's no law against natural creatures crossing from the wild side, but you won't be allowed back."

Bear came aboard, followed by Elle and Goaty. The man kept a wary eye on them all as he untied the ropes that held the boat stable against the pier.

Once they got into the middle of the river they lost sight of both banks. They could hear the creak of the winch pulling them along the cable, the slap of water on the hull, and the occasional sneeze from Goaty. Even Elle's eyes could not penetrate the mist. It was eerie and clammily cold. Rage had the feeling that they were not moving at all.

They drifted separately along the deck to meet behind a pile of crates, out of sight of the ferryman and his crew.

"I am afraid there might be trouble on the other side," Rage said in a low voice.

Bear grunted. "There is always trouble when humans are involved."

"Mama, you must convince them that you are a wild thing," Billy said urgently, stroking her arm. "There's no use just growling at them."

"I will do what needs doing," Bear said, shrugging away his hand. She moved to the edge of the ferry, sat down, and stared across the swirling water. She looked very bearish in the dull light.

"That man said Mama is out of Order," Billy murmured. "Seems like Order covers a lot of things."

"I think in this case it means Bear is not in the place the keepers want her to be," Rage whispered. "Let's talk to that ferryman and see if we can find out anything that will help us."

After making a few meaningless, casual comments about the river and the mist, Rage asked the ferryman, "What will happen to the bear on the other bank?"

He shrugged. "If it is a true beast, it will be sent to the provinces."

Rage said lightly, "What if it turns out to be a wild thing?"

"It will be set free." He gave her a speculative look. "What's it to you what happens to the beast?"

"Nothing, except I thought it was a wild thing and pitied it," Rage answered. "But if it is a natural animal, I guess it will be well looked after in the provinces."

To her surprise, the man's face darkened and he opened his mouth. Then he seemed to think better of what he had intended to say. He finally said mildly, "Some say there is sickness in the provinces."

Rage did not know what to say to this, but the ferryman returned to the previous subject awkwardly. "Time was, everyone petted and marveled at the wild things. Keepers didn't much like the magicking of them. Felt it showed disrespect to the true animals the wizard had put here. Maybe people did think the true beasts dull in comparison to wild things, but that was just the novelty of them, see? There were no rules or laws about who could go where and do what. No objections if a girl wanted to study magicking, and no provinces, either. Humans, natural animals, and wild things went where they liked it best. Live and let live."

"Why did things change if everyone got along so well?" Rage asked, curiosity making her forget caution.

The ferryman frowned at her. "Don't the folk in your village teach history to their children? The keepers never liked the making of wild things, like I said. Rumbled and complained enough that the women who did the magicking left Fork and set up their own settlement in Wildwood. Keepers didn't like that, either. Eventually they set up the provinces on the other side of the river and moved all the natural animals there. The witch women, as they came to name themselves, paid no heed to the keepers. Claimed the wizard would have let them know by now if he objected to their doings. By then the wizard had got reclusive and difficult anyway. Matters stayed that way until magic started to dry up on the wild side of the river. The witch women went to see the wizard about it. A hard, strange journey it must have been, through that Deepwood the wizard magicked around his castle, but when they got there, there was no one home. He had gone."

"So the keepers accused the witch women of driving him away with their magicking," Billy guessed.

The ferryman gave him a strange look. "Stands to reason, eh?"

"Do *you* think the wizard left because of the witch women?" Rage asked.

"Why else would he go?" the ferryman asked, but Rage had the impression he was being careful rather than truthful. She wondered suddenly if, like the baker's sister and the centaur, he suspected them of being keeper spies.

"Then what happened?" Billy asked. "Girls started being forced to come to Fork?"

The ferryman looked at him. "Are you not bringing this young lady to the city for banding of her own free will?"

Billy looked taken aback, and Rage could tell that he had become so interested, he had forgotten their ruse. "Of course I am," he said boldly. "But in the outer villages we never hear much of how things come about. We were told girls had to come to the city and stay until they were too old to have babies. That it was now keeper law."

"Well, it is," the ferryman said, apparently mollified.

Maybe he had decided they were not spies, for now he said, "The keepers had cause to clamp down hard on the witch women, what with them draining the wild side of the river of magic. Folk supported the laws, which said they must come to the city and give up magic, but the witch women refused to leave Wildwood. So the keepers formed the blackshirt brigade and set them to hunt down the witch women and bring them in to be banded. But of course they still had woodcraft enough to evade their followers. All but a few escaped, but they have a price on their heads."

"How exactly does banding stop the witch women doing magic?" Billy asked lightly. "I've always wondered."

The ferryman shrugged. "Don't rightly know myself. It's something about iron. Once a girl's hands are banded, she can't draw the magic up into her mind for the working of it. Welded on, they are, and there's no way of removing them, save with the same heat that sealed them. The first couple of bands are only lightly welded because they have to be replaced as the wrists grow. But once girls become women, the weldings are made to last."

Rage felt sickened at the thought of the heavy bands she had seen on the arms of the baker's sister being welded onto the arms of the little girls in the cart. "If all the magic is gone from the wild side of Valley, I don't suppose the witches will bother the keepers for much longer."

The ferryman shrugged. "There are still a few pockets of magic left, but the fact that the witch women have begun sending the wild things to beg for keeper mercy tells how desperate they have become. Mercy is as scarce in Fork as magic is on the wild side of the river. The keepers won't stop until all wild things have faded and all witch women are dead or in chains. That female wild thing and her faunish friend we've got aboard don't look too bad, but most of the creatures that come over the river to plead are pale and hunched in their bits of rag, and near faded away."

Despite her own worries, Rage's heart went out to the wild creatures she had met—the centaur, the laughing sprite, and the winged lions. All her life she had loved to read of such fabulous things, and here she was in a world where they existed, only to discover they were dying. Not that they had looked sick to her, but perhaps she had been too dazzled by their beauty to notice. She felt a surge of anger. Her desire to find the wizard had been for her own reasons, but now she thought that she would ask him why he did not help the wild things, since it was his magic that had made Valley and everything that lived in it.

"You can't help but pity the poor things," the ferryman said. "But cold as the keepers are, I don't see they have any choice. If the witch women were allowed to use up the magic on the tame side of the river to feed their pets, they'd die soon enough anyway, along with the rest of us."

"Die?" Billy echoed, sounding as confounded by this as Rage felt.

The ferryman gave a great snort. "That village leader of yours ought to be whipped for your ignorance, lad. Of course all of us. What do you think holds Valley together but magic? What is left is barely enough to keep Valley intact. The River of No Return is nibbling at the edges of Fork even now. I don't wish harm on the wild things, but like I said, if they don't die now, they'll die later when the magic runs out. But we have a choice. We don't need to use the magic up."

"What has the river to do with anything?" Rage stammered.

The man gave her a look of disgust. "Valley was taken from the bottom of a great and terrible river. The River of No Return is a small part of that river, bound to flow through Valley by magic. If the magic is used up, Valley will return to the bottom of the river. Everything here will be engulfed by the waters from which the wizard took it."

"The wizard could stop it, couldn't he?" Billy asked.

When the ferryman spoke, he was blunt, as if they were too stupid to be spies. "The witch women claim he could restore magic to Valley, but the keepers say he won't return until the wild things are all gone and there are no more witch women. My own opinion is that the wizard left for his own reasons. Who knows what moves a wizard to do anything? It is said that he loved Valley above all things, yet he abandoned it. Why should we imagine he means to return?"

His words gave Rage a peculiar feeling. Here was another man who had gone away, leaving those behind to suffer.

"Why would the witch women use up the magic if they will die when it is gone?" Billy murmured. "It doesn't make sense."

The ferryman glared at them and said loudly enough to make Rage jump, "Do you accuse me of consorting with the witch women? I did not say I spoke to them. Nor do I know their business. I have heard rumors, is all." He turned away, muttering about work to be done. Several crewmen cast furtive looks at Rage and Billy.

"Look!" Elle cried, distracting them. Rage turned to see the other bank materializing out of the mist. It was immediately clear that this side of the river was vastly different from the wild side. A stern promenade of black cobblestones ran in a wide path alongside the water. Beyond this lay an enormous, dark city. In the distance, stone skyscrapers were swathed in mist. Between the skyscrapers and the river were a higgledy-piggledy mass of small black-roofed houses and twisting streets. There was not a spot of green anywhere—no trees, no flowers, no grass. The air smelled of wet stone and rust.

Rage went to the edge of the ferry and stared out in disbelief. She had known Fork was a city, yet this was so huge and uniformly dark that it seemed less a collection of streets and buildings than some vast, slow, cold creature. Unlike Leary City or even Hopeton, there were no lights in windows, no flashing neon signs, no helicopters, and no traffic noise. No ambulance or police sirens. No music. No sign of life despite the fact that most of the population of Valley lived here.

Rage shivered, thinking how hard it must have been for children to come from their pretty, sunny villages to this gloomy metropolis. She did not wonder that Fork left its mark on those who dwelled there. She wondered if the wizard had created the city, and she shuddered at the thought of a mind that could spawn such a place. Not for the first time, she tried to guess what they would do if the wizard turned out to be evil or indifferent. But he was their sole hope, and so she must go on searching for him. She didn't believe the ferryman's suggestion that the wizard had left Valley altogether, and wished that they had asked him about the Endless Sea. Too late now.

Just then it came to Rage with a little shock that the

lines of verse on the hourglass might actually refer to something other than the real shore of a real sea. After all, the verse spoke of a door. How could there be a door on a beach? It was far more likely that there was a tavern or a shop called the Endless Sea, maybe even named for the children's myth the woman in the cart had mentioned. The wizard might be living there under another name. Though why he would stay hidden when Valley was in danger, she could not imagine.

Unless he planned to appear at the last minute to save his creation.

Goaty and Elle had shifted closer. Rage didn't have the heart to tell them they ought to keep their distance. The city, looming ever nearer, drew her eyes again. It was like Mam's imaginary city without cars and roads, but it was also without light and brightness and greenness.

"Where are the people?" Elle asked in a surprisingly timid voice.

"It's too early for humans to be up from their beds," Billy said.

All too soon they were approaching a wall of blackened boards that formed a solid barrier between the bank and the ferry. There was a metal gate in the barrier, and through it Rage saw a group of men in black trousers, boots, and shirts. Her skin rose into goose bumps at the sight of them. Blackshirts! Mr. Walker had been right about people who made rules needing soldiers.

The men she glimpsed had a grim resemblance to the visitors from the child-welfare department who had come to talk to Mrs. Johnson after the accident. One was a man and the other a woman, but they had been alike, even down to the dark suits they wore. When Rage said she could look after herself and had often done so before, it was as if she had not spoken. If Mrs. Johnson had not insisted on having her, she would have been taken away and put who knew where.

The iron cables drew the ferry with a thud against fat rubber bolsters alongside the barrier. An authoritative voice called through the iron gate, "Any passengers, riverman?"

"Aye. Humans and wild things," the ferryman answered.

Rage leaned forward in time to see surprise register on the flat features of a blackshirt. Perhaps it was unusual to have passengers so early in the day. The surprised man's shirt had a thin red line down the front, and she guessed he was the leader of the group.

The ferryman told Goaty and Elle that wild things had to disembark first. Then he asked, "Where is the bear?"

Only then did Rage realize that Bear was nowhere to be seen.

7

There was no place that a creature of Bear's size could be hiding aboard the ferry. Even as Rage saw how Bear had solved their dilemma, Billy gave a howl of anguish and rushed to the edge.

Rage ran at him and caught his arm, afraid he might hurl himself over. "You have to stay calm," she told him fiercely. "We still have to get off this ferry."

"But Mama—"

"Can swim," Rage said, squeezing his arm desperately. Fortunately, the gate was narrow enough that they were hidden from the blackshirts. Billy was pale as milk, and she could feel him trembling. She turned to find the ferryman watching them.

"The bear went overboard," he said in a queer, emotionless voice. "Keepers won't like that. I'll be blamed for it."

"You needn't tell them," Rage said, abandoning any attempt to pretend they were not traveling with Bear.

"Maybe not, but the crew won't keep quiet without reason for it."

Seeing he wanted some sort of payment, Rage's heart

sank. There was only one valuable thing she possessed apart from the hourglass, and that was Mam's locket. One day it was to be Rage's to give to her own daughter, just as it had been given to Mam by her mother. It was precious because it was a link between all of those mothers and daughters. But if the ferryman told the blackshirts about Bear, they might never get home. Mam would have given the locket up in a second for Bear.

In the end, things are just things. They don't care about you. They don't love back, Mam's voice whispered to Rage.

Rage dug the locket out, took the photographs from it, and slipped them into her pocket. Then she held the empty locket so it dangled on its golden chain and glimmered in the light of the ferry lanterns.

"A pretty trinket," the ferryman said, making no move to take it.

Rage saw that he was trying to make her offer something more. "I have nothing else," she said desperately. She could hear Billy's teeth beginning to chatter with the strain of controlling himself.

"That bear is old," the ferryman said. "Why take her to Fork? You could have let her live out her life on the wild side of Valley."

"We had to come," Rage said desperately.

The blackshirts shouted to the ferryman to lower the ramp so that the passengers could disembark. Rage took a deep breath and did something she never would have dared do before. She reached across and dropped the locket into the ferryman's pocket.

"Say nothing of the bear," she said.

She feared he might fling it back at her or shout out to the blackshirts, but he only gave the whey-faced Billy a final, penetrating look before turning to instruct his crew to let the ramp down. Elle and Goaty went down it and through the gate in the barrier. Rage moved so that she could see what happened. Her heart was in her mouth as the blackshirts inspected them, but the men made no attempt to touch or even speak to either of them. It was as if they were afraid of being contaminated. One of the blackshirts was pointing away from the river, and Rage guessed the animals were being directed to the High Keeper.

She breathed a sigh of relief. She had been afraid that wild things might be escorted directly to the High Keeper. "Three to go," she muttered, praying no one would search her. It had seemed simpler to hide Mr. Walker. But if he had pretended to be a wild thing, he would be safe now. Beside her, Billy was rigid with tension.

"You'd best make haste," the ferryman advised, coming to stand beside her. "The bank is steep this side of the river." He said all of this without looking at her, without expression.

Thinking that she had taken such risks that another scarcely made any difference, she said, "I am not banded. Will they take me away immediately?"

There was a short silence. The ferryman asked in the same quiet voice, "Are you from the witch women?"

"No," Rage said, startled. "The bear is my friend."

"Then it must be great need that brings you all here. You might not be taken to a banding house if you can convince the blackshirts you have family or relatives to stay with. Go ashore now, lest they grow suspicious." The ferryman turned away.

Rage gathered her wits and whispered to Mr. Walker, who had begun to wriggle, that he must be still now or see them all thrown into the River of No Return.

Steeling themselves, Billy and Rage made their way across the ramp, through the metal gate in the barrier, and onto the bank. The blackshirt with the red stripe stepped smartly forward and asked Rage's name. He had thick, powerful arms and small, cold green eyes.

"My name is Rage Winnoway," she said meekly. She had rolled up her sleeves so that it was immediately apparent she had no bands.

"You are almost a woman," he observed.

"I am from an outer village," Rage answered, hoping he wouldn't ask which one.

"Who are you?" the leader of the blackshirts demanded of Billy. Rage crossed her fingers, but he answered well.

"I am Billy Thunder, protector of Rage Winnoway until she is banded. The leader of our village sent me with her to make sure no witch women tried to recruit her."

The blackshirt nodded approvingly and turned to Rage again. "I will assign two men to escort you to the banding house. The next banding is tomorrow evening at the Willow Seat Tower. You will not need this fellow any longer."

The obedient part of Rage almost wanted to do what the blackshirt ordered, but the new, stubborn part of her silently asked what right he had to tell her to do anything. Aloud she said calmly, "We are to stay with my uncle." Behind the blackshirts, she could see the ferryman ordering his crew to make ready to depart. There were no return passengers.

The guard frowned. "Your uncle should be here to collect you, then. Where is he?"

Her heart felt as if it were thudding in her throat. She thought fast, fingering the tiny photographs in her pocket. "I could not tell him exactly when I would come because I did not know how long the journey would take. His name is . . . Samuel Winnoway. He will be expecting us." She was afraid that the guard would ask where her uncle lived. She must not be separated from the others, especially with Bear lost.

Pleasepleaseplease. She willed the blackshirt to let them go on their way. Perhaps if there really was magic in the land, she could draw it up with her longing. *Please let us go*. She grew hot, and a bead of sweat trickled down her spine.

To her stunned delight the blackshirt suddenly shrugged, seeming all at once bored. "Very well. Be with your uncle by nightfall and make sure you register at the nearest banding house early tomorrow."

Rage felt physically weak with relief as she and Billy walked away from the pier and down the nearest street. The minute they were out of sight of the blackshirts, Billy stopped and said in a hoarse voice, "I must find Mama."

Rage bade him go ahead and let Mr. Walker out of her pocket. He shook himself, then trotted alongside her as she hurried after Billy, who had vanished around the nearest corner. Despite her concern for Bear, Rage could not help but stare at the houses. They looked like buildings out of an old storybook, except that they were all black. The uneven cobbled road—empty of cars, buses, or even horse-drawn carts—was black as well, and it twisted here and there like an eel. It struck her that there were no lights nor any other signs of life from the houses: no sound, no smoke from a fire, no door closing. The silence of the city was as palpable as the mist coiling along the cobbles.

They made their way back to the riverbank. It was very dark away from the ferry lanterns. Would morning light never come? The bank turned out to be every bit as steep as the ferryman had warned. It was set with big, smooth green-black stones to stop it from eroding. Rage knew there was no way Bear could climb it without help. Yet there was no sign of her in either direction.

Billy sniffed frantically, then said in an anguished voice, "I can't get her scent!"

They made their way downstream, peering anxiously out into the river, but after some time Billy stopped and turned to look back upriver. Rage guessed he was wondering if Bear had managed to reach the bank closer to the pier. She did not like to say that such a swift river could have carried Bear some considerable distance if she had not got to the shore quickly.

"Maybe she swam to the other bank," Mr. Walker said, but without great conviction.

"No," Billy said. "It is too far. We must go back and search nearer the pier."

There was no point in arguing that they might be seen. As they retraced their footsteps Rage noticed that the houses facing the water had dark windows that showed nothing behind them. She shuddered at the thought of unseen eyes watching them, though she had the queer sense that the houses were empty.

Once the pier and the departing ferry were in sight again, Rage caught hold of Billy. "We must not let the blackshirts see us!"

"I have to find Mama," Billy cried.

"You know she can swim," Rage insisted. "It is just a matter of—"

"Look!" Mr. Walker hissed, and they both turned to

see a dark bulk move within a mass of shadowy reeds at the waterline, not far from where they stood.

Billy gave a groan of relief. "Mama!"

Bear emerged from the reeds and used her claws to drag her sodden mass onto the flat lip of the bank. It took all of their combined strength to push and drag her the rest of the way up onto the cobbled promenade. By the time they had managed it, their breathing was nearly as labored as hers.

"We have to find somewhere she can rest and get warm," Rage said, alarmed by Bear's utter exhaustion.

"I'll see what I can find," Billy said determinedly.

He ran off, and Rage reflected on how independent the animals had become. Was that because they had been transformed, or had they always been that way, without her knowing?

Trying to squeeze some of the water from Bear's thick fur, Rage felt her begin to tremble in shock. How much punishment could the old dog endure without being permanently injured? The journey was clearly taking a harsh toll on her, yet there was nothing Rage could do but push her to continue.

Elle and Goaty arrived, the latter looking deeply relieved.

"It is hard to smell far here," Elle said. She looked at Bear and sniffed. "She smells bad."

For once Goaty had nothing awful to add, which made Rage feel even more worried. What did *bad* mean? Sick? Tired? Dying?

"It took us a while to find her," Rage managed to say calmly. "She was in the water too long."

There was the sound of running feet and they all froze, but it was only Billy. He had found a small park farther along the riverbank. "It's not much better than this, but at least there is shelter," he panted.

Bear was in no state to be moved, but they dared not delay. They roused her enough to get her on her feet and led her to the park. This was filled not with real green trees but with black stone carvings of trees. Of all the things she had so far seen in the city, this horrified Rage the most. Why would anyone prefer black stone trees to living trees? On all sides of the park more of the small houses clustered together like black, crooked teeth. Again, it seemed to her that they were not separate houses but part of the same entity: this black city that seemed to have some sort of malevolent life of its own.

"I don't smell any people," Elle whispered uneasily.

Bear cast herself down under a stone tree with an overhang of drooping branches and lay as one dead. She had not said a single word since coming out of the water. Billy lay his jacket over her and lifted her head onto his knee. He stroked her fur, his face haggard with fear.

Rage knelt down beside them. "Billy, stay here with Bear and the others. I'll go and see if I can find out anything about the wizard."

Billy looked up at her, eyes brimming with unshed tears. "I'm afraid for Mama," he whispered.

Rage saw that all of his new power to think, and his delight in it, had been consumed by fear for Bear. She thought of her own mother but dared not dwell on her. She was responsible for herself and the animals being in Valley. It was time for her to think and act instead of letting everyone else do it for her.

"Bear's old and the water wasn't good for her, but she'll be all right if she rests," Rage told Billy with a mixture of Mrs. Johnson's kindness and Mr. Johnson's gruff certainty. She had to be firm because she knew the voice of fear must even now be whispering to Billy. "You must keep her warm. I will be as quick as I can."

She motioned to the others to withdraw and talk.

"The river did it," Elle said, looking more troubled than Rage had ever seen her before.

"It got inside her," Mr. Walker added.

Drawing a deep breath, Rage told them her plan. "I'm going into the city to see if I can find out where the wizard has gone."

"But we know that already. He has gone to the shore of the Endless Sea," Mr. Walker argued.

"Yes, but maybe the Endless Sea in the riddle isn't the real Endless Sea, if there is such a thing. Maybe it's the name of a place right here in Fork."

"Wouldn't those women in the cart have told us if it was?" Elle objected.

Rage shrugged. "It's a big city. And I asked about the Endless Sea, not about a place called the Endless Sea. Anyway, we have to do something." She directed a pointed look at Bear.

"All right," Elle said. "But you'd better not go alone. It might be dangerous."

"I'll take Mr. Walker in my pocket," Rage offered.

"He can't fight for you! He can't protect you!" Elle cried, but Rage was firm.

"Mr. Walker can hide in my pocket and come back for help if I get into trouble. Billy will need you here."

Rage felt a lot less sure than she sounded. But there was no point in burdening the others with her uncertainties. And maybe luck was on her side. She still found it hard to believe that the blackshirts had simply let her find her own way to her uncle's house.

Once she was out of sight of the park, her steps slowed and she tried to decide which direction to take. All of the houses looked exactly the same, and there was no sign of any people, nor of the circular, black Willow Seat Tower, to which the animals had been directed by the blackshirts.

Rage made up her mind to keep the river at her back and the skyscrapers in front. Surely such imposing buildings would be at the heart of the city, and among them she would be bound to find groups of people in which she could mingle and eavesdrop. She had no fear that she would not be able to find her way back to the others because the river would be her guide.

She had been walking for perhaps an hour when she entered a street that ran up a steep incline. At its apex, a perfectly round black tower stood in the center of a flat, open area paved in blocks of gleaming black marble that glittered as if studded with pieces of mirror: the Willow Seat Tower.

There were no signs of shops or stalls or anyplace where one might buy food or clothes. But here, for the first time, were people. Most of them were clad in long white gowns. Rage guessed these were keepers.

The thought of the High Keeper rejecting the pleas of the sprite and the winged lions made a cold, cruel picture in her head, even if it was true that Valley would be doomed if the wild things were fed any more magic. Still, something drew her toward the tower. Obeying the compulsion, she was careful to stay in the shadows and move as slowly as everyone else.

Rage was close enough now to see that all the people in the white gowns were men. But there were also men, women, and groups of boys and girls in plain gray tunics and trousers. Not a single spot of color was worn by anyone. No one spoke loudly or moved quickly. This crowd of harmoniously dressed people moving slowly and silently ought to have been beautiful, but the scene was strangely stiff and unreal. Everyone moved as if they were part of an old and complicated dance with many rules and tiny, intricate steps. No one looked happy.

This was a dance of obedience, Rage thought, each person doing only and exactly as he or she was bidden. This was Order, and clearly there was no joy in it.

"Have you noticed there have been no streetlights these past few nights?" Rage overheard a man observe to his neighbor in a low voice.

His companion nodded. "I heard there were orders that they should not be switched on, to conserve magic."

"Powering the lights doesn't consume magic any more than the enchantments that keep the provinces in Order. Besides, we don't need to conserve magic. It's those witches who need to do that."

There were indeed unlit streetlights—balls of glass on iron stalks attached to the walls lining the streets. Rage was intrigued by the news that there was more than one way to use magic. Apparently the keepers had some way of working it to organize the provinces where natural animals were kept. If what these men said was true, the keepers' working of magic did not deplete it. Rage wondered if the creation of the wild things was what had used magic up on the other side of the river. It must take more complex enchantments to create a living, thinking being than to organize animal habitats. If she was right, it would explain the keepers' dislike of wild things. But unless the witches were mad, there had to be more to it than that.

An ornately carved litter, borne on thick poles by eight muscular men, drew up beside the entrance to the tower. Rage watched closely as it was set down carefully by its bearers. Two men emerged from it, both elderly and clad in white. One, bent almost double with the weight of the years he carried, wore a tunic edged in gold trim. A troop of blackshirts marched toward the tower and saluted the two men. Rage scuttled hurriedly into a lane. It was too dangerous to stay here. She turned her back on the circular tower and began to walk in the direction of the black skyscrapers again.

"Where are we going now?" Mr. Walker asked, poking his head out to look around. He was a bit pale, but she supposed it was none too comfortable riding in her pocket.

"I am looking for a place where there are people. A market or a square," she told him.

"We must find an inn," Mr. Walker insisted. "You can buy some ale for someone, and they will tell you about the wizard."

Rage felt exasperated. "I haven't seen anything that looks like an inn, I don't know if they have ale here, and I have no money to buy it, even if they would serve someone as young as me!"

Mr. Walker looked disgruntled. "Those sorts of things never matter in stories."

"Well, this is not a story," Rage snapped. She had gone only a few more steps when Mr. Walker spoke again.

"You could knock at one of these houses and say you are trying to find your uncle Samuel, who lives near the big market. Then you could get directions."

It was a good idea, but before she could say so, the

little narrow street ended at a broad avenue, and as if at some hidden signal, dozens of front doors opened simultaneously, and dozens of gray-clad men and women emerged. The doors closed behind them soundlessly and almost in unison, and Rage had a dazed vision of all the doors in Fork opening up at the exact same moment and hundreds and hundreds of gray-clad people pouring into the streets in a silent flood.

Glancing around, she was shocked to see the black Willow Seat Tower in front of her again. How could that be possible when she had been walking away from it? Yet there was no mistaking the tower. The streets must twist about very strangely for her to have come back so close to it.

Not daring to walk boldly along the avenue, she peeped out and sought another lane. When there was a gap in the flow of people, she darted across the avenue and ran down the lane, until once more it ended at a broad avenue. This happened three more times before she recognized a pattern. The avenues all radiated out from the tower, while the lanes ran around it like the concentric rings in a tree trunk. But no matter how far she ran along an avenue before entering another lane, there was the Willow Seat Tower again, the exact same distance away!

Finally she gave up trying to make sense of the city. It had been built in an enchanted valley, so perhaps ordinary rules didn't apply. Taking any turn not filled with people, she walked and walked, always turning her face away from the Willow Seat Tower. But the black tower proved as hard to leave behind as the skyscrapers were to approach.

Then, all at once, she turned a corner, and there they

were, the skyscrapers, right in front of her. They were not modern skyscrapers after all, but ancient-looking towers made from huge blocks of rough-dressed, greenish black stone, with only a few unglassed windows set high up. Each tower had a tall iron door at street level, with a long lever worked by a complicated mechanism of cogs and meshed teeth instead of a doorknob. Over the doorways were spidery markings that reminded her of a picture she had seen in a history book of the writing on the walls of Egyptian tombs.

As Rage stood dumbfounded, a woman in gray came rushing around the corner and cannoned into her.

"What on earth are you doing here?" the woman demanded crossly. Her eyes fell to Rage's wrists, and in a flash she pounced. Rage found herself being marched briskly back the way she had come. In minutes they were approaching the black tower.

Rage began to struggle, though she could not bring herself to scream and draw the attention of all the silent walkers.

"Be still, child," the woman snapped, tightening her already viselike grip. "You are out of Order. By the look of your barbaric attire, you come from one of the outer villages. I suppose, being a bit older, you just thought you'd slip away from the banding house and do a bit of exploring."

Rage opened her mouth to tell the woman about the uncle she was supposed to stay with, but then she found herself being marched smartly *past* the door to the Willow Seat Tower!

Her relief that she was not going to be made to face the High Keeper was so great that she felt dizzy. She decided that she would not try to get away from the woman after all. She had no idea how to negotiate the strange, magical city, nor how to find information about the wizard. The banding house might be the very place to learn what she needed, especially if it was as easy to slip away as the woman's words implied. Far better to go there than wander stupidly in circles looking for some sort of public place. Anyway, if she did wrench her hand free and manage to get away, the woman would just summon the blackshirts and they would begin to comb the city for her, perhaps finding Bear and the others as a result.

They had walked no more than fifteen minutes when the woman stopped at a wooden door in a high stone wall and rapped at it imperiously. A young woman wearing a white apron over her gray clothes appeared.

"This girl is unbanded!" Rage's captor announced accusingly.

The young woman's eyes fell to Rage's wrists and widened. "I see, but what do you wish me to do? She was not registered here by the blackshirts. We are not expecting any new children before the next ceremony."

"She ought not to be wandering the streets! Look how close she is to womanhood."

"Her placement is the responsibility of the black-shirts," the younger woman said stubbornly.

"I will tell the brigade captain that you said as much. No doubt he will investigate the lapse in Order," the older woman snapped. "Meanwhile, the girl will remain here." She gave Rage a push that sent her stumbling into the arms of the younger woman, and departed triumphantly.

Inside the dimly lit hallway, the woman took a small notepad and pencil from her apron pocket. "What is your name?" Rage told her, and she wrote it down. "You may have to sleep top-and-tail tonight. The banding house is growing smaller, and there is less space than usual."

Rage was hardly listening. Instead, she contrived to drop a little behind as they walked so that she could ask Mr. Walker if he could stand to remain hidden a while longer.

"Not for too much longer," he whispered in martyred tones.

"In here," the woman said, and they entered a large, bare room with high, slotted windows that let in daylight, though Rage could not look out of them. Like everything else in the city, all of the surfaces were black and unpatterned.

The woman turned to Rage again. She was beautiful, with dark, lustrous hair smoothed into a bun and big, long-lashed eyes.

"My name is Niadne," she said. "I am one of the banding-house attendants. Are you hungry, child Rage?"

"A little," Rage admitted, puzzled that the woman did not ask how she had come to be wandering the streets.

"Nearly everyone is hungry when they arrive in Fork. And you have come very far. I don't suppose you were properly provisioned for the trip?"

"Not really," Rage said. "I didn't know how far I was to come when I set out."

"That is often the way of journeys," Niadne said serenely. "Especially journeys that lead to Fork. But come. You must wash your face and hands before you eat, and perhaps I can find you a gray tunic. You will have a proper gray gown for the banding. You will need to be fitted for it today, since the ceremony is tomorrow night. We must also find time to cut your hair. The High Keeper does not like hair to be so wild and curly. Too witchy."

Rage said nothing. She had no intention of being in the banding house long enough to have her hair cut.

8

Splashing her face and arms with warm, scented water, Rage was delighted to hear Niadne ask if there was anything she wanted to know. "I am aware that little is known of Fork in the outer villages," her companion added.

Rage's mind swarmed with questions, but she decided to begin simply, and asked if Niadne had been born in the city.

"I came from one of the villages on the other side of the river. Not an outer village like yours. But that is so long ago, it seems a dream."

"I suppose you love Fork now?"

There was a silence. "No. I could not say I love it, but I have grown used to it here." A hovering attendant handed Rage a simple gray shift and a pair of sandals, and watched as she stripped off her clothes to don them.

"These are queer garments," Niadne said, examining one of the ripple-soled hiking boots curiously.

"Can I keep my old things?" Rage asked.

"Of course you may," Niadne said kindly, which saved Rage having to try to think of what to do about

Mr. Walker, who was still in her coat pocket. Niadne watched her bundle the clothes up very gently before saying, "You probably won't ever wear them again, but there is no reason you should not keep them as mementos."

"Why does everyone in Fork wear gray or white or black?"

"The High Keeper wishes us to live in harmony with one another. To do so, we must give up selfishly asserting our individuality, even in our attire."

"What will happen after I am banded?"

"You will live in one of the childhouses, or if you have family here who claim you, you will be assigned to live with them. You will be given work to do and classes to attend each day, for idle hands make much mischief. But because you are older, and indeed almost a woman, an offer may be made for you. If that happens, you will go to live in the house of your future husband."

Rage's feelings must have shown clearly on her face. First they kept saying she was on the verge of womanhood, and now they were talking about marriage. She had barely begun secondary school! Niadne gave her a look of mild pity. "I suppose in your village girls and boys still choose their own partners, but here we are more efficient. The keepers will listen to proposals from boys or their fathers and then choose the most appropriate match for you."

"I'm too young to get married," Rage protested.

"You will not be wed immediately, but it is the High Keeper's belief that women are better growing in the will of their husbands from an early age."

All the better to stop them leaving Fork, Rage thought, wondering if Niadne had any thoughts or opinions that were not given to her by the High Keeper. But she reminded herself that she was supposed to be finding out about the wizard, not making judgments.

"Where is the Endless Sea?" she asked baldly, sick of trying to find clever ways to avoid asking outright for the information she needed.

Niadne smiled indulgently. "There is no such thing. It is part of a myth about the River of No Return. The story claims that once the river leaves Valley, it pours into a vast sea that laps between all worlds."

Rage's mouth fell slack. The ferryman had claimed that the River of No Return was connected by magic to the very river from which the wizard had drawn Valley. But what if it did flow to the Endless Sea? Common sense told her it was more likely that the Endless Sea was an inn, but this was a world held in place by magic! Why shouldn't it contain a river that flowed to a magical sea? In fact, where else would a river that flowed endlessly from a magical land go but into an enchanted sea?

"What is the matter?" Niadne asked.

Rage discovered that she had stopped halfway through putting on a sandal. "Nothing. I was just wondering about boats."

Niadne's eyes widened in outrage. "Who would speak to an innocent, unbanded girl about such dreadful things?"

Rage blinked, confused. "A boy on the road said I could see them here," she said quickly. In her experience, boys said all sorts of outrageous things, only some of which were true.

"Oh, a *boy*," Niadne said, looking both relieved and exasperated. "Well, it would be best if you forget what he said. Other than the river ferry, boats are only used by the blackshirts. I will not speak of the purposes to which they are put."

"I just wanted to see them," Rage said, twisting her face childishly in the hope that this would cause Niadne to elaborate.

Niadne just pressed her lips together in disapproval. "Your mother will have told you something of her own banding, but you should know that this High Keeper is very strict. He will not look tolerantly on mistakes. You must be very careful to move slowly and keep in Order with the other girls as you walk up to the Willow Seat, and do not speak to any of the other supplicants during the banding. The High Keeper does not like women to talk. He believes it is a flaw in womankind that we chatter rather than think deep thoughts. Do not speak to the High Keeper at all. And do not look into his eyes."

Rage was surprised at how much she resented all of the rules made by the High Keeper. Back home, rules had always made her feel safe. It had not occurred to her that there might be bad rules as well as good ones, and she had obeyed them without question. The High Keeper sounded as harsh and mean-minded as the rules he made. *What would he do if I refused to obey them?* Rage wondered hotly, then realized she had spoken aloud.

Niadne regarded her gravely. "This is not a game, child Rage. The High Keeper might see your boldness as an omen. The best thing is not to be noticed. Make yourself utterly inconspicuous."

Or what? Rage wanted to ask, but she only said, "You can be sure I won't speak to the High Keeper." She had no intention of even seeing him. The more she thought about it, the more certain she felt that the River of No Return flowed into the Endless Sea. It made strange but compelling sense. She couldn't wait to hear what Billy thought.

Niadne was still regarding her anxiously. "Can I have something to eat now?" Rage asked.

Her question wiped the lines of worry from the woman's lovely face. "Children are always hungry," she said happily. "Come."

A little later, eating horribly sweet porridge out of a thick earthenware bowl, Rage studied the girls seated at her table. Most were a lot younger than her. Other than being slightly subdued, they appeared content to be in Fork. Maybe they took comfort from the company of their friends. From what she could gather, they had all come from their villages in twos or in groups, having been collected by the white-faced guardians.

The little girls Rage had seen on the road recognized her at once, and the one who had invited her to ride with them insisted she join them. Her name was Ninaka, she said, and her two friends were Sarry and Bylan.

"Where is *your* friend?" Bylan had asked pertly after Rage introduced herself.

"Friend?" Niadne asked. "There was another?"

"A boy," Rage said quickly. "He came to escort me, but now he has gone back."

Niadne seemed mollified and told Ninaka that boys did not come to this childhouse, which was a temporary refuge for those to be banded.

"My brother is coming to Fork soon, but he will not stay in a childhouse," another girl said. "He will go to the keeper academy. He says the villages are dead and one day Wildwood will just be another province ruled by the keepers."

"My brother wants to be a blackshirt," another said.

"My brother *is* a blackshirt!" yet another offered.

"Hush," Niadne said. "Good girls do not boast or speak loudly, even of their brothers."

The little girls exchanged abashed looks.

"What *do* girls do?" Ninaka asked. "Can we be keepers and blackshirts, too?"

Niadne shook her head. "Keepers and blackshirts must be strong and give orders and make rules. Girls are not good at such things."

Rage gritted her teeth and vowed that she would never obey another rule or voice without first deciding that it was wise.

"Why is everything so black and dark in Fork?" Sarry asked in a mournful voice.

All of the little girls sat cross-legged in a circle around Niadne, who folded her hands neatly in her lap. "In the beginning," she said primly, "the wizard used his great magical power to draw Valley from time. He made it to be fruitful. He filled it with natural beasts, and he made the river to flow through it and the moon and the sun to shine on it. He brought high-minded men to keep Order, and women to be their obedient helpmates. He made the great city of Fork for them to live in. At that time, Fork was shining and filled with music and color, and there were bridges of glass and sculptures of silver and gold."

"Why did it become black?" Sarry asked, sounding sadder than ever.

Niadne gave her a reproachful look. "You must not interrupt in such a rude and aggressive way, child Sarry. You must wait until I have finished speaking, and then, if no one else is speaking, you may speak."

"Why *did* it become black?" Rage repeated in the silence that followed this soft scolding.

Niadne looked at her in disapproval, but this time she answered. "The city blackened to reflect the disappointment the wizard feels at what became of Valley."

"You mean, because of the magic being used up?"

Niadne pressed her lips together for a moment, then nodded stiffly.

"But how could Fork reflect what the wizard feels when he left Valley so long ago?" Rage asked.

"Valley is held in place by the wizard's magic. He knows what is happening here. That is why we must strive so hard for Order. Perhaps, in time, he will forgive us and return," Niadne said piously. "Only then will the city grow light again."

She rose and directed them to rinse their plates and spoons and dry them. Another attendant summoned them to practice the banding ceremony. Rage began to follow the other girls, but Niadne asked her to remain behind.

"The ceremony is not so very complex that you need worry about lacking practice," she said. She led the way through a door and down a passage that brought them to a long room where women sat sewing and ironing. "Practice is needed for the little ones, since they forget things easily. But you are old enough that you need only be shown once or twice. Tonight and tomorrow morning there will be practices, and those will be sufficient. Now you must be fitted for your banding dress."

"Why do the little ones have to be banded so young?" Rage ventured.

Niadne gave her a quick look. "Well, it was not

always so, of course. In your mother's time and mine, as I am sure she told you, only women who came to Fork were banded. The keepers would not have magic worked this side of the river. But when magic began to die on the other side of the river, the High Keeper announced that all girls must be banded, so that there was never any possibility of their drawing magic from the land and harming Valley."

"The keepers use magic in the provinces, don't they?"

Niadne shook her head. "They do not work magic. They channel it."

Rage was confused. Maybe channeling was like making a river flow to a different place, while the making of wild things and magical food was like taking the water away in buckets and drinking it or letting it evaporate. But even then water was never really used up. It was transformed into mist or moisture and eventually would return as rain.

"I don't understand why the witch women keep on wanting to work magic if it is destroying Valley."

Niadne looked aghast. "Child Rage, you must not speak of . . . of those women here. The High Keeper has decreed that they are not to be mentioned. You must learn to curb your tongue. There are many unpleasant punishments for women, and even children, who speak or behave in forbidden ways."

Rage was puzzled that mention of the witch women seemed to occasion more alarm than the possibility that Valley would be destroyed. "If the wizard comes—"

"He will not come until Order is restored in Valley."

Rage was suddenly sick of hearing about Order. "It seems to me that Order is whatever the High Keeper decides it is. I can't believe a wizard who made all of

Valley and Fork would want all curly hair to be cut and everyone to wear gray."

Niadne paled. "You must not speak so, child Rage. The wizard is not here, and so the High One keeps Order in his absence. It is not for us to question the rules he imposes."

Not even if they are stupid, mean rules? Rage thought, but she held her tongue and kept her face meek as she was measured by two slender young women with downcast eyes. She thought darkly of how, in stories, people left in charge often ended up wanting to go on being in charge. Sometimes they even plotted to murder or imprison the true ruler, to make sure they would not return to claim their place. What if the keepers, who seemed so fond of making rules, had done something to the wizard? But the keepers would be no competition for a powerful wizard. Yet it did seem possible to her that the keepers might be glad that the wizard had gone, despite what they said.

Rage remembered the two men she had overheard talking about the loss of magically produced power in Fork and the rumor of sickness in the provinces. A queer thought occurred to her: what if the magic on *this* side of the river was fading as well?

"How does anyone know there is magic on *this* side of the river?" she asked without thinking.

Niadne's lovely face grew stern. "You will suffer the discipline of silence if you go on speaking so thoughtlessly, child Rage," she said.

Rage decided she had better not provoke the woman and tried to look penitent. Besides, if the magic *had* died on this side of the river, Valley would have gone back under its river and they would all be dead. If it had begun to fade, the keepers who looked after the provinces would have noticed.

The two women who had measured her knelt and unrolled a bolt of gray silk. Their scissors flashed through the lengths, then they pinned the pieces together around her, their hands darting like quicksilver, their touches as light as a butterfly landing. At last they stood back and surveyed their handiwork with tilted heads. Turning her to face a mirror, they began to unbind her matted plait and comb out the snarls with fine combs and slim, gentle fingers.

Rage stared into her own face and realized she had not seen herself since leaving her own world. Was it her imagination, or did she look different? Certainly her face was less round and her chin more pointed. Her eyes were more watchful, too. But she knew she had changed inside much more than outside. She was less frightened of things. She could hardly remember why she had been so nervous of leaving Winnoway, talking to the other children at school, or telling the Johnsons she wanted to visit Mam. Was it possible that the journey through the bramble gate had changed her, too, if not as obviously as the animals? Or was it just that she had come so far alone and had faced so many difficult decisions and dangers that many of the things that had once frightened her seemed silly?

Like Niadne's, the hair of the two attendants was plaited and fastened closely and sleekly about their heads so that not a single stray hair floated free. They clearly intended to do the same to Rage's hair, but before long it stood out all around her head in a wild aureole of moonbeam-colored spirals.

Finally one of the seamstresses murmured, "I do not

think this will be tamed into Order."

"It will be cut tomorrow when she is being readied for the banding," Niadne said dismissively. "It is not the sort of hair that will lie down and be still."

Nor will I, Rage thought. Her amber eyes flashed in the mirror.

"As she is older, we will embroider silver and pearl beads all over the hem and here at the neckline," one of the seamstresses told Niadne. "It will glitter and shimmer in the sun. She will be so beautiful, an offer will surely be made."

"The High Keeper will be pleased," Niadne said.

I bet he will be, Rage thought. She wanted to tear the lovely gown off and flee the cloying, perfumed air, but she made herself stand passively while they removed the dress, piece by careful piece.

Collecting her bundle of clothes, Rage felt Mr. Walker stir, and hoped he was all right. She yawned widely and asked Niadne in her meekest voice if she could sleep.

"Of course," Niadne said kindly. "You may rest until supper, and then you will be fresh for the evening practice."

She brought Rage to a tiny, cupboard-sized room containing a single pallet bed with white sheets and gray blankets, and a bucket with a lid. Rage had expected to find herself in some sort of dormitory, and her heart sank when the door was locked from the outside. It would be impossible to escape the windowless cell at night. That meant she must risk slipping away during the evening practice or at suppertime. It would not be long before her absence was discovered and an alert sent out to the blackshirts, but there was no alternative.

When Niadne's footsteps had faded, Rage shook her clothes, and Mr. Walker came out, looking cross and rather ill. "That is the last time I am going in anyone's pocket," he announced. "It is *too much*."

Rage smoothed his disheveled fur and made soothing noises until he calmed down, then she gave him a piece of bread she had hidden in her sleeve. When he had eaten, Mr. Walker sighed and said, "We must get away before they cut your hair. Once a woman cut my fur and nipped me on the ear. Having your fur cut is a very bad thing."

"Having your hair cut is not quite the same thing as having your fur trimmed, though I expect the High Keeper would make sure it was a very ugly haircut. But I don't suppose it would be the end of the world," Rage said.

"You never know when magic and hair might be mixed up together," Mr. Walker said. "Hair is very odd stuff. Look at what happened to Samson when his was cut. Then there was that princess who grew into a giant when her hair was cut."

"Ragewinnoway whose name is also Stupid!" a voice taunted.

Mr. Walker began to growl ferociously. Rage woke, wondering where she was. Memory flooded back, and she hissed at Mr. Walker to be quiet. "What do you want?" she asked the firecat softly.

There was a pause full of anger, then the wall began to glow red above the bed. Mr. Walker gave a yelp of fright and launched himself into Rage's arms.

"It's only the firecat," Rage assured him.

"Only! *Only?*" it mimicked furiously.

"Yes, only," Rage snapped, wondering why it had ever made her feel nervous. After all, other than tricking her into coming to Valley and setting them to find its master, it had done little but sneer and refuse to answer questions. Incredibly, she had hardly thought of it since coming to Fork.

"Not taking hourglass to shore of Endless Sea!" the firecat said vehemently.

"I am doing my best," Rage answered.

"Not taking. Locked in little room! Stupid, stupid Ragewinnoway!"

"I may be locked in, but at least I know how to get to the shore of the Endless Sea," Rage said sharply.

Mr. Walker looked up at her. "Do you really?"

"How getting there?" the firecat asked warily.

Rage considered refusing to answer, but after a hesitation she said, "We have to go down the River of No Return."

"Ragewinnoway will go down river?" the firecat asked in such a queer, tense voice that any doubts Rage felt about whether the river would bring them to the Endless Sea vanished. But if the firecat had known this, why hadn't it said so? She decided not to antagonize it by asking it directly.

"I'll go down the river if I can find a boat to carry us," she said. "Maybe you could help us find one."

"Clever Rage is finding out all things on ownsome," the firecat purred. "Doing what must be done. Good. Brave."

Its voice seemed to be fading, and Rage remembered she wanted to ask it about the magic in Valley. "Is magic really dying here in Valley?" she asked.

"Of course not dying. Why such stupid thinking?" It

scoffed so firmly that Rage thought it must not know about the magic fading.

"Can you get us out of this place?" she asked, but the glow on the wall winked out. "Wretched creature!" she muttered.

Suddenly the key in the lock turned. Mr. Walker barely managed to dive into her coat before the cell door swung open.

9

Instead of Niadne or one of the other attendants, a gray-eyed girl only a few years older than Rage entered.

"We meet again," she said.

Rage was startled to recognize the voice of the youngest of the three guardians who had been in the cart that brought the little girls to Fork. Last time they met she had been masked in the white paint that made her teeth look yellow, and she had seemed much older.

"You are . . . Ania?" Rage said.

"You have a good memory, Rage Winnoway. I have come to help you escape the banding house. But we must make haste, for the blackshirts will soon arrive to check the names against their list of all who dwell here."

"Niadne has written down my name already, and the blackshirts have it, too."

Ania smiled. "I can do nothing about the blackshirt list, but names in Niadne's book do not necessarily remain there. As long as we hurry, the blackshirts will never know you were here. Quickly, gather your belongings."

"You work for the keepers!" Rage accused.

"I may work here, but I assure you that I do not serve the High Keeper or his minions."

Rage hesitated. The last time she had accepted an offer of help from a stranger, she had ended up in Valley. On the other hand, she would be a fool not to jump at the chance to be free of the banding house. She dragged her coat on over the gray shift and gently bundled up the rest of her clothes. Despite her care, Mr. Walker groaned. "Where are we going?" she asked quickly, to cover the noise.

Ania was not listening. She walked over to the nearest wall and peered at the seam where it joined the floor. Glancing in both directions first, she knelt and pressed her palms flat to the floor. Rage could see no lever or button, yet there must have been one, for a section of the floor slid soundlessly aside, revealing a set of rough-hewn steps leading down into darkness.

"Where do they go?" Rage asked.

"Down," said Ania. She might have said more, but they heard footsteps coming along the corridor. "Quick!" she hissed urgently, slipping into the opening. Rage followed, and the moment she was clear, the floor above slid shut, leaving her standing in pitch blackness.

Several sets of boots sounded directly overhead, and gradually the voices of their owners became audible.

". . . latest arrivals have been fitted with their banding gowns and are now practicing their movements for the ceremony." It was Niadne. Rage tensed, but her name was not mentioned.

When the boots and voices had faded away, Ania's hand pressed at her shoulder. "Make no sound as you climb down, for this stairway runs by places where we could be heard." She sounded breathless and apprehensive, which did much to reassure Rage that she was not working for the keepers.

The steps led to a tunnel, which led to more steps and finally to some kind of cellar. Ania bade her wait. A thick, dank odor rose in her nostrils, as if Ania had opened a trap door in the very earth. Then Rage smelled something sharp and acrid that made her want to sneeze. Ania told her to kneel and pushed her toward a wall. "There is another tunnel in front of you. It is low, so you must crawl. I will follow."

Rage obeyed awkwardly, trying to be careful of Mr. Walker. Under her hands, stone became mud. Rage wished she weren't wearing a tunic, for it made crawling difficult. They crawled for miles, or so it seemed, turning now left and then left, then right, in no discernible pattern. At last she felt stone under her palms again, and Ania stood up, panting hard. Rage stood, too, her knees and palms stinging. It was still very dark, but chinks of light penetrated the small room into which they had crawled. Rage could dimly see Ania's features and dark-pupiled eyes.

"Here we can talk without fear of being overheard," Ania said, holding up her arms to bare her bands. "These are not metal. They are made by magic to seem so."

"You are a witch woman?"

"I will deserve that title when I complete my apprenticeship, but I can already draw magic from the land and work it in small ways," Ania admitted.

"You are here stealing magic for the wild things?"

"Magic cannot be stolen or used up by what I do, Rage Winnoway."

Rage did not want to go into this argument. "Why you are helping me?"

"I was bidden to do so by my mistress, the Mother of the witch folk. But tell me, where are the five that traveled with you? Are they safe?"

"They are hiding." Rage decided not to bring Mr. Walker out and complicate matters. "Why does your mistress want to help us?"

"I do not know," Ania admitted. "But I am not the only one in Fork who was bidden watch for a girl called Rage Winnoway who traveled with five nonhumans that smelled of magic."

Rage had told the centaur and the sprite that they were trying to find the wizard. She supposed they had reported it to the witch Mother.

Ania continued, "I was told only to say that what you desire, the Mother desires also: the finding of the wizard so that Valley may be saved."

"I thought Valley would be safe as long as no more magic is used up."

"Magic is not like a loaf of bread that can be used up, Rage Winnoway. It is a flow like water. Better to say that the flow of magic here is afflicted. First it was afflicted in Wildwood, and now it is the same here in Fork. Each day the River of No Return becomes more ferocious as it begins to rejoin the great water from which it was taken. When magic ceases to flow, the river will consume Valley."

"The keepers think that the witches—"

"At least some of the keepers know that the magic flow in Fork is fading," Ania interrupted sternly. "They will not tell the people, for it means admitting they were wrong about the witch folk. Or that they lied. But in time, all will know the truth. Our only hope is that the wizard will return to save Valley."

"Wait," Rage said, and she wriggled out of the sodden gray tunic and pulled on her own clothes. She turned to Ania. "Show me where the boats used by the blackshirts are kept."

Ania looked as shocked as Niadne had been at the mention of boats. She took a deep breath and seemed to brace herself. "I will take you, but it means traveling through the oldest part of Fork, to the other side of the city. Are you willing?"

"What do you mean?" Rage said suspiciously. "The river flows this side of the city."

"The river goes on both sides of the city because it splits above Fork," Ania said. "The part you crossed to come here is only a portion of the flow. Farther down, it splits into many smaller threads and feeds the wetlands. The main strength of the river passes to the other side of Fork, and soon after flows out of Valley."

"All right. Let's go," Rage said, barely able to control her excitement. With Ania's help, she might even be able to steal a boat and hide it before fetching the others.

Again Ania knelt and put her hands flat against the floor. Beside Rage a block of stone swung away, revealing a set of ascending steps. In minutes they were both standing in the open. It was twilight, and the sky was a brilliant swirl of cloud and color, the sun visible between buildings and low in the sky. Rage was horrified to think she had wasted almost the whole day in the banding house. "You know the way?" she asked as Ania set off briskly.

"It is not a matter of knowing the way," the other girl said over her shoulder. "With Fork, one must know one's destination. Then you need only walk and the city will bring you there."

Rage was fascinated. "You mean, if I thought of the boats, I would just be able to walk and end up where they are?"

Ania shuddered. "The boats are artifacts. They are not part of the city. You must know the *place* you are seeking. You see, the city understands itself. If you do not know where you want to go, the city cannot fathom your desire. If you are confused, you will find Fork confusing."

It gave Rage an odd feeling to think of the city as some sort of living, thinking entity, and yet hadn't she felt exactly that when she first saw it? She had not only thought of it as a live beast but also a sinister one. "Is the city's magic good?" she asked.

"One can no more think of magic as good or bad than one can call an ax good or bad. But the purposes to which they can be put may be good or bad. Fork's magic reflects what occurs within its walls and streets."

Niadne had said something similar about Fork being made from responsive magic, but she had claimed that the blackness reflected the wizard's disapproval at what had happened in Valley. Rage did not know which version to believe. She was more concerned with finding a boat to take them out of the city and, she hoped, out of Valley. "Why does everyone act so strangely when I ask about boats?" she asked.

"You will see soon enough." Ania refused to be drawn out further on the subject.

They were now moving along narrow, cobbled paths that ran between the somber stone towers with their queer markings and levered doors. There were no people around, and Rage asked the witch girl about the emptiness of the streets.

"There are only certain times when people are permitted to leave their homes or places of work or training," Ania explained. "Of course, that is one of the High Keeper's rules."

"Of course," Rage muttered darkly.

"A lot of the houses and towers are empty," Ania continued. "The city grows and shrinks and changes shape constantly."

Rage wondered what would happen if one was standing in a bit of the city that decided not to *be* anymore. But maybe the city always knew where people were, and left them alone. "Those tunnels and stairs we just used . . . ," she began.

"Oh, the city made them because I asked it with my own magic," Ania said casually.

"You mean, when you put your hands on the ground, you were drawing magic out of it?" Rage asked excitedly.

Ania smiled. "I know exactly what you are imagining now—all manner of wonders that magic could let you do and be and have. But magic is not so easy to hold nor to shape in your mind. It is like trying to remember a very, very difficult and tricky tune. It takes much training and discipline to learn how to perform even the smallest working. And you have to be in touch with the earth the whole time. The moment you stop, the flow ceases and so does the working."

"Is that why you made the tunnels so low back there?"

Ania nodded. "I can just manage to reach the flow through floors. It is better if I can touch dirt. Or mud." She grimaced at her filthy dress and hands.

"But what about the wild things? How do they exist if the witches who created them aren't constantly touching the ground? Why don't they vanish?"

"Their creation is the result of a different way of using magic. But what they do does not use magic up."

"Why did the witch women make the wild things in the first place?" Rage asked.

Ania shrugged. "Why does anyone create anything that is beautiful and difficult? It is the striving that counts, and the making of something wondrous and exquisite. And the witches who used this magic had to bind the spell of creation up with a little of their own souls. One cannot create life without cost. But they don't make them now."

"Because of the wild things starving?" Rage guessed.

Ania smiled slyly. "The wild things are hungrier since magic stopped flowing through Wildwood, but we do not let them starve. They are sent here by the witch Mother to petition the High Keeper for mercy, and he allows it because he is cruel and proud and it pleases him to see them fading. Once their pleas have been rejected by the High Keeper, we witch folk who dwell here in secret feed them and they return to Wildwood."

"The keepers think the wild things are dying out."

"That is what the Mother wishes them to think. When they come to Fork, the wild things carry enchantments that make them appear sickly. They also avoid humans so as to seem scarce. The real reason witch women no longer create wild things is because Valley is in danger and they do not wish to create beasts only to see them perish."

"Did the wizard really take Valley from time?"

"So they say."

"*Why* did he?"

Ania shrugged again. "Who knows why a wizard does anything? Some say he saved Valley from a terrible flood. Others say he wanted a place to use as a sanctuary for the animals he brought here. But if that was so, why bring humans?"

"To keep everything in Order?"

"So the keepers preach, but what need have wild animals of Order?" Ania stopped to survey another of the wider streets, then said as they crossed it, "I have told you I work magic, but you should not think I will be able to use it to protect us if we are caught by blackshirts. The keepers believe a girl must be full grown before she can work magic. In reality, we have the potential for magicking from the moment we can think and imagine. If the keepers understood this, they would band us from birth. If we are caught, I will admit to being a sympathizer, but no more than that. I will deny all that I have told you, no matter what they do to us."

Rage realized with a sick feeling what Ania was trying to say. "You mean they'd torture us?"

"It is better not to voice such possibilities," Ania warned. "But if we are caught, remember that you would only be punished for being a sympathizer. There is a much more terrible fate for anyone caught working magic in Fork, and it may be that the keepers would judge your use of magic to come here as a high crime."

If mere sympathizers were tortured, Rage did not dare to imagine what the punishment might be for a "high crime." It terrified her to think that someone might deliberately hurt her. She didn't know how she would have the courage to keep silent about Ania if that happened. *I'd better not get caught*, she told herself.

They walked several more blocks between the stone towers in silence. She thought about the hourglass in her pocket and considered telling Ania about it, but some part of her rejected the idea so forcefully that she felt disoriented. Maybe it was because the hourglass was her sole link to the wizard and her only means of winning his help for Mam.

Thinking of her mother made Rage feel strange. It had been so long since she had seen her. Guiltily, it came to her that she was getting used to making decisions and being on her own. Sometimes many hours went by without her even thinking of Mam. "Tell me about the provinces," she urged Ania, because if she thought any more about her mother, she would cry.

"What about them? A place for everything and everything in its place, that's what the provinces are about. The keepers say that is what Order means. They made the provinces so that each animal has its own place. Habitat magic in the land keeps any animal from hurting another or straying out of its own territory. But it is no different from cages. We witch folk think all creatures, natural and magical, should be left to run wild and free. There should be no keeping and no territories but the ones animals carve for themselves. The Mother says that is what nature and the wizard intended. The keepers ask, what are keepers for if not to keep Order?"

Poor Mr. Walker began to fidget violently in Rage's pocket, which was his way of saying he needed to get out. When they turned the next corner Rage hung back and set the little man down, whispering for him to follow but stay out of sight.

"What is the matter?" Ania called back.

"A stone in my shoe," Rage answered, and caught up with her.

A group of adolescent boys in white robes came out of a street. Several glanced at them, frowning.

"Why did they look at us like that?" Rage asked when they had gone out of sight.

"They're keeper apprentices, and they looked like that because we are girls. They've been taught that the seed of dis-Order is in all females."

This did not accord with what Niadne had said about the keepers saying girls were naturally weak and obedient. It made Rage see all over again that the High Keeper's rules were shaped to punish girls who were strong. In a way, Mam had done the same thing in telling her over and over to be quiet and good, Rage thought sadly.

She was so busy with her thoughts that she did not notice it was getting more and more damp until she slipped on the wet cobbles. Before she could ask if they were nearing the river, a man in a black robe crossed the street in front of them, leading an elephant and its baby. Rage was dumbstruck by the sight. It was only after the trio had vanished down another street that she saw the hides of both elephants were marred by livid, scabby patches.

"They were sick," she murmured, remembering what the ferryman had said about sickness in the provinces, and wondering if the fading of magic was the cause of that as well.

"Animals are brought in from the provinces to be treated at the conservatorium when they are ill so that if they are contagious, an entire species won't be wiped out," Ania murmured.

Another group of boys entered the street and marched slowly toward them. One smiled fleetingly at Ania, though the rest gave her disapproving looks.

"That was my friend," Ania said shyly when they had gone.

"A keeper's apprentice is your friend?"

"Not all of them think keeping is about controlling and Ordering. Some, like my friend, think it just means watching over and healing. He became a keeper because he believes you can't change things from the outside. Maybe he's right, but I'm afraid that by the time he's high enough in keeper ranks to make a difference, it will be too late for all of us."

Rage was very much surprised to hear that all keepers were not harsh and controlling. "Does he know that the flow of magic is dwindling here?"

Ania shook her head and looked troubled. "The Mother has forbidden us to speak of this to anyone but witch folk. I do not know why."

The street they were walking along ended suddenly at the edge of a wide canal running swiftly with water. Ania turned and followed the path running alongside the canal until they reached a small bridge that allowed them to cross to the other side. They had not gone far when they came to another canal, and then another. All of the canals were bridged and before long it seemed to Rage that there were more canals than streets.

"This part of Fork is built over the river," Ania explained.

Rage lost count of the canals and bridges they crossed after that. The air and the buildings became increasingly wet, and in some places the stone was so eroded that it had a diseased look. As they moved deeper into the canal district of Fork, there were fewer of the forbidding stone towers and more buildings with turrets, cupolas, differently shaped windows, and funny flights of stairs and balconies. The stone here seemed less black than gray, and the area was more run-down than the rest of Fork. Rage wondered why the city had not repaired itself, but perhaps it did not see the erosion as ugly. Nor was it, any more than the wrinkles of an old woman made her ugly. In truth, Rage thought the area far nicer than any other part of the city she had visited.

"This is Old Fork," Ania said. "The new part, where the Willow Seat Tower stands, is called Outer Fork or

Newfork. Then there's Lower Fork, which goes down to the wetland provinces, and a section that goes up to the desert and mountain provinces, called Upper Fork. I like this part best because even though it is so damp and crumbling, there are no people living here anymore and the city may be whatever it chooses."

"Is it true that the wizard made Fork?" Rage asked, again wondering about the mind that had created such a city. Niadne had said it was beautiful in the beginning. Did the degeneration of the city mirror that of the wizard?

"Don't judge the wizard by what Fork has become," Ania said, seeming to read her mind. "It was very different when he made it. There were gardens and trees and lawns, white cobbles rather than black ones, and all of the buildings were different. They say it was so lovely a melding of nature and city that bridges sang and natural animals lived in it as easily as in a forest."

"Niadne said Fork is like it is now because the wizard became disappointed with Valley."

The other girl shook her head. "The city reflects what exists within its boundaries. It was infused with accommodating magic, for the wizard intended it to be a city that shaped itself to people who lived in it, and their needs. He thought it would go on being lovely and light and beautiful, but he did not reckon on the keepers. Fork altered gradually to match their stony hearts. It became dark, and the black towers started appearing. The bridges fell silent and the birds vanished. Some parts of Fork are very bad," she added in a low voice. "Especially where blackshirts and keepers gather."

The pier, Rage thought, remembering the malevolent feel of the city as they had approached the bank. She glanced at a wall and wondered if the city was listening to their words, if it was capable of resenting them or taking revenge. But even if it was, this part of the city seemed less malicious than sorrowful.

"Why do you think the wizard brought people like the keepers here?"

Ania shrugged. "Perhaps for companionship. They were not like they are now, I suppose. But if company was what he wanted, he soon enough regretted it. The witch women say the keepers almost drove him mad, going there and wanting him to decide this or that, or to judge their disputes and mediate their arguments. To keep them away he made Deepwood grow and enchanted it so that it would be almost impossible for anyone to reach his castle."

Glancing behind, Rage caught sight of Mr. Walker lifting his nose and concentrating intensely. She sniffed, too, and noticed a strong seaweed odor in the air. It must come from the reddish lichen that grew on the walls of the canals just above water level, for there was no other kind of plant life. Certainly, it was not caused by the sea, and yet the smell reminded her vividly of the windswept seaside town where she and Mam had lived before they went to Winnoway. Rage had been small, but she clearly remembered the massive crash of the breaking waves, the cries of the seagulls as they dived for leftover bits of food.

The memory was so clear she seemed to hear the roar of the ocean. Then she realized she *was* hearing it. "What is it?" she asked.

Ania merely pointed ahead. They came to a corner, and when they turned it, Rage stopped and gaped.

There was a handrail in front of her. It was all that stood between them and a broad, savage river that rushed to the rim of an abyss, then roared in a tumbling white broth over the edge and out of sight. There was nothing at all beyond it. It was like being at the top of the world's highest waterfall. The air shimmered with a mist that made the river look as if it were steaming, and droplets clung to Rage's skin and hair. Under her feet the ground vibrated with the sheer force of the water thundering past and under the city.

It was both thrilling and terrifying to witness the elemental force of the river and the waterfall after the quiet of the somber, black city. Rage's hair blew back from her face in the wind coming off the water. She felt breathless.

Looking back along the river's banks, she saw that the city was built on platforms that stood on immense pylons sunk into the riverbed. There must once have been many more buildings, but the platforms that supported them had been eroded by the water until they crumbled. Not far away half a building stood sagging on the edge of a platform, and even as she watched, the water tore at its jagged edges.

"Be careful." Ania pointed to the rail, and Rage saw that it was almost rusted through where she was leaning. She swayed back, the blood draining from her face.

Fear thickened into despair as she saw the end of her quest. The death of hope. No one could sail a boat down the River of No Return and live. It was not possible to reach the Endless Sea. She felt too sick with despair even to be angry at the firecat or to wonder why it had bidden her to do the impossible. Maybe it had hoped there was another solution and that she would be smart enough to find it. But if there was, Rage did not know what it could be.

Ania plucked at her arm and pointed to an unmanned raft careering wildly along the river. There were no passengers aboard, but a dark bundle was lashed to it. The raft was drawn inexorably to the outer edge of the fall, where it teetered at the very brink before being smashed to splinters on hidden rocks. The shattered remnants and the bundle were swept from view over the falls.

A second later the sun fell in orange splendor into the horizon and gray dusk fell like a cobwebbed cloak around them. Ania tugged at her arm. Numb, Rage let herself be led back down the lane and through an open doorway into the ruined shell of a building. There was nothing inside but a mess of moldering timber and wet, broken stone covered in spongy black moss, but the walls cut the din, so they did not need to shout.

"The boats are tethered upstream, near the blackshirt towers. They are used for the execution of ultimate sentences meted out by the High Keeper," Ania said.

Rage shuddered in horror, thinking of the bundle. "There . . . there was someone alive on that raft we saw?"

Ania nodded grimly. "Let us go from here. I cannot imagine why you wished to see the boats."

They abandoned the ruin and went back through the streets and over the canals and bridges to Newfork, the roar of the river slowly fading behind them. Even after they had passed out of hearing of the water, Rage's ears still hummed, and her heart beat too fast. Now what were they to do?

They came in sight of the Willow Seat Tower, gleaming darkly in the wan light of a rising moon. The city had bent to bring them here quickly. It struck Rage that the moon was exactly the same size as the night before and the one before that. Though it rose and set, it had neither waxed nor waned. What did that mean? Then she wondered what it mattered, since she would never be able to go home again. Never see Mam.

"There will be a search when you do not appear at the banding tomorrow evening," Ania said. "I removed you from Niadne's list and from her mind, but I do not know which blackshirts to deal with, and I am not sure their minds would be weak enough to mold."

Part of Rage still wanted to ask questions about Niadne and about Ania's use of magic, but the knowledge that there was no hope of returning home kept getting in the way.

Ania broke into the unhappy flow of Rage's thoughts, saying, "I must go now, but be very careful. The Mother bade me cast a spell to make you hard to see. Give me your hand. The spell will work best if you stand still when you are in danger of being seen."

Too depressed to speak, Rage offered her hand. Ania took it and dropped to her knees, pulling Rage down with her. She pushed Rage's hand flat against the earth between the cobbles and spoke a word.

In an instant, Rage was thrown across the lane and against a stone wall. Still kneeling, Ania gaped at her in horrified disbelief. "I—I don't understand," she stammered. "I felt something push against the magic. . . . That couldn't happen unless you are . . . a wizard."

Rage stood up, her head spinning. She felt sick and her whole body tingled, but she was otherwise unhurt. "I promise you, I'm no wizard," she said shakily. "It's probably because I'm a stranger to Valley. Thank you for . . . for trying to help me, but I . . . I have to go." She really felt dreadfully ill and had only walked a little distance out of Ania's sight before she vomited.

Mr. Walker came running up to her. "What did she do to you?"

"She tried only to work some magic, to make me hard to see, but somehow it backfired," Rage gasped. Then she thought of what she had seen. Mr. Walker must have seen it, too. "It's hopeless," she said bitterly. "There is no way we could survive a journey down that river."

"Let's go back to the others. Maybe Billy will know what to do," Mr. Walker said, his tail drooping.

Rage nodded and scooped him up. It took little time to return to the stone park because Rage knew where she wanted to go. But there was no sign of the others. Then Goaty emerged from the shadows and waved frantically. Rage heaved a sigh of relief. But when she was close enough to see him clearly, she saw that his long, thin face was pale and he wept.

"What's the matter?" she demanded, setting Mr. Walker down. "Is it Bear?"

"It's all of them. Bear and Elle and Billy—they have been taken away!" Goaty cried.

10

"Who took them?" Rage demanded. She ought never to have left them alone!

"Men in black clothes, like the ones that met the ferry," Goaty wept.

Blackshirts!

"Tell me exactly what happened," Rage told him. "Start from where Mr. Walker and I left."

"We were hungry and Elle wanted to go and search for food, but Billy Thunder said no one must go anywhere until you came back. Bear was awake, but she started coughing and some blood came out of her mouth. Elle said she was going to find you, but Bear said no. Elle tried to leave and Billy ran after her, and then the men in black came and saw them. Elle fought, but there were too many of them. One hit her over the head, and she fell down. Then some more of them came to the trees. I ran back to Bear. I tried to make her get up and run and hide, but she had gone to sleep again and she wouldn't wake. I was so scared. I . . . I hid, and I saw them take her, too."

"They carried her?" Rage said in disbelief.

"They fetched a board and a whole lot of them carried her on it, grunting and groaning. They took her one way, and some other blackshirts took Elle and Billy another way."

"Did they say where they were taking them?" Mr. Walker asked urgently.

"They said Bear must go to the conservatorium, but Billy and Elle were to be imprisoned. I heard one of them say that the High Keeper would have to decide what is to happen to them, since wild things are supposed to be harmless and Elle bit one of the blackshirts," Goaty said miserably.

Rage patted his arm, thinking that Bear was safe enough for the moment. Ania had said sick animals were taken to the conservatorium to be healed. "We'd better find Elle and Billy first," she announced. The blackshirt prison was sure to be close by the place where the rafts carrying condemned prisoners were launched, and she would use her memory of the river to bring them to that side of the city.

"Even if we do find them, how will we free them?" Mr. Walker asked. "There will be blackshirts guarding them, and they might even be in chains!"

"We'll figure it out once we see where they're imprisoned," Rage said. If she had to, she'd find Ania and demand the help that the witch girl had offered on behalf of her mistress.

"I'm coming with you," Mr. Walker declared.

Rage agreed, but she told Goaty to wait in the park. He hung his head in shame. "It's because I'm a coward, I know."

"It's not that at all. Someone has to be here in case Elle and Billy manage to escape on their own and come here."

Goaty only looked more depressed than ever.

Rage debated what to do. Her instinct was to rush off at once, but there would still be people awake and out in the streets. Better to wait until later, when the streets would be dark and deserted. Mr. Walker must have been exhausted, for when she told them what she had decided, he immediately curled up and fell asleep.

She heard Goaty sigh, and shifted closer to him. "I don't think you're a coward," she told him. "If you had done anything other than hide, the blackshirts would have taken you away as well. Then no one would have been here to tell Mr. Walker and me what happened. Hiding was the most sensible thing to do."

"Billy and Elle would not have hidden and let the blackshirts take me," Goaty said sadly.

Rage took Goaty's hand and they sat quietly, watching the thin moon rise higher and higher.

She was playing hide-and-seek. She charged at the dogs, and they raced away, barking wildly with excitement. Slipping into the undergrowth, she giggled to think how puzzled they would be, but instead of coming out on the other side of the shrub that ran between Winnoway and the Johnsons', she found herself caught in a mass of dark, rubbery leaves.

As she pushed deeper into them, their peppery smell grew stronger and the air became hot and damp. The barking of the dogs faded to a dim echo, and Rage saw that the forest was transforming itself around her, growing and thickening.

All at once she came to a clearing amid trees bigger than any she had ever seen. They soared up, their leaves high above linking and twining to block out all but a few stray beams of sunlight. The air was a deep greenish color, and shafts of light sliced through it like cables of radiance anchored to the ground.

Without warning a man stepped into the clearing. Very tall, he was, with dark-tanned, muscular arms. He wore faded jeans, a grubby T-shirt, and battered hiking boots. He carried a big, lumpy, beaten-up backpack with all sorts of things hanging off it. His hair grew down to his shoulders in a wild tangle of curls like Rage's, except it was black. This was not hair that would lie down and stay in Order, she thought, nor did the man look as if he would be easy to order around. His mouth had a harsh set, and the expression in his eyes was hidden by sunglasses that had been repaired with tape. A sweat-stained hat was pulled low over his forehead.

He stared at Rage in amazement. "Where the hell did you come from?"

His voice was muted, as if it came from behind a thick wall, but she heard it quite clearly. He looked exactly the sort of dangerous man that teachers warned against when they forbade talking to strangers, but Rage didn't feel afraid of him.

"I'm from Winnoway Farm," she said, and the man's mouth fell open with astonishment. "My mam was in a car accident and she can't wake up, so I'm trying to find some magic that will help her."

"What is your name?" the man asked urgently.

"I'm Rage Winnoway," Rage said. "Who are you?"

Before the man could answer he vanished. Billy emerged beside her, but he was no longer a dog.

"We couldn't find you anywhere," he said, pushing the toffee-colored lock of hair from his eyes.

Rage hissed at him to be quiet. She could hear a voice calling her name. Was it the dark-haired man?

"What was that?" Billy asked.

"Shh," Rage whispered. She listened hard. Sometimes when you heard a voice a long way off, it sounded like it was your name being called, even when it wasn't. But no, she was certain someone was calling her. Thinking about it seemed to make the voice louder. It was a man's voice.

"Who is it?" Billy whispered.

"Ra-age," the voice cried again.

"Who's there?" she shouted. "Who's calling me?"

The air shimmered, and the long, glowing lines of sunlight penetrating the green dimness wavered and became streamers, winding tighter and tighter into a greater brightness.

"Can . . . hear me?" The voice was coming out of the twisted sunbeams.

"Who . . . what are you?" Rage whispered, thinking of the firecat.

Beside her Billy began growling. Suddenly he was a dog again, and all the fur along his back had stiffened into a crest. She rested her hand on his head. He was trembling with tension.

"Don't trust . . ." The man's voice faded into a crackling sound, and there was a loud groan of pain.

"Who are you?" Rage asked again.

"Can't . . . ," the voice said haltingly, as if it were in pain. "Spell . . ."

Rage had read enough stories to know what this must mean. "Someone cast a spell of silence on you?"

"Yes," the voice said, sounding relieved. "Only . . . some things . . ."

"You can't say some things?"

No answer. She thought for a minute. "What do you want?"

"To tell . . . to warn . . ." The voice groaned very loudly.

"Break . . ." Another burst of static drowned out the next words.

"You want me to break the spell that is holding you?" Rage asked.

"Break . . . break . . ." The voice faded into a wheezy scream.

"How?" Rage cried.

There was a bright ruby flash of light and a violent hissing sound.

Rage opened her eyes to find she was staring up into Goaty's thin, worried face. "Are you sick?" he asked. "You were groaning in your sleep."

Rage sat up feeling very muddled. "I was having a dream," she said. She had been in a forest that kept changing. Then there had been a man wearing dark glasses, and a voice begging her to break a spell of silence. How peculiar it was that dreams stole bits of the day and wove them into stories that made sense while you were dreaming but none when you woke.

She shrugged, for she had far more serious things to worry about than a dream. Waking Mr. Walker, she told him they must go. Then she hugged Goaty, reminding him again to stay hidden until they returned.

"I'm afraid," he admitted, nearly weeping again. "I don't like being alone."

"Be brave," Rage said gently. "It gets easier each time you do it. Besides, maybe the others will escape and come back and then you won't be alone."

He took a deep breath and straightened his shoulders. "I'll try."

The streets were even darker than they had been in the

early hours of the morning. A river mist had risen, damp and clammy, blurring the edges of every solid thing with shifting shadows. In the distance the black towers again looked like skyscrapers.

Rage carefully pictured the outer edges of the city and began to walk. Her mind drifted to wondering where the wizard had got the men and women who peopled Valley, and why some of their descendants had ended up being like Ania and others like the ruthless High Keeper. Maybe there was no answer. Sometimes in a family one of the children was nasty and sullen or a bully, while the others were especially nice, but they all had the same parents and lived in the same house.

Rage stiffened as the Willow Seat Tower came into view. Thinking of the High Keeper must have been enough to encourage the city to bring her here. The street seemed too narrow and close around her, and Rage had the eerie sensation that she was being watched by unfriendly eyes. She noticed that the buildings around the Willow Seat Tower looked wrong. It was as if their shadowy outlines were distorted, so that one side of a wall was higher or wider than another, and windows were not properly square or round.

Unnerved, she turned her back on the tower and summoned up a mental picture of the place Ania had taken her to see the boats. Resisting the urge to run, she walked purposefully, and gradually the feeling of malevolence faded until she could smell the seaweed odor of the red lichen again.

She stopped when she came to the first canal and looked down at Mr. Walker. "The blackshirts keep prisoners in this part of the city, but almost no one else lives here. Can you smell people in any direction?"

Mr. Walker sniffed, turning his nose this way and that. "I think there are people that way." He pointed across the bridge.

Rage started walking toward it, but Mr. Walker did not move. "What is the matter?" she asked.

"Trolls," Mr. Walker said. "Everyone knows they live under bridges and that they especially love to eat goats. They will smell Goaty on us."

Rage wanted to shout that there were no such things as trolls and that they probably did not live under bridges even if they did exist, but she mastered her impatience. "I've already crossed this bridge today and there was no sign of any troll!"

Still Mr. Walker refused to budge, saying that everyone knew trolls only came out at night because they couldn't bear the sun.

"That's vampires, and anyway, when I came back across this bridge the sun had set." Rage and Mr. Walker were still arguing when she heard the sound of boots marching along the cobbles. Knowing there was no time to waste, she snatched him up, ran across the bridge, and pressed herself into a doorway on the other side, holding her hand over his mouth.

Not a moment too soon. A pair of black-clad men marched purposefully along the canal and crossed the bridge. Mr. Walker ceased his struggles and began to tremble in her arms as the men approached. Rage stroked his head and listened intently. She caught a snatch of the conversation and was elated to hear one of them speak of prisoners. It was too good an opportunity to miss. She set Mr. Walker down and hurried after them, leaving him to follow or not. The blackshirts walked so fast, she almost had to run to keep up. She prayed they would not hear her. Luckily, they were deep in conversation. Even so, Rage stayed close to the walls, darting from alcove to alcove and across bridges swiftly and lightly, prepared to freeze if either man glanced back.

Then, without warning, she lost sight of them.

The men had been striding along a broad street beside a canal. They had not passed any bridges, though there were a lot of tiny lanes running off to the left. Rage guessed the men had turned into one of them. She stopped and listened but could hear nothing other than her own wildly beating heart.

She went on cautiously, stopping to peer down every lane. They were all empty. A chilling thought struck her: what if the guards had become aware of her and were hiding somewhere, waiting to grab her?

Mr. Walker caught up, puffing hard. "I don't like the smells here," he whispered.

Rage swallowed her own rising panic. "Can you smell anyone hiding nearby?"

He sniffed in all directions, then began to sniff his way along the stones of a narrow lane. He stopped at the corner of another street.

"What is it?" Rage hissed. "Did they go this way?"

He didn't answer her at once. He began sniffing the building on their right—a tower like the others, except for the door, which looked new and very solid, its lever gleaming as if it had been polished.

"Do you smell that they went in there?" Rage prompted. The building was surely too small to be a prison.

Mr. Walker looked up at Rage in triumph. "I smell them! Billy Thunder and Elle."

Rage hugged herself in elation, but *finding* Billy and

Elle was a long way from rescuing them.

"Their smell is not very strong," Mr. Walker said. "I wouldn't have noticed it at all if you hadn't asked me to smell for someone hiding."

Rage took a few steps back and looked up, deciding that the men she had been following must have gone inside the tower. There was a single lit window, about halfway up. She tried the door but couldn't move the lever an inch. There was no way to get round the back of the building because it was built right up against the ones alongside.

"Here," Mr. Walker cried, peering into what looked like an air vent in the wall. "I can get in here," he announced.

Rage hesitated, not wanting him to go in alone. Bitterly she realized that she had no choice. "All right," she agreed. "Just see if you can find them and come straight back. Don't let anyone see you."

"No one ever sees me," Mr. Walker said.

Seeing his gallant, solitary little figure in the moonlight, Rage wondered for the hundredth time how the family who had owned him could have taken him to the dog pound.

"Be careful," she called, but he had already gone.

She knelt down and tried to see into the vent, but it was too dark. Then she searched along the street until she found a crumbling building where she could wait unseen for Mr. Walker. There was a hole in its rear wall that opened into another lane: a perfect escape route if she needed one.

With nothing to do but wait, she sat down in the doorway, keeping an eye on the tower. Something dug into her. She wriggled and reached into her coat pocket until her hand closed around the hourglass. It felt hot.

She took it out, and there was a gust of wind, then a sliver of mist shimmered and blew into a spiral that blushed red before her. A face appeared like a hologram; a shifty feline face with the suggestion of pointed ears and beautiful red eyes slitted with yellow, catlike irises.

The firecat.

"What do you want?" Rage demanded coldly.

The smoky image blinked at her. "Ragewinnoway not hurrying," it accused.

Rage wanted to shout that she was in no hurry to sail over the edge of a waterfall, but she held her tongue. The firecat was likely to vanish once it understood that she had no intention of going down the River of No Return.

"I can't go down the river until my friends are free," she said slyly. "They are imprisoned in this tower, and I must get them out."

"Ragewinnoway must take hourglass to wizard. Wizard helping friends."

"I won't leave the others, so if you want me to deliver the hourglass, you'd better do something to help them," Rage said bluntly.

"*Can't* do something," the firecat burst out.

Rage felt her anger fade because the firecat's frustration sounded genuine. Giving up all pretense, she said, "Look, no one can go down the river without being killed. You know that, don't you? You might as well tell me the truth about the hourglass and what it measures." She had no expectation that it would answer her question. But she was wrong.

"Hourglass is measuring life," the firecat spat. "Wizard's life. When sand runs out, no more wizard and no more magic for waking mother of Ragewinnoway."

It vanished.

Rage stared at the hourglass in horror. Most of the

sand had fallen to one side of the hourglass. She told herself that the firecat had lied to pay her back for refusing to go down the river. But what if it had told the truth and the wizard really would die if he did not get the hourglass before the sand ran out? Yet it made no sense that a wizard powerful enough to create a magical land would bind his life to the sand in an hourglass. And what part did the firecat play in all this? Despite its violent desire for her to obey the riddle etched on the base of the hourglass, it had never shown the slightest sign of love or fear of its master.

Of course there were no answers, only more questions. And the answers no longer mattered. Whether or not the wizard's life was at stake, Rage knew she would not survive a journey down the lethal River of No Return.

She thrust the hourglass back into her pocket, dismissing all thoughts of the wizard, the firecat, and the hourglass. Right now, the important thing was to get her friends out of the hands of the blackshirts. She left the safety of the crumbling building and paced up and down the street, wondering what was taking Mr. Walker so long.

She was in front of the doorway to the tower when it suddenly burst open and a group of blackshirts crowded out. Rage froze. But to her astonishment, they didn't seem to see her. Ania's spell must have worked after all, though she did not understand how Mr. Walker and Goaty had been able to see her—unless it was that she had not wanted to hide from them.

Rage dared not move as the blackshirts milled around her. Ania had said that the success of the spell depended on this. A trickle of perspiration ran down between her shoulder blades.

"Come on!" one of the blackshirts shouted back into the doorway.

Rage could see stone steps going up. She heard the sound of boots and four more blackshirts appeared.

"We should have relieved the others guarding the ferry pier half an hour back!" the man holding the door ajar said angrily. He had a red stripe on his shirt.

"It's not our fault that the tunnel collapsed," one of the latecomers said.

They marched away. On impulse Rage ran softly forward and grabbed the edge of the door to stop it swinging shut. In a twinkling she was inside and creeping up the stairs, hardly able to believe her luck.

She climbed and climbed, wondering what could be in the lower part of the building, since these steps were the only way in and they went straight up without a single doorway leading off them. They brought her to a long stone corridor, and she saw light flowing from a doorway ahead. This must be the room with the lit window she had seen from the street. Summoning her courage, she made her way to the door.

"*I know what you are up to!*"

Rage nearly jumped out of her skin as the voice and a burst of sneering laughter cut through the silence. But there were no footsteps. Whoever had spoken had to be inside the room.

"What do you suppose they were up to?" another man asked in a conversational tone.

Rage pressed herself to the wall and edged closer to the door.

"I've no idea. They both look human to me, but the female is furred, so she must be some kind of wild thing. The boy looks completely human, but what boy would associate with witches and wild things?"

"Maybe the witches made some wild things that could pass as human."

"I didn't think there was enough magic left in Wildwood for any more making."

"Unless Boone is right and they've found a way to get it from this side of the river. They do say the river is getting worse."

"Well, it's for the High Keeper to decide what they are, when he gets round to taking a look at them."

"Boone said there's no hurry."

"They'll die like the other ones if they're here too long. If they're wild folk, I mean."

The other man laughed harshly. "One less wild thing to bother about."

The two men were silent for a time, then there was a slapping sound.

"Is it true that the real animals in the provinces are getting sick?"

"Maybe, but who cares if a few animals die? Ahh! *Now I've got you!*"

There was another period of silence and some more slapping. The sound was tantalizingly familiar. Rage had a vision of herself playing Snap with Mam. The men were playing a card game! Figuring this out made her feel bold, and she went right up to the door and peeked into the room.

The men were seated at a table. There was nothing in the room but the table and two chairs. Rage withdrew. The conversation of the blackshirts suggested they were guarding Billy and Elle. But where were they? And where was Mr. Walker?

Rage took a deep breath, then ghosted past the door and down the shadowy hallway. It turned sharply to the left, and she peeped around the corner. There was a window in the outer wall, and in the blue-tinged moonlight she could see metal bars set in the wall opposite.

Creeping up to the bars, Rage saw a small stone cell. A man in it was sleeping soundly, his back turned to the bars. She craned her neck and saw another two cells, empty, but the third had three fairies in it, all with delicate dragonfly wings. Only one of them was facing the bars, its tiny mouth opened in a perfect O of amazement at the sight of her.

Rage put her finger to her mouth, wondering what crime the little creatures could possibly have committed. The fairy nodded and poked at her two companions. All three crept to the bars, close enough for Rage to see that they were pale and notice that they smelled bad. Her heart twisted in pity. The poor fragile things were clearly sick, despite what Ania had said about none of the wild things dying of hunger.

"Are you from the secret coven?" one of the fairies whispered through cracked lips.

"No, but I'm going to try to get you out," Rage said softly. She examined the bars. There was no lock. In fact, there didn't even seem to be a door.

"When they put us in here, the bars slid aside," the fairy said.

This reminded Rage of a movie she had seen about men in a prison. When it was breakfast time, all of the cell doors had opened simultaneously at the flick of a single switch in the office of the prison warden.

"I have an idea, but first I must see if my friends are all right," she whispered.

"The not-dogs?" another fairy asked, coming up to the bars. Then she flinched and drew back as if the metal had burned her.

"They are down at the end," the other said, pointing carefully through the bars.

Rage hurried along the corridor to the last cell,

where Billy and Elle stared out at her happily, their fingers curled around the bars. "We could smell you," Elle said joyfully.

Rage put her hands on theirs and squeezed hard. "I am so glad to see you both," she said fervently, blinking to stop herself from crying out of sheer relief.

"How did you find us?" Billy asked, bringing her down to earth.

"Mr. Walker sniffed you out," Rage answered. "Have you seen him?"

Billy shook his head. "I thought I could smell him ages ago, but not now."

Elle nodded confirmation. "He was near and then he had a going-away smell."

Rage decided that the vent Mr. Walker had used to enter the building must have led to the lower level of the tower. He'd probably gone outside by now and was heading back to Goaty. At least she hoped so.

"Have you found Mama?" Billy asked eagerly.

"She's been taken to a place where they look after sick animals. We'll search for her when I've got you two out of here."

"What are you going to do?" Billy asked.

"Just be ready to run," Rage said. She went back to the fairies. "Are there any more wild things in here?"

The fairies shook their heads. One said sadly, "There were others, but they faded. It was the iron bars."

"What about the man in the other cell?" It would be a problem if all of the cells opened and he attacked them or started shouting.

"The blackshirts brought him in last night," a fairy said. "He was groaning, but he hasn't made any noise today."

The smallest of the fairies held out a tiny bag to Rage. "It is witch's dust," she whispered. "It's for making us look sick when we come to Fork, but you can use it to wish the guards asleep. You have to throw it over them, and you mustn't breathe any in yourself."

"It doesn't last very long," another warned.

Rage pocketed the tiny bag and crept back to the room where the blackshirts were playing cards. This time she noticed another open door behind the one to the guards' room, and stairs going down. She wondered if this led to the tunnel the departing blackshirts had talked about.

". . . don't see why we can't just go in and clean Wildwood out once and for all," one of the men said. "It would be more merciful than letting the creatures die slowly, and it would teach the witches a lesson. That's what Boone thinks we ought to do."

There was the sound of cards being shuffled.

"Keepers would never abide it. They don't want their hands dirtied with violence."

"Their hands wouldn't have to be dirtied, would they? Besides, wasn't it the High Keeper himself who wanted to see what would happen if wild things were kept behind iron bars?"

Another slapping sound.

Rage peeped around the corner again. The men hadn't moved from their seats. She poked her head right into the room and saw that there was a big wheel set into the same wall as the door. It might be a central control for the cell gates, but even from that distance she could see that there was no way to turn such a wheel quietly. She thought of the little bag of witch's dust.

"I heard the witch folk claim it's not them using up

magic from the land," said the guard with his back to the wheel.

Rage took a deep breath and stepped into the room. The lanterns hung on the wall gave off a bright but flickering light, but if she could move quietly enough, perhaps Ania's spell would stop the men looking her way until it was too late.

Pleasepleaseplease, she thought, and again she grew hot with anxiety.

She took another step into the room, legs shaking.

The blackshirt with his back to her groaned, and the other gathered the cards up with the same burst of sneering laughter she had heard from the hallway.

She took a step nearer. She was so close to them now, she dared not breathe, but neither lifted their eyes from the cards.

"What about the man in the first cell? What did he do that he's locked up here?"

Rage waited, curious despite her fear.

"He's a keeper, if you can believe it. Boone said he was found in the provinces snooping around. There's some suggestion he's mixed up with the witch women."

"A keeper working with the witch women!" the other exclaimed. He lifted his head so that he was facing Rage.

She gasped. She couldn't help herself. The blackshirt's eyes widened and focused on her. She hurled some of the witch's dust over the two men, who instantly toppled sideways under the yellow shower.

Still holding her breath, Rage shoved the pouch into her pocket and ran to the wheel. There was a blue arrow on it, pointing up to the roof, and another blue arrow on the wall. If she was right about the wheel controlling access to the cell doors, she must have to turn the wheel arrow to match the arrow on the wall.

She took hold of the wheel and tried to turn it. It was terribly heavy, and she only managed to shift it a little. Struggling, she dragged it another fraction. Unable to hold her breath any longer, she breathed in with a loud gasp.

Nothing happened. The witch's dust must have settled. She put both hands on one side of the wheel and, bracing herself, tugged down as hard as she could. The wheel shifted another fraction, then it simply wouldn't turn anymore.

She heard a sound behind her and was aghast to find the two blackshirts beginning to stir. She tugged frantically at the wheel. In seconds they would be properly awake!

The wheel would not move.

One of the men sat up. He groaned and climbed groggily to his feet, his back turned to her. Rage didn't know what to do. To throw more dust, she would have to get closer, and maybe there was too little left to affect the men. If it didn't work, she would be trapped in the room.

Part of her wanted to run, but she set her teeth together and pulled violently at the wheel. It still wouldn't budge. The second man woke and saw immediately what she was about. "Stop her," he cried in a slurred voice.

The other guard turned unsteadily, but at the same moment a tall man with a bloodied face stepped through the door holding a boot. Rage gaped at him in astonishment.

"Don't think you can trick us," the nearest black-shirt sneered at Rage, then his face changed comically as the newcomer hit him on the head with the boot and he slipped back to the floor. The man did the same thing to the second blackshirt before turning to Rage. "That should keep them quiet for a bit. How did you open my cell?"

Wordlessly, Rage pointed at the wheel. The man took two steps across and turned it the rest of the way with a great heave. "Come on. It won't be long before more blackshirts come."

They dashed out into the hallway to see the fairies limping fearfully out of their cell. Clearly their wings were too weak to use. "Come, little ones," the man said gently, and scooped all three into his arms. Further down the hall, Billy and Elle emerged, and Rage waved them to come.

When he had ascertained that there were no other prisoners, the man bade them follow him and ran lightly down the hall. He descended the stairs two at a time, the fairies clinging to his shoulders and gazing at his face in awe.

Rage followed with Elle and Billy close behind her.

At the bottom, the man opened the door and peered out. "No one. Come on."

They followed him outside, and then they all heard the sound of boots coming along the cobbles.

"This way!" Rage cried, and ran along the street to the ruined building. She meant to lead them through it to the lane, but as soon as they were inside the deserted shell, the man caught her arm and shook his head. He squatted down and held his finger to his lips. After a slight hesitation, Rage and the others did the same. They heard the boots come closer, the sound of the door being opened. Then more steps and a *clank* as the door shut.

The man rose. "There is a back way out of this?"

"There is a hole and it opens to another lane, but I don't know where that leads," Rage said.

As they climbed through the rubble, Rage thought of Mr. Walker and hoped that he had gone back to the river. There was nothing she could do to help him now.

When they were clear of the ruin, the man took the lead again and began to walk very quickly, urging the fairies to climb inside his voluminous jacket. It was all Rage could do to keep up with him. When she began to lag, Billy and Elle each took one of her hands and pulled her along.

The man did not stop until they had left the region of canals and entered the drier territory of Newfork. They came to a sliver of space left between two small buildings. A real tree grew there, though it was gray and sickly-looking. The man stopped under its branches and turned to Rage. "I don't know what you are doing in Fork or how you came to be in that prison, yet I thank you, girl, for setting me and these little ones free."

"I heard one of the blackshirts say that you are a keeper. Is it true?" Rage asked.

"I *was* a keeper," the man said. "Now you might say that the witch women and I have interests in common." He glanced around. "I would like to repay your help, but I have no means, and right now I must get these three and myself across the river before the blackshirts raise the alarm. I would advise you to come with us, for my escape is likely to cause a furor."

"We can't!" Billy cried. "My mother is here in Fork."

"And Goaty and Mr. Walker," Elle said.

A bell began to toll loudly.

The man looked at Rage with regret. "I'm afraid it's too dangerous for any of us to stay out in the open like this. You must go your own way now, or come with me and cross the river."

Rage shook her head. "I can't. We must find our friends."

The man nodded. "Well then, I wish you luck. Maybe we'll meet again someday."

He turned, but Rage caught his arm. "Wait. One of our friends is a true animal. She was hurt, and the black-shirts took her to the conservatorium. Do you know where that is?"

The man looked horrified. "She was taken there? That means she is to be killed and stuffed!"

"No!" Billy screamed. He rushed at the man and shook him. "She's my mother! They can't. They mustn't!"

The man looked at him in pity and wonder. "I don't know how a beast can be your mother, but if you would save her, lad, if she is not already dead, you must go there as fast as you can."

"Where?" Billy demanded, tears streaming down his face.

"The conservatorium is behind the Willow Seat Tower. You will know it when you see it. It is like no other place." He would have said more, but Billy had already dashed away. Rage and Elle ran after him.

"Good luck. . . ." The man's voice faded behind them.

11

Billy ran wildly ahead. All too soon the Willow Seat Tower loomed before them like an accusing finger. Elle growled under her breath at it, and Rage caught hold of Billy before he could rush off again. "We have to go carefully now! We can't help Bear if we're caught."

He gasped, and she saw the effort it cost to calm himself. "All right," he said in a strangled voice.

"That man said the conservatorium was behind the Willow Seat Tower. Let's try walking around it, but let me go first. There is a spell on me that will stop anyone noticing me as long as I see them first and stand very still." Rage hoped it was still working.

They made a wide circle around the tower. Rage felt as if there were eyes peering from the windows. Surely those within must have heard the alarm bell. But there was no sign of any activity, and somehow this was more troubling than if the place had been swarming with blackshirts.

They did a second circuit and still could not see a building that announced itself as the conservatorium. Rage stood still and craned her neck, trying to look past the tower, but this was curiously hard to do. It was as if the building insisted on being looked at. She persevered and, for a moment, caught sight of something looming dark and huge behind it.

Her breath caught in her throat, and whatever she had seen dissolved into the general darkness. Elle began to growl loudly. Rage again looked past the tower, and this time she clearly saw a huge, squat black dome. It was so big that it was impossible they could have missed seeing it, and yet none of them *had* seen it until now. They walked slowly toward it but found themselves lost in a twisting maze of streets that wound and coiled around its base.

Rage went on picturing the dome, even when it vanished from sight. Before long it was visible again and closer than ever. Then the streets began to narrow dramatically. When they finally reached a street that ran to the base of the dome, it was no more than a sliver of an alleyway.

Elle made a little whining sound. "What is it?"

"The conservatorium," Rage answered. She knew Elle had been asking her more than that. But she did not know what to say. The dome was only a building, but she sensed it was also the sick, pulsing heart of all the darkness that inhabited the city. Every instinct bade her flee from it as fast as she could.

Rage noticed uneasily that the distorted architecture she had noticed earlier in buildings around the Willow Seat Tower was far worse here. A dozen different styles of buildings were jumbled together. Minarets and spires and chimney stacks and crenellated openings warred with one another for space. But nothing made sense. Stairs led nowhere; balconies were without guard rails or were fixed upside down onto walls. Windows opened onto walls or doors or other windows. Crooked, half-completed walls listed drunkenly, and paths led to nothing. Things were half completed or finished with impossible and lunatic detail. It was as if a strange frenzy had filled the mind of its designer.

Yet the grotesquerie of the streets, however horrible, did not arouse in Rage the same dread as the black dome.

They stopped and looked at one another.

"Mama is inside that place. I have to go in," Billy said determinedly.

"We will all go in," Elle announced, and Rage was never more glad of her indomitable courage than at that moment.

They walked side by side to begin with, but soon there was room only for two, then one—the alley had reduced itself to no more than a crack. The conservatorium still looked as distant as when they had first seen it.

Rage swung around. The alley behind them appeared wide and inviting. "This is some sort of trick," she said. She felt the crack begin to close on them.

"I can't fit!" Billy shouted.

"We must go back and try another way," Elle said.

Rage shook her head. "No. That's what it wants us to do. There is no other way, and if we try again I think it will find a way to stop us getting even this close."

"But we can't go forward," Elle protested. Then she said in a strange, rigid voice, "I'm trapped! I can't move!"

Inside Rage, the voice of fear urged her to save herself, but she ignored it. No matter how malicious it seemed, the city was made of responsive magic. Even the dome. That meant it could respond to them as well as to the keepers.

It came to her what they must do. "We have to imagine the street opening up and letting us through."

"I don't know how to imagine things," Billy said in a strained voice.

"Just make a picture in your mind of the city letting you through. Imagine the crack opening up," Rage called.

"I . . . I can't!" he cried. "My mind is not big enough for that yet."

"Animals can't imagine things," Elle said in a muffled voice.

"I will do it," Rage said. She concentrated on imagining the city Ania had described: Fork as it had been when the wizard created it, with a wide, graceful street leading up to the dome.

The crack began to close around Rage's shoulders. She could feel the hateful black pressure of the dome as it resisted her vision. The keepers' influence was too deep, too strong. Elle and Billy said nothing, and Rage dared not think of what was happening to them. She had to make the city listen!

I am Rage Winnoway whose name is also Courage! she cried out in her mind. She let her imagination run wild, picturing towers of glass wound with threads of silver and gold and studded with pink pearls; wide, straight streets where there were trees and flowers; graceful rooms filled with air and light and butterflies; a city where antelopes and winged lions wandered freely in and out of buildings filled with human laughter, where bridges sang.

A groaning, as much the sound of crumbling stone as a howl of inhuman anguish, filled Rage's head. She felt the agony of the city so keenly that she had to stop herself from screaming. But she did not stop visualizing the city as it had been, as it could be, as it should be. The city was not evil. It was like someone who had been forced into a bent and crippled position for so long and knew of no other way to be. She offered her vision of the city to free it, and despite the brutal pressure on her arms and shoulders, the imagining became easier. Rage went on dreaming of Fork as it could be, mixing up Mam's carless city with the things Ania had said and with her own ideas. Despite her fear for Elle and Billy, a kind of elation filled her, for surely imagining so hard and so brightly was a kind of magic, too.

There was a loud crack, then the walls on either side of them crumbled and collapsed softly and silently into powdery rubble. Before them, the alleyway was wide and perfectly straight.

"Look!" Elle gasped, and they stared in amazement as blooms as red as blood burst through the piles of shattered stone.

There was no time to wonder at them. Billy scrambled over the debris and was approaching the dome. Rage followed. The door to the black tower was a great heavy slab of what looked like marble. Billy reached for the lever, and the door sprang open at his touch. Behind it was a set of steps going up into darkness. Billy and Elle staggered back, gagging and coughing.

"Whatever is it?" Rage asked.

"Can't you smell?" Elle sounded appalled.

"Something rotten," Billy gasped.

Rage shook her head and entered. As in the blackshirt tower, there was no access to the bottom part of the dome. The steps led to an enormous room that occupied an entire level of the conservatorium. Windows in every wall looked out over Fork. The room was empty and deathly quiet, with wide pillars stretching up to the ceiling. Something about the room, about the muted light, was familiar to Rage. She racked her brain until it came to her.

It reminded her of the Museum of Natural History.

Billy walked to the nearest pillar, and Rage tried to reach him. But she was too late. He gave an anguished cry and started back in horror. Rage was close enough now to see that there was a glassed-in box set into the pillar. A group of tiny, squirrel-like animals, all stuffed, stared blindly and pitifully out into the darkness.

"Mama!" Billy cried, falling to his knees.

Rage thought she heard something. "Wait here with Billy," she whispered to Elle, and crept across the room with a thudding sense of fear. She heard a man's voice, muffled as if through a thick wall.

"Are you sure we should not reconsider?"

Rage could not see any doors, but she heard footsteps. She crept around the pillars, searching until she found a stairwell. The voices grew louder. The speakers were coming up the stairs!

Rage darted behind the nearest pillar just as an old man emerged from the stairwell. He wore a white tunic edged in gold, like the man who had alighted from the litter at the door to the Willow Seat Tower. Maybe this was the High Keeper himself. Studying the man's cold, haughty expression, his small, pouting mouth and glittering black eyes, she could easily imagine him demanding that a man or woman or child be tied to a raft and sent to a horrible death.

The keeper turned and spoke down the stairs: "I see no need to reconsider my decision, Hermani." He had a beautiful, deep voice that compelled attention.

Another old man emerged from the stairwell, carrying a jar in which something dark floated. He wore a plain white tunic. "High One, it is just that we do not know what the beast is yet. That is why I—"

High One! Niadne had referred to the High Keeper of Fork as the High One.

"It is a form of dog."

Rage's heart jumped into her throat. Surely they meant Bear.

"High One, there are aspects of the form that do not seem to fit into our list of canine characteristics. If this is a new species and we conserve it—"

"What is it that you want, Hermani?"

The other man hung his head. "To tell you the truth, High One, I don't like to conserve things that might be saved. The creature is old but—"

"The longer she lives, the more trouble we will have in conserving her well. The coat will dull and become threadbare. The claws will blunt and perhaps fall out, not to mention the teeth. If it is a new species, there is all the more reason to conserve it at its peak. You saw the pelt. It is already considerably scarred."

"Someone has ill-treated the poor beast."

"Witch women," the High Keeper hissed, eyes black and small with hate. "The blackshirts that brought it in said it was with two wild things. I will interrogate them myself."

Rage shuddered at the thought of Elle and Billy in the clutches of the High Keeper.

"High One, the witch women would not ill-treat a true beast any more than they would harm one of their wild things. And why would they send it here, in any case?"

"I don't like to hear you talking this way, Hermani,"

the High Keeper said icily. "You should know by now that the witch women are capable of anything. They are a constant danger to the wizard's Order, and our only hope that he will return to us lies in obedience to his will."

"If he does not return soon, there will be no one to admire our obedience, High One." He waved his arm. "All will be lost when the river reclaims Valley. Surely anything would be better than that. Perhaps if we approached the witch Mother—"

"Silence!" the High Keeper roared, and Hermani shrank from the fury contorting his master's face. But the High Keeper smiled now, the change of expression so complete as to be terrifying.

He is quite mad, Rage thought.

"Do not concern yourself with the river, Hermani," the High Keeper said pleasantly. "Once Wildwood is emptied of blasphemy and witches . . ."

It seemed to Rage that Hermani forced himself to speak, though his voice quivered. "High One, forgive me, but in the last seven days the waters have risen rapidly. Some of the deeper blackshirt tunnels have become saturated and are in danger of collapsing. Even tonight there was a report that a tunnel running to the ferry pier had collapsed. Yet there is no magic in Wildwood for the witch folk to draw on. It cannot be their fault. Something else must be—"

"Enough," the High Keeper thundered. "I am disappointed in you. Let us proceed with this conservation. I am weary. Another five minutes and the beast will no longer be alive for you to—"

Rage had been creeping steadily nearer the two men, and at these cold words a great fury rose up in her heart. She groped in her pocket for the slender pouch of witch's dust and hurled the remainder of it as hard as she could at the two men.

They crumpled soundlessly, just as the blackshirts had done.

"Elle!" Rage cried. "Come and tie these two up and follow me! Billy, hurry before it's too late!"

Not waiting to see if they obeyed, she hurtled down the steps, only to find herself in another huge room with more glass cases in pillars, except there were no windows in the walls, and it was brightly lit. There was a square hole in the floor, which must lead down to yet another level.

Then she saw that there was no need to go further.

Billy cannoned into her.

Incapable of words, Rage pointed to an enormous glass case set against the far wall and lit from above. Bear was inside it, lying on a bed with wheels. A tube from a metal tank fed into the side of the case, and a hissing noise filled the air.

"No!" Billy screamed. He lifted the metal tank with a deep-throated groan and heaved it at the glass case with all of his might. There was a tremendous shattering crash, and then the air filled with a sickly sweet smell. The hissing sound became louder.

"Hold your breath and let's get her out of here!" Rage gasped.

Billy crunched over the broken glass and tried to shove the bed, but Bear's bulk was too much for him to move alone.

"Elle!" Rage screamed.

The Amazon came running down the stairs. "It took me a while to find something to tie—" She paled at the sight of Bear.

Somehow they managed to get the unconscious Bear

to the top of the stairs. Rage saw that Hermani had awakened. He said in a slurred but urgent voice, "You heard the bells before? It means someone has escaped the prisons. Blackshirts will pour through the tunnels into the conservatorium any minute, wanting instructions from the High Keeper."

Ignoring him, Billy peered into Bear's face and patted her loose jaw. She did not respond. Rage laid her head on the old dog's chest with a feeling of dread and heard a heartbeat tap against her cheek. It sounded uneven and too slow, but it was there.

"She's alive!"

Billy burst into tears and kissed Bear's gray-flecked muzzle and forehead.

"You must listen to me," Hermani cried frantically. "There is a chute over by where you came in. Under the pillar with the case of squirrels. The pillar can be pushed aside. It will bring you to a tunnel that lies below the network of blackshirt tunnels. It's your only hope."

"Why would you help us?" Rage demanded.

The keeper looked at his master, who had begun to stir. "Because I would save the beast," he hissed, nodding at Bear. "Go, or it will be too late for all of you."

"They're coming," Elle said. "I smell them."

Rage could hear nothing, but she ran to the gleaming case with the stuffed squirrels and pushed on it. It slid aside with a faint sigh, and there was the promised chute.

"How can we trust that man after what he did to Mama?" Billy demanded.

"We have no choice. Help Bear down the chute, and you two go after her!" Rage commanded.

"What about you?"

"I'm coming, too, of course. Now go!"

Leaving them to drag Bear over to the chute, Rage ran back to the two keepers. The High Keeper's eyes were fluttering. "How do I close the pillar back over the chute?" she demanded of Hermani.

"A lever on the underside of the case. Push it and you will have just enough time to jump through before the pillar moves back into place. Now go! He mustn't know I helped you."

Rage did not waste time on thanks. In seconds she was hurtling down a smooth chute in pitch darkness. At first the speed was terrifying, but then the tunnel leveled out and flattened so that eventually she simply slid to a halt.

Elle and Billy were leaning anxiously over Bear, but they looked up at Rage in puzzlement. She realized that the faint source of light that bathed them all was coming from her. Looking down, she was astonished to find her pocket glowing. Reaching in, she found the hourglass. It was warm to the touch and radiated a bright ruby light. How strange! She held it before her like a beacon and saw that the chute became a proper tunnel that ran away into the distance.

Bear started to retch and cough violently.

"Mama!" Billy turned his attention back to his mother.

The old dog struggled to sit. "Where are we? What has been happening?" she rasped.

"There's no time to explain now," Rage said. "We need to go on if you can." They had to find Goaty and Mr. Walker, and they had to get out of the tunnel in case Hermani had betrayed them. After that, there was really nowhere to go but back over the river to the wild side—if they could get on the ferry.

"What did you do to it?" Billy asked, glancing at the

glowing hourglass as they helped Bear to her feet.

"Nothing," Rage said. "It did that on its own." Was it possible that she had somehow invoked the wizard's magic? Taking the hourglass and holding it high to light their way, she took the lead.

Billy's mind must have been on the same track. "Maybe the hourglass gives wishes if you just think about something. Like the bramble gate tried to make us human after you wished for it. Did you want it to be light?"

"I don't think I thought about light."

"Try wishing for something new," Elle suggested.

Rage doubted it would be that easy, but she said in a loud, formal voice, "Please take us to Goaty!" When nothing happened, she told the others what the firecat had said about the sand representing the wizard's life.

"But it has almost run out," Billy said, looking aghast.

Rage nodded. "I don't think we can do anything to save the wizard, if what the firecat said is true. We can't survive a trip down the River of No Return to find him."

Elle, Billy, and even Bear stared at her. Rage remembered that she hadn't told them about what Ania had shown her. So as they walked she explained all that had befallen her since they had parted in the park of stone trees.

"A waterfall," Billy murmured. "But it must be possible to go down it safely, if the wizard went there."

"He had magical powers to protect him," Elle said.

"If the wizard could use his magical powers, he would have come back to get the hourglass and save himself," Billy said. "That means he went down the river without magic."

"We don't know that. He might have got there some

other way altogether. He might have even used a gate like the one that brought us here," Rage said. "But *we* have only one way to get there, and that would kill us."

"Maybe," Billy said. Then he sighed. "Well, who knows what is true, anyway? The firecat might have lied about the sand showing how much time the wizard has to live. Before, it said the hourglass contained all that the wizard knew."

"It might have lied about everything," Rage said. "But I do believe it wants us to take the hourglass to the wizard. I just wish we knew why."

They walked in silence for a while.

"When I was in that prison cell, I kept wondering why the firecat just didn't magic itself to the wizard with the hourglass, like it magicked itself to us," Elle said presently.

Rage was surprised—usually Elle wasn't interested in thinking about things. But then again, she wasn't usually stuck in jail.

"I was thinking about the firecat, too," Billy said. "I don't think it can magic itself anywhere. I think it only magics an image of itself to us. That's why it won't appear properly and wouldn't unlock your door in the banding house. It can't."

"But if it's not following us physically, how does it know where to send its image?" Rage asked. Then she stared at the glowing hourglass.

Billy nodded. "It has to contain some sort of spell that lets the firecat see us. It knows the hourglass is the one thing you wouldn't lose or give away. You said yourself that it warned you to be careful not to break it."

Rage did not know what to say. Any of their guesses could be right or completely wrong, depending on which part of the firecat's story was true—if any. Rage's thoughts went on turning this way and that, like the tunnel, never reaching any conclusion. When they came round a bend and found the way split into three identical tunnels, she felt it was a perfect symbol of their journey. Every question to do with the wizard and the firecat led only to more questions.

Now that they had stopped, Rage was alarmed to hear how raggedly Bear was breathing. "Let's rest for a bit while we decide which way to go," she said lightly. It was a measure of Bear's exhaustion that she did not even argue. She slumped to the ground, and when Billy lifted her head onto his lap, she did not push him away.

Rage turned to Elle. "What can you smell down the tunnels?"

Elle sniffed the first. "Buildings, people, and metal." She sniffed the second. "Flowers, trees, earth . . ." She frowned. "Animals, too, but their smell is old and faded, as if they were there once but have long gone. I smell . . . sadness."

She turned her attention to the third tunnel. "Water," she said. "And something else . . . I don't know what it is. I've never smelled it before. It makes me want to sneeze."

She turned to Rage expectantly.

"I don't know what to do," Rage admitted. "I thought it was hopeless to try to find the wizard, once I saw the waterfall. But maybe I was wrong about the riddle. Maybe it means something completely different."

"Well, we can't stay in the city," Elle said. "Those blackshirts will be looking everywhere for us."

"Especially since we stole Mama out from under their noses," Billy said. "The High Keeper will want to know how we escaped."

"I think we have to go back over the river and see the witch Mother. Ania says she wants to help us because she wants the wizard found, to save Valley. Maybe she will be able to figure out the riddle on the hourglass. And she might even know something about the firecat."

"So, which tunnel?" Elle asked.

Rage studied the first tunnel. It led to people, so it probably came out somewhere in Newfork, which was the last place they wanted to be just now. The second tunnel? She liked the sound of trees and flowers, but the smell of sadness was daunting. The tunnel probably led to one of the provinces, where there was clearly something wrong. And anyway, there would be lots of keepers there. The third tunnel led to water. That sounded most promising. It might even lead them to one of the tunnels Hermani had mentioned, which had become saturated with water seeping from the encroaching river.

Rage hesitated, worried about Bear. "I think we should take the tunnel that smells of water, but I will go down it alone to see where it leads."

Billy said anxiously, "Don't let's split up again."

Rage bit her lip. "But, Bear—"

"I can walk," Bear said gruffly, struggling to her feet.

12

They had been on the move for half an hour when they came to a grille embedded in the walls of the tunnel, completely blocking their way. Rage stared stupidly at it, knowing they would have no hope of shifting it. Bear was swaying on her feet, eyes cloudy and unfocused.

"We'll have to go back and try one of the other tunnels, but I think we might as well rest here," Rage said. "I've been thinking that if we take long enough, the blackshirts will think we've gone over the river, and they'll give up searching."

"What about Goaty and Mr. Walker?" Elle asked.

"If anyone questions them, they'll simply say they're wild things and they'll be left alone." Rage said this with more confidence than she felt. The blackshirts were bound to be suspicious if they found two wild things wandering about when they had already taken three as prisoners. But they could not go on with Bear in such a state. Given everything, it was sensible to stay where they were for the time being, though she dared not look at the sand in the hourglass.

The old dog lay down with a profound sigh. Billy

took her big, misshapen head onto his lap and ran his fingers over her soft ears. Again she did not reject his caress.

"I wonder what is happening to Goaty," Elle said wistfully, peering through the grate. "He will be afraid if he is all alone."

"I hope he is *not* alone," Rage said. She leaned back against the sloping side of the tunnel, wishing Mam could see Bear and Billy together. It had always upset her that Bear was so cold to Billy. But Mam seemed so far away. It was becoming harder for Rage to imagine being home with her again. Having entered a magical world, she had somehow lost touch with her own world. The longer she was away from it, the less real it seemed. She closed her eyes and slipped into a deep sleep.

A voice was calling her name.

Rage opened her eyes and found she was sitting on the grassy lawn at Winnoway Farm. The dogs were sleeping around her, and she could see Goaty standing on the Johnsons' fence and eating the new buds off the plum trees. She shook her head, thinking Mr. Johnson would go mad when he saw the damage.

"Ra-age!"

Someone was calling, but there was no one in sight.

"Who is it?" she cried, wondering if Mam was calling her from inside the house. Strangely, the dogs remained asleep.

"Help me," the voice called.

It was the same voice that had called her before, out of the streamers of light in the forest.

"How can I help you?" Rage asked.

"Break . . . release . . . before . . . too late . . ."

"I don't know how to break the spell," she cried.

"I already told you. Who are you? Where are you?"
But there was no answer.

Rage woke to find herself sitting in the cold tunnel by the metal grille.

"Rage!" a voice called.

"I must be going mad," she muttered to herself. "First I dream of a voice calling me, and then when I wake up, I can still hear it."

"Rage!"

Rage looked through the grille and was astounded to see a pixie-sized woman wearing a tight-fitting brown catsuit and flat-heeled, high-topped boots. Her hair was a floating cloud of yellow, like spun sugar, and it shimmered in the light of the tiny lantern she carried.

"You must move back so that I can open the grille," she told Rage, waving the lantern with a shooing action.

Billy had been sleeping with his face pushed up against the grille. Wakened by their voices, he opened his eyes and gave a yelp of surprise. "What are you?" he asked.

"I'm Kelpie."

The small stranger lifted her lantern, the sole source of light in the tunnel. Rage glanced anxiously at the hourglass. It was safe where she had left it, but it had gone dull.

"It's a kelpie," Billy told Elle, who had woken, too, and was sniffing through the grille.

"Kelpie is my *name*." The woman giggled. "And you are Billy Thunder."

"How do you know our names?" Rage demanded warily, wondering if the little woman was a wild thing.

"Mr. Walker told me."

"Mr. Walker!" Billy cried in delight. "Then he's safe."

"I will bring you to him as soon as you let me open the grille." Kelpie tapped her tiny fingers impatiently against the metal. Billy woke Bear, and they all moved back down the tunnel. Kelpie knelt and pressed her hand to the ground. There was a grinding noise, and the grille swung open like a gate.

Rage was intrigued. She had supposed Kelpie was a wild thing, yet she was drawing magic from the earth just as Ania had done, and wild things weren't supposed to be able to do that. After they had all come through the grille, it swung back into place with a gritty screech.

"Come," Kelpie said imperiously, dusting off her hands.

"Wait just a minute," Rage said firmly, refusing to be dazzled into acting without thinking. "Before we go anywhere, you'd better tell us how you met Mr. Walker."

"He fell down a shaft and found us."

"And how did *you* find *us*? Mr. Walker didn't know we were coming here," Rage said. *"We* didn't know we were coming here."

"The Mother foresaw it," Kelpie answered. "Now we must hurry. She awaits us with Mr. Walker, in the Place of Shining Waters."

"The witch Mother foresaw us trapped in a drain?"

Kelpie nodded.

Rage did not know what to think. Obviously someone with magical powers might be able to look into the future, but if that was so, why hadn't Ania said that the witch Mother had foreseen *them* meeting?

Rage glanced at the others. Elle and Billy were eager to go, while Bear looked exhausted and ill, but none of them said a thing. They were leaving it to Rage to choose.

Kelpie turned to hurry away down the tunnel, and Rage led the way after her. Though rested, Bear moved slowly. She was still suffering from having breathed in the High Keeper's poisonous gas. Rage hoped she had not suffered any permanent damage. After a time the tunnel began to narrow. Rage's heart sank, but she told herself sternly that her experience outside the conservatorium had made her oversensitive.

"It doesn't get much smaller, does it?" Billy asked Kelpie nervously.

"A bit," she answered cheerfully.

"Why didn't Mr. Walker come with you?" Elle asked.

"The Mother foresaw *me* finding you," Kelpie answered proudly.

This was not really an answer. Rage wondered if the Mother hadn't deliberately kept Mr. Walker with her to ensure that the rest of them came with Kelpie. She had heard nothing bad about the witch women, except from the keepers, and the witch Mother had enabled her to get away from the banding house. But Rage had expected a long, difficult trip back to Wildwood to see the witch Mother. It was unnerving to find that she was here, waiting to see them. And why was she in Fork? If she had come in the hope that Rage had located the wizard, she was about to be bitterly disappointed.

"What about Goaty?" Elle asked, interrupting the flow of Rage's thoughts. "Did the Mother foresee anything about him?"

Kelpie giggled. "Oh, he is waiting for you as well. Mr. Walker told us where to find him. Goaty was very afraid of us at first. He shivered and shook and thought we meant to eat him. 'I must be brave,' he kept saying."

Her imitation of Goaty was so accurate, Rage relaxed. No matter what was going on, at least they would all soon be together again.

Billy and Elle went on questioning the woman, but

she only repeated, in various ways, that all of their questions would be answered by the Mother. Rage had returned the dulled hourglass to her pocket. She ran her fingers over it, wondering again why it had glowed. Had it really answered their need, or was there another reason?

Perhaps the Mother would know.

The way split again, and without hesitation Kelpie chose the left-hand tunnel, which was so low that everyone except Rage and Kelpie was forced to stoop. Bear only just fit. If the way became smaller, she would not be able to go on.

"How much further?" Billy asked worriedly, again voicing Rage's fear.

"I smell something," Elle said.

The tunnel turned a corner and opened out into a vast cavern that seemed to have no walls. The air was filled with an emerald glow, and at first glance Rage thought the cavern held a lake of luminous green water. But as they came closer she saw that there were hundreds of rivulets of shining water flowing around a multitude of small islands. The cavern was a vast subterranean wetland!

Her skin began to prickle as they approached the water. She looked down at her arms and found the hairs were all standing on end, just as they had when she approached the bramble gate.

"The Place of Shining Waters," Kelpie announced reverently, before leading them along a path where the ground was higher and quite dry.

"The witch Mother is here?" Rage asked, for the cavern appeared deserted.

"We must go beyond the hills," Kelpie said, pointing past the shining water to the darker end of the cavern.

Bear was at the end of her strength by the time they

reached the first of the dark hills, which proved to be carpeted in a thick moss. She staggered and then lay down panting, tongue lolling from her mouth.

"She must rest," Billy told Kelpie, and he sat by his mother's head and stroked the fur around her ears tenderly. Rage sank onto the soft moss, too.

Elle wandered over to peer into a streamlet of the glowing green water. Sniffing, she squatted down and cupped her hands.

"Don't drink it!" Rage cried in alarm.

Elle looked over at her in puzzlement. "Why not? It doesn't smell bad."

"I don't think it's bad. I think it's magic, and who knows what it would do if you drank it."

"You are wise to be wary of the waters, Rage Winnoway," came a woman's voice, cold, sharp, and familiar.

Rage looked around and saw the baker's sister, Rue, coming over the hill. She now wore a long, floating dress of russet brown, and her unbound hair hung in a wild and shining tangle to her knees. Woven through it were leaves and flowers, and a plait circled her brow like a crown. She looked younger than she had in the village, but no less severe. With her were two younger women in similar attire, carrying lanterns that gave off a buttery yellow light.

Kelpie went to her with an expression of shy adoration. "Mother," she murmured, and reached out to stroke Rue's hand.

"*You* are the witch Mother?" Rage said in amazement.

Rue smiled, and suddenly she was very beautiful, though her eyes remained stern. "I am."

"Your bands are—" Rage began, but Rue interrupted her gracefully.

"False, of course. But all questions that can be answered will be answered in good time. Now you must come to the place where your friends wait anxiously for your arrival." She looked at Bear with compassionate eyes. "Let the great beast sleep here. These witches will watch over her. Later she will be brought to join us."

"I will stay with her," Billy said.

"No," Rue said. "You can do nothing for her now. The witches will tend her ills, and they will work best if left to their own devices." Such was her serene authority that Billy did not argue. He took a long and longing look at his mother before leaving her side.

Rue caught hold of one of the yellow lanterns and began to walk back over the hill, holding Kelpie's hand. Billy and Elle followed, emanating excitement.

"Is the baker really your brother?" Billy asked the witch woman.

"I am Rue, who is sister to the baker and who cooks and cleans for her keep," the witch woman answered. "Unknown to my brother, I am also a witch who dwells in Wildwood when I can."

"Why are you called Mother?" Elle asked.

"To remind me that I do not rule the witch folk for my own pleasure or gain. Like a mother, I love and I serve and I nurture. Occasionally I scold."

Rage swallowed a lump in her throat.

As they left the wetlands behind, they also left the shining waters, and it became very dark and silent. The rivulets that flowed into the hills were set deep, so that they shed little light. Yet there was enough to see that there were plants growing here and there, bushes and shrubs. Rage did not know how such things could thrive without sunlight and fresh air. It must be the magic in the water. The cave did not smell the least bit musty. If she had not known better, she would have believed she was outside on a dark night.

"How did you know we had stopped back there?" Billy asked.

"There are watchers here who serve me, unseen but seeing all," the witch woman answered. "It was they who summoned me."

They reached the summit of the third and highest hill in the cavern and found themselves looking down into a small, deep valley. A grove of trees grew at the bottom, and light flowed within it, yellow like the lantern light and quite different from the eerie illumination of the magical water. This was obviously their destination, and despite all the strange and wondrous things that had happened to Rage since leaving Winnoway, something about the grove of trees in this cavern deep under the earth thrilled her to the depths of her heart and lifted the black despair that had sunk its claws into her in the dank tunnel. It was true that she was no closer to finding Mam, but she had rescued Billy and Elle from the blackshirts, and they had saved Bear from a horrible death. They were free, and together, and maybe at last they had found someone with the power to help them.

Light was thrown from lanterns suspended from tree branches and from a large bonfire in a small clearing in the grove. There were hundreds of people milling around under the trees. Only when they were closer did Rage see that the crowd consisted not only of witch folk and wild things but also, astonishingly, of gray-clad Fork citizens. Some were little older than Rage. Most looked grave and worried, but a few had wary, suspicious expressions.

There were also natural animals. A leopard with pale blue eyes, several intelligent-looking squirrels, and a number of horses were standing with a handsome male centaur. A monkey with yellow eyes sat on the centaur's back, chewing at its fingers and looking anxious. Another surprise was that some of the witch women, with their long hair and tattered robes, were not women! Apparently men could be witches as well, or at least align themselves with them. In fact, there were representatives in the grove of all the factions in Fork, except for keepers.

Rue went to the center of the clearing, where the fire was lit, and everyone began to draw nearer. She let go of Kelpie's hand and turned to Rage. "There are many things that must be dealt with at this gathering, but first you must greet your old friends." She made a gesture and two sprites came from the trees, leading Mr. Walker and a shyly smiling Goaty, his ringlets plaited with little blue flowers.

"Goaty!" Elle cried, and rushed to hug him so ferociously he gasped.

Rage knelt down and gathered Mr. Walker up, cuddling him for a long, glad moment. "I was so afraid when you didn't come back."

"I couldn't!" Mr. Walker said, twitching his feathery tail in agitation. "That vent led to a pipe, and I couldn't stop myself sliding down it. It went on and on, and I thought I was going to slide forever. But I came out and landed on a pile of soft rags. The Mother—"

"Foresaw that you would drop from a drain and arranged for a soft landing?" Rage finished the sentence for him, sitting back on her heels.

"How did you know?" Mr. Walker demanded.

Rage did not answer because a hush had fallen over the grove. The witch Mother lifted her hand, but before she could utter a word a little man the size of a three-year-old child darted out and took her hand. He bowed with a flourish and kissed her hand extravagantly. Like the fairies he had dragonfly wings protruding from the back of his brown shirt.

"Welcome, Mother," the fairy man said to Rue in a deep, elegant voice that hardly matched his comical face and plump form.

"I *wish* you would not make such a fuss, Puck," the witch Mother said crossly, sounding more like the baker's sister than a leader.

"It is in my nature to revere that which is worthy of reverence," the winged man said, and he bowed again to her. "Was I not made so?" he demanded pertly.

"I fear so," the witch woman said, but now her eyes were amused. "A miscalculation on my part, no doubt."

"I can be irreverent, too, when it is needed," he responded with a sly smile. He snapped his fingers, and two sprites ran forward with a stool for the witch.

Rage stared at the little man in confusion. Puck was a character in a play she had seen with her drama class. Rue must have named him after that character. Something about this idea seemed tremendously important, but there was no time to tease it out.

Now seated, Rue addressed the gathering. "Witch folk, wild things, citizens of Fork, natural beasts, thank you for coming. I know it is dangerous for all of us to meet in this way, and I know that some of you were reluctant to do so. Yet as I said in my message to you, Valley is dying, and we have very little time in which to save it and ourselves."

"Whose fault is that?"

Rage turned around to see a man in gray glaring at Rue.

"What is this place?" another Fork man demanded.

"Why was it necessary for me to be blindfolded to come here?"

"I was in the middle of bathing when your people came for me," a woman complained. "Why was I given no warning?"

"It would have been too dangerous to set a meeting place and time in advance," Rue said calmly. "Someone might easily have spoken out of turn, alerting the black-shirts." She paused but no one spoke. "This is the Place of Shining Waters, and it is the source of all magic in Valley."

Rage was no less astonished than the Fork people. "The wizard gave Valley its magic—" a Fork man began.

"That is true," Rue agreed. "He stood in this very grove and infused the waters in the cavern with pure magic. He knew that it would flow, as water does, up through the land, to succor all things."

"Magic no longer succors Wildwood!" a gray-clad woman said.

"The flow has all but ceased in Wildwood," Rue agreed mildly. "As it has begun to cease in the provinces, and as it will soon cease in Fork."

There were exclamations of disbelief, but there were also nods and cries that it was true, that magic *was* dying in Fork.

"In order to know the truth of what ails Fork, you must know other truths," Rue said in a voice that was suddenly chilly and majestic. "The High Keeper claims that witch folk offended the wizard and made him abandon Valley. This is not true. The wizard wearied of ruling and retreated to his castle and his arcane researches. Then he vanished. I do not know where he went. Witch folk went to dwell in Wildwood after his withdrawal to Deepwood, for we did not desire to live by keeper rules, or Order our lives as they commanded."

There was a mutter of disapproval from the Fork citizens, but Rue ignored it. "We continued to create wild things and to use magic to feed them. But I say to you that the working of magic to free wild things does not remove magic from the land."

"Then why is it that Wildwood lost magic first?" a Fork woman called truculently.

"Because the High Keeper decided it should," Rue answered flatly.

There was a loud rumble of disbelief from the crowd of Fork citizens, who had drawn together into a group. *No doubt to give themselves courage to speak*, Rage thought.

"I *knew* that the High Keeper was bad," Mr. Walker hissed.

"He smelled of badness," Elle agreed.

"*Why* did he stop the magic?" Billy muttered.

"*How* did he stop it, I'd like to know," Mr. Walker said.

"Shh!" Rage hissed, for the centaur had turned to glare at them.

"The High Keeper knows of this cavern," Rue continued, and many of those gathered looked about in alarm. "He knows it is the source of magic in Valley because the knowledge is passed from each High Keeper to his successor. I do not know why the wizard showed this to the first High Keeper. Perhaps in pride, for it was a mighty deed to freeze the moment in time within which Valley exists. Yet it was inevitable that there would come a High Keeper with arrogance enough to try to use the pure magic. The man who is now High Keeper of Fork used the power here to block the flow of magic to Wildwood. He wished to punish witch folk for their disobedience."

"I do not believe this," a man in gray exclaimed. "How do you come to know so much of the High Keeper's doings, you who have always dwelled in Wildwood?"

Rue looked suddenly weary and older. "I have dwelled in Fork. Like many, I was forced here as a girl and unwillingly banded. I made no secret of my unhappiness, and soon agents of the witch folk sought me out. I believed them when they told me that witch folk were not responsible for the harm being done in Valley, and I agreed to help them seek out the source of magic. The witch who was Mother then believed there was some blockage in the flow. She did not dream it had been done deliberately. But she knew there was no point in approaching the High Keeper for help. His hatred of us seemed to grow daily. When I was sixteen, my bands were to be replaced, and the man who was supposed to weld the permanent bands on my wrists gave me false bands. He was an ally of the witch Mother.

"Thereafter, I was secretly trained in the working of magic. Eventually I found this place, and it was here that I first saw the High Keeper dip his hands into the shining waters."

Rue paused, a challenge in her eyes, but no one spoke. "I heard him cackle and shriek like a madman afterward. He ranted his hatred of the witch folk and his horror of the wild things. I heard him command the magic to cease its flow through Wildwood. He vowed he would not reverse his order until all witches and wild things had been wiped from Valley."

She stopped. The anger in her eyes became weariness. "He was a fool not to see what any witch apprentice could have seen. One cannot stop *part* of a flow. When the High Keeper prevented magic flowing through

Wildwood, he began the process that would one day stop the flow of magic in all of Valley."

"You are saying magic is dying here because of an accident?" This from one of the witch women.

"Is it an accident when the wrong done is greater than the wrong intended?" Rue asked. "I do not think so, for wrongness is a flow, too."

"I do not believe the High One did this," a Fork woman shouted. "I did not come here to hear him accused! I—"

"You came to hear how to save Fork and yourself," snapped Rue. "Therefore listen. The High Keeper saw us as evil—"

"Yet it is he who is evil and does evil now." A new voice. The crowd drew back to reveal the speaker. Rage was amazed to see the elderly, white-robed keeper who had assisted the High Keeper in the conservatorium.

"Isn't that—" Elle began, but Billy shushed her as the old man shuffled through the crowd to Rue's side.

"Evil is only another kind of illness, Hermani," Rue said in a surprisingly gentle voice.

"Once the High Keeper was my friend," he said in a quavering voice. "He spoke with such poetry of the need to keep and Order Valley. When Wildwood lost its flow of magic, I agreed to the pogrom against witch folk because I believed you were endangering the true beasts in our care. I believed it was your fault that they had to be kept in provinces, for why else would magic have died in Wildwood? But then the High Keeper began to band children and to forbid travel. He set curfews in the city and allowed the blackshirts to punish anyone who disobeyed him or spoke out against his methods. Fork became dark. Yet I held my tongue, for I truly thought all would be healed once Wildwood was emptied out."

He paused for breath, his face haggard with grief. "But then the High Keeper began to bring natural beasts in from the provinces. He killed them and had them stuffed, claiming they could be better kept in Order dead than alive." Tears began to run down his wrinkled face. "The conservatorium grew and grew. Only now do I understand that his madness began here."

"His madness began before he used the shining waters," Rue said coldly. "It began with his hunger for power."

"At first I made excuses for him," the old man said in a broken voice. "I told myself that the animals were old or ill. That they had lived good lives. I could not admit to myself what was happening. You see, I have loved him, and to face the truth meant that my whole life had been a lie. But I could not go on seeing the animals die. I began to work with others to secretly remove from the provinces animals in danger of conservation and to transport them back over the river to Deepwood." He bent his head forward and wept in earnest. Rage felt her own eyes fill with compassion at his terrible despair.

"Do not torture yourself," Rue said, and now there was pity in her face.

At a signal, a sprite brought another stool, but the stricken keeper turned to face those assembled. "I came to this meeting because the High Keeper is mad, and I can ignore it no longer. Magic is dying in Fork, and all keepers know it. I believe the Mother speaks the truth when she says it is the High Keeper's doing. If there is hope for Valley now, it lies with the Mother and her kind."

Rue laid her hand on his shoulder, and he sat. Then

she examined the pale faces of the Fork citizens. "Many of you came here seeking someone to blame. If we can save Valley, then it will be worth understanding how this came to pass. Only then can we ensure that it will not happen again. But now we have very little time in which to act."

"How long, Mother?" a witch man asked.

"We have perhaps six months before the flow of magic is weakened so much that Valley will slide back into time."

13

"What can we do?" the centaur demanded.

"Can't we use the power in the waters here to make magic flow through Valley again?" a gray-clad woman called.

"Have you heard nothing?" Rue asked. "The magic must flow to us through the land before it can be drawn upon. Anyone attempting to reverse what the High Keeper did by using the shining waters will also be driven mad, and even so will fail. Only a wizard is strong enough to work magic against magic. Only the wizard who created this land we call Valley can save it."

"But you have already said that you do not know where the wizard went," someone pointed out bitterly.

"I said that *I* do not know where he went," Rue said softly, yet a hush fell. "There is one here among us who does know, and on that one rests our only hope." Slowly the witch woman's eyes came to rest on Rage. "Will you speak of your quest, child?"

Rage felt everyone turn to stare at her. She had never been the center of so much attention. Standing on rubbery legs, she was infinitely grateful when Billy and the others stood with her. Even Goaty stood.

"I . . . I am Rage Winnoway," she began.

"Speak up!" someone called impatiently.

She licked her lips. "I am Rage Winnoway, and these are my friends. I came from my world to Valley through a magic gateway. I wanted to see the wizard, but when I got here I learned he had vanished. I was given a riddle to solve that would lead me to him."

"Say the riddle," Rue commanded.

"'Bring me to the shore of the Endless Sea, step through the door that will open for thee.'"

There was a burst of derisive laughter. "There is no such place as the Endless Sea," someone cried.

"Oh, but there is," the Mother said, her eyes holding Rage's.

Rage opened her mouth to say that the riddle had been engraved on the bottom of the hourglass given to her by the firecat, but to her astonishment she could not speak. She tried again. Nothing came from her mouth. There *was* some sort of magic stopping her! No doubt this was the firecat's doing.

"Who gave you this riddle?" Rue asked.

"I . . . I can't say," Rage said, and was relieved to find she had not been silenced altogether.

Billy gave her an odd look and opened his mouth, but nothing came out. He could not speak of the firecat, either.

"Then we will not press you," Rue said. "But you have solved the riddle, have you not?"

"I thought I had," Rage said, and despair welled in her anew. "I thought that since all rivers flow to the sea, then maybe a magical river would flow to a magical sea."

"The Endless Sea," Hermani murmured.

"I thought it would be possible just to get a boat and go down the river—until I saw it."

"You would not make this journey for the sake of your mother?" Rue asked.

"I would gladly, for her sake and for the sake of Valley," Rage said, feeling the weight of all those eyes on her. "But it wouldn't be any use. No one could travel down the River of No Return and *live*."

"It is not fitting to ask a child to undertake such a dangerous journey," Hermani said with quiet dignity. "I will attempt it. Perhaps some of the rivermen who have been working to save the true beasts can accompany me."

A man stepped forward, and Rage was not too surprised to see that it was the ferry captain. "Aye, we will aid you, keeper. It would be a quest worthy of a bard song and a nobler end than dying in a flood of water, if it comes to that."

"A noble end indeed," Rue said with some asperity. "But it is not heroic deeds for bard songs that we need. I tell you bluntly that you will not attempt this journey. You would fail. Death is the destination of any here who would attempt to reach the end of the River of No Return."

There was a silence, and faces fell.

"You brought us here to tell us of our doom?" Hermani asked.

Instead of answering him, the witch woman turned to Rage. "Child you are, Rage Winnoway, yet more than that, too. I did not speak idly before when I said that upon you rests our only hope."

Rage stared at her. "But . . . you just agreed that no one could survive the journey."

"I said no one here. Look." On Rue's palm lay a pink-gold locket.

"Mam's locket," Rage murmured, glancing over at the ferryman.

"It is very old, and strong with images of many kinds of love and sorrow. Perfect as a focusing object. I saw the accident that hurt your mother, child. But know that her illness, this sleep, was not caused by that accident. It is the result of a deeper, longer affliction."

Rage stared silently at the witch woman. The witch woman must be mistaken. Mam was certainly asleep because of the terrible head injuries inflicted on her in the accident.

Rue continued. "I saw you and your quest here. I had thought the Endless Sea a myth, but then I dug deeper. Finally, in an old tome, I found mention of it as a true thing. It was not difficult to discern that you believed the wizard had gone to the Endless Sea. But I could not guess how you meant to get there."

"Why didn't you send someone to ask me, or come yourself?" Rage asked.

"We witch folk have learned to move slowly and carefully in all things, but especially where magic is concerned," Rue said. "For all I knew, your journey was wound about with delicate enchantments, which my interference would undo. I sent my people word to give you what help they could and to tell you that my desire was yours: to find the wizard and let him know that Valley needs him. I thought that if you reached the wizard, you would surely tell him this."

"Why did you bring us here now?"

"Before you appeared, I had come to believe that no single group in Valley would be able to come up with a way to save us," Rue said. "That it would take all of us to find an answer, and this gathering was long planned to that end. But once I reached Fork and learned from Ania of your shock upon seeing the River of No Return, I knew what I had hoped. Only then did I perform a difficult and costly working of magic, using that trinket as a focus. It was during this working that I saw Mr. Walker fall into the drain near one of our secret places, and you and your other companions trapped behind a grille in the lower tunnel system that leads to this cavern.

"I made arrangements for Mr. Walker to be met, and I sent Kelpie to find you and bring you here. It was Mr. Walker who told us of Goaty waiting for you by the river, and so I had him brought here, too." Rue's voice cracked. She made a motion that brought one of the sprites with a cup of water.

"I don't understand why you say that *I* can survive the journey when no one else could," Rage said.

"I performed the magical working to ask if there was any way in which Rage Winnoway could survive a journey down the River of No Return."

"What did you learn?" Billy asked eagerly.

"I learned what I had sensed all along," Rue said. She turned to look at those gathered. "Only in unity can we save Valley." There were confused looks and muttered questions and exclamations that eventually dwindled to silence. "My vision told me that Rage Winnoway and her companions had the best chance of negotiating the river and finding the wizard, but that *we* must provide for her a vessel that will endure the journey."

"But how?" a Fork man asked. "No boat could survive the waterfall."

"I do not speak of any ordinary boat," Rue said. "I

mean we must create a magical vessel. Such a thing can be provided only at great cost."

"What cost can be too great for the saving of Valley?" Hermani cried.

"Time," Rue said flatly. "It will cost time. These vessels can only be created from magic, but this working will do what we witches have long been accused of doing—it will drain magic from Valley, to the extent that the six months or so we have left will be reduced to a few days."

There was an aghast silence.

"You ask us to sacrifice the little magic now flowing in Valley to bring this girl and her companions safely down to the Endless Sea?" the ferryman asked. "Why not send only her? There will be less of a drain for a vessel for one than for six."

"The chances of Rage Winnoway fulfilling her quest will decrease if all of her companions do not travel with her. I do not know why, but that is what I saw. To know more would cost more than I will pay," the witch answered evenly. "Also, I do not know how long the journey to the Endless Sea will take, nor if Rage Winnoway will find the wizard. I know only that she *may* succeed where no other would."

"Why her?" someone called. "She is a stranger to Valley."

"This I tried to learn, but my vision was obscured in ways I do not understand. I saw only that there is some link between Rage Winnoway and the wizard, which increases her chance of finding him."

There was a loud buzz of troubled talk. Rage knew that the link was the hourglass she carried, but of course she was unable to say so.

"We have no choice," said Puck. "We will certainly die in six months if we do nothing. If we help her, we might die in a few days, but we might also save ourselves. We would be fools to choose six certain months of life over the possibility of living full lives."

"Yet we may find our own solution in six long months, and remember, the witch woman has not said that the girl and her friends *will* reach the wizard, only that they have the best chance of reaching him," a Fork man argued, sounding troubled.

"Maybe the wizard knows of all that besets us and will return at the last moment," Hermani suggested.

"We must quickly make a decision about whether or not we will aid Rage Winnoway, else there will not be magic enough to do it without destroying Valley," Rue said. "I will give you one hour to talk, and then we will see what has been agreed upon."

"There is no point in us talking. We have never been able to agree on anything." Hermani sighed. "I say the witch Mother will decide for us."

There were cries of "yes" and "no," mixed with groans of uncertainty. Rage had no idea what to say. She wasn't even sure how she felt, because a queer numbness seemed to have stolen through her senses. The only thing she knew was that if there was a hope of her finding the wizard—the merest bit of hope—she would go.

Rue said nothing until all the shouts and murmurs faded. "Even if you wish it, I will not decide for you," she announced. "I am Mother, yet you are not children. You must take responsibility for yourselves. Again I say, go and talk among yourselves. Seek for an answer together. In one hour I will hear what you have decided."

She turned without waiting for a response and

walked briskly away into the trees. After a moment of bewilderment, in which no one seemed to know quite what to do, the crowd broke up and began walking this way and that or sat in groups. A buzz of talk arose and became steadily louder.

"They will have to give us the vessels," Elle said, her eyes gleaming with excitement.

"They don't have any choice," Billy agreed.

"But that man was right. The witch Mother only said we would have the *best chance* of surviving the journey," Mr. Walker protested. "She didn't say we *would* survive it."

"She didn't even ask if we agreed to go," Goaty said timorously.

"She didn't have to," Elle said. "If we stay, we'll only have six months to live, like everyone else. This way we have a chance at life. And besides, Rage must get to her mam."

"I'm scared," Goaty whispered.

"It will be a great adventure," Elle said, clasping his shoulders.

Billy had a peculiar look on his face. Rage asked him what he was thinking. "I was wondering how Mama is," he said, seeming to read her mind. Rage felt a stab of guilt, and he saw that, too. His expression changed. "It's not your fault Mama is exhausted, Rage. I'm not sorry we came."

"You're not?" Rage asked in disbelief.

"If we had not come, Mama would be the same as she was before. She lets me come close to her now, and sometimes she tells me things. Last night she said she dreamed of me when she was inside that killing box in the conservatorium. She dreamed that I was calling her. . . ."

Elle leaned over to them. "I've just been thinking. If they refuse to magic a boat, I will use the six months to visit Wildwood and see the winged lions again. Then Goaty and I will go to the mountain province."

Goaty gave her a look of adoration.

"I would go to the castle in Deepwood," Mr. Walker said dreamily. "Perhaps there is a magic mirror there. I have always wanted to look into one."

"I would like to see the outermost villages," Billy said.

He looked expectantly at Rage, but before she could speak, Kelpie appeared. "The Mother has asked me to bring you to her."

They followed her through witch folk and gray-clad humans, wild things and true beasts, all talking earnestly and shaking their heads or pounding hands or paws or hoofs, and into the dense trees, which smelled of pine needles and sap. Silence descended around them, and the only sounds were of twigs snapping under their feet and their own breath.

Through the greenish black darkness Rage saw an ancient, thick-waisted tree with great serpentine roots coiling in and out of the ground. A chattering streamlet of the magic water ran close by, bathing the gnarled arms of the tree in a bright emerald glow. Beneath it sat Rue, with Puck and several sprites. The leopard lay dozing at her side, the nervous monkey curled between its paws. Rage was startled to see that in the midst of this exotic tableau, the witch woman was sipping tea out of a flowered teacup.

"Sit, and be welcome," Rue said.

"Do you know what they will decide?" Rage asked.

"I do not, nor will I seek to know what a little patience will give me."

"I taught you patience," Puck said, and leered winsomely at her.

Rue smiled and stroked his shaggy hair. "I have learned much from you and your kindred, little one." She looked at Rage again, her eyes gentler than before. "I am sorry I snapped at you, but the price a witch pays to foresee each glimpse of the future is the loss of that much of his or her own life. So you see, it is not done lightly. Now eat, for that is why I invited you to join me."

She pointed to a picnic cloth laid with buttered scones in a silver tin and more teacups, a plate piled with thick sandwiches, and another with rock buns and little iced cakes with cherries on the top. "You need not fear that it will bind you or enslave you, as so many stories claim of magicked food." She addressed these words to Mr. Walker, who had drawn back in alarm.

Her words rekindled a question that had occurred to Rage when she first heard Puck's name. "How do you know so much about fairy tales and plays from my world?"

Rue quirked an eyebrow at her. "I know nothing of the stories from your world. I spoke only of stories here. Perhaps the same stories are told in all worlds," she said lightly. "Or maybe the wizard learned them from your world and taught them to the first people he brought here. My ancestors."

"There are no wizards or magic in my world," Rage said.

"Our wizard must have been in your world for some time if he created a magical gateway there," Rue said as a sprite poured more tea from a flowered teapot. "And perhaps there are others of his kind in your world. After all, wizards are only people who have discovered how to draw on the power that flows between all matter."

Rage tried to ask about the firecat, but again she was unable to say a word. She gave up and asked, "Why do you think the wizard left Valley?"

Rue shrugged. "I do not think he was evil. If he knew what had happened here, I have no doubt that he would return." She gestured to the food again. "Now, eat!"

Elle and the others did not have to be asked twice. In no time the picnic had been consumed down to the last crumb. Rage managed only to nibble at it politely. It seemed to her that hours had already passed, and all she could think of was that the decision made would decide whether or not she would see her mother again. She refused to contemplate that they would not survive the journey. Rue would not let them go unless there was a good chance they would succeed.

As if she felt Rage's thoughts, the witch woman looked up. Then she said, "I would ask something of you. I sensed that there had been images inside the locket. May I see them?"

Rage groped in her pocket until she found the two tiny photographs, and she handed them to Rue.

"This is the boy for whom your mother grieved so deeply," Rue murmured, looking at one.

"That is my uncle," Rage said, leaning closer. "It was taken a long time ago. He went away and never came back." She wanted to ask if the witch could see where he was and what he was doing, but having learned the cost of looking into the future, she knew she could not.

The witch examined the other photograph with a strange expression. "This is your grandmother?" Rage nodded. "I thought so. This woman is connected to the wizard."

"But—but that's not possible," Rage stammered.

"I sensed it before I saw this image. But now I am

positive," Rue said. "Perhaps they met when he was in your world."

Rage tried to explain that the photograph of Grandmother Reny had been in the same pocket as the wizard's hourglass, but again she was unable to utter the words. She tried to take the hourglass from her pocket but could not. The effort made her so hot she began to sweat.

"I do not know why I cannot see the connection clearly." The witch sighed as she gave the photographs back.

"Someone comes," Puck announced, and Rage looked up to see the renegade keeper they had met in the blackshirt prison. Accompanying him were a sprite, a timber wolf with an enormous ruff of silvery fur at his throat, and a witch bearing a lantern.

"Thaddeus," Rue said, and her sharp face was softened by a new warmth. She stood and embraced the man. "It has been too long."

"Too long indeed. I have not seen you since you were a girl fighting Order in Fork. I never knew you had become the Mother to whom I sent my secret messages. The fairies I brought here told me. Do you know, it was you who originally made me begin to wonder about the provinces? All your endless questions. I was just now on my way to Wildwood, having escaped the blackshirts, when I met a witch who told me that the long-planned meeting was to take place. I hastened here with her, thinking I would speak of what I had seen in the provinces, but I am told you have a more important voice than mine to testify to what is being done to the natural beasts."

"No less than Hermani. I did not dare hope he would

be brave enough to come to this meeting."

"He is not a coward. He found himself in an agonizing position, having to kill natural beasts for the High Keeper."

"He continued to support the High Keeper though he knew him to be evil," Rue said coldly.

"He was not evil in the beginning," Thaddeus said.

"Few are, but his nature was clearly flawed. It was madness to name him High Keeper."

"Peace, dear one," Thaddeus responded gently, and he kissed her palm. "He was brilliant and full of zealotry and bright ideals. He made us feel that we were doing something worthwhile and beautiful in keeping Order. Something necessary and honorable."

"How some people do love to control the worlds they live in," Rue said with sudden bitterness. "Ever does it lead to repression and pain."

Thaddeus shook his head. "Rue, at the time he seemed the answer to our lost sense of purpose."

"It is a pity you could not simply live," she said coolly.

He sighed. "People can change. Even keepers. Am I not proof of that? But tell me, how is your brother?"

"Sweet-hearted and stubborn as ever. He would be glad to see you. Come and eat. You have missed the meeting but not the picnic." All at once the plates were piled with food again, only there was more of it, and even a cake with cream and strawberries.

"A magic tablecloth!" Mr. Walker sighed ecstatically, and reverently took another iced cake.

"I am pleased to see you have come to safe hands," the man said to Rage. He looked back at Rue. "Is it true what they have been telling me? This child and her companions are our only hope of reaching the wizard?"

"What you have been told is true, but let us leave speaking of these things. I am weary with speculating most of all."

"I don't understand about the animals in the provinces," Billy said. "The ferryman said there was sickness among them."

The renegade keeper gave him a sorrowful look. "It is true, but it is not magic's fading that hurts them. It is nothing more than that they are natural beasts and do not thrive while penned away from one another, protected, sterilized, and controlled. It has been so since the provinces were created, I am afraid. It was thought they would adjust in time. But natural animals must be wild, and things grew steadily worse. They breed badly and do not thrive in captivity. This was why the High Keeper's practices found favor."

"I don't understand why the High Keeper just went on pretending it was the witches' fault that magic was fading in Fork. He must have known that wiping out witches and wild things wouldn't save Valley," Billy said.

"I don't think he was capable of reason by the time Fork began to be affected," Rue said. "You heard Hermani. In the beginning the High Keeper was no more than a zealot. Once he drank the shining waters, I doubt he was able to see beyond his hatred for those who opposed him."

Rage wanted to ask where the keepers had come from and why they had been given charge of natural animals in the first place, but Rue stood. "They are ready. Let us return to the clearing."

Rage's heart thumped as she followed in the Mother's wake. If the folk of Valley voted not to help her find the wizard, she would never see Mam again. But if they voted to help them, then she and the others faced a terrifying journey into the unknown. And what if they got to the Endless Sea and the wizard was not there?

There was silence as the Mother walked to the center of the clearing to stand by the fire. "You have made your decision. Is it unanimous?"

A chorus of voices confirmed that it was.

"Who shall speak for you?" she asked.

"I will," the centaur said in his deep, thrumming voice. He stepped forward. "It has been agreed that Rage Winnoway and her companions shall be given the means to travel down the River of No Return in search of the wizard."

14

A group of wild things and witches appeared, carrying what looked like three enormous soap bubbles. Rage stared at them in disbelief. Surely these were not the invulnerable vessels whose creation had reduced the life span of Valley to mere days!

Rue ordered that the bubbles be set down by the cavern wall. Everyone gathered to examine them.

"This is what the magic produced?" Thaddeus asked worriedly.

"It is," Rue said. "I asked for a mode of travel that would survive the journey and keep those within safe."

"Perhaps there was not enough magic," Hermani murmured.

"There was enough. But Valley has only two days remaining."

Rage looked around at the people of Valley, understanding that it had taken great courage to agree to help them. She and the animals were about to undertake a possibly fatal journey, but in a way all of Valley would share the danger. Their sole hope was for her to find the wizard and convince him to return to

Valley. And it had to happen within two days.

Rage ran her hand over the surface of the nearest bubble. It gave beneath her fingers, and she quailed inwardly at the thought of facing the savage River of No Return in such a flimsy vessel. Beside her, Goaty was as pale as his ringlets and trembling visibly. She could not think of a thing to say to comfort him.

Elle went to him and put her arm around his shoulders, looking as fearless as ever. She whispered something in his ear and, surprisingly, he ceased shivering and gave her a shy smile.

"They don't look very strong," Mr. Walker muttered.

"No more are they," Rue said tartly. "The raft boats are strongly made, but they are smashed to pieces. The secret of the river is that one cannot fight and master it, for it is too powerful. One must accept its strength and bend to it. One must face all of its magnificent power with humility. These bubbles are the humblest of crafts, and they will carry you safely with the flow of the river. There is magic in their making that will allow them to bear your weight and keep upright. You will have to ride two apiece."

Looking at the transparent spheres, Rage thought of how fragile they were to carry such a weight of hopes. Yet Rue's words made sense: one could not oppose violence with violence. Rage had only to remember Grandfather. He had fought the sorrow of losing his brother with a harshness that had only driven his son and daughter away.

The tops of the bubbles were lifted away. Rage watched as Elle, Mr. Walker, and Billy tried them out. Bear watched Billy, her expression impossible to read. After some rearranging, it was decided that Goaty and Elle would go in one bubble, Mr. Walker and Bear in another, and Billy and Rage in the last. Rage got in when the others were settled. The bubble felt hard and slippery, like a glass in soapy water.

"Will you magic the bubbles to the river from here?" Elle asked Rue when they had climbed out to say goodbye.

"There is no need," Rue told her. "The river passes on the other side of this wall of stone. I will open the wall with magic."

"Won't water pour into the cavern?" Mr. Walker asked anxiously.

"Will it be dark under the river?" Goaty asked in a tremulous voice.

"What if the bubbles hit something?" Billy asked, moving closer to Rage.

"You will see," the witch said. She looked at Rage. "Are you ready?"

Rage swallowed a lump of fear lodged in her throat. "I'm ready," she said.

"Then I will open the way." The witch knelt and pressed one hand to the earth.

Rage heard a loud ripping sound as the stone wall opened in a wide seam and out of it came a deafening roar. The lanterns flared, and all at once she could see the river thundering by, cloudy with froth and debris. But it was not flowing horizontally. It was flowing downward.

It took some seconds for Rage to realize the water was falling rather than flowing. Then she understood. They were looking out onto the underside of the waterfall.

The witch woman came to stand beside her, and the wind from the falling water blew her hair into a dark halo as she turned. "Thank you," Rage said.

"It is I who thank you, Rage Winnoway," Rue responded serenely, and that was all.

Rage had half expected a speech. "I will do my best to find the wizard and make him listen," she promised, wishing that she had been able to speak of the hourglass and the firecat. "I will tell him everything that I have seen and heard."

"Let us hope it does not take long," Rue said. "Make yourselves ready."

Rage and Billy settled themselves as best they could in a shape with no bottom or sides, and Rue motioned for the top to be replaced. As it sealed seamlessly with the rest of the bubble all exterior sound was cut off, including the roar of the river.

"I hope there is enough air in this," Billy said to Rage. His voice sounded thin and strange in the enclosed space.

"I wish it were over already." Rage felt half suffocated.

All three bubbles were carried carefully to the brink of the opening. Rage experienced a moment of pure mindless terror as she looked down into the black abyss.

"It will be all right," Billy said. He smiled reassuringly at Rage, and she struggled to match his pretense, seeing that it was another kind of courage.

The bubble containing Mr. Walker and Bear was the first launched. With her heart in her throat, Rage watched Thaddeus and the ferryman push it over the edge. Immediately the water bore the bubble down and out of sight. Billy squeezed her hand so hard it hurt.

Then it was their turn. Their palms were slippery now, but they held on tight. Rage looked back at the Mother, and their eyes met for a second before there was a lurching sensation. Then they were falling, and the river was falling with them and around them.

Rage fought against her fear, knowing that if she gave in to panic, she would go mad. She wanted to stand up straight and stretch out her arms and legs and breathe freely. She wanted to scream.

Suddenly there was a great thud and they were under the water with bubbles and debris.

And darkness.

Now they were swept forward. The bubble stayed upright, but they were thrown violently from side to side. Finally, Billy put his arms around Rage. They pressed together, bracing their feet against the bubble to stop themselves being battered.

Rage discovered that she was no longer afraid. It was as if she had felt all the fear she was capable of feeling. A numb dullness stole over her and, incredibly, she began to fall asleep. She tried to stay awake, but her eyelids felt as if they were weighed down with lumps of steel.

"Billy," she muttered, surprised at how loud her voice sounded in the silence of the bubble. Maybe she was getting sleepy because the air in the bubble was being used up.

"Sleep," Billy said, kissing her forehead. "I'll hold on to you. I'm not tired."

She knew he was lying, but she did not have the strength to resist his kindness. And so, in all that flooding darkness, she slept. Her last waking thought was that perhaps it was the river that was endless, and not the sea.

Rage dreamed that she was on a roller coaster. Billy was with her, in his human form, and she could smell popcorn and hot chips and hear the sound of music and the screams of people behind her.

Then she heard her name being called.

"Ra-age!"

"Who is it?" she asked, and suddenly she was standing on the ground and there was no sound but the wind, and nothing but a dark rise in front of her. It took her a moment to recognize the hill above Winnoway. It was night, and the stars were so bright they might have been pressing themselves toward her.

Rage should have been frightened, but she wasn't.

"What do you want?" she called. Looking around, trying to see who had cried out, she saw a falling star.

"Help . . . ," the voice called. It was quite loud, but there was a violent crackling that made it almost impossible to hear. "Break . . ."

It was the voice she had heard in the forest, urging her to break the spell that held it prisoner. "Who are you?" she called.

"Break . . . ," the voice begged.

"I don't know how," Rage cried.

The dream shattered into pieces around her, and she fell through it into another.

Now she was walking through a strange house. A strong wind blew. Her cotton nightie flapped and fluttered against her bare skin. There was no furniture in the rooms and nothing on the walls. The floor was made of some kind of pale, knotty wood with a bluish tinge, and the walls were all white. There were no doors, only open doorways. There was no glass in the windows, but long white curtains coiled and flagged wildly in the wind. One of them brushed Rage's cheek. It felt like someone's fingers touching her face.

She heard her mother's voice. "Mam?" she whispered eagerly.

"Rage!" Mam called, and somehow the wind was in her

voice. "Sammy?" She sounded like a little girl. "Sammy?"

Now Rage was standing on the deck of a ship. The sound of the sea filled the air. Again it was night. A full moon hung among the glittering stars. A man was staring up at it. Rage saw that it was the man with the black, shaggy hair whom she had seen in the jungle. He was not wearing dark glasses now, and she was amazed to see that his eyes were the same color as hers. Winnoway eyes. She reached out to touch him. He started and looked her way, but it was clear that he did not see her.

He reached into his pocket and took out a letter. He stared at it for so long that Rage became curious. She peeped over his arm and was stunned to see her own address written there in a scrawled and childish hand.

The ship hit something, and Rage was thrown hard to the deck. She lay there with her eyes closed, finding it curiously hard to open them or to move. She knew she was lying still, but at the same time she felt as if she were rolling over and over.

Is the ship sinking? *she wondered, dazed.*

Someone shook her arm, and the world behind her eyelids grew red and bright, the air warm.

"Rage!"

It was Billy calling her. Rage forced herself to open her eyes. She was sitting on a white beach, facing a perfect blue sky. An endless blue ocean unrolled heavy and gleaming onto the shore before turning into froth that was so white it glowed as it sank hissing into the hot sand.

"The Endless Sea," she murmured.

"It's an endless beach as well," Billy said. "There's nothing in either direction but sand and more sand."

Rage turned and saw the graceful undulation of sand

dunes. The beach all around them glittered with shards of broken glass.

"The bubbles exploded just before we hit the shore," Billy explained. "Mama and Mr. Walker saw us land, but Elle and Goaty haven't come yet."

Rage noticed that Bear was sitting behind them, licking her paws. Mr. Walker was standing by her, staring out to sea with a dazed look on his face.

They heard a call, and she turned and saw two dark specks approaching. "It's Elle and Goaty!" Billy said in relief.

"What now?" Mr. Walker asked when they had all got over hugging one another and exclaiming about their incredible journey. Even Bear suffered being hugged by them all, and Rage was astonished to see her sit down and rest her head on Billy's lap of her own accord. He stroked her brow with reverent tenderness.

"We will wait," Rage said, taking the hourglass from her pocket. There was a single grain left. It fell very slowly, even as they watched.

"If this means the wizard's life is nearly over, he'd better hurry up," Mr. Walker said.

"Wasn't it strange how we couldn't talk about the firecat or the hourglass to the witch Mother," Elle said. "The firecat must have cast a spell on us."

"I guess it didn't want anyone to know about it or the hourglass," Rage said. "Maybe it was scared the witch Mother would take it from us."

"How much time do you suppose it took us to get here?" Mr. Walker asked Billy.

"No more than a few hours, but maybe Valley time is different from time here," he answered.

"Like in Narnia," Mr. Walker said eagerly. "You might be away for only a little while, but when you return, any amount of time might have passed. Even years." His face fell as he heard what he was saying.

"It might work the other way," Billy said. "Years might pass here, but only a few minutes there."

"Or maybe no time at all," Rage said. "Remember how the witch Mother told us that the wizard took Valley out of time?"

"We have to do something!" Elle declared. "Shouldn't we search for the wizard?"

The air popped and buzzed. A bright orange creature shimmered into existence on the sand nearby.

It gave off such an intense, hot light that Rage was forced to step back. Squinting against the brightness, she saw the flaring eyes and sharp teeth of the firecat.

"No need for worrying. Firecat being here." The smoky voice of the creature insinuated itself into the bright air.

Rage realized she had been half expecting it to appear. "Where is the wizard?" she demanded.

"Only a little more doing before finding him," the firecat promised.

"We are not doing anything else or going anywhere until you answer some questions," Rage snapped, fed up. "You've lied to us and you've kept things from us, and then you cast a spell so we couldn't even talk about you. Why did you choose us to bring the hourglass here, and what is it for, really?"

"Ragewinnoway wanting to talk or wanting to find wizard?" the firecat asked with silky malice. "Time running out for sleeping mother."

"All right," Rage said stiffly. "Where is he?"

"Stand," the firecat said, a note of triumph in its voice. "Take hourglass. Speak these words: 'Night gate! Appear!'"

Rage obeyed. The hourglass glittered in the sunlight as she spoke the words. They echoed oddly in the air, as if they were being repeated again and again, by many different people.

A slab of pure darkness appeared.

Rage moved back, then stopped. The lines engraved on the hourglass said to step through a door on the shore of the Endless Sea. This darkness was a door. The hair on her arms prickled just as it had by the bramble gate.

"Ragewinnoway must go through night gate," the firecat commanded.

"It doesn't smell like the bramble gate," Elle said, sniffing at it.

"It doesn't smell of anything," Mr. Walker said.

"Ragewinnoway must take the hourglass through night gate *now*," the firecat insisted.

Rage didn't trust the firecat one bit, but what else was there to do? She hadn't come so far just to turn away from the final step of her quest.

"Where will it take me?" she asked.

"To wizard!" the firecat shrilled in fury. "If not going now, then never going."

"I don't like this," Mr. Walker muttered. "Why is it so eager for you to go?"

"It's a liar, and it stinks of lies," Bear growled.

"I don't have any choice, Bear," Rage whispered. "I'm scared, but I have to go."

"Now or never," the firecat hissed. There was a desperation in its voice that told Rage this really was the last moment in which she could act.

"I am Rage Winnoway whose name is also Courage," she said, and stepped toward the door.

"No," Billy cried, grasping her arm and pulling her back. "I'll go first."

"Let *me*," Elle insisted, pushing them both aside.

A violent crackling sound filled the air. Then an explosion threw them all to the ground.

The firecat screamed: *"No!"*

"What happened?" Billy asked groggily.

"A trick! I knew it was a trick!" The firecat's voice sizzled with fury.

"Mama!" Billy howled, and Rage knew that Bear had gone through the gate while they were arguing.

"Where is she?" Rage demanded angrily of the firecat. "Where did you send Bear?"

"Gone!" it hissed venomously. "Gone forever into the black and the nothingness. Gone!"

Then there was another explosion. Rage flew sideways, as if a giant hand had slapped her. She fell into darkness.

15

"Rage . . ." It was the voice that kept asking her to break the spell that bound it.

"I don't know how to help you," Rage muttered. Something heavy was pressing down on her. Something monstrous and unbearable.

She felt a hand on her cheek, and a prickling tingle ran through her body.

She opened her eyes to find a man staring down at her. He was very thin and rather old, with faded amber eyes. He wore jeans and a white T-shirt, and his gray hair was pulled back into a ponytail. Around him the night sky bloomed with stars.

"You . . . you are the wizard, aren't you?" she said. "It was *your* voice that I kept hearing in my dreams."

"I could only make contact when you were asleep, because of the trap spell I was under. But I gave what magical help I could on your journey."

"What help?"

He gave a slight smile. "Light when you needed it in the tunnels under Fork, mental manipulation of black-shirts at the pier, a little direction in the city when you were seeking your friends in the blackshirt prison. And I was able to make you hard to see on several occasions."

"That was you?" Rage said slowly. "But how did you know . . . where . . ." She stopped, remembering all the times the hourglass had grown inexplicably hot. The fire-cat had told her the truth when it claimed that all the wizard knew lay within the hourglass.

"*You* were trapped in the hourglass!" she groaned. And that, of course, explained why Ania's spell had backfired.

"All riddles look simple with hindsight," the wizard said. "I was trapped within that form until the sand ran out, or until it was broken."

Rage sat up and saw that although they were still on the beach, there was no sign of the others.

"I am afraid I have much to answer for," the wizard went on. "I apologize for the things that you have endured since using the bramble gate. I should not have left it there. Yet if you had not used it, Valley and all of its life would be lost."

"Why did you put the bramble gate there?" Rage asked. "And how did you come to be trapped in the hourglass?"

He held up his hands. "Dear girl, I cannot answer a thousand questions at once. It will take time."

"Time!" Rage gasped. "I forgot. There is no time! Sir, the keepers, the river . . . they only have two days, and maybe most of that has already—"

The wizard shook his head and held a finger against his lips until she fell silent. "Have no fear. I will return to Valley in time to save it from destruction. Remember that I know all that you know, Rage Winnoway. Was I not a secret companion on your journey? I know exactly what the sharp-voiced Mother of the witch folk wanted said to me. And I know what the High Keeper has become. I know the stories told of me by Niadne in the banding house, and by the baker in the village. If you could only know how it felt to be unable to speak or act. Never have I felt so helpless!"

"Did you really make Valley?"

The wizard shook his head. "Rue had it most accurately when she said I took Valley from time. The original valley exists in your world, but I seized the moment of its existence *before* it was flooded, and I turned it into a land with its own inner time."

"I don't understand."

"Valley is like that lagoon you swam in by the river," the wizard explained. "It was once part of the flow, but now it exists apart from it."

Rage nodded slowly, thinking she understood, though it was very complicated. She remembered another question she wanted to ask. "Did you really bring women to Valley to serve the keepers?"

The wizard laughed out loud. "Of course not. Look at Rue and Ania. Do they seem obedient and willing to serve?"

"Then why do the keepers—"

The wizard shook his head. "The keepers! You know, when I brought their ancestors to Valley, they were young idealists, weary of a world in which nature was squandered. I bid them take better care of it, but they quickly moved from loving and nurturing to keeping and Ordering." He shook his head. "I did not want to repress the keepers and control them. I thought that they would work it out for themselves, given time."

"Then you didn't tell them to keep Order?" Rage asked, wanting to be clear.

"Of course not! I brought humans to Valley because

I wanted to share my love of it. But the zealots among those I brought to Valley felt useless. All that energy and hunger to be doing something. First they bothered me endlessly. The pettiness of their questions and complaints! The idiocy of their ideas of improving Valley! I felt I would go mad. Generation after generation of them were the same."

"You must be very old," Rage murmured, her mind reeling at all she had been told. To think she had not even believed that magic existed!

The wizard sighed. "Those who dwell in Valley age according to Valley time. I have always spent time outside, and so I seem immortal to the Valley folk."

"I still don't understand why you made Valley into a land if it wasn't for the keepers," Rage said.

"I froze Valley to preserve it. I could not bear to think of it buried under thousands of tons of water. Lost forever to sunlight and greenness. All that natural beauty drowned for no better reason than the rules of economics and politics."

"But you made Fork," Rage said, thinking that any city buried land.

He nodded. "I did, so that the rest of Valley would remain in its natural state. Yet I sought to make a city that lived and shaped itself to nature and life. Oddly, Fork might be the most wondrous thing I have ever made. When I was in your pocket inside the hourglass, I saw that it is not only a city that reflects life but one that is truly sentient. It lives, just as Valley lives. It has been so long since I was in Fork that I had not seen this. I will restore it to light and life. The streets will be green again, and the bridges will sing."

"What will you do with the keepers?"

"I do not know," the wizard admitted. "I see no point in punishing them or locking them up. Some of them might be capable of changing, but some . . . Perhaps I will return them to the world from which their ancestors came. But I must be careful. I do not want to overreact."

"Will you stay in Valley?"

The wizard sighed. "I wish I could swear that I would, but I know my own nature. In time, curiosity and my studies will lure me elsewhere. But I will leave it better able to fend for itself. The time has come for me to atone for the things I have neglected or abandoned."

"Nothing you do will bring back the animals that the High Keeper killed," Rage said, suddenly disliking the wizard. "It won't bring back the wild things that died in the blackshirt prison or the people who were sent down the River of No Return on the death boats."

The wizard sagged before her eyes, and something began to nag at Rage. Something to do with the absence of the animals. Where *were* Billy and the others?

"Don't force your memory," the wizard advised, his eyes watchful. "When the trap spell broke and released me, you took the full weight of the shock because you were carrying the hourglass. You have been unconscious for hours. It is almost dawn."

"Where are the others?"

"Sleeping in the dunes. They were exhausted, and I said I would sit with you. It was windy down here, but I shielded you with magic. It was best not to move you."

Rage had the sensation that something heavy was lying against her forehead. "Where is the firecat?"

"It vanished as soon as it saw I was free. It was afraid of what I would do, of course. But it will return eventually. It won't be able to stay away from me."

"Then it was the firecat that trapped you inside the hourglass?" Rage's head had begun to ache. She rubbed at her temples to ease the pain.

"I am afraid I trapped myself," the wizard said. "I was so eager to be rid of the firecat that it was able to trick me."

"You are not its master?"

"Better to say I am its creator." The wizard sighed. "I was interested in what the witch women were doing in creating wild things. I wondered what would result from the creation of a thing out of pure magic. I was less experienced then, and too foolish to be aware that the things I was experimenting with were dangerous. The firecat is a thing that has no soul. It has no compassion or goodness. You see, I gave none of myself into its making."

"How did it . . ."

"Trick me? I wished to be rid of it, for it had caused endless trouble and mischief over the years."

"What did you do?" Rage prompted.

"I was determined to trick the firecat into unmaking itself. It could use magic, but the deepest workings eluded it. I told it that it could master magic if it gained a soul, and I invented a quest for a soul—the very quest you have undertaken and whose directions were in-scribed on the hourglass. But the firecat did not trust me. It demanded that I bind myself into the hourglass that it was to carry to the shore of the Endless Sea. Like a fool I did so, thinking it would not matter, for soon I would be free of the hourglass and the wretched firecat. I never imagined it would force you to undertake the quest I had set it!"

"Why did it choose me?"

The wizard hesitated. Emotions fled over his face: fear, guilt, sorrow. Finally resignation settled there. "It seems you will have the whole story from me. Well, perhaps it is time."

Rage's head started to ache again, and she lifted her hand to her brow.

The wizard looked concerned. "This should wait. . . ."

Rage was sick of being put off. "Does it have something to do with Grandmother Reny? Rue said there was a connection between you and her. Did you meet her when you were in my world? Did she fall in love with you, and then you left her? Is that why she married Grandfather Adam and then was so unhappy that she faded away?"

The wizard looked as if she had punched him in the stomach. He sat down right where he was standing. "Oh, child! Every word you say is a knife to my heart," he gasped.

Rage was astonished and embarrassed to see a tear roll down his grizzled cheek. "I—I'm sorry," she stammered.

"No. It is I who am sorry. Although I speak of atonement, and mean it, some things cannot be healed. Sometimes it is too late." He paused and wiped his eyes and cheeks with a crumpled handkerchief.

Rage did not speak. She did not know what to say.

"You ask if your grandmother Reny loved me. She did, but only as a friend. It was Adam she loved." He looked into Rage's eyes. "My brother, Adam. I am your great-uncle Peter."

"But how can you be Grandfather's brother?" Rage demanded. "You're a wizard!"

"I discovered magic as a child. Most wizards and

witches begin before they are adults. It seems adults are incapable of making the mental leaps that magic demands. I did not plan to leave my world, but when the government diverted the river to flood the valley . . ."

Rage gasped, suddenly understanding. "*Valley* is the land that used to be part of Winnoway!"

"It is a moment from the life of that valley. The last moment," he added sadly.

Rage frowned. "But Valley is much bigger than the flooded land back home."

He nodded. "I used magic to make Valley bigger within than without."

Rage stared at him in awe. Then she frowned, her excitement fading. "Why didn't you ever go back to Winnoway to see Grandfather Adam?"

The wizard's face fell into lines of grief. "We were so close as boys. He used to follow me everywhere." He shook his head. "I didn't know that my going would mean so much. I always meant to contact him. That was why I left the bramble gate open. I even created the magic mirror so that I could see him, but I never used it."

"You didn't care that he loved you," Rage accused, angrier than she had ever been in her life.

"You are a child," the wizard said, drawing back. "You don't understand."

This was a wizard with terrifying powers, but Rage was reckless with fury. "I'm not old and I can't work magic or create it, but I understand better than you do that when you hurt someone who loves you, it doesn't end there, because love is a flow, too. How come you know so much about magic but you don't know *that*? What use is magic if you can't care about people who love you?"

The wizard looked pale and shaken. "You are right,"

he whispered. "I loved my brother, but I loved my research more."

Rage's head was pounding now, and she was beginning to feel sick. "How can you ever make up for all the harm you've caused?"

"I can't," the wizard said. "My brother died of grief while I was trapped inside the hourglass. I saw it in my magic mirror, even as the firecat held me trapped in the hourglass and scried for you."

"Me?" Rage was taken aback. "The firecat was looking for me?"

"For someone that I would care about. Family. It knew the mirror connected me to my past. It sought my brother out first, but he was close to death. The firecat sought your mother next, but by the time it figured out how to activate the bramble gate, she was . . . well, as she is now. Your uncle Samuel, of course, had gone away."

"Why did you put the night gate *here*?" Rage asked.

"I had to magic a gateway that I could key to nothingness. The firecat was to come to the shore of the Endless Sea and command the night gate to appear. Then it was to leave the hourglass behind and go through it if it desired a soul. The glass would break, I would be freed, but the firecat would cease to exist."

"It was right to mistrust you," Rage said, disliking the wizard more and more. But some terrible awareness was growing in the back of her mind, pushing aside her anger and disgust.

"I told myself that lying to a soulless creature filled with malice and mischief did not truly count as a lie," the wizard said.

Rage felt a great wave of sorrow engulf her as her memory returned of the moments before the explosion. "Bear! *Bear* went into the night gate!" she cried.

The wizard nodded, his pale eyes seeming to glow.

"This is all your fault!" Rage cried. "You are a hateful, selfish man! You are worse than the High Keeper!"

"Yes," he said in a low, sad voice.

Rage could not bear to think of him as her great-uncle. "Bring her back!" she screamed at him. "Use your magic!"

"No magic can return your friend. She went out of time when she entered the night gate. She is beyond time."

"No!" Rage wept, but she had heard the truth in the wizard's voice. They had saved Bear from the river and from the conservation tank of the High Keeper only for her to die anyway.

"It may help you to remember that Bear chose to take a risk so that no one else would have to," the wizard said gently.

Rage stood up and turned her back on him. That was when she saw Billy, sitting alone at the top of a dune. His outline in the dark blue sky was unmistakable.

She went slowly up and sat by him. He said nothing. He did not look at her. Rage put both of her arms around him and held him as tightly as she could. "Oh, Billy. My poor Billy," she whispered, pressing her face into his neck.

He gave a great, wrenching sob and buried his head in his hands. Rage wept for him and for poor, sad Bear, whose life had been so full of pain and hardship. They cried until they were both exhausted, then they sat close together, holding hands as they had in the bubble.

One by one the stars vanished until the sky was a perfect sheet of darkest blue, growing lighter at the edges. It was almost dawn.

"You know, I felt that she . . . she was coming to be able to care for me," Billy said at last in a husky voice. "Coming to Valley healed her."

"*You* healed her," Rage said. "You just went on loving her and caring for her, no matter how cold and hard she was to you. These last couple of days she watched you all the time, as if she was hungry for the sight of you."

He laughed softly. The sound of it was so sad that Rage felt her eyes fill again. Letting the tears trickle unchecked down her cheeks, she felt strangely empty. She thought of something the wizard had said. "You know, she went through that door to stop you from going."

"Us," Billy said gently. "She went for all of us."

Rage brushed at some more tears. From the corner of her eye, she saw Elle and Goaty cuddled together with Mr. Walker in a dip in the sand. The sight of them asleep together squeezed her heart, for she loved them all so. As if they felt the intensity of her gaze, they began to stir, and then they were trudging across the shadowy sand to join her and Billy.

"Are you all right?" Elle asked. It wasn't clear which of them she meant, for she looked at them both with concern. Her eyes were red, too.

Billy said nothing.

"I'm sorry," Mr. Walker said, his big, soft ears and tail drooping down. He patted Billy's hand, then climbed into Rage's lap.

Elle sat down on the other side of Billy. "She always growled at me, but I can't imagine never being able to smell her again."

"I could never forget her smell," Billy said hoarsely, and Rage felt her heart must break.

Goaty said in a low, miserable voice, "She was so brave. Maybe if I had known her better, she could have taught me to be brave, too."

"I don't think anyone really knew Mama," Billy murmured. "Not even me, though I tried so hard. She showed such a little bit of herself, but I always felt that inside her was some vast, wonderful country just waiting for the sun to discover it."

That made them all silent for a long time.

"She was good," Goaty said at last. "I was never so good."

A few faint smears of dull orange on the horizon and then the sky was afire with color. They watched the sun rise without speaking, and the beauty of it, reflected in the silver skin of the sea, was so great as to hurt Rage. This was only the first of many sunrises that Bear would not see.

"I want to see it again," Billy said suddenly. He stood up. The new sun painted him golden red all over, and his hair hung over his forehead like a lick of pure bronze.

Rage got up, too. "See what?"

"The gate she went through." Billy pointed.

Rage had not noticed it earlier because they were facing the side of it. The wizard was further along the beach, sitting and staring out to sea. He turned as they approached the night gate, so at the same instant they all saw that the blackness in it had changed.

It was now filled with stars.

"What happened?" Rage whispered. It was as though they were looking at a gateway that truly led to night.

The wizard had come to stand by them, staring into the gate with a look of astounded awe. "I don't know how this could be, but it has become a world gate."

"A what?" Elle asked.

"A world gate. A gateway that can be used to travel from one place to another."

"Then Bear . . . ," Billy began with heartbreaking hope, but the wizard shook his head.

"I'm sorry, son. When Bear went through it, it was a night gate. A way to nothing." He frowned. "Somehow, her going in has made it a world gate. I have no idea how or why. It shouldn't happen. It *couldn't* happen unless . . ."

"What?" Billy asked.

The wizard shrugged. "Unless she was actually dying at the moment she entered the gateway."

Rage stared at the wizard, but she was not seeing him. She was hearing Bear pant and gasp in the tunnels under Fork, hearing the vet say she should be given an easy time, hearing Goaty say blood had come out of her mouth after they had pulled her from the River of No Return.

"She was sick," Elle said slowly. "I could smell it on her."

"She was so tired," Billy said. "She smelled tired all the time."

The wizard turned back to the door. "It has to be what happened. The night gate became a world gate because her soul magic went into it."

All of them stared into the gateway.

"Maybe the sun did come to that country inside Mama after all," Billy said, and though he was crying, he was smiling, too.

Rage thought of her own mother, waiting to be wakened.

"We want to go home," Rage told the wizard bluntly. She could not bring herself to plead with him or think about the fact that they were related. It had never mattered to him before, and it was too late for it to matter now.

"I can send you," he replied gravely.

"Will you give me magic to wake Mam?"

"No," the wizard said gently. "You see, there is no such thing as waking magic."

Rage stared at him, so devastated that she would have fallen if Billy wasn't close behind her.

The wizard only smiled sadly. "You are wise for your age, Rage Winnoway, and you have great courage, but you do not know everything."

"I don't understand," Rage said.

"Rage, your spirit shines more brightly than you can ever know. What Adam and Samuel did to Mary is what I did to my brother. They made her believe that she is not worthy of being loved. They made her feel she is unnecessary."

Rage made a strangled sound that was partly a moan and partly a cry of protest. "She is necessary to *me*! Doesn't she care about that?"

"She cares deeply for you. But she does not think you need her. She thinks her loss won't hurt you."

Rage wanted to cry at the thought that her mother would just go to sleep and leave her all alone, just as her mother's brother had done to her. One part of Rage grew cold and even angry at Mam, because a mother ought to love her daughter more than a brother. But Mam hadn't chosen to be sick. Rage thought about how Billy had just gone on loving Bear, no matter how she acted. That was real courage.

She took a deep, shaky breath and then pushed all of the coldness and the sadness out of her heart. "I am Rage Winnoway whose name is also Courage," she told the startled-looking wizard. "Send me home."

16

"I cannot summon up a world gate to send you home from here," the wizard said. "We must return to Valley and to the castle first. It will take some days, but you can—"

"No," Rage said, suddenly certain that there was no time to lose. "Can't I go through the night gate? You said it had become a gateway that would take you from one place to another."

The wizard looked troubled. "It is a world gate, but I don't know where you would end up if you went through it. You see, most gates are made by, and are therefore ruled by, the wizards who command their obedience. But this gateway . . . well, it made itself and it rules itself. *It* will decide where to send you, if anywhere."

Rage looked into the star-filled gate and smiled. "I'm not afraid. I don't believe Bear would ever hurt us."

"But it's not Bear," the wizard said. "You mustn't think that."

Billy said, "I'm not afraid, either."

"I am," Goaty said in a humble voice. "It's a terrible

thing, I know. But I can't help being a coward."

Elle said quickly, "It's not cowardly to be afraid. Sometimes it is wise." She looked at them all and said proudly, "I have named him, and you must not call him Goaty anymore."

Rage remembered her whispering into Goaty's ear just before they entered the bubbles in the Place of Shining Waters. "What is your name?" she asked him.

Goaty gave Elle a smile of shy pride. "I am Gilbert."

"Gilbert," Billy echoed. "That's a good, strong name."

"It was the name of one of my litter brothers," Elle said.

"I do not think any of you should go through this gate," the wizard broke in. "It is too unpredictable."

"I have to go," Rage said, but she looked at Goaty, who would not meet her eyes.

"Perhaps Gilbert would prefer to come back to Valley with me, rather than going through the night gate to his own world and resuming an animal life," the wizard offered.

Rage thought that there were many times in life when you had to make hurtful choices. But sometimes there was no other way to do what was right. *That* was why they had taken Billy from Bear when he was tiny. It had hurt all of them, but it had been the right thing to do.

She turned to the animals. "I have to go back, but I think all of you should go and live in Valley."

"No!" Billy said.

"Listen," Rage insisted. "You know what it's like in our world, being owned by humans and ordered and kept by them. Remember how your family gave you away, Mr. Walker?" He nodded. "And Elle, remember how they were going to kill you, the very day Mam took you from the pound?" Elle nodded, too. "And Billy, think how my grandfather treated Bear."

The wizard shifted and seemed about to speak, but then he shook his head and remained silent.

"But we belong with you," Billy said stubbornly. "We're in no danger. You'd never give us away or hurt us."

"*I* wouldn't," Rage said. "But I might not have any choice. I'm just a child, and I don't have much more say than an animal in our world. They are likely to take you all away from me because it will be a long time before Mam can come home from the hospital. I'll probably have to go into a home."

The animals stared at her soberly.

"But if your mother doesn't wake," Mr. Walker said softly, "you'll be all alone."

"I *will* wake her," Rage vowed. "But I wish I could go back there knowing that you are in Valley—all of you— living in the castle, picnicking with Kelpie and the other wild things, exploring the provinces."

"We will never see you again," Mr. Walker said in a small voice.

Rage swallowed hard. "I'll never forget any of you. Never." She looked at Billy, who had not said a word. His face was white under the brightness of his hair. She turned to the wizard. "Go now to Valley and take them with you."

"If you must go through the night gate, I think you had better go through it before we leave. It might vanish when I go."

"Yes, you go first," Billy urged in a queer, fierce voice. "At least let us see you go."

Rage fought to hold back tears and made herself smile as she took his hands and looked into his dear face.

"I love you, Billy. I love all of you, and I'll think of you every day."

She hugged each of them. Then she turned to the gate, hardly able to see it for her tears. "What now?"

"You must enter the gateway with a clear picture in your mind of where you want to go," the wizard said gravely. "If you are sure."

"I am sure," Rage said, and she was, but again she looked at Billy and felt torn in two by the thought that she would never see him again. He was staring at her so hard, she had to turn away from the pull of his eyes.

Taking a deep breath, she jumped through the night gate, but at the same time she felt something hit her hard in the back.

Then she was among the stars and she was not afraid or sad.

She was just floating.

And all at once she heard a child's voice.

What are you? it asked.

I am a girl, Rage said, or thought or dreamed. *I am Rage Winnoway.*

What is a ragewinnoway?

I am, Rage laughed, and the stars seemed to shiver at the sound.

What is that you just did?

I laughed, Rage said.

I like it. May I remember it?

Yes.

May I remember you?

Yes.

Rage felt something run through her like an enormous electric shock, only there was no pain.

So, the voice said, and now it was older and gruff and

247

familiar. *So that was what I was before.*

Bear, Rage whispered.

Your mind told me that this was once my name. I am more than I was then. Now I must find a new name. But I would like to give you a gift for your laughter. What do you wish for?

I want to see Mam.

Goodbye, said Bear, or whatever it was that Bear had become.

Then Rage was on the grass beside a sign that read HOPETON GENERAL HOSPITAL.

Something hit the ground beside her with a great gasping thud, and she looked around to see Billy Thunder. He gave a bark of joy and flung himself on her, licking her wildly, whimpering and wagging his tail with delight.

"Oh, Billy!" Rage cried, remembering the thump in her back and understanding suddenly that he had never intended to let her go alone.

She buried her face in his silky coat and breathed in the doggy smell of him. "Oh, I'm so glad to see you, and so sad!" She looked into his eyes, thinking of all that brightness and curiosity that had grown in him, now lost. "Do you remember everything that happened? I wonder."

Billy gave a single bark and stared at her very hard.

Her skin prickled, for his eyes looked cleverer than before. "Do you understand what I'm saying?"

He barked again, and she hugged him. Somehow, she knew, he had not lost his new ability to think. Perhaps that had been a gift from his mother. After all, he, too, had come through the night gate, and Bear must have recognized him. But he would never be able to tell her what his mother had said to him.

Billy wriggled free of her arms and barked, then pawed at the sign urgently.

"Mam!" Rage gasped. "Of course. Come on." She started to run toward the main entrance, but Billy whined and growled and tugged at the hem of her coat. "What is it?"

Billy barked again and sniffed loudly, then went a few steps in the other direction and looked back at her.

"You know where she is? You can smell her?"

He raced off.

"Wait!" Rage cried, and ran after him as he made his way around the side of the hospital to a second building. He stopped and sniffed at a door, then ran a bit and sniffed at another doorway.

"Are you sure you will be able to find her?" she asked doubtfully. He seemed to be sniffing for a long time. He looked back and growled, then barked again. He trotted to a nearby window and looked at her expectantly.

"In there?" Rage asked. He whined before sinking into a crouch and lowering his head onto his paws beside a door that said NO ENTRY. STAFF ONLY. Rage slipped through it and found herself in a shiny white hall. There was a desk in an alcove, and behind it sat a nurse. Rage's heart sank. The nurse looked exactly like Mrs. Somersby! Fortunately, she was concentrating very hard on whatever report she was filling in. Rage began to creep along the hall toward the desk, step by careful, silent step, wishing she had some of the witch's dust.

She froze when the phone on the desk rang, but the nurse took the receiver without looking up. "Somersby. Yes?"

Rage had to force her legs to move.

"*Whose* brother?" the nurse demanded of the phone. Rage was shaking so hard that it was a wonder she could walk at all, but she was almost past the desk.

"I've never heard of such a thing," the nurse said in disapproving tones. "How do they know he's who he says?" A pause. "Incredible! And they believe that?"

Rage was in the first doorway now, but all of the beds in the room were empty. She walked to the next door quickly, now out of sight of the nurse. There were two strange men and two empty beds. She went along to the third door.

"No, she hasn't woken. . . ."

Rage hesitated, suddenly certain the nurse was talking about Mam.

"No, the doctor was here this afternoon, and he said there is very little chance of her waking now. Her vital signs have dropped, and I think it's only a matter of time. Have they found the child yet?"

Rage refused to let herself lose heart, because hope was another kind of courage. She looked into the third room. There was a young woman with bandaged eyes in one bed, and Mam, head bandaged, in the other, exactly as pale and still as Rage had dreamed.

Her heart gave a great lurch of love and terror as she approached the bed. Next to Mam, a big square machine on wheels emitted a steady beep. Wires ran from the machine to the bed and were taped to the inside of her thin wrist.

Rage took her hand and shook it very gently. "Mam?" she whispered.

Still there was no response. Outside a dog barked once. Billy.

Rage blinked back tears. "Mam, please wake. I love you. Billy and I need you. So much has happened. . . ." She wasn't making sense now. Tears were getting all mixed up with the words she wanted to say.

She won't wake, the firecat's voice sneered in her mind.

"What on earth is going on in here?"

Nurse Somersby stood in the doorway, hands on hips. "What do you think you are doing in here? I know who you are, Miss Rebecca Jane Winnoway! Look at you. How can you have got into such a state!" The nurse strode across the room, took Rage's arm, and began to pull her to the door.

"Mam!" Rage cried, pulling uselessly against the viselike grip. Outside, Billy began to bark wildly.

"What is happening here?" A doctor appeared in the doorway. "Nurse, if you can't keep control, I'm afraid—"

"This child is a runaway, and her mother is the comatose patient in bed twelve. I'll just take her out and call the welfare people."

Rage wrenched her arm free and ran back to the bed. "Mam, I know it hurt you when your brother left. I know sadness has been poisoning you for a long time. But he didn't leave you. Grandfather drove him away. Oh, Mam, if you don't wake, it'll be like you're leaving me, too!"

"You don't seem to understand that this sort of thing is likely to harm your mother!" the nurse scolded, dragging Rage away from the bed. "There are rules here. A good girl would obey them."

Rage grew very calm. She realized that the nurse, like Niadne, believed that rules were there to be obeyed, never questioned. There was no way to argue with anyone who thought like that.

She looked at the doctor. He had talked about keeping control, but his eyes were kind. "Sir, I need to be with my mother. I don't think a rule that stops me from seeing her can be a good rule."

His brows lifted. "You are impertinent."

"Is it impertinent to question a rule that seems wrong to me?"

The doctor blinked, taken aback. "Well, I suppose I see your point, but the rules here are made for the safety of our patients. All of this shouting and struggling . . ."

"I'm sorry about that," Rage said sincerely. "I was upset. But I will be very quiet if you just let me sit with her. You won't even know I'm there."

The doctor's mouth twitched. "Yes, perhaps just for a little while."

Rage resisted the urge to hug him. "Thank you, sir," she said softly.

"Doctor, really, I must object," the nurse began.

He shook his head at her. "I think the rules can be bent on this occasion. After all . . ." He didn't finish his sentence as he ushered the nurse out, but Rage knew what he meant. *After all, the patient is dying.*

Rage went to the bed and took Mam's hand again. It felt small and cold. She sat by the bed and began to tell her in a soft voice all that had happened since she had left Winnoway.

She had just got to the part of the story where Goaty was telling her that Billy and Elle had been caught by the blackshirts when the nurse came in. With her was a police officer and a woman in a dark suit who was one of the child-welfare agents who had come to see Mr. and Mrs. Johnson.

She looked down at Mam, who had not moved or fluttered an eyelash.

"Come, Rebecca," the welfare agent said, gently but firmly. "It is time to go now."

Rage wanted to shriek at her that she wouldn't go, that she had to stay with Mam. But she made herself speak softly. "Please, mightn't I stay with her? They say she's dying."

The adults looked shocked, as if by naming death she had said a swear word.

"I really think—" the police officer began, but the doctor entered.

"*Now* what is going on here?" he asked in an annoyed voice.

"Doctor, the police have come for the girl. I called them. I told you she was a runaway," the nurse said.

The doctor gave her a cool look. "I am sure you were only doing your duty, Nurse Somersby. You may leave now."

The nurse paled and hurried out, and the doctor turned to Rage. "Child, I am afraid you will have to go with the officer."

Rage saw there was no point in arguing, because there were rules he had to obey, too, and more rules that the police officer and the child-welfare woman had to obey. She told herself that if she went with them meekly, maybe they would let her come back on another day. But even as the police officer's hand settled on her shoulder, she had the deep, sad feeling that tomorrow might be too late.

"Officer?" the doctor called.

The policeman turned. "Doctor, I'm afraid the law—"

"Officer, in this hospital, I am the law. Let the girl go." His voice was a whiplash of authority, and the officer released Rage.

"Come here, child," he called, and Rage obeyed.

"You see this?" He pointed to the little television screen on the machine beside the bed. "This shows us how your mother is doing. Not long ago, things looked very grim. But right now I think you've pulled her some way back from wherever she has been all these weeks, because this little line is doing what we want it to. Now, why don't you sit down and try to pull her the rest of the way back."

He drew up a chair. Rage sat in it and took Mam's hand again. She thought the dark, curly eyelashes trembled on her cheeks.

"Speak to her. Let her hear your voice," the doctor said calmly.

"Mam?" Rage said softly, hope opening in her heart like a flower. "Mam, I love you. Please come back to me. I need you."

This time the eyelids definitely fluttered. Then Mam opened her eyes and looked straight at Rage. "My darling, I . . . I was having the strangest dream. You were in it, and Billy Thunder. You were searching for someone. . . ." Her eyes fell closed again.

Rage looked at the doctor apprehensively, but he only patted her hand in reassurance. "She's sleeping now. A proper, natural, healing sleep, and I promise you, this is a sleep she will wake from."

"It's a queer thing. The same day you ran off, that goat of ours disappeared," Mrs. Johnson said.

"It's as if he knew I'd finally called the butcher to come and get him," Mr. Johnson grunted. "Well, I suppose him and those other dogs will turn up eventually."

Rage looked at Billy, and his ears twitched—his version of a nudge in the ribs. She hid a laugh in her mug of milk and ate up the last mouthful of pie.

"Have some more, Rage dear," Mrs. Johnson said. "I've baked another one for tomorrow night, when your uncle Samuel gets here. I wonder what he'll look like after all these years. Last time I saw him he was a teenager, but he'll be a grown man now. Just fancy him coming back out of the blue like this."

"Funny, him turning up right now after all these years of nothing," Mr. Johnson grunted, blowing on his coffee. "He didn't know anything about the accident until I told him. He was calling from some strange country I've never even heard of. Said he'd been doing research and was of a mind to call. Hmph. Wonder what put it in his mind."

Rage drank her milk and thought she knew exactly what her uncle would look like. He would be tall and tanned. His hair would be as black as Mam's: the sort of hair that would never lie down and be still. He would wear dark glasses over his amber eyes.

Turn the page for a preview of Book Two
of the Gateway Trilogy.

Rage gazed over the long dam. It had once been a magnificent wilderness owned by Grandfather's brother, her great-uncle Peter, before he had become a wizard and abandoned their world for one of his own making. She had been to the dam a few times since returning from Valley. She had tried to imagine it as green and vibrant as it must have been before the government flooded it. It was impossible to believe that only a thin curtain of magic separated the dam from Valley. The water shimmered like pale pink satin in the afternoon light. Long, narrow shadows of the drowned trees that poked out of the water lay in charcoal slashes across it. Perhaps in the parallel magical world of Valley, these very trees were flourishing.

Beside her, Billy growled, and Rage automatically dropped her hand to his collar. In the same moment, she realized that the dam ought to have been frozen and bordered by snowy hills. Then she saw what Billy was growling at, and her mouth fell open in surprise. For sitting on a bare, flat stone right at the edge of the water was a tiny hourglass, the very same hourglass that Rage had carried during her whole perilous journey through Valley. But this could not be *that* hourglass, no matter how much it looked like it, because that hourglass had shattered on the shore of the Endless Sea.

This is just a dream, she thought.

"Jusst a dream," sneered the slinky, sulfurous voice of the firecat.

"If *you're* in my dream, then it must be a nightmare," Rage said coldly.

"Nassty ragewinnoway," the voice accused.

"Go away," Rage said crossly. No wonder that Billy was growling. None of the animals had ever trusted the wretched creature, and their instincts had been right.

"Sstupid ragewinnoway," the firecat said.

"I thought I told you to go away," Rage snapped.

The air by the dam shimmered and distorted, and Rage squinted her eyes against the hot brightness as the firecat appeared. It was impossible to look at it properly. All Rage could make out was a suggestion of slitted red cat's eyes, radiant with fury above needle-sharp teeth.

"Firecat bringing warning!" it sizzled at her.

"You ought to warn me about yourself," Rage retorted, turning away with deliberate rudeness, though she was careful to keep the firecat in the edge of her sight. No telling what it was capable of doing. Billy was still growling and his hackles were up, so Rage kept a firm grip on his collar. He might get burned if he attacked.

"Sstupid dogboy," the firecat hissed. "Why sstaying him in that sstupid shape?"

"He can't be a boy in my world," Rage said coldly. "Go away, or I will let him bite you."

"Wizard needing ragewinnoway," the firecat snarled urgently.

Rage pointed at the hourglass. "Have you managed to trap him again? How clever of you! Where am I supposed to take him this time? Not to the shore of the Endless Sea again? Maybe to the bottom of the bottomless ocean? Or to the next-to-last star?"

There was a long silence. Long enough for Rage to reflect that she was silly for getting mad with a dream.

"Firecat . . . needing wizard," the firecat spat with such furious anguish that in spite of herself, Rage was touched. "Can bringing you to him!" it added eagerly, as if it felt her weakening.

Her heart hardened at this familiar offer. "I know this is a dream, but even in a dream I'm not going anywhere with you. And I honestly don't care enough about your master to want to help him if he has gone and got himself into trouble again." Rage was startled to hear the strength of her dislike of the wizard in her words.

The firecat made a sound of spitting fury and frustration. "If not caring for wizard, maybe caring for your sstupid world, sstupid ragewinnoway."

A bell began to ring insistently and the dream slipped away. "I am waking . . . ," she murmured.

"Yesss! Waking to nightmare, sstupid ragewinnoway," the firecat snarled after her.

Acknowledgments

My sincere thanks to Mallory Loehr, who was a meticulous and tender editor and the perfect companion on my journey back to Valley. Thanks also to Kristin Hall and all of the others at Random House, for making my time there so special. And thanks to Bear, Goaty, Billy, and my brave little Mr. Walker, for love and inspiration.

MURDER
PLAYS HOUSE

Berkley Prime Crime Books by Ayelet Waldman

NURSERY CRIMES

THE BIG NAP

DEATH GETS A TIME-OUT

A PLAYDATE WITH DEATH

MURDER PLAYS HOUSE

MURDER PLAYS HOUSE

Ayelet Waldman

BERKLEY PRIME CRIME, NEW YORK

MURDER PLAYS HOUSE

A Berkley Prime Crime Book
Published by The Berkley Publishing Group
A division of Penguin Group (USA)
375 Hudson Street, New York, NY 10014

Visit our website at www.penguin.com

First edition: July 2004

Library of Congress Cataloging-in-Publication Data

Waldman, Ayelet.
    Murder plays house / Ayelet Waldman.— 1st ed.
        p. cm
    "A Berkley Prime Crime book"—T.p. verso.
    ISBN 0-425-19635-6
        1. Applebaum, Juliet (Fictitious character)—Fiction. 2. Women
detectives—California—Los Angeles—Fiction. 3. House buying—
Fiction. 4. Jewish women—Fiction. 5. Housewives—Fiction. I. Title.

PS3573.A42124M87 2004
813'.54—dc22
                                                              2003063739

PRINTED IN THE UNITED STATES OF AMERICA

10 9 8 7 6 5 4 3 2 1

Acknowledgments

My thanks to Sylvia Brownrigg, Peggy Orenstein, Micheline Marcom, and Susanne Pari, brilliant writers and fine editors all; to Natalee Rosenstein, Esther Strauss, and Rebecca Crowley for taking such good care of me; to Lisa Desimini for such delightful and original covers; to Jan Fogner for details of the real estate business (all errors are my own, of course); to Kathleen Caldwell for her unending support; to Mary Evans, not just a remarkable agent, but a good and loyal friend.

Sophie, Zeke, Ida-Rose and Abraham give me something to write about, and their father makes everything possible.

To my girls,
Sophie and Ida-Rose

One

As I huddled in the six inches of bed that my three-and-a-half-year-old son allowed me, I comforted myself with the knowledge that at least I was marginally more comfortable than my husband, who had been reduced to camping out on the floor. We didn't normally permit Isaac to evict us from our bed, but since he'd made his toddler bed uninhabitable with a particularly noxious attack of stomach flu, we'd been forced to let down the drawbridge and allow the barbarian through the gate.

"Are you sure you don't want to sleep on the couch?" I whispered to Peter.

He grunted.

"Honey? Do you want to try the couch?"

"Yeah, right," he muttered.

"It's not *that* wet," I said defensively.

He groaned and rolled over.

It wasn't my fault that the dryer broke down two loads

into laundry day. Perhaps it was shortsighted of me to use the couch as an impromptu drying rack, but how could I have anticipated a night of vomiting and musical beds?

I jumped as Isaac jammed his foot into my stomach, and reached a protective hand around my bulging belly. I patted at the tiny elbow I felt poking up just north of my belly button and murmured to the little girl swimming in the warm dark inside of me. This was likely just the first of many beatings she would suffer at the hands of her older brother.

"Juliet?" Peter said softly.

"Mm?"

"Is he asleep?"

"Like the dead." I heaved myself over so I could see Peter's shadowed form on the floor.

"You win," he said.

"Good," I replied. Then, "I win what?"

"You win. We buy a house. A big house. With lots of beds. At least two for each of us."

I sat up in bed. "Really? Really? Oh sweetie, that is so great. You will not be sorry, I promise. I'll start looking tomorrow. I'll find something with enough room for all of us, and even a special place for your collection."

The truth was, I'd staffed looking for a house months before, and Peter probably knew it. I had paid little or no attention to his insistence that our entire family could continue to fit comfortably into a two-bedroom apartment, even with the pending arrival of our surprise third child. Peter was just nervous about spending the money on a house. He preferred the flexibility of a month-to-month lease, comforting himself with the notion that if his screenplays ever stopped selling, we could just pack up our children and his twenty cubic feet of vintage action figures still in the original blister packs and move into the trailer next to his mother's. Yeah. Like that would ever happen. While it's possible that there has been born a man both cruel and strong enough to force this particular Jewish American Princess into a double-wide in Cincinnati, Ohio, it is certainly not the sweet, sensitive, grey-eyed guy I married.

Anyway, I knew the moment I saw the double pink line of the pregnancy test that we were going to buy a house, and since then all of Peter's protestations and carefully constructed arguments about mobility and low overhead had had about as much effect on me as flies buzzing around the ears of a hippopotamus. Sure, they were irritating, but did they prevent me from wallowing in the mud of the Los Angeles real estate market? As my six-year-old daughter would say, "I don't *think* so."

I drifted off to a sleep enchanted by dreams of second bathrooms and front-loading washers. Alas, it seemed as if I had only just managed to close my eyes when I was awakened by an insistent whine in my ear.

"Come *on*, Mama. It's seven fourteen! We're going to be late for school." As I had every morning since Ruby's sixth birthday, I cursed my mother for buying my overly conscientious daughter that *Little Mermaid* alarm clock.

I hauled myself out of bed, scooping Isaac up with me, and prodded Peter with one toe. "Bed's all yours, sweetie," I said.

Peter leapt up off the floor and burrowed into the newly vacant bed. I sighed jealously and herded the children back to their room. My husband works at night; he finds the midnight hours most conducive to constructing the tales of mayhem and violence that characterize the particular style of horror movie for which he has become marginally well known. That leaves the morning shift to me, a system that works well, by and large, although on the mornings following nights punctuated by the cries of sleepless children, I sometimes wonder if I'm getting the short end of the stick. Before allowing myself to become awash in a sea of self-pity, I reminded myself that since I barely earn enough with my fledgling investigative practice even to pay a babysitter, it is in my interest to make it possible for my husband to get his work done.

I left Isaac wrapped in a blanket in front of the television set, a sippy cup of cool, sweet tea propped next to him, and a plate of dry toast balanced in his lap. He had strict instructions to wake his dad if he felt sick again. He had already started to nod off when his older sister and I walked out the door.

"Mama, what's in my lunch?" Ruby said as we drove down the block to her school.

"Peanut butter on whole wheat, pretzels, half an apple, and a juice box, of course." I always packed Ruby the identical lunch. She is a picky child, and I'm a lazy mother, and once we figure out something that suits both of us, we stick with it.

She sighed dramatically.

"What?" I said.

"Well, it's just that that's an awful lot of carbs."

I nearly slammed into the car in front of me. "What did you say?"

"You know, carblehydrapes. Like bread and stuff. They make you fat."

"First of all, it's carbo*hydrate*s. Second of all, they do *not* make you fat. And *third of all,* you don't need to worry about that, for heaven's sake. You're only six years old!"

I could feel my daughter's scowl burning into the back of my neck.

"Honey, really. You *don't* need to worry about your weight. You're a perfect little girl."

"Miss Lopez says I'm fat."

Now I really did leap on the breaks. "Your teacher called you fat?" I was very nearly shouting.

"Not just me. All of us. She says there's a eminemic of fatness."

"An epidemic."

"Right. Epinemic. We're all fat. The whole first grade."

I pulled into the drop-off area of her school and turned to look at my child. Her red curls were tamed into two pigtails on either side of her narrow face. She was wearing a thick sweater and jeans, so it was impossible to see the shape of her body, but I knew it better than I knew my own. I knew those knobby knees, the narrow shoulders, the tiny rounded belly. I'd memorized that body the moment it came out of me, and had been watching it ever since. She wasn't fat. On the contrary. She was lengthening out into a skinny grade-schooler who looked less and less like my baby every day.

"Sweetheart, there might be an epidemic of obesity—that means fatness—in the *whole country.* But not you, or your friends. You guys are all perfectly shaped. You don't need to worry about your weight. All you need to worry about is being *healthy,* okay?"

Ruby shook her head, sending her pigtails bobbing. "You worry. You worry all the time about being fat."

"No I don't," I lied, feeling a vicious stab of guilt. I had obviously done exactly what I swore never to do. I had infected my lovely little girl with my own self-loathing. Despite all my promises to myself, I had handed down to her my sickening inability to see in the mirror anything other than my flaws. Was it too late? Was Ruby already doomed to a life of vertical stripes and fat-free chocolate chip cookies?

She unclipped her seatbelt and bounded out the door, dragging her Hello Kitty backpack behind her.

I rolled down my window and shouted, "Don't forget to eat your lunch!"

She didn't bother to reply.

AS I waited in traffic to get on the freeway, I called my partner, Al Hockey. Al and I had worked together at the Federal Public Defender's office, in the days when I imagined that I'd spend the rest of my life representing drug dealers and bank robbers, cruising the streets of Los Angeles looking for witnesses who might have seen my clients anywhere but where the FBI claimed they had been. Back then, I'd been a fan of the leather miniskirt, and thought of child-bearing as little more than an excuse to buy cute maternity suits and garner a little extra sympathy from the female members of my juries. It had never occurred to me that once I had my kids I'd end up shoving all my suits into the back of my closet and spending my days in overalls and leggings, ferrying squealing bundles from Mommy and Me to the park, and back again.

Al had once told me that lawyers like me, the ones who seem to get off on squiring the lowlifes through the system and giving the prosecutors a run for their money, invariably end up growing old on the job. I remember that I felt a flush of pride at his words, but replied that I wasn't getting off on it—rather, I loved being a public defender because I did *justice*. Al had looked up from the evidence we were sifting through and held up a photograph of our client pointing a gun at a terrified bank teller. I'd muttered something about the Constitution protecting the guilty as well as the innocent, and had gone back to preparing my cross-examination.

I had surprised both Al and myself by deciding not only not to spend my life as a public defender, but also to quit work altogether to stay home with my kids. On my last day at the office, I swore to Al that I'd be back someday, but neither of us had imagined that the work I'd return to would be as his partner in a private investigation service run out of his garage in Westminster. Al and I specialize in criminal defense investigations, helping defense attorneys prepare their cases. We interview witnesses, track down alibis, take photos and video of the crime scenes, and do everything we can to help earn our clients the acquittals they may or may not be entitled to. As partnerships go, we have a good one. His years as a detective with the LAPD taught him top-notch investigative skills, as well as the delicate art of witness intimidation, and my criminal defense experience makes it easy for me to anticipate what an attorney will need when trial rolls around. Given the spotty quality of the private defense bar, sometimes I end up crafting the defense from start to finish, even going so far as to give the lawyer an outline for a closing argument.

We work well together, Al and I, even if ours is an unlikely match. I'm a diehard liberal, and Al's, well, Al's something else altogether. I pay my dues to the ACLU, and he pays his to his militia unit. He belongs to a unique band of gun-toting centralized-government-loathers. Although some of their rhetoric is a bit too close to that of the white supremacists seeking to overthrow the U.S. government, Al and his colleagues are an equal-opportunity bunch. They'd have to be. Traditional groups would have tossed Al out as a race-mixer, and despised his children as mongrels. Al's wife, Jeanelle, is African-American. Al's positions are purely political and entirely unracist. He feels that all of us, white, black, brown, and green, are being screwed over by a government concerned with maximizing the wealth of the very few. The difference between Al and normal people who might at least sympathize with that opinion, especially come April 15, is that Al expresses his belief by amassing guns and marching around in the woods with a cabal of similarly committed loonies.

"What have we got going on today?" I asked Al, when he snarled into the phone. Not a morning person, my partner. That's one of the few traits he shares with my husband, although Peter would take issue even with that. He hates to think he has anything in common with Al. Peter just doesn't find the whole libertarian-militia-black-helicopter thing as charming as I do.

"Rats. Rats is what we've got going on," Al said.

"Those rats pay our bills," I reminded him. Al is a notorious despiser of lawyers, preferring to call my fellow members of the bar either "liars" or "scum," and referring to every firm we do business with, somewhat tediously, as "Dewey, Cheetum & Howe."

"Not your kind of rat," he said. "Real rats. Big, fat tree rats, all over the office. My idiot neighbor took down his palm tree, and they've all migrated into my garage."

I felt my stomach heave. "Al," I groaned. My rat phobia probably stems back to the time my mother let me take my kindergarten class gerbil family home for Christmas vacation. I woke up on New Year's Day to find that Penelope, the mother gerbil, had eaten her children. Also the head of Squeakers, her husband. I found her belching over the remains of Squeakers's body. All these years and two children later—while there are certainly days when I sympathize with Penelope's impulse—I still cannot abide rodents. Even rabbits are too whiskery and slithery for my taste. And rats are beyond the pale.

"I'm not coming to work today," I said.

"I figured as much. Anyway, why should you even bother? It's not like we've got any business."

Al isn't a guy inclined to self-pity, which made his woeful tone of voice all the more worrying. Our business *had* been limping along lately. We'd certainly experienced flush moments, but it had been far too long between well-paying gigs. Al's optimism had been less and less apparent, and now I feared it had seeped entirely away.

"When is the exterminator due?" I asked.

"Today, but who knows if he'll be able to do anything. They're everywhere."

"So what do you want to do today? Come up here and work out of my house?"

"No point. Nothing to do. I'm calling this day a loss and heading on over to the shooting range as soon as the rat guy shows up."

"Good idea." Firing a few rounds into a paper mugger was just what Al needed to improve his mood. By tomorrow he'd be chipper again. I hoped.

I decided to take advantage of my newly acquired day off and do some house hunting. I had already gone around with a realtor a few times, in a more or less desultory manner, just to see what was out there, and what our money could buy us. Not as much as I'd hoped, it turned out. Lately, I'd taken to cruising the nicer neighborhoods, more to torture myself with what I couldn't afford than for any other reason. Although there was always the chance that I'd pass a house at the same time as an ambulance pulled away, bearing its owner to his final rest, and setting in motion a probate sale.

I pulled into a Coffee Bean & Tea Leaf, bought myself a mocha freeze (promising the baby that this would be the last jolt of caffeine I'd expose her to for at least a week), and pulled out my cell phone.

"Kat Lahidji," my realtor murmured in her slightly breathy voice.

"Hey Kat, it's Juliet."

"Hi! Are you on your way to class?" Kat and I had met at a prenatal yoga class on Montana Boulevard. I liked her despite the fact that she, like every other pregnant woman in that part of greater Los Angeles, didn't even *look* pregnant when seen from the rear. She was in perfect shape, still doing headstands in the sixth month of pregnancy. She had sapphire blue eyes and nearly black hair that she tamed with a collection of silver and turquoise pins and clips and wore swirled into a knot at the nape of her neck. Only her nose kept her from being exquisitely beautiful. It looked like something imagined by Picasso—a combination of a Persian princess's delicate nostrils, and the craggy hook of a Levantine carpet merchant. Kat had once told me that her mother-in-law was on a tireless campaign to convince her to explore the wonders of rhinoplasty.

Kat and I had become friendly, meeting weekly for yoga, and even once or twice for lunch, although Kat never did much more than push her food around her plate. Despite the fact that her food phobia made me feel compelled to double my own consumption in order to compensate, we enjoyed each other's company. We had the same slightly off-beat sense of humor, were plagued by similar insecurities about the state of our careers and the quality of our parenting, and shared a fondness for crappy chick flicks that disgusted our husbands to no end. I had been surprised to find out that Kat was a real estate agent—she seemed entirely too, well, *real,* for that dubious profession. She did have the car for it, though. She drove a gold Mercedes Benz with the embarrassing vanity plate, "XPTD OFR." When she had caught me puzzling out the plate's meaning, she had blushed a kind of burnt auburn under her golden skin, and told me that her husband had bought her the car, plates and all, as a present to celebrate her first year's employment in his mother's agency.

"You work for your mother-in-law?" I had asked, shocked.

"Yes," Kat sighed.

"The nose-job lady?"

"The very same."

I had wanted to ask my friend if she was out of her mind. But I had also wanted her to show me some houses, so the question didn't seem particularly appropriate.

Kat responded to my invitation to join me on a morning of house-hunting with her usual professional excitement. "God, do you really want to bother?" she said. "I mean, what's the point? There's nothing but dumps out there."

"There's got to be *something*. I finally got the official go-ahead from Peter; I've graduated from a looky-loo to a spendy-spend."

She sighed heavily. "All right. I'll see what I can scrape up to show you. At least it will get me out of here for a couple of hours."

Kat was a truly dreadful real estate agent. Perhaps she kept her loathing for her job hidden from clients who didn't know her personally, but I doubted it. She lacked the fundamental realtor ability to seem upbeat about even the most roach-infested slum. On the contrary. She had a knack for telling you as you pulled up in front of a house exactly what was wrong with it, why you were sure to hate it, and why she wouldn't let you buy it even were you foolish enough to want it. Her standard comment about every house was, "Who would ever live *here?*" Sometimes she just shuddered in horror and refused even to step out of her car, forcing me to explore on my own. It made for entertaining, if slightly unproductive, house-hunting.

I actually might have considered the first house Kat showed me that day. It was a crumbling Tudor whose prime was surely in the 1920s or 30s, but the kitchen and bathrooms still had the original art tiles, and the master bedroom had a killer view of the Hollywood Hills. It could have worked for us, except for the fact that in the gaggle of young men hanging out on the corner in front of the house I recognized one of my old clients. He'd weaseled his way out of a crack cocaine conviction by ratting out everyone both above and below him in the organization. Given that in the thirty seconds I was watching him, I saw him do two hand-offs of what looked suspiciously like glassine packets, I figured he had resumed his original profession. Either that or he was still working for the DEA, and was just pretending to deal.

"Nice neighborhood," I said to Kat.

She laughed. "My mother-in-law calls it 'transitional.'"

"Transitioning from what to what?"

"Slum to crime scene, apparently," she said. That kept us giggling through the next couple of inappropriate dives.

"Okay, I've got one more house on my list, but there's probably no point. It's not even really on the market," Kat said. We were attempting, with the assistance of another round of frozen coffee drinks, (no reason not to start breaking promises to this baby early—her childhood was most likely destined to be a series of failures on my part, and if Ruby and Isaac were anything to go by, caffeine exposure would surely be the least of her problems) to recover our senses of smell from assault by a 1920s Craftsman bungalow with four bedrooms and forty-two cats.

"I don't think I can stand it, Kat," I said.

"I *told* you they all sucked." She heaved her feet up on the dashboard and wriggled her toes with their violet nails. "My legs are killing me. Look at these veins." She traced her fingers along the mottled blue lumps decorating her calves. Kat was only six months pregnant, a month or so behind me, but already she had a brutal case of varicose veins, the only flaw in her otherwise perfect pregnant persona. I had been spared that particular indignity, but had plenty of others to keep me occupied: ankles swollen to the size of Isaac's Hippity Hop, most notably, and a belly mapped with stretch marks like a page out of the Thomas Guide to the city of Los Angeles. I was desperately hoping the lines would stop at the city limits, and not extend all the way out to the Valley.

"It's kind of nice how your toenail polish matches the veins," I said.

"I paid extra for that. Anyway. One more. I'm sure it's no better than any of the others, but I haven't seen it yet. My mother-in-law asked me to go check up on it for her. Apparently it belongs to the boyfriend of the son of her cousin. Or something. She wants to make sure they've got it in shape to show it. We could just pretend we went, and go catch a movie or something."

My ears perked up. "Gay owner?"

Kat nodded, stirred her straw in her drink without sipping, and held out her hand for my empty cup. "Yup."

"That's terrific!" I said. Gay former owners are the Holy Grail of the West LA real estate market. Who else has the resources, energy, and taste to skillfully and painstakingly decorate every last inch of a house down to the doorknobs and crown moldings? Single women generally lack the first, straight men always suffer from a dire shortage of the third, and straight couples with children definitely have none of the second.

"Movie time?" Kat said, hopefully.

"No. Let's go see the house."

"But it's not even on the market. And it's bound to be hideous."

"Come *on,* Kat! Gay owners! Let's go!"

I wasn't disappointed. We pulled up in front of a large, stucco, Spanish-style house with wrought-iron miniature balconies at every front window, tumbling purple bougainvillea, and a small but impeccably maintained front garden. The house was only about ten or so blocks from our apartment in Hancock Park, in an even nicer neighborhood called Larchmont.

Even Kat looked strapped for something negative to say. Finally, she grumbled, "I'm sure it's out of your price range."

I jumped out of the car and raced up the short front walk. The house was a little close to the street, but the block seemed quiet, at least in the middle of the day. I was already imagining how the neat square of grass would look with Ruby's bike overturned in the middle and Isaac's plastic slide lodged in the flowerbeds.

The front door was of carved oak. In the middle of the broad, time-darkened planks was a knocker in the shape of a gargoyle's head. I grabbed the lolling tongue and rapped once. Kat came up behind me.

"There's a lock box," she said. She reached into her purse, pulled out a keypad, and snapped it onto the box attached to the door handle. Then she punched a few numbers into the keypad, and a little metal door at the bottom of the box slid open. In the box was a security key that looked like it belonged in the ignition of the Space Shuttle rather than in the front door of my dream house. The house I planned to live in until I was an old lady. The house I intended for my children to call 'home' for the rest of their lives. My house. Mine.

"Open it, already," I said.

Kat rolled her eyes at me. "Playing hard to get, are we?" It was real estate love at first sight. The front door opened into a vaulted entryway with broad circular stairs leading up to the second floor. A heavy Arts and Crafts style chandelier hung from a long chain. It looked like the pictures of the Green & Green mansions I'd seen in books about early Los Angeles architecture.

The living room took up the entire right side of the house. At its center was an enormous fireplace tiled in pale green with a relief of William Morris roses. The walls were painted a honey yellow and glowed from the lights of the ornate wall sconces with hand-blown glass shades that were set at regular intervals around the room. There was a long, rectangular Chinese carpet in rich reds and golds.

"I wonder if they'll leave me the carpet?" I said.

Kat shook her head. "Don't get so excited."

"What?" I said. "This is my house. It's perfect. I'm buying it."

"I'm sure there's, like, a twenty thousand dollar pest report. And a brick foundation. Plus, Larchmont is known for car theft because it's so close to Beverly Boulevard. It's a car jacker's fantasy—the lights are all perfectly linked. Anyway, you can't afford it. Let's go get some lunch."

"You're really good at this, you know?"

She just followed me across the hall to the dining room. There was another fireplace in this room, smaller but just as beautiful as the one in the living room. The walls were papered in what had to be vintage floral wallpaper, tangled ivy, and vines dotted with muted roses. I immediately began fantasizing about all the dinner parties we'd give in this room. The fact that we'd never actually given a dinner party, and that my culinary skills are limited to pouring skim milk over cold cereal, interfered not at all with this flight of the imagination.

"Oh my God," Kat said, from behind the swinging doors she'd passed through. I followed her into the most beautiful kitchen I'd ever seen. The centerpiece was a restaurant stove as big as my station wagon. Across from the stove was a gargantuan, stainless steel Sub-Zero. The appliances were professionally sleek, the counters zinc, and there were more cabinets and drawers than in a Williams Sonoma outlet. One half of the huge space was set up as a sitting room, with a deep, upholstered couch, and a wall unit that I just knew hid a television and stereo system.

I sighed, and turned to Kat. "There's no way I can afford this place."

She rifled through some papers. "There isn't even an asking price yet."

"It's definitely going to be more than I can afford."

"I told you. Should we even bother going upstairs?"

"Why not? I'm already depressed. A little more won't kill me."

There were three small but adorable bedrooms on the second floor, with a shared bath, and a master bedroom that nearly made me start to weep with longing. It was so large that the owner's massive four-poster bed fit into one small corner. There was an entire wall of built-in bookcases, a fireplace, and not one, but two upholstered window seats. But it was the master bathroom that really got to me. It was Zelda Fitzgerald's bathroom. Two oversized pedestal sinks, a built-in Art Deco vanity with dozens of tiny drawers and a three-panel mirror, black and white tiled floor and walls, and the largest claw-foot tub in the known universe. It was so big it could easily fit a family of five. Or a single pregnant woman.

"I hate you," I said to Kat. "Why would you show me this house? I can't afford it, and nothing else will ever seem good enough after this."

She sighed. "I know. It's totally hopeless. Let's go see the guesthouse."

"The guesthouse?"

She began reading from the printout in her hand. "Two room guesthouse with full kitchen and bath, located in garden."

"Guest house like office for Peter, and even office for Al and me so we can escape the rats in Westminster?"

But she was already headed down the stairs.

The guesthouse was as beautifully restored and decorated as the main house. We opened the door into a pretty living room with wainscoted walls and leaded glass windows. However, unlike the main house, which was immaculate to the point of looking almost uninhabited, the guesthouse was clearly lived in. There was a jumble of shoes next to the door—Jimmy Choo slingbacks, Ryka running shoes, and a pair of black clogs with worn soles. The tiny galley kitchen with miniature versions of the main house's lavish appliances was filthy—there were dishes on nearly every surface, and a month's worth of crumbs on the counters.

"Ick," I said.

"Some people," Kat said. "It would have killed the tenant to clean up? The place is probably infested with mice. Or rats. Definitely cockroaches."

One corner of the living room was set up with a long wooden table scarred with rings from glasses and what looked to be cigarette burns. On the table was a brand new Mac with a screen larger than any I'd ever seen. There was also a huge, professional-quality scanner, a color laser printer, a printer designed specifically for digital photographs, and a thick stack of manuals and reference books. I lifted one up—"The Mac Genius's Guide to Web Design."

"Check this out," I called. "I bet there's like twenty thousand dollars worth of computer equipment here!"

"Hmm?" Kat said.

There were two large stacks of eight-by-ten photographs on the table. One showed a generic-looking blond woman, her hair teased into a halo around her head, and her lips shiny and bright with gloss. An illegible signature was scrawled across the bottom with black marker. The other stack was of a more peculiar photograph. It was clearly of the same woman, but showed her from the back, with her face turned away from the camera. Her arms were wrapped around her body, her fingers gripping either shoulder. The bones of her spine stuck out like a string of large, irregularly shaped beads along the center of her back. These photographs were also signed with the same indecipherable scribble.

A bulletin board hung crookedly on the wall, and I winced at the hole I was sure the nail had made in the thick, creamy plaster. The board was full of what appeared to be fan mail, much of it in the ornate curliques of young girls' handwriting. I stood up on my tiptoes to read one of the letters, but Kat stopped me.

"Come on," she said. "Don't be so nosy."

I flushed. That's certainly one of my worst qualities. Or best, if you consider my job.

"She must be an actress," I said.

"Probably."

"With a knack for self-promotion. And a really good website."

Kat shrugged, not particularly interested, and led the way

down the small hallway next to the kitchen. We walked into a surprisingly large bedroom, with French doors opening to the garden. Dappled light shining through the windows illuminated the piles of clothes and gave the veneer of dust on every surface a golden luminescence.

"Pig," Kat said.

"Yeah, but it's a gorgeous room anyway, don't you think?"

"Hmm."

"Is that the shower running?" I asked, but Kat had already pulled open the door to the bathroom and begun to scream.

Two

ALICIA Felix's was not the first dead body I'd ever seen, but I think it would take years of experience in crime-scene investigation before one became inured to the sight of a naked woman slumped against the wall of her bathtub, her chest and belly defaced with a scrawl of stab wounds. I reached the bathroom door in time to catch Kat as she tottered backwards. I held my friend up with one arm as I stared at the grim scene in the small, white-tiled room. Kat sagged against me, her face buried in her hands, her chest heaving. I looked at the dead woman for only a moment, but what I saw seared itself into my memory. This was a hideously violent murder. The poor woman's torso had been hacked and torn, nearly shredded. Her wide-open eyes had a milky quality, as though a haze had lowered over them as life seeped away. Her body looked rigid, almost like a grotesque statue, particularly around the neck and jaw. Her skin was mottled; above the flesh was white and waxy, but what I

could see of the bottom was purple, the color of a deep
bruise. Postmortem lividity, the pooling and settling of the
blood in response to gravity. The shower was still running,
washing her body with a constant stream, and thus there
was very little blood spilled anywhere at all. I could see only
the smallest smudge just underneath the woman's shoulders
and neck, which were bent to one side by the protruding
taps of the shower.

What made the starkest impression on me, however, was
not so much what had been done to her, although that
was certainly awful, it was rather the *shape* of the woman's
body. She was, in a word, emaciated. Her legs were long and
horribly thin, withered as if by a wasting disease. Her knees
bulged larger than her thighs, contrasting starkly with her
skin-draped femur and tibia bones. Her ribs and the gullies
between them were clearly visible even despite the stab
wounds. Her clavicles stood out from her neck, nearly fram-
ing her bony jaw. The only hint of fleshiness about her body
was the one breast, the right, that had not been horrifically
mutilated. It sat, perfectly round, obviously fake, in the
brutalized expanse of her chest.

I slowly backed out of the doorway, pushing Kat behind
me. I settled her on the edge of the bed, but then remembered that the room was a crime scene. The whole house was
one, and Kat and I had wandered through it freely, stomping across the floors and carpets, handling everything, probably obliterating all signs of the murderer. I grasped Kat
more firmly around the shoulders, heaved her off the bed,
and together we stumbled out to the courtyard. I sat her
down in one of the wrought-iron lounge chairs in the garden. She leaned her head back on the white muslin cushion,
her eyes still closed. I don't think she had opened them since
she'd first seen the body. I reached into my purse, pulled out

my cellphone, and dialed 911. Then I called Al. He asked
no questions, just took down the address and hung up the
phone.

Kat and I sat in silence while we waited for the police to
arrive. A gnarled and lush jasmine vine grew up a trellis
nailed to the side of the guesthouse, and the air was redolent
with the blossoms' heady fragrance. I closed my eyes and inhaled deeply, relishing the smell, the steady beat of my heart,
and the sun warming my flushed cheeks. It felt, for a moment, as if Kat and I were ensconced on a tiny island of sweet-
smelling tranquility, the twittering of birds and the steady
hum of our breath the only sound that disturbed the silence.

In a few minutes, however, I heard the faint shriek of police sirens, and got up to open the front door to the four uniformed officers that were the first of the hordes that soon
invaded; their loud voices, heavy footsteps, and barking ra-
dios banishing every trace of that odd moment of serenity.

THE supervising detective seemed a bit taken aback at
the sight of two heavily pregnant women rolling around
in the middle of his crime scene. In addition to asking us
the same long series of questions about who we were, what
we were doing there, and what we had seen, that we had already answered for the uniformed officers who arrived first
on the scene, and again for the detectives who had shown up
fifteen minutes later, he grilled us about how we knew each
other, even going so far as to request a description of the
prenatal yoga class in which we'd met. I watched him carefully jot down the name and address of the yoga studio, and
did my best not to express frustration at the thoroughness of
his inquisition. This was, after all, his job. He had no way of
knowing at this stage of the investigation what clues, what

individuals, would come to be important. Kat and I, as the discoverers of the body, were, of course, his first and so far only possible suspects.

I was in the middle of recounting, for the third time, what we had been doing in the house, when Al arrived.

My partner walked into the yard, flanked by police officers. One of them, a grizzled man who seemed too old to be a cop at all, let alone a uniformed officer, called out to the detective, "Hey, this is Al Hockey. He used to be on the job. He knows the redhead."

I gave Al a relieved smile, and he winked at me. He extended his hand to the detective, whose brusque manner had already begun to dissipate.

"My partner giving you some trouble?" Al asked.

"Your partner?" the detective said.

"I've been doing some private security work since I retired. Juliet works with me."

"Al left kicking and screaming," the older officer said. "Bullet took him out, but he'd still be here if it weren't for that."

The detective nodded. "I'm about done with my questions," he began. Just then, we were interrupted by a piercing shriek.

"What's going on here? What are you all doing here?" A small woman with pitted olive skin meticulously covered by a smooth sheen of expensive make-up, was standing in the French doors, hands on her hips, her face twisted into an anxious scowl. "What happened?" she yelled.

The detective heaved himself laboriously to his feet and walked over to the woman. At the sound of her voice, Kat had finally roused herself from her stupor. She had not been able to answer the police officers' questions with much more than whispered monosyllables, and I was worried that she was in some kind of shock. Now, she glanced over at the woman and groaned, "Oh, God."

"What? Who is that?"

"My mother-in-law."

Nahid Lahidji's eyes were hidden behind a vast pair of Jackie O sunglasses, but she certainly didn't seem old enough to be Kat's husband's mother. She had the clothes for it, though. She looked exactly like what she was, a fabulously successful Beverly Hills real estate agent. Her trim body was encased in a chartreuse Chanel suit with large gold buttons and matching stiletto pumps. Her black hair was sprayed into a bobbed helmet, and her diamond earrings flashed in the sun. Her thin wrists were heavy with bracelets and bangles, and her lipstick was fire engine red.

Mrs. Lahidji blew by the detective as if she hadn't even noticed his presence. "Katayoun! What's happened here? Why are the police here? What have you done?"

"What?" I asked, dumbfounded at the absurd accusation. I turned back to Kat, expecting her to blow up at this tiny, designer-clad, green goblin, only to see her close her eyes once again.

"Katayoun! I'm talking to you!" the woman said sharply.

By now the detective had caught up with her. "Excuse me, ma'am," he said, "I'm going to have to ask you a few questions."

She spun on one elegantly appointed heel. "One minute. I'm talking to my daughter-in-law!"

"Mrs. Lahidji," I interrupted. "I'm Juliet Applebaum, and Kat was showing me the house. I'm afraid we found a body in the guesthouse."

"A body!" she shrieked. "The house isn't even on the market yet!"

I was not quite sure what to make of that comment. Was it standard procedure to dump a body only *after* the house had an official MLS listing?

The detective finally managed to refocus Kat's mother-in-law's attention on him.

"Ma'am?" he said. "I'll need to know your name."

"My name?"

"Yes, ma'am."

"Nahid Lahidji. And who might you be?"

The cop identified himself and asked her whether she knew the name of the deceased.

She replied, "A woman? Blond? Fake boobs?"

"Well, I, uh, I couldn't make a definitive call about the breast implants," he said, looking a little embarrassed. "But yes, a blond woman."

"In the guesthouse?" Nahid barked.

He nodded.

"Then it must be the owner's sister. God knows there wouldn't be any reason for another woman to be on the property."

"Do you know her name?"

"Of course I do. This is my listing!"

"Nahidjoon, please." Kat whispered. Nahid paid not the slightest attention to her.

"Ma'am?" the detective asked softly, almost tentatively. Why, I wondered, did the man seem so utterly cowed by this miniature tyrant?

"*Felix,* like her brother. Her first name is Alicia. She's an actress."

Three

I felt terrible leaving Kat in the clutches of her terrifying mother-in-law, but by the time the detectives released us I was desperate to get home. I'd called Peter and asked him to pick Ruby up from school, and had found out that Isaac's stomach flu had returned with a vengeance. I hated the idea of Peter taking him out, even just to do a carpool run, but not even Al could convince the detective that I was needed at home. In fact, he didn't intimidate the supervising detective anywhere near as much as the diminutive Nahid Lahidji did. It was Kat's mother-in-law who got us sprung. After she had engaged in a conversation with the detective in which she'd asked as many questions as she'd answered, she turned to me.

"Business card," she snapped.

"Excuse me?" I said. By then I'd become as silent as Kat.

"Give me your business card. And your driver's license, too."

I proffered the requested documents wordlessly.

"Katayoun!" she said. Kat roused herself, reached into her purse, and handed Nahid her wallet. The older woman rummaged through it, *tsk*ing at the jumble of cards and bills until she found Kat's driver's license. She then reached into her trim gold purse and pulled out a sparking card case. She snapped it open, removed a thick business card printed on creamy ochre paper, tapped all the cards into a neat pile, and handed them to the detective.

"Check the names against the licenses," she said. "And then we're leaving. My daughter-in-law and her friend need to get home. As you can see, they are both in a delicate physical condition."

The detective leafed through the small stack of documents and then handed our driver's licenses back to us. "We'll be needing to talk to you again," he said.

"Of course," I replied.

"We'll see," Nahid said. She poked Kat and said, "Katayoun. Up. We're going home."

Kat struggled to her feet, and I reached out a hand to help her. She shook her head at me, rubbed her eyes once, and then stood up. "I'm okay. Nahidjoon, I'm fine."

Nahid clucked her tongue. Then she turned back to the detective. "I assume when you're done here you'll clean up after yourself. I'm planning an open house for next week, and I can't have you making a disgusting mess here."

His jaw dropped, but by then the woman had spun on her heels and was halfway across the yard to the outside gate, dragging my friend along behind her.

I turned to Al, expecting him to escort me out, but he shook his head slightly. "I'm going to hang out here for a while," he whispered to me. "See if I can't get in to see the body. You go on."

Kat and her mother-in-law had already driven away by the time I got out to the front of the house, and it was a moment before I remembered that I'd left my car in the parking lot at the Coffee Bean & Tea Leaf. Nahid had hustled Kat into her own car, and Kat's Mercedes was still on the street in front of the house. I debated waiting for Al to drive me, but, it wasn't more than a fifteen or twenty minute walk home. In the middle of the trek, I realized that while I'd routinely walked dozens of blocks when I lived in New York City, since Peter and I had transplanted ourselves to the City of Angels—and of SUVs—my walking had been pretty much limited to trips to and from various parking lots, and the odd, desperate perambulation with a stroller, trying to convince a crying baby to nod off. I'd certainly never attempted a mile or so in this late stage of pregnancy. But the walk, or should I say waddle, was good for me. By the time I got home, I had managed to calm myself down sufficiently to fool the kids, if not my husband. We spent what remained of the afternoon playing Chutes and Ladders. Peter seemed to understand that I wasn't in any shape to be alone, so he hung out with me and the kids. He hadn't cleaned up the bathroom after Isaac's latest adventure in emesis, but only because we have always had an unofficial division of labor that makes disposing of the children's various effluvia my purview. There are other household unpleasantnesses my husband assumes responsibility for, including dealing with the cars, plumbing problems, and his mother. Trust me, it's an even trade.

It was only after we got the kids to bed that I could collapse on the couch and recount to my husband the horror that I'd witnessed.

"So the shower didn't have any effect on the progress of

the rigor?" Peter said, when I was done describing the state of the actress's body.

"Peter!" I said.

"What? It might come in handy some day."

I shook my head. You'd think after eight years of marriage I'd be used to my husband's voracious appetite for the disgusting detail.

He suddenly seemed to remember that we were talking about a real person, and not one of his celluloid corpses. He reached an arm around me and snuggled me closer to him.

"It was pretty awful," I said, leaning my head against his chest. "Mrs. Lahidji said the woman was an actress. Alicia Felix. I've never heard of her, have you?"

He shook his head. Then he reached under the couch and pulled out the laptop he'd stashed there when I'd walked in the door. I had pretended not to notice that he had been sitting on the couch playing on his computer while the kids wrestled on the carpet, and I didn't comment now. He tapped on the computer for a while. Peter had set us up with an Airport, so we could get a wireless connection to the Internet from anywhere in the house.

"Here she is," he said. "I found her on TV-Phile."

I lifted my head and looked at the screen.

The headshot that decorated Alicia Felix's page on TV-Phile.com, a website devoted to the minutiae of canceled television shows and former personalities, was the same one I had seen in her apartment. It showed a gamine-faced blond woman with a thick head of tousled hair and a pout that somehow managed to look both sexy and innocent at the same time.

Alicia had an impressive list of television credits. She had appeared in guest roles on almost every major sitcom and drama in the late 1980s and early 1990s. She had even had a recurring role in a short-lived drama that I remembered watching when I was in law school. It had featured a cast of stunningly attractive prosecuting attorneys, and a few of us had gathered weekly to watch the show in the student lounge. We weren't fans; rather our purpose was to jeer with our newfound expertise at the glaring errors and misrepresentations in the cases on the television lawyers' make-believe dockets. I couldn't honestly remember this Alicia; there had been too many young blond females in the cast.

Beyond the early 1990s, there were fewer and fewer entries for Alicia. The last listing was in 1997: she had had nothing since.

"What happened after 1997?" I asked Peter.

"Maybe she moved into film." He clicked over to the part of the site devoted to filmographies. Inputing Alicia Felix's name resulted in no hits.

"Does that mean she didn't do any movies? Do they have every single actor listed online? Or could she have had some small roles that don't show up?" I asked.

Peter wrinkled his forehead. "I think the site is pretty thorough. I mean, I know that the casting agents on our movies use it to dredge up information even on the most unknown person who auditions for us. I think this has got to mean she never made a movie."

"Huh." I leaned back on the couch and heaved my legs into his lap, pushing aside the computer. "Will you rub my feet, sweetie? Is helps me think."

Peter lifted my left foot. "It's like a little, tiny sausage bursting out of its casing," he said, poking the swollen skin. His finger left an indentation on my ankle.

"That's nice, honey." I jerked my foot away. "Way to make me feel good."

"Oh stop it." He took my foot back in his warm palms

and began rubbing. "You know I think you're fat little feet are adorable."

"Yeah, right."

He tickled my toes and I giggled. "I do," he said. "You're the cutest pregnant woman around."

I sighed. "You wouldn't say that if you knew Kat. She's gorgeous. She looks like a supermodel who happens to have swallowed a basketball. A very neat, petite little basketball."

Peter reached his arms around my waist and heaved me on to his lap, grunting loudly. "I prefer women who look like basketballs, not women who look like they swallow them."

I leaned against his chest, first checking to make sure that I wasn't crushing the life out of him. Why am I one of those pregnant women who blows up to cosmic proportions? Why can't I be like Kat, or like the other Santa Monica matrons at my yoga studio?

"How about a root beer float?" Peter asked.

Aha. The answer to my question. "Sure," I said, rolling off his lap.

I followed my husband out to the kitchen, and while he scooped vanilla ice cream into the soda fountain glasses he'd bought me for our anniversary the year before, I mused aloud about Alicia Felix's career.

"Maybe she stopped getting parts because she got too thin," I said. "It was disgusting. She looked like an Auschwitz survivor."

Peter popped the top off four different bottles of root beer. He was involved in a systematic and painstaking analysis of all commercial root beer brands, including ones available only over the Internet at shocking prices. There were literally two hundred single bottles and cans of root beer taking over our pantry. Every night we had to taste-test at least a few. And I wondered why I was so fat. He carefully poured root beer into the ice cream–filled glasses, careful not to the let any liquid foam over the top.

"I doubt that's why she stopped getting cast," he said. "There's no such thing as too thin in Hollywood. You would not believe what some of those starlets look like in their bikinis."

Peter's most recent film, *The Cannibal's Vacation,* was shot on an island in Indonesia. He was currently pretending to be hard at work on the prequel, *Beach Blanket Bloodfest.*

"Oh really? And just how careful an analysis did you make of these gorgeous women in their bathing suits?"

Actually, I was only pretending to be jealous. My husband is adorable, in that kind of thick glasses, mussy hair, skinny, and pale-skin way that seemed lately to have become so fashionable. He pretty much epitomizes nerd-chic. I'm okay-looking, for an average woman. Pretty even, when I'm not bloated with pregnancy. However, in Hollywood, pretty in a normal way just doesn't cut it. Everyone here is beautiful, and if they aren't naturally so, they pay top dollar to get that way. It's enough to make anyone insecure.

"Oh, you know me," Peter said. "Ogling all day and all night. Actually, if you want to know the truth, I did spend a lot of time looking at them. But it was more scientific curiosity. There's something almost extra-terrestrial about those skinny girls with the big boobs. They don't look *human.*"

I leaned over and kissed my husband on the lips. "Thanks, honey. You're so loyal."

He buried his head in my chest. "At least I know these are real." He sat up and handed me a root beer float. "Taste this one."

I slurped.

"This one any better?" He handed me the other glass.

"I guess so. But honestly, honey, they all taste more or less the same to me."

He shook his head and sighed. "You have such a primitive palate."

I took another long sip, and said, "Delicious. So, if the concentration camp look isn't a deterrent, then why hasn't Alicia Felix been able to get any work for the past five years?"

Peter lifted his head and got his own drink. "How old was she?"

"I don't know."

He went to the living room and retrieved his computer. He clicked back to the TV-Phile site.

"Says here that she was born in 1973."

I wrinkled my brow. "So she's thirty?"

"Maybe, but I doubt it."

"What do you mean?"

"Her first credit is as "Bereaved Young Mother" on *St. Elsewhere* in 1983. Something tells me that by 'young' they didn't mean ten years old. She's got to have been at least twenty then. Or been able to play twenty. That makes her birthdate no later than 1963. Or 1964, if she could play old."

I leaned forward and stared at the screen. "No way. She took ten years off her age?"

"It's pretty common," Peter said. "You wouldn't believe who shows up when we put out a casting call for a high school student. Women *your* age walk in and try to fake seventeen!"

"That old and decrepit, huh?" I said.

"You know what I mean. You're young and gorgeous, but, baby, I hate to break it to you, you ain't seen twenty in a long, long time."

"Fifteen years," I said.

"Yeah, well, for an actress like Alicia Felix, thirty-five is old, and forty is the kiss of death. If she was that old, that explains why her career dried up."

I sighed, slurping up the rest of my drink. "That just sucks," I said.

Peter nodded.

"Why is it okay for some of these ancient actors to play virile young men well into their sixties and seventies, but a forty-year-old woman can't get work?"

Peter opened his mouth, but I didn't allow him to get a word in edgewise. I was on a roll. "I mean, do they really expect us to believe that some gorgeous thirty-year-old would ever be married to Sean Connery, or Michael Douglas? Those guys are like sixty years old!"

"Um, babe?"

"What?"

"Catherine Zeta Jones. Married to Michael Douglas."

"Oh. Right. Still . . ."

"It's unfair," Peter said. "But that's Hollywood. Just be grateful you're not in the business."

"Poor Alicia. It doesn't look like she was in the business anymore, either."

Four

"I want a hard-boiled egg. And a Tab," Ruby said.

"And what?" I was pouring breakfast cereal into bowls, tying Isaac's shoes, and carefully padding Ruby's class project, a diorama of her grandfather on skis (long story), with wadded paper towels so that it wouldn't get crushed in transit to school. All at the same time.

"A Tab."

"A tab of what?" I asked, wondering if it was really possible that LSD had made it to the first grade set.

"A Tab of soda."

"Ruby!" I said, more sharply than I should have. "Speak English."

"I am!" she yowled in righteous indignation. "I do not want cereal! Cereal is yucky! I want a Tab soda and a hard-boiled egg!"

I dropped Isaac's foot, carefully set the shoebox diorama down on the counter, and turned to my daughter, doing my best not to yell. "A *diet soda?*" I said through gritted teeth.

"Yes. Milk is sugary. And sugar makes you fat. And cereal is just stretch, and stretch makes you fat, too. I want an egg, and Tab."

"First of all, it's starch, not stretch, and second of all, how do you even know what Tab is?"

"It's the best diet soda. Better than *Diet Coke.* Madison says so. Madison's mommy lets *her* have it. She buys it at a special store. A store for skinny women." She paused and looked at me critically. "I don't think you've ever been there."

I counted silently to ten, poured milk into the two cereal bowls, and set them in front of my children. Isaac picked up his spoon and began eating. Ruby scowled down at the little yellow balls bobbing in the milk.

"Eat," I said.

She rolled her eyes at me.

"Now."

"Whatever," she said, and lifted her spoon to her lips.

I sat down at the table next to her. "Honey, what's going on with you? Why are you thinking so much about diet stuff? Is it because of Madison? Did she say something to you?"

Ruby didn't answer.

"Honey?"

She picked up her bowl, drank her milk and cereal down in a few huge swallows, and clambered down out of her chair. As she walked to the sink to deposit her bowl and spoon, I looked at her sturdy legs, her bubble butt (something she inherited from her mother), and her waist, still untapered.

"Rubes, come here," I said.

She came over to me, leaned against my legs, and put her

head on my belly. "Hi, baby," she said, sounding a little glum.

"Tell me what's going on, Ruby?"

She sighed and, without lifting her head of my stomach, said, "Madison, Chinasa, and Hannah are on diets. And I want to be on a diet, too."

"Why, sweetie? Why would you want to go on a diet? You're gorgeous. Your body is perfect! You're strong and powerful. You're not fat at all!"

"I know," she said.

I lifted her face in my palms and forced her to look at me. "Well if you know that, why do you want to be on a diet?"

"Because *everybody* is on a diet. All the girls in first grade. Everybody wants to be like Madison's mom. She's really skinny. She can wear Madison's pants!"

"No way!"

"Yeah, she can!"

It's a measure of how sick *I* am that for a brief moment I felt admiration for a thirty-something-year-old woman who could fit into her six-year-old's clothes. Then I came to my senses. "I don't believe that. And if it's true, then it's just sick. Honey, normal women can't wear their little girl's clothes. Normal women just aren't that small."

"Madison's mom isn't *normal*," Ruby said, with disgust at the very idea. "Madison's mom is a *model!*"

"Well, that explains it. Models are insane. All of them. They have a grave mental illness. And I don't want you listening to Madison anymore. Tab! Please. You're a beautiful girl with a beautiful body. And that's the end of it. Okay?"

Ruby shook herself free of my hands. "Okay," she said, and wafted morosely out of the kitchen.

At that moment, as if to punctuate her exit, there was the sound of a huge crash, immediately followed by jack-hammering. Our neighbors were beginning the demolition of their house. We'd received notification a few months before that the young couple who had bought the duplex from the elderly brother and sister who had lived there for the previous sixty years planned to raze the place and build a McMansion on virtually the entire lot. We hadn't paid much attention—after all, we were renters, and had little interest in the effects of the neighbors' activities on property values. For some reason the sheer *volume* of the construction project had not occurred to me. I wrapped my bathrobe around my waist and ran down the steps to our front door, hoping to catch the workers before they woke my husband.

"Excuse me!" I shouted at the hard-hat-clad young man wielding the jack-hammer.

No reply.

"Excuse me!" I shouted, again.

This time he raised his eyes, but pointed at his ears and shook his head. That's when I noticed that he was wearing heavy plastic earphones. Lucky him. I waved my hands in the air, and he finally switched off the machine and took off his earphones.

"Yeah?" he said.

"Can you guys wait to do that? My husband works at night, and he sleeps in the morning. You're going to wake him up."

"Huh?" he said.

"My husband isn't going to be able to sleep if you guys keep jack-hammering!" I said.

"Lady, we're working here."

"I know that!" I said, exasperated. "But isn't there some more quiet thing you could be doing? Couldn't you leave the jack-hammering until after lunch?"

He shook his head. "Lady, city ordinances allow us to begin construction at 8 AM."

"I'm not asking you to stop. I'm just asking if there isn't something more quiet you could do in the mornings."

He shook his head, put his earphones back on his head, and revved up his machine again.

Defeated, I walked back up the stairs to our apartment. I found Peter huddled at the kitchen table, his head in his hands.

"I went to bed at four," he said.

"I know, honey. I'm really sorry. There's nothing I can do. The city lets them start at eight."

"How long is this going to go on?"

"I don't know. Months, I imagine. Maybe even longer. I mean, they're taking the thing down to the ground and rebuilding from scratch."

"Juliet," my exhausted husband whispered. "Please go find us a house. Any house. As long as it's quiet."

I thought of the bucolic garden in which Kat and I had waited for the police. The jasmine plants. The twittering birds. And the house! The giant tub. The Sub-Zero. The mangled corpse. I pushed that last image firmly from my mind and picked up the telephone.

"You don't want that house!" Kat said, dumbfounded.

"Yeah, I do."

"But someone was killed there! We found her body!"

"I know."

"How could you live there after that?"

I looked over at my husband, drooping in misery over a cup of steaming coffee.

"Easily."

She let out an exasperated groan. "Anyway, you can't afford it."

"I couldn't afford it two days ago, but I'm betting there's some wiggle room in the price now, don't you think?"

"That's sick!"

"Kat, just do me a favor. Find out what the asking price is. And help me make an offer. I want that house."

"Oh, all right. But you know what?"

"What?"

"You are a *sick* person. Really."

I laughed. "I'm not sick. I'm just *cheap*."

Five

WITH Peter awake and able, more or less, to help me get the kids into gear, we were dressed and ready for school almost on time. Before I had kids I never had the problems with tardiness with which I've been plagued ever since. I used to blithely juggle court dates, visits to prisons, interviews of witnesses, and appearances before the appellate court with an aplomb that I thought came naturally to me. My first inkling that parenthood was going to have a drastic effect on my competence was the first time I showed up late for jury selection. I had actually made it to the courthouse in plenty of time. It was the twenty minutes I spent crouched in the ladies room, trying to haul my maternity pantyhose back up over my bloated thighs and mountainous belly, that made me late. My favorite moment wasn't waddling into court, sweat streaming from my forehead, the crotch of my stockings hovering at about knee level. It wasn't even reassuring my client that all was well while I tried surreptitiously to make sure my skirt wasn't tucked up into the waistband of my underwear. No, the crowning moment of my career was when the judge called me up to the sidebar and made me explain my tardiness. And forgot to cover the microphone with her hand.

My attempts to balance work and home kind of went downhill from there. Thus I found myself, six years later, working only a few hours a week, and paying more in late fines to my son's preschool than the monthly tuition—they billed me ten bucks for every ten minutes I was late to pick the little guy up. Extortion, if you ask me.

Peter succumbed to the children's entreaties and agreed to drive them to school. Actually, I think what got him out of the house wasn't really a burst of paternal devotion, but rather the realization that it was Wednesday, and if he ran the morning carpool he could make it to Golden Apple as soon as it opened and be the first uber-geek in line to buy the brand new Promethea and Top Ten.

I took a more languid shower than usual—three minutes rather than thirty seconds—and called Al while I was getting dressed.

"So?" I said my voice slightly muffled by the oversized T-shirt I was pulling over my head.

"So what?" he answered.

"So did you see the body?"

"Yeah."

"And?"

"Typical sex crime. At least that's what it looks like now."

I shivered. "And what's going on with the rats?"

He sighed.

"Are they still there?"

"Yup."

"And?"

"And now it seems some of them are dead. At least it smells that way. We don't know where they are, though. Maybe under the floor, or in the walls."

I gagged, which made putting on lipstick something of a challenge. "No way I'm showing up, Al."

"So what else is new?"

I felt a flash of defensive indignation, but the truth was, he was right. The days I actually made it in to work were dramatically outnumbered by the days I didn't. Still, it wasn't like I took any money out of his pocket. I billed the clients for the hours I worked. The very few hours I worked.

"Anyway, what have we got on today?"

Al sighed. "Barely more than nothing. Just that witness investigation out of Texas. The referral from that friend of yours from law school. I tracked down the address of the witness. He's up by you. In Inglewood."

One of my best friends from law school, Sandra Babcock, had become the terror of the Texas bar. She was an aggressive and talented defense lawyer, operating out of Houston. That made her something of an anomaly in a state where it often seems like most indigent defendants are represented by attorneys whose sole qualification for a career in criminal defense is their ability to catch a nap at counsel table. The appellate court for the Fifth District, perhaps because it understood that it would otherwise force two thirds of local counsel out of business, actually ruled that sleeping through trial does not qualify as ineffective assistance of counsel, a decision which has been a real boon for the hung over and narcoleptic members of the Texas bar, and something of an aggravation for Sandra, whose pro bono clients outnumber her paying ones three or four to one.

She had called a week before, asking for help on a case. One of her clients, a young woman, had been fingered by a

DEA informant who claimed to have passed her three kilos of cocaine for processing into crack. The defendant, a twenty-one-year-old college student, had insisted that she was in Los Angeles visiting family at the time the deal was supposed to have gone down. Sandra had called and asked us to track down the family members with whom she was staying and get witness statements from them. She was hoping that the statements would help in her motion to dismiss the charges. Meanwhile, because it was Texas, the poor kid was rotting in jail, bail not being something the judge felt obligated to provide to an African-American in a drug case, no matter how patently false the charges.

"Why don't I do it?" I said. "There's no reason for you to schlep all the way up here, and, anyway, who knows when or if we'll get paid for this case." Sandra would bill the government for our time, but if she were to receive reimbursement at all, it wouldn't be for a good long while.

"Okay," Al said. "You're better at chatting up regular folk, anyway." That certainly is true. There's no one like Al for getting the low lifes to spill their guts, but somehow his skills often fail him when confronted with decent, law-abiding citizens. I think the truth is that after twenty-five years on the force, Al just has a hard time believing that there's any such thing as an honest person. My years as a public defender certainly infected me with this cynicism, and it has been more than validated by my experiences sticking my nose into private investigations. I've seen some pretty straight-seeming people do some pretty awful things. Still, unlike my partner, my belief in the fundamental integrity of at least some members of the human race has not gasped its final breath. Who knows how long that will last?

Inglewood is one those strange Los Angeles neighborhoods whose benign, even charming, appearance belies its frightening crime statistics. Little cottages flanked by palm trees and jacaranda bushes nestle on small squares of lawn. There are bicycles leaning against porch steps, and kids playing hopscotch and basketball on the sidewalks. It's only at second glance that you notice the metal bars on the windows and doors, and realize that there are few if any older people sitting out on their porches, even in the warmth of a Los Angeles winter morning. They are bolted and barred in their houses, too afraid of flying bullets and warring children to risk the sun-dappled streets. The young people are out, congregating on the corners, leaning against the broken streetlights and staring at the passing cars with eyes vacant of any expression other than vague menace.

In my years at the public defender's office I'd represented many boys like these. And they *were* boys, still in their teens, although they had lived through enough violence and fear for men twice their ages. It had taken me many hours to get through to these young men, to convince them that I, a white woman from a background so dissimilar to their own that it might have been another country, another era, another world, would represent them not just honestly, but passionately. I'm ashamed to say that many of them never believed me. The ones to whom I got through weren't necessarily those who ended up being acquitted. Like most public defenders, I had relatively few of those—my clients were pretty much always guilty of the bank robberies and drug deals with which they'd been charged. Every so often, however, I made one of them understand that I cared about him, that I knew that underneath the tough hoodlum he presented to the world was a young boy with the same fears and dreams as any other boy, from any other neighborhood, including my own. Those guys stayed in touch with me, writing me long letters from prison, occasionally bragging of their successes in getting their GEDs, or maintaining contact with their girlfriends and children. Many if not most of them ended up back in prison after their releases, but every once in a while there was one who turned his life around. I wasn't arrogant enough to believe I was the cause of the transformation, but I knew it didn't hurt that somewhere in the system he had met someone who took the time to care about him.

I pulled up in front of a small pink house set back from the street. The owners had given up the fight against crab grass and LA drought, and had ripped up their lawn, laid down cement, and painted the whole thing an almost ironic shade of grass green. They'd done their best with window boxes of nasturtiums and geraniums, and there were a few bright blooms poking out from behind the wrought-iron bars covering the windows. An ancient and impeccably maintained Lincoln Continental hunkered down in the driveway, its fins casting sharp shadows across the flat, emerald pseudo-lawn.

I pulled into the driveway behind the Lincoln, careful not to get too close to the highly polished rear bumper. I flipped down my mirror, applied some modest, girly pink lipstick, and buttoned my white cardigan up to the neck. Different witnesses respond to different things, and I'm always careful to look the part—whatever that might be. Given the tidy house, window boxes, and thirty year old car, I was betting that the house contained an elderly couple who would be most likely to confide in a nicely but unassumingly turned out matron. And I was right.

The door was answered by a woman in her late seventies, wearing a flowered dress and a cotton sweater that was the twin of my own. Her sparse white hair was arranged carefully on her head, not quite concealing the mahogany sheen of her scalp, and she had an ironed pink handkerchief tucked into her sleeve. The only affront to the impeccably maintained order of her person was the puffy, veined ankles protruding from a pair of pale blue terrycloth slippers. She had crushed down the backs of the slippers, and her heels hung, cracked and swollen, over the edges. I wriggled my toes as best I could in my too-tight Joan and David navy blue pumps. At this stage of my pregnancy, my feet looked more like those of this old woman than I cared to contemplate.

"Hello," I said, extending my hand. "My name is Juliet Applebaum, and I work for your niece, Lara."

The woman shook my hand firmly and moved aside to let me in. "Yvette Kennedy. Very pleased to make your acquaintance. My sister told me that someone might be coming to talk about her poor child. You come on in."

She led me into the front room, a small neat parlor with carpeting the precise color of the cement lawn. I perched on the edge of a pale pink sofa, marveling at how long it had been since I'd felt the sticky tug of clear vinyl slip-covers beneath my thighs. The only seat in the tidy room not thus protected was a taupe Barcalounger whose cracked pleather seemed not to warrant defense against assault by the human behind. Or, perhaps, it was simply that the recliner had never been empty long enough to allow it to be wrapped in protective sheeting. The old man ensconced in its depths appeared to have been there for the last two or three decades.

"Mr. Kennedy," the old woman said, gently, waking the man from his slumber. He startled, and wiped the corner of his mouth with one large hand. His fingers were smooth and bloated, twisted with age and arthritis. Nothing could hide, however, the massive expanse of palm, and it was clear that this had once, a long, long time ago, been a very powerful man. "We have a visitor."

He looked at me, and then at his wife. "Mrs. Kennedy?" he asked. His voice was deep and hoarse, but time and sleep had rendered it more of a purr than a growl.

"It's about Etta Jean's girl. You know."

He grunted and pushed a bar on the side of his chair. The leg rest swung down, and the back moved upright. He put his hands on his knees and turned his attention to me. He rubbed his gnarled fist across his cinnamon-colored cheek and said, "A gross miscarriage of justice, is what that is."

"I agree, sir," I said.

"I marched with Dr. King in Selma," he said, shaking his head. "You'd have told me then that forty years later we'd be looking at this kind of thing, I would have gone on home. Not bothered missing a day's work."

"Now you just stop, Mr. Kennedy," his wife interrupted. "One has nothing to do with the other."

He sighed loudly, and shook his head.

"Mr. Kennedy. Mrs. Kennedy," I said. "Your niece Lara claims she was here visiting you in August of this year. Is that true?"

"It surely is," the old woman says.

"Are you positive about the date?" I asked.

"Absolutely," her husband replied.

"Really?" I asked. Most people don't remember dates and times with quite this certitude.

The woman nodded, her stiff hair bobbing with the vigorous motion of her head. "There's no mistaking it. Mr. Kennedy is a deacon at our church, First African Methodist, over on Thirty-Seventh Avenue. Lara was with us during the summer baptisms. She came to the Lord, she did. Blessed be his name."

"Amen," her husband said, so loudly it made me jump.

This was about as good as I could ever have hoped. Better even. Nothing like a baptism for an alibi to turn a case around.

"Would you like to see the photographs?" Mrs. Kennedy asked.

I nodded, and to my delight soon found myself leafing through an envelope of pictures clearly stamped with the date and time. There was a series of photos of white-clad young people being dipped backwards into something that looked a lot like the birthing tubs I'd seen advertised for rent in the back of *Mothering Magazine*. Maybe those tubs doubled as baptismal fonts when they weren't being used by natural-minded home-birthers.

"That's Etta Jean's girl, right there," Mrs. Kennedy said, pointing a finger at a rail-thin girl whose robes hung loosely on her gaunt frame.

My complacent glee at the sureness of an acquittal ebbed. Lara had the telltale, hollow-cheeked, brittle-haired look of a crack addict. Her aunt must have noticed my dismay, because she clicked her tongue.

"She looks bad in this picture, I know," she said.

I didn't deny it.

"By the end of her time with us, she was much improved. Much. Isn't that so, Mr. Kennedy?"

Her husband nodded vigorously. "Indeed. That is the truth. She got off that plane, I didn't think she'd be able to walk to the car. Honestly I didn't. But she got back on it a few months later with a spring in her step. Yes she did."

"Was she . . ." I paused, not wanted to insult this sweet older couple. But there was no getting around it, Sandra had hired me to do a job, and do it I must. "Was she using drugs, do you think?"

"No! Of course not," Mrs. Kennedy said sharply.

"Now Mrs. Kennedy, you calm down," her husband said. "You can see why she would ask. Of course you can." He turned to me. "It wasn't the drugs got that girl. She was making her own self sick, no help from any drugs."

"What do you mean?"

"My sister sent her to us because Lara had been making herself ill," her aunt interrupted. "She'd put her finger down her throat, to make herself vomit."

"She was bulimic?" I asked.

"Yes, she was," Mr. Kennedy said. "And that Etta Jean was at the end of her rope. Never could control the girl. You know that's true," he admonished his wife, who had opened her mouth to object. "Never could do a thing with her. Well, we took that girl in, brought her to the Lord, and she kept her food down fine. Yes, she did."

Mrs. Kennedy smiled. "We fattened her right up. Look here." She pulled out another photograph. This girl in the picture was by no means fat, but she was a world away from what she'd looked like in the previous photograph. Her skin looked smoother, her hair was neatly ironed and turned under at the ends, and almost glossy. Her smile was broad. She looked happy. I felt a pang at the thought of what befell her once she'd returned home to Dallas. I was willing to bet all the money in my wallet that her bulimia had returned full force once she'd been thrown into jail.

I spoke to the Kennedys for a while longer, and then told them that I'd send typed witness statements for them to sign and return. I asked them if they'd mind if I took the photographs with me, promising that I'd be sure to have Sandra return them. I left confident that I'd helped Sandra win her case. The word of a deacon and his wife, and the timed, dated photographs, were surely all the alibi Lara would need to provide. Not even a Texas jury could ignore that evidence. There was even a chance that the prosecutor would see his way to dismissing the case before trial. Although, given that this would mean acknowledging what everyone else knew to be true—that his informant was a liar whose interest lay not in convicting actual criminals, but in protecting himself and keeping money flowing into his pockets—perhaps a dismissal was too much to hope for. When I'd worked at the Federal Defender, I'd come across all too many of this particular breed of informant scum. The most galling part of it all is the amount of my tax dollars the government blithely hands over to them as reward for their dishonesty. I'd been involved in cases where the confidential informant had earned millions of dollars setting up drug deals. Now, some of these guys certainly pulled in some actual drug dealers. After all, they were themselves involved in the business, and had been recruited precisely because of whom they knew. A shocking number, however, set up first-time offenders with no history of participation in drug crimes. I'd represented all too many of these folks, people whose sole involvement in the drug trade was at the behest of the informant. They were invariably facing ten-to-twenty-year sentences for their minor roles in drug conspiracies. At first I couldn't figure out why the informants would prey on this kind of person. Then it finally hit me; why turn state's evidence against some gangland thug who is bound to have someone track you down and exact retribution, when the DEA will pay you the same amount of money to set up a first-time loser? It's a simple question of personal safety, and your basic snitch is nothing if not wise in the ways of self-preservation.

On my way home from the Kennedys, I was overcome by an insurmountable urge. Right here, only ten or fifteen miles out of my way, was Beulah's Fried Chicken n' Waffles.

It really was too much to expect a pregnant woman to resist. On my way through the overwhelming LA traffic that was quite obviously conspiring with my obstetrician to keep me from my appointment with a platter of wings and thighs, I called Al.

"Where are you?" I asked him.

"Shooting range. Just leaving."

"Good. You're not too far. I'll buy you lunch. Beulah's."

He didn't even reply. He didn't need to. My favorite thing about Al is his encyclopedic knowledge of the lunch counters of the Los Angeles basin. We share a devotion to greasy, budget cuisine. It's what brought us together in the first place. When my first case was assigned to this gruff, sexist gun-toting ex-cop, I never imagined we'd end up friends. In fact, I vowed I'd never work with him again. I'm fairly confident he made the same promise to himself, when he saw me tripping through the office in a black leather miniskirt, acting like god's gift to criminal defense. A week later, after a day spent interviewing a passel of good-natured Hell's Angels, Al took me to Felipe's for a French dip. My first bite of the sandwich served to seal Al in my affections, and I think I earned my place in his when I devoured, in two bites, the purple pickled egg he handed me.

I was dipping my fried chicken in maple syrup when he walked through the door.

"Couldn't even wait?" he grumbled. But he grinned when a platter appeared before him as soon as his butt hit the chair. I'd gotten his order in at exactly the right moment.

While we gobbled our food, I told him about my success with the Texas case. When I was done recounting the tale, he waved a drumstick at me.

"Excellent luck. But will we get *paid?*"

"Sandra will file a request for investigation fees. We'll get something, I'm sure."

He wiped a stream of grease from his chin. "Well, thank God for that. Because we've got nothing on the calendar for the next two weeks."

"Nothing? Nothing at all?"

He shook his head. "Big goose egg. And I've got to pay for the rat problem."

I made a gagging sound. "I'll cover half."

"Nope," he sighed. "My house, my problem. Anyway, I hired a kid to help me out. Cheaper than the exterminator. Remember Julio Rodriguez? I've got him digging around under my house looking for the dead ones."

"He's out?" I asked. Julio was one of Al's protégés. He was a young kid with a talent for computers, who had used his skills in slightly less than legitimate ways. Rumor had it that it had taken upwards of a million dollars to close the holes he exposed in the Social Security Administrations computer system, and I'm pretty sure they never caught up to all the immigrants who benefited from Julio's early-amnesty green card program. The thing about Julio was that he never benefited, financially, from any of it. As far as any of us could tell, he did it all out of a kind of Robin Hood impulse, stealing legitimacy from the government to provide it to his family, friends, and neighbors. Money never changed hands at all.

"Yup. Supervised release, as of two months ago. Poor kid, damn probation won't let him work in the only trade he's got, so he's got to hunt rats for me." In hacker cases like Julio's, one of the conditions of release is always that there be no further contact with computers. It always seems sort of harsh to me. I mean, how's a guy supposed to get a job nowadays if he can't get near a computer? No wonder

Julio's reduced to scraping rat corpses out from under Al's garage.

Al patted his lips with a napkin and hunched forward in his chair. "We're in trouble, Juliet."

I nodded. I knew we were. "I've got five thousand dollars just sitting around in my separate checking account," I told him. "That should hold us for a couple more months. We could pay your salary, and the phone bill at least."

Al shook his head. "I'm not taking it from you."

"That's ridiculous. We're partners, Al. You've sunk money into this. Now it's my turn."

He dipped a finger into his syrup and swirled it around. "No can do."

"Al!" I said sharply. "I'm not willing to give up on us. We're just in a slump. Things were going great. We got paid a ton of money for the Jupiter Jones case. We had those worker's comp investigations. Sandra will get us paid. It's building. Slowly, but it's building."

He shrugged, and then changed the subject. "You doing okay?"

"You mean because of the murder?"

He nodded. Then, in a gruff voice, as if uncomfortable with his own attempt at empathy, he said, "I know it can be hard, first time you see something like that."

"Not as hard as being shot," I said. I spoke from experience. Bullet wounds were one of the few things Al and I had in common.

"I don't know. That's different," he said. At that moment, Al's cellphone rang, and he sent an inquiring glance in my direction. I nodded, and he licked the syrup off his fingers and answered the phone. I could tell by his tone that he was talking to one of his talented and beautiful daughters, the younger of whom was an FBI agent in Phoenix. He was probably in for a long chat, so I decided to do some calling of my own. I dialed Kat's number. She didn't sound entirely glad to hear from me.

"What's wrong?" I asked.

"Wrong? Nothing. I mean, nothing really. It's just that I don't think you're going to get that house."

"What do you mean?"

"My mother-in-law says they're not sure about selling. I mean, they aren't sure it's the right time. Right after Felix's sister's murder and everything."

I asked in frustration. "Why not? That's ridiculous. Don't they *want* to get out of there? Isn't the whole idea of living with such a horrible memory oppressive to them? I have to have it. We're bursting at the seams in our apartment, and that's even without the baby. Peter can't get any work done because of the construction project on our block. We have got to move. And damn it, Kat. That's *my* house."

"You are so morbid, Juliet. Really you are. Why would you *want* to live there?"

I didn't grace that comment with a response. After all, she had seen the living room. What was a dead body compared to hand-blown wall sconces?

"Let me show you some other houses," Kat said. I sighed. "Come on."

"You yourself said that everything out there is crap."

Now it was her turn to sigh. "Well, maybe something will turn up. I mean, this place did, right?"

I was just about to beg off another fruitless house-hunting expedition when I noticed Al trying to get my attention. "One second," I said to Kat.

"Possible insurance investigation," he said, holding his hand over the phone.

"Really? Where?"

"Pasadena."

I looked at my watch. "I've got to pick up the kids soon."

"Don't worry about it. I'll take the meeting myself."

I put my phone back to my ear. "Kat?" I said.

"So? Are you coming?"

"Sure. But is it okay if I bring the kids? I've got to pick them up from school in half an hour."

"That's fine," she said. "I've got Ashkon with me today. He and Isaac can entertain each other." Kat's son was a year younger than Isaac, and nearly three inches taller. He also outweighed my kid by a good twenty pounds. Isaac would never admit it, but Ashkon scared the bejeezus out of him.

"That'll be great," I said.

Al was wiping his mouth with a carefully folded napkin when I got off the phone.

"Good case?" I said.

"Probably not. But it's billable hours. And that's what matters, right?"

I nodded. "Call me and let me know how it goes."

six

KAT and I crammed our three kids into my station wagon, shoving the car seats in on top of each other in a mountain of straps, buckles, and velcro. Despite Kat's entreaties, I wasn't willing to risk the buttery leather of her Mercedes. I'd bought Ruby and Isaac bags of sour gummy bears as a bribe to ensure good behavior on our real estate rounds, and I knew from experience that at least two or three of the sugar-encrusted globs was going to end up adhered to someone's butt. Better that it should be my crud-mobile that suffered the consequences of my lousy parenting.

"Just a couple, Ashkon," Kat said, staring in horror at her son's beatific face as he jammed the candy into his mouth, licking his fingers and giggling maniacally. Given Kat's various food phobias, I suppose it was entirely possible that this was her child's first experience with sugar in his life. He had crammed two-thirds of his bag of candy into his mouth, and he sat in his booster seat with the blissed-out look of someone who has just found the secret to eternal life.

"Sorry," I said. "I probably should have asked you before I gave him those. It's just that since Ruby and Isaac had them . . ." my voice trailed off.

"It's fine, really," she said, looking nauseated. Thank goodness my friend was too polite to yell at me. It probably didn't hurt, I guess, that she was enough of a real estate agent to remember that she wanted at some point to make a sale.

"Okay, so. What do you have to show me?" I asked.

Kat reached into her bag and pulled out a folded piece of paper. "There isn't much new on the market. We saw almost everything the other day. But I found one place we haven't looked at yet."

It took a good forty minutes to wind our way up to Mulholland Drive. The house, when we finally arrived, didn't look too bad, if you happened to be a devotee of bad 1970s architecture. And who isn't, really? I could barely bring myself to get out of the car, and it was only Isaac's urgent need to get to a bathroom that convinced me to go inside.

The listing agent was waiting for us in the kitchen, and I was full of something akin to admiration when I saw the avocado green appliances and orange Formica cabinets. You've got to appreciate that kind of devotion to the palette of the period—and 1973 was such an *interesting* year for colors.

"It's beautiful!" Ruby announced, her voice almost reverent.

"What?" I said, staring at her.

"This house. It's just like *The Brady Bunch!* I want to live here, Mama. Please, can we live here?"

With Peter's purchase of TiVO he and Ruby had lately become devotees of all the television shows we used to watch when we were kids. Ruby was absolutely obsessed with both *The Brady Bunch* and *The Partridge Family,* and wandered around singing, "I Think I Love You," and howling 'Oh my nose!' at odd intervals.

"You're right, little lady, this is a beautiful home! Let's see if we can convince your Mommy to buy it for you!"

I shot the listing agent who had made this comment a baleful scowl. He smiled back. Unlike Kat, this realtor looked the part. His blond hair was sprayed and marceled into a high wave that perched on his head like a sparrow on a tree branch. He was impeccably turned out in a black linen jacket and matching pants. I'd never before seen linen so crisp and unwrinkled. A gold ring in the shape of a horseshoe flashed on one knuckle, and it was all I could do to keep from telling him that he had the thing upside down— all the luck would leak right out of it. Worst of all, I had never met anyone so perky, not even when I had tangled with a religious cult. He had greeted Kat with an effusive hug, and begun to rave about the house as soon as we walked in the door.

My frown at his comment to Ruby seemed to faze him not at all. "This place is a true gem," he shrilled. "Honestly, I can't even believe I'm letting you guys in! I should be saving it for my own clients." He waggled a reproving finger at Kat, as if my friend had forced him to open the doors of this dump to us.

"Now just look at this carpeting," he said, flinging open the double doors to the dining room. "It's in perfect condition, but if you don't like it, you can tear it right up. Who knows what's underneath. Could be parquet!"

Kat winced, and I nearly laughed. The mauve shag carpeting probably concealed something, but it was more likely to be bare cement than anything else.

The real magic of the house, however, was that it seemed to have been designed by someone with homicidal feelings toward small children. I'd never before been somewhere quite so kid-unfriendly. The circular staircases had no railings and led down to cement floor. I kept Isaac's hand tightly in mine, because I didn't trust him to avoid the spiky wrought-iron sconces that were placed just at the level of his eyes.

We drifted aimlessly through one hideous room after another, the children amusing themselves by making faces in the mirrors that lined every wall and some of the ceilings. The master bedroom was nearly the death of Ruby, although it was hardly her fault. How could she have expected that the sliding glass doors would lead to a sheer twenty-foot drop to the asphalt below.

"They must be redoing the balcony!" the agent said, Ruby swinging from his hand. I couldn't bring myself to thank him for grabbing her collar and saving her life.

Finally, once it had become obvious that unlike the listing agent, we were not the types whose cheerfulness could not be dimmed even by peeling bathroom fixtures and water-stained ceilings, he led us out to the garden.

"It's perfect for children. Perfect. There's even room for a play structure!"

I followed his pointed finger with my eyes. "Where?" I asked.

"Right there!"

"In those sticker bushes?"

"It's a xeriscape—a low-water garden. Very fashionable, and environmentally sensitive."

I murmured something noncommittal, then found my attention distracted by the shrieks of a child. Little Ashkon had managed to impale himself on the thorns of one of those succulents.

"Oh no!" Kat screamed, tearing through the garden, tripping over the rusted patio furniture.

"Stay right here!" I ordered my children, sitting them down on the back step—the only area not overrun with child-eating thorn bushes. "Do not move!"

I ran over to help Kat. She was trying to yank Ashkon's arm free of the barbs, but their gyrations served only to entangle him further.

"Wait!" I barked. I waded warily into the garden. Kat held her son still while I carefully disengaged him from his predator, thorn by thorn. Once he was free, Kat lifted him in her arms, and we trudged back to where my kids were sitting, quietly for once.

"Perfect for kids?" Kat snarled at the other agent, who had the grace to blush.

By the time we got back into the car, Ashkon had stopped crying, and had begun showing off his scratches to Isaac, who expressed a very satisfactory awe at his friend's bravery. I took off down the hill, as fast as I could.

"Fine," Kat said.

"Fine, what?"

"Fine, we'll get you the Felix house."

"Really?" I smiled at my friend. "Really?"

She had her arms crossed over her chest, and she looked grim. "I just warn you, it's not going to be easy. Nahid is planning a full frontal attack for when the boys decide to put the house on the market. She's lined up a psychic to do this insane 'ghost-clearing' ceremony, and she's already booked a dresser for the open house."

"A dresser?"

"You know, like a decorator."

"But the house is beautifully decorated!"

Kat shook her head. "If there isn't something gilded

in every room, my mother-in-law doesn't consider it done."

"Ah. She must *love* your place."

Kat laughed bitterly. "Not a holiday goes by that she doesn't try to foist some monstrosity off on me. You would not believe what she gave Reza for his birthday this year."

"What?"

"I don't even know what it's supposed to be. It hangs from the ceiling. It's covered in gilt sparrows."

"Ew!!"

"My sentiments exactly. It went right into his study, with every other present she's ever given us. At this point that room looks like Ali Baba's cave!"

"So what do we do? How do we get me my house?"

Kat shook her head. "I don't know. I have to think about it. If we wait until it goes on the market, we'll be screwed. Knowing my mother-in-law, she'll jack the price up and get a bidding war going. I wouldn't be surprised if she manages to convince people that a dead body is good *feng shui*. Our only hope is to get an accepted offer *before* it goes on the market."

"How do we do that? Isn't the owner's boyfriend Nahid's cousin's son or something? They're not going to sell it to us, especially not if they know she can make them more money."

Kat wrinkled her forehead. "I don't know. But that's our only hope."

We rode in silence for a while. Then I said, "What if I went to talk to Felix? What if I offered to help with the investigation of this sister's death? You know, in my capacity as an almost-licensed private investigator, and an experienced criminal defense attorney. I could act as his advocate with the police, that kind of thing."

"You're saying you want to ingratiate yourself with a

murder victim's brother, in order to buy his house on the cheap?" Kat said.

I glanced over at her. "Yeah."

She heaved her feet on the dashboard and tapped her toes. She looked positively disgusted with me. Finally, she said, "That could work."

Seven

WHEN we got home I foisted the kids off on their father with instructions to give me an hour's peace and quiet.

"And you know what would be great?" I said.

"What?" Peter asked, Isaac dangling upside down from his shoulder and Ruby wrapped tightly around his legs.

"An early dinner."

My husband glanced ostentatiously at his watch. My generally constant level of pregnancy starvation had resulted in our evening meals creeping closer and closer to the daylight hours. I couldn't help it. I just couldn't seem to make it past five. I suppose that wouldn't have been so bad if I weren't always hungry again by eight. Yes, all right, I'd been eating two full suppers since the first trimester of my pregnancy. Two breakfasts, too. Also two lunches. So sue me.

"How about if we make homemade pizza?" Peter asked.

"Mmm," I said, wondering how I'd survive until the pies came out of the oven.

"Don't worry," he said, "I'll make you an extra one for tonight. And have an apple if you're hungry now."

Thank God I'm married to an understanding man. So sympathetic was he, in fact, that he had taken, with each pregnancy, to matching me pound for pound. Alas for him he could not breastfeed the pounds away.

I waddled off to Peter's office and logged on to his computer. In a short while I had gathered a very detailed picture of Alicia's brother, Murray Felix. No surprise the man went by his last name only. The name Murray conjured up many things—a *bar mitzvah* boy, a certified public accountant, a podiatrist with bad teeth. But Murray, the fashion designer, on the cutting edge of every trend? I don't think so. So Felix it was. A name that was also a brand.

Felix had launched his label with a collection of old-school preppy clothes, *a la* Ralph Lauren, but with a twist. The men's suits were cut a little tight, with bright colored ties that would not have passed muster at the Harvard Club. The women's gowns looked like fairly conservative classics, but in black and white only, with necks so high and hems so low that they were nearly demure. Except they were each characterized by a plunging back nearly to the buttocks, or a cut-away section that revealed an unexpected peek of the side of a breast. The fashionistas had raved about Felix's quirky creativity, his lush fabrics, his unexpected vision. And the hordes had responded by buying, and buying big.

Within a few years, however, other quirky, unexpected, lush designers had come on the scene, and Felix's star had begun to fade. Then, last year, the man had come up with the marketing coup of all time. He hired as a spokesman an eighteen-year-old rapper from Compton named 9 MM and launched the line that made his career. 9 MM had a brother serving a life-sentence for murder, a mother with three crack cocaine possession convictions on her record, and more street cred than any other gangsta rapper in the business. The clothing line was called Booty Rags and, from the pictures I saw on the Web, seemed to consist primarily of gigantic cargo pants, tight shirts in vaguely Indian patterns, and dresses of torn spandex that revealed significantly more than they covered. Booty Rags were all the rage—everyone from Hollywood starlets, to teenage nymphets, to the well-maintained and impeccably toned matrons of Beverly Hills was prancing through their days draped in the torn and bedraggled finery. For those, like me, whose bodies would not stand up to the rigors of micro-mini-dresses and see-through tank tops, Felix sold T-shirts with 'Booty Rags' scrawled in a facsimile of graffiti tagging. No wonder Alicia's brother was selling his house in Larchmont. He had moved way beyond that pleasant neighborhood, and well into the land of gated estates.

The aroma of baking pizza interrupted my Internet reverie. I followed my nose out to the kitchen and found my husband and son swathed in identical white aprons. Their hair and faces were dusted with flour, and they had rigged up a catapult system out of wooden spoons and elastic bands.

"What's up, guys?" I asked, from what I thought was the relative safety of the doorway.

"Extra dough," Peter said. Isaac leaned back and fired off a grayish clump. The T-shirt I was wearing had ridden up over my round belly, revealing a strip of midriff. The dough caught me right there.

"Ick," I said, peeling off the cold clot. "Gross."

"Yeah!" Isaac squealed. "Really gross. Like brains!"

I winced. "Ick," I said again. "Where's Ruby?"

"She didn't feel like helping. She's down on cooking for some reason. She's in her room, playing computer games."

I left my men to their battlefield, hoping vainly that one or the other of them would become inspired to clean up. I found Ruby hunched over the iMac she had inherited when her father upgraded his system.

"What'cha doing, kiddo?" I asked, sitting down on her bed and picking a bit of pizza dough off my stomach.

"Barbie dress up."

Ruby's favorite computer game was a particularly vacuous one in which she spent her time crafting outfits for Barbie to wear. Her current project looked like a bra and panties in a lime green, with fringes.

"Cool outfit," I said, wondering if I shouldn't hire her out to Felix. She seemed to have his style down pat.

She leaned back in her chair and gazed at her handiwork appraisingly. "It's okay. Mom?"

"What?"

"I need a belly button pierce."

I lifted my eyes from my stomach and stared at my six-year-old, dumbfounded. "You need *what?*"

"I need a belly button pierce. Like Barbie." She pointed at her design. It was only then that I noticed that she'd decorated the doll with a thick gold hoop where her belly button would be. The thing is, though, Barbie is not particularly anatomically correct, and Ruby's ring sat on an empty expanse of virtual belly.

"You don't need your navel pierced, kid."

"Yes I do!" she said. "Barbie has one!" She poked the screen with one indignant finger.

"First of all, Barbie isn't real. She's a doll. And that's just a picture of a doll that *you* made. And anyway, if she *were* real, Barbie would be a lot older than you, Ruby."

"But I'd look really good with a belly button pierce." She lifted up her shirt and showed off her delicious rounded stomach. I scooped her up in my arms and kissed her exactly where she'd hoped to impale a bit of metal.

"Mom!" she objected.

"Sweetie, we're not having this argument. You're not getting your pupik pierced, and that's that."

"Pupik is not an English word, mama."

"I know sweetie. It's Yiddish. It's what your Bubbe and Zayde call a belly button."

She sat up in my lap and gazed at me, her expression carefully devoid of expression. "Okay, well. How about earrings?"

I stared back at her. Had this all been a ploy to get me to agree to pierce her *ears?* Was my little girl capable of that kind of craftily sophisticated manipulation?

"When you're twelve, Ruby. You know that."

She groaned in frustration and heaved herself off my lap. "When I'm *twelve?* I can't wait that long! I might already be ugly when I'm twelve! I might be . . ." she paused for dramatic effect. "I might be *fat!*" She whispered the word, as though it were too horrible even to say out loud. I could have been imagining it, but I swear she shot a horrified glance at the stomach peeping out from underneath my too-small shirt.

I was saved from launching into a defense of my prenatal weight gain by the chirping of the telephone. Peter had reprogrammed all the ringers on our various phones so they did anything but ring. They beeped, they twittered, they squawked.

I left Ruby to her fashion design and went to answer the phone. Kat didn't even bother to say hello.

"She says if I even *talk* to them she'll force me to manage rental units for the next thirty years."

"What?" I asked, perplexed.

"Nahid. My mother-in-law. My *boss,*" she snarled. "She

caught me going through the computer looking for Felix's phone number. She freaked. I mean, freaked."

"Why? What did you tell her?"

"I didn't tell her anything." Kat paused. "Okay, I told her that we'd decided to approach Felix to see if he'd be interested in a quiet sale."

"You what?" I'm ashamed to say I shouted. "Why? Why would you tell her?"

"You don't understand the woman," Kat shouted back. "She's a *djinn!* I couldn't help it. I had to tell her."

Now, Peter's mother and I weren't friends. I had never managed to muster sufficient interest in her Hummel figurine and Beanie Baby collections even to feign a relationship. Did I think Peter's mother was crazy? Sure. Did I find her irritating? Definitely. But even I had never thought of the woman who insisted on being called "Mother Wyeth" as being a demon capable of assuming both human and animal form. But then, perhaps I'd change my tune if I had to work for her.

"It's okay," I said to Kat.

"No it's not," she groaned. "You loved that house. We'll never find you anything like it again."

"Spoken like a true real estate agent."

"Oh, shut up."

We both sighed at the same time, and then giggled half-heartedly.

"I'm not giving up," I said.

"I am."

"Look, I'm not afraid of Nahid. She can't hurt *me,* I'm not married to her son."

"But I can't get Felix's number. And even if I could, I can't give you any kind of introduction. She'd kill me."

"There's got to be another way to get to him. Once he hires me, what's she going to do?"

"Sic the forces of evil on you. Curse you and all your progeny for a thousand years." Kat didn't exactly sound like she was kidding, but I laughed anyway.

"You, butt out, okay?" I said. "You're no longer involved. The next thing you're going to do is cash your commission check. Other than that, you're an innocent bystander."

She grunted. "Yeah, she'll believe *that*."

"She'll have to. It's the truth."

I hung up the phone and peeked a head into the kitchen. "How long until dinner?" I asked. Peter and Isaac were lying on their backs on the kitchen floor, their faces covered with flattened pancakes of raw pizza dough.

"Like, ten minutes," my husband said, his voice muffled.

"We're monsters that don't have any faces!" Isaac said, lifting up a corner of his mask. "Get it?"

"I do. You definitely scared me."

"But you didn't scream!"

I obliged with a howl of shock and fear, and went back out to the living room. After a minute, I dialed my friend Stacy, the one person I knew who was sure to have a way in to Felix.

Stacy and I have been friends since college, when our competitive natures and single-minded ambition forced us either to become enemies or intimates. We'd chosen the latter, and had spoken pretty much every day for the last seventeen years. We'd gone to graduate school together at Harvard—me to the law school and Stacy to the business school. She'd moved out to LA as soon as she'd graduated, taking a job at ICA, one of Hollywood's top agencies. She'd soared up through the ranks, swiftly becoming a star at the agency. Through the first years of our careers we were pretty evenly matched, Stacy and I, although she always made much more money than I did. Despite that financial disparity, we excelled at more or less the same pace. I won my first jury trial, Stacy signed her first major star. I appeared on NPR to discuss a Ninth Circuit appeal, she did an interview for *Entertainment Tonight* about hot young women directors. Unlike me, however, Stacy had not let pregnancy and parenting derail her career. She'd limited herself to one child, Zachary, who was brilliant and accomplished enough for a whole pack of siblings. Zach had inherited his mother's looks—he was sharp-faced and attractive, with the same thick head of dark brown hair growing low on his forehead that I vaguely remembered Stacy sporting before she'd begun dying it a succession of glittering tones. She had been a honey blond for years, and had lately taken to wearing her hair swept up in an artfully messy bun at the top of her head, clipped with one or two antique marcasite hair clasps.

It took a moment to convince Stacy's new assistant that she should put me through to her boss. I've been known to keep a pair of pantyhose longer than Stacy keeps one of these poor young things. They never last more than a few months—she chews them up and spits them out, much the worse for wear. To my friend's credit, however, her assistants invariably end up moving up the ranks of the ICA hierarchy, or into a better job at a studio or production company. The assistants might have a miserable few months in Stacy's employ, but she prepares them for a career in Hollywood, and she champions them forever after. Los Angeles is full of her castoffs, and no matter how severe their nervous twitches, or how bad their cases of hives, once they move on to bigger and better things they remember her, if not fondly, then with respect and admiration.

"Jules!" Stacy shouted. "I just got back from the Manolo Blahnik trunk show at Neiman's!"

"Lucky you," I replied, wishing that I, too, could indulge in the purchase of a pair of three hundred and fifty dollar stiletto heels I'd have no opportunity to wear. I have, I'm afraid, something of a shoe problem. For a woman who spends her life in maternity smocks and overalls, I have a rather stunning collection of pumps and strappy sandals. As indulgences go, it's not so bad, is it? And anyway, since I'd discovered Ebay, my shoe fetish had come to be satisfied with bargain basement bidding.

Once I'd managed to divert my friend's attentions from the delightful distraction of overpriced footwear, I said, "Felix. The designer. You know him?"

"Booty Rags? Of course. He's a friend." She paused. "Anyway, I've met him once or twice. On the phone. He dressed Fiona." Fiona Rytler was one of Stacy's latest mega stars, a waif-like blond with a classical Shakespearian education and a talent for comedy.

"He dressed her?"

"Yup. For the MTV Movie Awards. He had her in this amazing black dress, like a spider web. Didn't you see it?"

"Uh, Stace?"

"Right, right. What was I thinking? You don't watch award shows."

Peter and I had long ago made a vow that we wouldn't watch the Oscars or any of the other of the multitude of award shows unless and until he was nominated for one. I had a feeling we'd be spending the Oscar nights of our golden years catching reruns of *The Rockford Files* on TV Land.

"Anyway, we were on the phone for weeks working out the dress. He's a sweetheart."

"Can you call him for me?"

"Why?" she asked, suspiciously.

I explained about my investigation.

"Oh, Juliet. When are you going to give this nonsense up? I mean, you can't possibly be making any money at it, can you?"

"We're doing fine," I said, barely managing to keep the annoyance out of my voice. I knew Stacy had my best interest at heart, but she didn't approve of my burgeoning career as an investigator. She, like my mother, felt I should be working at what I was really good at: keeping criminals out of jail. She was convinced that I was wasting my time hanging out with the kids and playing at being a private eye. She was probably right, as I freely admitted to her. Still, I reassured myself that, unlike Zachary, my kids have never had to play a game of soccer with the nanny cheering from the sidelines, and no one else there to notice. In my more content moments I was confident that I didn't want to exchange that for Stacy's glittering career, no matter how bored and frustrated I found myself.

"Really? I mean, I can't imagine there's any money in the investigation business."

"Of course there is!" I said, refraining from mentioning that Al and I weren't earning any of it. "We bill out at more or less what an attorney charges. It's a great part-time job."

"But do you have any clients? I mean, *paying* clients?"

"Well, I might have one if you would just call Felix for me!"

"Is that *it?* You mean you have no other clients at all?"

I gritted my teeth. "We're doing fine, Stacy. I told you. We're in a bit of dry spell now, but it will pass."

She clucked her tongue sympathetically and I gripped the phone receiver to keep from smashing it down in its cradle.

"I'll call Felix for you. But, Juliet?"

"What?"

"I'm worried about you."

"Don't be. We're doing great, Al and I." I was plenty worried about us, myself. I didn't need her help.

Eight

STACY'S intervention inspired in me a sartorial crisis the likes of which I'd never experienced before. I must have tried on every piece of maternity clothing in my closet before flinging the last stretched-out smock to the ground in a fit of pique.

"Damn it!" I snarled.

"Mama!" Ruby said, pretending to be horrified at my language. I rolled my eyes at her. Unless her teacher was lying, she knew worse words than that one, and felt free to use them on the playground.

"What's wrong, honey?" Peter said from under the covers, where he and Isaac were building a fort out of blankets.

The only time Felix could see me was on a Sunday morning. While the rest of my family was playing amidst the pillows and sprinkling bagel crumbs in the sheets, I was forced to confront the terrifying paucity of my wardrobe.

"I have nothing to wear!" I wailed.

"What are you talking about? You've got piles of clothes in there."

I'd been wearing the same maternity and nursing clothes for the past six years, with ever-increasing dissatisfaction; and now that I'd been sucked into a more stylish orbit, it seemed I had an emergency on my hands. I threw a rolled-up sock at my husband's head. "Felix is a fashion designer! I can't wear your old Fantastic Four T-shirt to a meeting with a fashion designer!"

"So go buy something new," he said, entirely unsympa-thetically. The few times in recent years that I'd had to buy clothes had been exercises more in humiliation than any-thing else. It was no fun to shop for my rapidly expanding and slowly deflating body, and I had decided just to wait until I was back to something approximating a normal size before I hit the boutiques again. I was obviously going to have to reevaluate that decision.

I was on my way out the door when the telephone rang.

"Please hold one minute for Mr. Brodsky."

A few moments later a deep voice purred into the phone: "Ms. Applebaum. I received your name and num-ber from a mutual friend, Stacy Holland. I'm with the firm of Brodsky, Brodsky & Shapiro. I imagine you've heard of us?"

I had. They were a fairly well-known entertainment law firm in the city, and were not infrequently cited in the trades. "Of course. What can I do for you?" I crossed every finger and toe, praying that he had a case for us.

"My firm has lately been exploring the possibility of engaging in a relationship with an investigative office that specializes in criminal defense. The idea would be to have someone on call when our clients find themselves in unexpected difficulties. Difficulties that require a different kind of expertise to resolve than we possess."

I didn't scream and shout in a combination of joy and relief, but that's only because I clamped my lips shut.

"What kind of difficulties?" I said calmly.

He paused, and my stomach tightened. Had my question caused him to doubt me?

"Perhaps situations where claims are made against your clients, either in the press or simply as rumor?" I asked.

"That's one kind of situation."

"And I imagine there are the occasional brushes with the criminal justice system; situations where hiring a defense attorney might be premature, but where an investigation might prove useful."

"Precisely."

"I think we can certainly help you," I said. "My partner is an ex-police officer, and thus has both connections and experience that is invaluable in all kinds of different situations. And I am a criminal defense attorney, although I no longer practice in the courtroom. I can make sure that any investigation would not endanger future criminal defenses."

"That is what Ms. Holland led us to understand. She believes your firm would suit our needs nicely."

I sent a wordless blessing to Stacy.

"Do you, perhaps, have any references?" Brodsky asked.

I gave him Sandra's name, but I could tell he wanted someone, well, glitzier. I told him I'd need to consult my clients before handing out their names, but I was sure that I'd have something for him. Lilly would talk to him, I just knew she would. And then I made a terrible mistake. It was an understandable error, born as it was of my desperation to close the deal, of my concern for Al, and for my own professional future, but I regretted the words as soon as they left my lips: "I've just taken on a rather high-profile case," I said. "Of course I can't go into detail, but it's a murder investigation involving a number of well-known individuals."

"A high-profile murder investigation? Going on right now?"

"Yes."

"The Felix case? The murder of the fashion designer's sister? You're investigating that? I know Felix quite well. We represented a company that sought to acquire his a few years ago."

I gulped and said, "I'm so sorry; confidentially prevents me from saying any more."

"Of course, of course. Well, Ms. Applebaum, that certainly is impressive. My partners and I will be watching to see how that case turns out. Why don't we plan on speaking once things are resolved? At that point we'll all have a good idea if working together would be in our mutual best interests."

It was all I could do to keep from strangling myself with the phone cord. Had I really all but told the man that I represented Felix? I had. And had he really made our hiring contingent on resolving Alicia's murder? He had. Of course, Felix hadn't even hired me yet, and even if he did, who knew if I was ever going to be able to solve the case? What a fool I was. What a complete and total fool.

In a terrible funk, I made my way to Liz Lange, a maternity clothing store that was so expensive I'd never done more than casually browse the window displays. A meeting with the founder of Booty Rags justified a more intensive scrutiny of their wares, and my misery was more than enough excuse for some retail therapy. Thirty minutes and over two hundred dollars later I flounced out of the store wearing a tight, black, long-sleeved T-shirt that showed off my belly, and a gray skirt that did much the same to my rather corpulent behind. The salesgirl had assured me that tight clothes were in for pregnant woman. The idea, I guess, is to celebrate the vastness, not disguise it. Since I was well aware that any attempts at concealment were at best fruitless and at worst pathetic, I was ready to jump on the celebratory bandwagon. Still, I was not quite willing to buy myself a pair of maternity thong underpants—every girl has her limits. A pair of high-heeled black boots that I'd brought with me completed the ensemble, and I felt great, panty lines and all.

The door to my dream house was answered by a small man with a thick shock of black hair and the largest brown eyes I'd ever seen in my life. His sooty lashes were so long they looked tangled, and his lips were full and red. He was beautiful, although certainly not traditionally handsome. He was far too petite for that. He looked like a miniature movie star, a fashion model writ two sizes smaller than normal.

"Hallo," he said, in a vaguely European accent.

"I'm Juliet Applebaum," I said, extending my hand.

"Farzad Bahari," he said, taking it in his own. His grip was surprisingly firm, for such a delicate man.

He led me through the vaulted entry way and into the long living room. A cheery fire was burning in the green-tiled fireplace, and the many sconces were lit, despite the bright midmorning light shining through the leaded glass windows. I surreptitiously buried a covetous toe in the thick Chinese carpet, and determined to convince Felix and his pretty boyfriend not only to sell me their house, but also to toss in the rug.

"One moment. I'll let Felix know you're here. He's in his room. Resting."

"Of course," I said. "This must be very difficult for him. Losing his sister."

Farzad pursed his voluptuous lips for a moment, and then nodded, almost grudgingly. He left me alone in the room and ran quickly up the stairs. I took advantage of his absence to look once again around the room. When Kat and I had been through the house I'd been far too interested in the tiles, wood floors, moldings, and fixtures to look at the pictures on the walls. Now I could examine the black and white photos at my leisure. There was a long row of them, matted and framed behind museum glass. There were one or two that looked decidedly like Robert Mapplethorpes—few other photographers capture the male body with quite that erotic artistry. The others were dramatic, stylized fashion photographs, including two large prints of ethereal models wearing clothing that bore the unmistakable mark of Booty Rag ghetto-chic.

"Those are Avedons," a voice said. I leapt back—I'd had my nose pressed altogether too close to the glass.

"Wow!" I said. "The real deal?" I turned to look at Alicia's brother. He was a tall, thin man with fair hair cropped close to his scalp. His narrow face was dominated by a sharp beak of a nose, made all the more prominent by the diamond stud nestled in the crease above his nostril. He was wearing a black T-shirt in a soft clingy fabric that looked like silk. His narrow hips were having a hard time holding up his voluminous cargo pants, and a pair of black silk underwear peeped above the drooping waist.

"I'm so sorry for your loss," I said.

He nodded, and collapsed into an oversized wing chair, leaning his head back into the nubbly leather. "So you're a friend of Stacy Holland's," he said.

At that moment Farzad came into the room carrying a tray with three small cups and a matching coffee pot. He put the tray down on a sidetable. Without asking me how I took mine, he spooned generous portions of sugar into each cup and handed them to his boyfriend and me. I took a tentative sip, and then smiled. The coffee was rich and sweet, but plain and strong, too. Much better than the milkshake-like concoctions I'd been drinking lately.

"Mm," I said.

"Farzad makes a fabulous cup of coffee," Felix said, smiling at the smaller man. Farzad sat down on the couch and tucked his legs up under him. He nodded graciously at the comment, clearly understanding that it was no more than his due.

I took another sip, and then warmed my hands around the small cup. "I've known Stacy forever," I said. "Since college."

"Oh?" Felix said, in a voice entirely devoid of interest.

"Did she explain to you why I wanted to meet you?" I asked.

"Sort of. But I'm not sure I really understand. She told me that you were the one who . . . who found Alicia."

"Yes," I said softly. I told him how Kat and I had come to be in the house that morning.

"I told Nahid that lock box was a dreadful idea!" Farzad interrupted. I looked over at him. His face was flushed and he looked angry. "She wouldn't listen. She is just like my mother. Does what she wants."

"You hadn't asked her to put the box on?" I asked.

"Of course not!" he said. "It's a ridiculous idea. Putting your key on the door so anyone can walk in! What's the point of having a five thousand dollar alarm system if you leave the key for anyone to find?"

"Why did she want the lock box, do you know?"

Felix reached across to the couch and laid a calming hand on his boyfriend's arm. "We were just about to put the house on the market," he said to me. "Nahid wanted to be able to get in when she needed to, and to send other agents by to look at the place while we were out of town. She had one of her handymen come and install the box."

"You were out of town?"

He nodded. "At our place in Palm Springs. We'd been there for a couple of months. That's why we wanted to sell the house. To move down there, permanently."

"You'd planned to leave LA?"

He nodded. "Farzad's been dying to get out of the city. And we've fallen in love with Palm Springs. The desert has wonderful energy. So creatively inspiring. We were there working on the preliminary sketches for my autumn collection when we found out about Alicia. So much for the collection," he said, waving his hand as if to bid it goodbye. "I'm not likely to get any of it done now."

"Of course you will. You'll be ready to go back to work in a week or two. It will be a good distraction for you," Farzad said, managing to sound both tender and bossy.

Felix shook his head. "I don't know. I doubt it. Maybe you'll have to do it for me, sweetie." He laughed humorlessly. "It's not like anyone would know the difference."

I gently brought them back to what we'd been talking about before. "So you were out of town when Alicia was killed?"

"Yes," Felix said. He suddenly narrowed his eyes and looked at me. "I'm not sure I understand, Ms. Applebaum. Exactly why did you ask Stacy if you could meet me?"

I explained to Felix that I was an investigator, and that I was eager to help in any way that I could. "I guess you could say that finding her body makes me feel like I have a kind of personal stake in finding out who murdered your poor sister," I finished, lamely.

Felix nodded, not looking entirely convinced. He said, "How can you help? The police are investigating her murder."

"Well, in addition to being an investigator, I was a criminal defense attorney. I can act as your advocate with the police, help you navigate their questions, follow leads they might not be interested in pursuing. I'd be on your side, acting in your interests. You can't necessarily rely on the police for that." I thought of Harvey Brodsky and had a sudden inspiration. "My partner and I provide these kinds of services for people in situations like yours. High-profile individuals for whom relying on the good will of the police is simply not an option, but for whom engaging a criminal defense lawyer might not project the right image."

Farzad nodded, although Felix still looked perplexed, and perhaps a little suspicious.

"Why would I need an advocate with the police?" Felix said.

"Because the police are bound to think you killed Alicia!" Farzad said. "They always blame the family." He turned to me. "Don't they? Don't they always blame the family?"

"Well, statistically, murders are most often committed by someone the victim knows. So yes, they do look to the family."

"But we were in Palm Springs!" Felix said.

I nodded. "And I'm sure the police will rule you out once they verify that."

"No they won't," Farzad said. "They'll just say we paid someone to kill her."

I was surprised by his vehemence. Why was he so sure that he and his partner would become suspects in this grisly murder?

Felix once again patted his boyfriend's arm. Then he smiled at me, uncomfortably. "Farzad was born in Iran. He doesn't have exactly warm feelings towards the police."

I nodded sympathetically. "Of course not."

"He's basically pathologically suspicious of authority," Felix said.

"Have you done this kind of work before?" Farzad asked.

"Yes, I have. Of course my work is confidential, so I can't give you references, but rest assured my partner and I are experienced in this area." Lilly's case qualified as experience, didn't it? "This isn't a service for everyone," I said, hoping my voice wasn't slipping into too oily a register. "Only individuals with a certain public profile can afford this level of protection, or even need it. Most people simply muddle through. Ours is a service appropriate only for the select few." I was definitely going to need a shower when I was done with this interview.

I wasn't wrong in my assessment of Felix's vanity. I've found, in fact, that it's very difficult to overestimate the narcissism of the average wealthy Los Angelino.

"I suppose it wouldn't hurt to have someone on our side," Felix said. "I do have a public profile I need to protect." Then he narrowed his eyes. "But what do you get out of this?"

I was not willing to confess my hope to buy his house on the cheap, and I was getting more and more uncomfortable with my own ulterior motives.

"We pay her," Farzad said. "That's what she gets out of it."

I nodded. "That, and the knowledge that I've done what I can to help find whoever did that to your sister. Finding her is not something I'm ever going to be able to forget." I wasn't lying. The image of Alicia's violated body was there, in my memory, forever.

"How much, exactly, do we pay you?" Farzad asked.

I outlined Al's and my rates. They were reasonable, considering how much money Felix obviously had.

After a moment, Felix nodded. "Okay. We can give it a try. See if it works out."

I hoped my huge sigh of relief was not audible. I leaned forward. "You won't be sorry," I said. "Can I ask you a few questions about your sister? To give me some context for my investigation?"

Felix told me that he and Alicia had grown up in Miami. "My dad owns a Chevrolet dealership. The first thing I did when I got out of there was buy a European car."

After a brief stint at the Fashion Institute of Technology, Felix had followed his sister out to Los Angeles. She'd gone to UCLA and majored in acting. By the time her brother joined her in Hollywood, it was clear to them both that her star was rising.

"She had auditions almost every day, and seemed to get a lot of the parts she tried out for. It was mostly commercials and little one-time roles on TV shows, but she was doing really well. And she was leading this total Hollywood lifestyle. She and her friends would spend every night at parties, or at clubs. She was dating guys you'd recognize from TV, even if you didn't know their names. To a kid like me, it seemed like the coolest scene ever." He shook his head ruefully. "Alicia was terrific. She put me up for almost a year—I slept on this stinky little pull-out futon in her living room. She introduced me to people, even set me up with guys she knew."

"Hey!" Farzad said.

"That was all before you, baby."

"Did the rest of your family know you were gay?" I asked. "Or just Alicia?"

Felix snapped his fingers in the air. "Oh honey, I've been out of the closet my whole life. My mother caught me with our Cuban gardener when I was about fourteen years old."

"Wow!"

He smiled, ruefully. "Let's just say she was *not* surprised. I'd been cutting up her dresses and restyling them for her since I was nine years old. Not many hetero boys can manage a straight seam in velvet."

I thought of my husband and his wardrobe of jeans, khakis, and T-shirts.

"That's certainly true," I said.

"Anyway, I was lucky. My parents were fine with it. They just told me to keep my hands off the help."

Farzad snorted into his coffee cup.

"So Alicia was getting a lot of parts," I said.

"For a while," Felix said. He then told me what I already knew about the downturn in her fortunes.

"That must have been difficult, coinciding as it did with your success."

He shook his head. "It was awful. I mean, not that Alicia was necessarily jealous. She was glad for me."

"She certainly liked having someone to borrow money from," Farzad interjected.

"Farzad! You know full well how much I owe Alicia," Felix said, raising his voice.

The younger man shrugged and made a zipping motion across his lips.

I paused for a minute, and then said, "Alicia borrowed money from you?"

Felix glared at his boyfriend. "Not exactly. I mean, I never expected her to pay me back."

"And you gave her a place to live?"

He nodded. "She worked for that, though. She was our personal assistant." He shot a warning glance at his boyfriend, and I wondered exactly what he was worried the indiscreet young man would tell me.

"What did she do for you?"

"She took care of the house while we were gone, for one. And she did errands and things."

"What kind of errands?"

"You know. Picking up the dry cleaning. Doing the grocery shopping. Making dinner reservations, booking travel. That kind of stuff."

I nodded, imagining what it would feel like to be one's younger brother's maid and errand girl. I don't think I could have tolerated it for a minute, and I felt terribly sorry for Alicia. While my career might not be going anywhere fast, it certainly wasn't sinking into the kind of oblivion that had forced her into this awkward and surely unpleasant situation with her brother.

"What was Alicia planning on doing once you moved to Palm Springs? Was she going to come with you?"

Felix shook his head. "No. She couldn't have. Not if she wanted to keep auditioning and appearing with her comedy troupe. She'd have found some other work, I guess."

"Was she upset at the prospect of your move?"

"She wasn't thrilled. I mean, it meant a lot of changes for her. But Alicia was a flexible person. She would have been fine." He heaved a huge sigh. "I don't know what's going to come of all that now."

"All what?" I asked.

"Palm Springs. The move. Everything."

"Don't be silly, darling," Farzad said. "There's even less of a reason to stay here, now."

Felix rubbed his eyes with his hand. "I can't bear the idea of selling this house, of leaving, with everything so unresolved. I don't know. I just don't know." His voice trailed off.

I felt my tenuous grasp on my dream house slipping away.

We sat in silence for a few moments, and then I changed the subject. I asked for the names of some of Alicia's friends, and after a short pause Felix came up with one.

"Moira Sarsfield. She's known Alicia for ages. They kind of rose and fell together, if you know what I mean."

"Do you have her number?"

He shook his head. "No, but she works at Franklin's, the restaurant in that Best Western, the one right before you get on the 101 in Hollywood. You can probably find her there."

Before I left, I gave Felix and Farzad a printout that Al's wife Jeanelle had made for us of our fee schedule and expense reimbursement policy. My embarrassment at taking the job solely to get my paws on that house kept me from asking for a retainer, and I mentally crossed my fingers, hoping that Al wouldn't kill me when he found out.

Farzad saw me to the door.

"You have a beautiful home," I said.

He raised an eyebrow. "That's right; you were looking at it with a real estate agent. So, had you planned to make an offer? Before all this, of course."

I gazed at him for a moment, and then I said, "You know, Farzad, I'd still like to make an offer. That is if you still plan on selling the house. It would be perfect for me and my family."

He waggled his head in something between a nod and

a shrug. "Well, we'll see how all this pans out. Perhaps you will figure out who murdered poor Alicia, and Felix will be so grateful that he'll sell you the house!"

My plan exactly! "Perhaps," I said. "I'll do my best."

Nine

WHEN I told Al about Harvey Brodsky's call, and about the possibility of us receiving a lucrative contract from him, Al expressed a momentary excitement. I felt terrible when I was forced to explain that it all hinged on how we did with the Felix murder.

"It's most likely a sex crime, Juliet! We aren't qualified to investigate a murder like that."

"I know."

"You solve those crimes forensically!"

"I know."

"With teams of detectives, crime scene experts, medical examiners!"

"I know."

"Not two people operating out of a garage!"

"I know."

He sighed.

I pulled over to the side of Melrose Avenue. This was not

a conversation I could have while driving. "We don't have to solve the crime," I said. "Our job is to help Felix and Farzad navigate through the system. You know, be their representatives to the police. That kind of thing."

He sighed again.

"That's what Brodsky's interested in! Not if we solve the murder or not. He can't possibly expect that."

"Let's hope not," he said.

"Hey, how'd that meeting with the insurance company go?"

"They offered me a job."

"Great! A paying client!"

"No. They don't want the agency. They want me to go work for them. To head up their investigation unit."

"Oh." My stomach sank. Was it all going to end like this? "Oh. Well, then this whole Brodsky thing isn't really important, is it?"

"I turned them down."

"You did what?"

"I turned them down. I don't want to work in some office with some vice president breathing down my neck. I've had enough of that."

"You'd rather work out of your rat-infested garage?"

"Damn right I would. What, do you want me to take the job? Are you trying to weasel out of our partnership?"

"No! No!" I said.

"Good. You're stuck with me, lady."

I smiled and merged back into traffic. After Al and I hung up, I called Peter. The first thing he did was fill me in on the state of the neighbor's construction.

"Jack-hammering. All day. I'm losing my mind."

"I'm so sorry, honey. We'll move. Soon. I promise."

"God, I hope so. Anyway, we're on our way to the Santa Monica pier to ride the carousel."

I was free to continue my perambulations around the city. I'd been sure that my husband would not approve of my plan to investigate Alicia's murder, but to my surprise he was remarkably easy going about my efforts. He merely wished me luck, and reminded me that my first priority was to find us a new house. I don't think he thought much of my chances of parlaying an investigation into a house purchase. But he hadn't been out in the real estate trenches like I had. He didn't know just how little there was out there.

I took surface streets over to Franklin's, hoping that I'd find Moira at work. I debated calling the restaurant first, but decided that the benefit of a surprise appearance outweighed any inconvenience of schlepping all the way to Hollywood. I was more likely to catch Alicia's friend in a gregarious mood if I caught her unawares.

Franklin's is one of those dives that for some reason periodically becomes fashionable among Hollywood's almost-elite. The place certainly has a seedy charm to it, with the cracked vinyl booths and Formica counter. But the food isn't much to speak of, and the listless snobbery of the wait staff has always made it and other restaurants of its ilk something of a turnoff to me. It's not that I don't feel sorry for the Juilliard and Royal Shakespeare Company graduates who are forced to earn their livings pouring ranch dressing onto iceberg lettuce salads and swabbing countertops with foul-smelling rags. I was a waitress myself, back in my pre-lawyer days. I have nothing but sympathy for food servers. It's just that I'm never really able to understand why their professional despair need express itself in an ill-concealed disdain for my food choices, my clothes, and me as a person.

Moira was working, if you could call it that, and more than happy to pull herself a cup of coffee from the vast metal urn and sit with me while I ate my BLT.

"It's such a nightmare," she said, dragging the back of her hand roughly across her eyes. It hadn't taken much to start her tears flowing. The mere mention of Alicia's name was enough to jumpstart her grief.

"I'm so sorry," I said again, patting her arm with one hand while the other balanced my leaking sandwich. I swabbed at the dripping mayonnaise with my tongue and put the sandwich down. "Had you seen Alicia recently?"

Moira nodded. "I see her all the time. Like every couple of days. She's my best friend." Her tears were flowing thick and fast, now. "God, Aziz, that's the manager, he's going to kill me. I've been crying pretty much constantly since I found out. The customers aren't real excited about being waited on by some wailing hag."

"You're not a hag," I said. "But maybe you should take a little time off. It's got to be really hard trying to work while you're feeling this way."

"Yeah, that might be nice. But if I don't work, I don't eat and I don't pay the rent, so it's not like I've got a choice."

I nodded sympathetically. "It's not an easy life, acting."

"You could say that. Although I'm not really sure I can consider myself an actor anymore. I mean, I haven't gotten a single part in three years. I'm pretty sure that that makes me just a waitress."

"That's kind of what was going on with Alicia, wasn't it?"

She nodded and tucked her stringy blond hair behind her ear. I noticed a fine, white scar extending along her crown and scalp. Had her hair been clean, and not dragged back on her skull, it would have been entirely covered. I'd seen scars like that once before—on Stacy's mother when she was recuperating at Stacy's house after one of her many facelifts. Mrs. Holland's had been red and fiery, but they'd faded over time. Like Moira, she now looked a bit pressed and pulled, but not too bad. The only difference was that my friend's mother was in her sixties, and Moira was surely not much older than I.

"It's just really hard for women in Hollywood," she said, sighing into her cup of coffee. "A guy is considered young and sexy until he's, like, seventy. But once a girl hits thirty, things start getting really tough. And my God, don't even talk to me about forty." She laughed mirthlessly. "I'll probably just shoot myself before I get there."

It didn't sound like she was kidding, and I patted her on the arm again. There was no comfort I could provide. She smiled wanly. "I'm okay," she said. "You know the saddest part? Things were starting to turn around for Alicia."

I leaned forward in my seat. "What do you mean?"

"Well, she had this new boyfriend, Charlie Hoynes. Have you heard of him?"

I shook my head.

"He's a producer. Film and television. He's pretty huge. He's done lots of things, but what he's most famous for are those vampire movies. The *Blood of Desire* series? They started on cable?"

I'm afraid my familiarity with horror movies borders on the encyclopedic, not a surprise given to whom I'm married. "Those adult ones? Basically soft-core porn?"

"Exactly. He's done other features, but the vampire movies are his biggest. Now he's putting together a one-hour adult drama based on those."

"Based on the porn movies?"

"They aren't really pornography. Just adult entertainment. I mean, there's a difference, isn't there?"

"I guess so." Horror movies I can catalogue, but pornography is a bit out of my field.

She looked defensive. "I don't think Alicia would have done porn. I mean, I know she wouldn't have. It's the fastest way to oblivion. Once you shoot a porno, there's just no way to get back to mainstream film and TV. So the series must be tamer than the original cable movies were."

"She was cast in it?"

Moira nodded. "All but. I mean, she met Charlie at an open call, and she pretty much started dating him right away. I'm sure he was going to give her a part. I mean, he kind of had to, don't you think?"

"I suppose so," I said, no more familiar with the ways of the casting couch than I was with contemporary pornographic cinema.

I wrote down Charlie Hoynes's name in my little notebook. "Was that the only iron Alicia had in the fire, do you know?"

Moira nodded. "Well, I mean, except our improv group. Do you know about that?"

Suddenly, a dark man with a thick bushy mustache and matching eyebrows appeared at our table. "Moira!" he said. "You are only sitting with customer! You are not working, not at all!"

She glared at him. "Can't you see I'm on a break? I'm not some Moroccan slave, Aziz. Here in America we have *coffee breaks*." She raised her mug at him and shook it slightly. Coffee slopped over the side and onto her hand. "Ow!" she squawked. "Now look what you made me do!"

"Oh no, so sorry," the man said, dabbing at her hand with the damp and dirty dishcloth he held.

She shook him away and he slunk back in the direction of the kitchen.

"Sorry," she said to me.

"No problem. But if you have to get back to work . . ." my voice trailed off.

"Oh, please. Like I care what Aziz wants me to do."

I felt a pang of pity for the poor, beleaguered Aziz. I wanted to follow him into the back and reassure him that all Americans weren't as spoiled and ill-mannered as his employees, but I had work to do, and alienating Moira surely wasn't the best way to elicit information from her.

"You were telling me about your improv group?"

"Right. You've probably heard of us. The Left Coast Players, Spike Steven's comedy troupe?"

I smiled noncommittally, and she chose to interpret it as a yes.

"We've been in the LCP for years, Alicia and I. It's pretty much a feeder program for *New York Live.* Kind of like Second City in Chicago."

"Really?" It had been years since I'd watched the midnight comedy show *New York Live,* but in college I'd been a devoted fan.

"Yeah, like half the casts of the first ten years or more of *NYL* were LCP alumnae. There are a couple of folks on the show right now. Jeff Finkelman. And, well, of course, Julia Brennan. No relation." It was obvious from her tone that *the other Ms. Brennan* wasn't one of Moira's favorite people.

"Do you know them?"

"Who? Jeff and Julia? Sure. We're really good friends. I mean, Julia's a nightmare, and Alicia and I hate her, but we've been friends for years."

Ah, Hollywood, the only place on earth where the definition of 'friend' includes someone you've hated for years.

"Why do you guys hate her?"

Moira opened her mouth to speak, and then snapped it shut. "Look, I can't talk about it."

"Talk about what?"

"Any of it. Julia, the whole thing. Alicia's dead, and it doesn't matter any more. *NYL* has auditions all the time, and the last thing I need is Julia Brennan finding out I've been trashing her."

"Moira, your best friend is dead. If we want to find out who did this to her, we're going to have to ask some really hard questions. Like who might have had a grudge against her. I know you want to protect your chances of getting on the show, but what's more important; that, or finding Alicia's murderer?"

Moira stared into her coffee cup, and I had the sinking suspicion that the answer to that question was not as obvious to her as it was to me.

She sighed. "You know Julia Brennan's *NYL* character, Bingie McPurge?"

"No," I said, vaguely horrified.

"Well, she does this whole bit. Bulimia jokes. Anorexia jokes. Anyway, that's the character that got her the slot on the show. And it's incredibly funny. There's only one problem."

"What? The tackiness factor?"

She smiled politely. "Okay, two problems. The big one, though, is that it's not Julia's character."

"What do you mean?"

"I mean, she didn't make it up. Alicia did. Bingie McPurge was Alicia's character. I mean, that's not what she called her. Alicia just called hers Mia, but she developed her in the improv group. She performed her in our workshops and on our open mike nights. She made it up, she wrote the jokes. Everything."

"Are you serious?"

"Yes. Julia stole the character, and made it on to *NYL* with it. And we just heard she's got a movie deal with Fox. Alicia's Mia is going to be *huge,* and she is never going to get any credit for it at all."

"Was Alicia doing anything about it? Was she going to sue Julia?"

Moira nodded. "She wanted to. But it's really hard to get a lawyer in Hollywood to take on a major studio like that. Everyone she talked to told her it was too hard a case to win. But Alicia wasn't going to give up. She'd never give up. That's just not the kind of person she was."

Moira began crying again, and I gave her a minute. Then I asked, "Moira, was Alicia bulimic?"

"Oh God, no."

"Really?"

"She'd never make herself throw up like that. Too gross. And you have to binge to purge. Alicia would never allow herself to eat that much."

"Was she anorexic?"

Moira considered the question. "I don't *think* so."

"Could she have been?"

She shook her head, but not with any sense of certainty. "Maybe when she was a kid, or something. But not now. Not as an adult. I mean, she was really careful about what she ate—she never ate in front of people, because she thought that was just kind of gross, but she didn't starve herself or anything."

I thought of her emaciated corpse. "Are you sure, Moira? Is there any chance that she was anorexic, and just kept it a secret from you?"

Moira shook her head again, this time firmly. "No. No, I just don't believe it. I mean, we were best friends. We knew everything about one another."

I nodded. Then I said, "Moira, I hate to even ask this question, but you probably understand why I need to. And I'm sure the cops have asked you, or will ask you already." I paused.

"Where was I when Alicia was murdered?"

I nodded.

"Right here," Moira said. "Working with Aziz. Where I always am. Where I'm probably going to be for the rest of my life. In this grease pit with a boss who watches me every goddamn minute of every goddamn day."

"You work nights?" I asked.

"I work all the time. Aziz lets me pull double shifts. It's the only way I can afford to pay for my apartment, my car, and my answering service. Plus the more I work the more he feels like he owes me, so if I ever do get an audition again he won't have any choice but to give me time off to take it."

"The police will probably want a record of it."

"I punch a time clock. They can look at that. And they can talk to old Aziz. He'll tell them I didn't do more than walk outside once or twice for a cigarette, if that."

"Would you mind if I just checked the time clock? I trust you absolutely, but this way I can just cross you off the file, and make it look like I'm doing my job." I used my best beleaguered-working-girl voice and topped it off with a 'you know how it is' shrug.

She called Aziz over, and the obviously good-natured manager supplied me both with Moira's time card and his own firm recollection that she'd been working by his side all evening. He even let me use the office copy machine to make photocopy of the time card. I left the restaurant knowing a little more about Alicia Felix, and with at least one potential suspect firmly in the clear.

Ten

I was still arguing with Stacy when I walked into my house.

"Why *not?* You're being totally unreasonable," I said into my cell phone.

"Why not? Because Charlie Hoynes is a creepy little dope and I'm not going to allow my name to be raised in his presence."

"I won't mention you when I *meet* him. Just on the phone to get him to take my call!"

"Not good enough. You just don't understand how this works, Juliet." She wasn't exactly yelling, but I had to hold the phone a few inches away from my ear nonetheless.

"Sure I do," I said. "If I use your name to get to Hoynes, then he's doing you a favor by talking to me, and if he does you a favor, he'll expect you to do one for him in return."

"Precisely. And what he'll ask for is that one of my clients agree to be in one of his sleaze-fests. And that's just not going to happen."

"So, you just say no! What's so hard about that?"

"He'll *call* me. And I'll have to take his calls! That's what's so hard. Look, girlfriend. We're done here. You can't use my name, and that's that. End of story."

"But I don't know anyone else who knows Charlie Hoynes," I said, but she had hung up the phone.

"I know Charlie Hoynes," Peter said pleasantly.

"What?" I snapped my head up. I was still standing in the entryway to our apartment, my cell phone in my hand. Through the arched doorway into the living room I could see Peter and the kids tumbled together on the couch. Isaac was asleep, his head resting on his father's chest, and a string of drool connecting his pooched-out lower lip to the red plaid of Peter's flannel shirt.

"How do you know Charlie Hoynes?" I whispered.

"You don't need to whisper, he's totally out," Peter said.

"Yeah, Mama, watch this." Ruby reached across Peter's chest and smacked her brother in the head. He didn't stir.

"Ruby!" I said.

She rolled her eyes at me and turned her attention back to the TV. They were watching *Thumbtanic.* Peter and Ruby had rented *Thumb Wars* ("If there were thumbs in space and they got mad at each other, those would be *Thumb Wars*") and watched it pretty much non-stop for two weeks. Now they were on to the all-thumb version of James Cameron's romantic classic. Nothing cracked my daughter up like an ocean full of drowning thumbs.

"How do you know Charlie Hoynes?" I repeated.

"Remember those two producers who pitched me that idea for the abortion movie?"

I groaned. When Peter and I had first arrived in Hollywood, he had been hungry enough to take meetings with pretty much anyone who would see him, including a producing team that had an idea for a horror movie in which aborted fetuses came to life and attacked a city. It was supposed to be a comedy. Needless to say, Peter didn't take that job.

"Please don't tell me that that's Charlie Hoynes," I said.

"Indeed. Wait a second, it's the 'King of the World' part." He and Ruby poked each other and snickered.

"I'm the king of the world!" Peter said.

"I'm a dentist!" she replied.

Peter turned his attention back to me. "You want me to call him?"

"You don't mind?" I asked.

"Why should I mind?"

"Well, he'll have your number, and you'll owe him a favor."

"Please. Who cares? Go get me the phone."

My generous spouse was somewhat less sanguine when Hoynes not only took his call, but insisted that we join him for dinner the following evening at Spago.

"Ick, Spago," I said, when Peter hung up the phone.

"Don't ick me. This is your fault."

I sighed. "I'll go call a babysitter."

"Nobody old!" Ruby shouted. At her piercing howl, Isaac finally woke up, crying, as usual. Neither of my children has ever managed to arise from an afternoon nap without at least twenty minutes of hysterical tears. I used to wonder if the couple of hours of bliss while they slept was worth the drama of their rising, but then Ruby stopped napping and I quickly realized that an entire, uninterrupted thirteen-hour day with a child is significantly longer than your average human adult can tolerate. The break a nap provides is worth any amount of weeping.

Eleven

THE next day, after the usual Monday-morning horror—
why am I constitutionally incapable of remembering to buy
lunch-making materials when I'm at the grocery store?—I
dropped the kids off at their respective schools and made
my way to Silver Lake. I'd left a message for Spike Stevens,
the director of the Left Coast Players. I hadn't imagined that
I'd reach him early on a Monday morning, but Moira had
given me his home address, and I wanted at least to give
him warning that I was on my way.

Spike lived near the "lake" for which his neighborhood is
named, a reservoir strangely denuded of trees and surrounded by a high fence. His apartment building was a typical LA *dingbat,* an early-sixties multi-unit monstrosity,
mostly carport, with an overhanging second floor and an
outdoor staircase. Generally the only time people outside of
our fair city see those buildings is in the wake of an earth-
quake, when the rubble of crushed cars and piles of cement

is broadcast on the news. Al met me out in front of the building. He hadn't thought much of my idea to interview Spike—he didn't think much of any part of the case, frankly, but Brodsky was too important to us for Al just to ignore what was going on. And it wasn't like he had anything else to do.

I rang Spike's bell, to no avail. While I was writing a note to put in his mailbox, Al pushed open the wrought iron gate that passed for a security system. The lock was rusted open.

"Al!" I said, but he was already halfway up the stairs. Spike lived on the second floor, behind a steel door painted a noxious shade of ultramarine. I tried to avoid looking at it. I'd remained true to my promise that morning and had had no coffee. The combination of caffeine deprivation and the assault on my senses of that garish color was enough to rekindle my morning sickness.

After a few minutes of pounding, a middle-aged man attired solely in pajama bottoms answered the door. His skin was colored an unnatural orange, with streaks along the side of his bulging waist, and I recognized the inexpert application of tanning cream from my own ill-fated exploration of the product. His belly spilled over the waistband of his pants, despite his immediate effort to suck it in. His swift inhalation served only to expand his narrow chest and push his double chin to the fore.

"Can I help you?" he muttered, pushing his lank hair out of his eyes with one hand.

"Spike?" I asked.

"Yeah?" he said suspiciously, rubbing his eyes. He glanced at the flecks of sleep on his fingers and flicked them away. I flinched, trying not to leap out of the way of what Isaac and Ruby so accurately called "eye boogers."

"I'm Juliet Applebaum. I left you a message?"

"Yeah?"

"This is my partner, Al Hockey. We're investigators. We work for Alicia Felix's family."

"Oh, wow. Bummer. You guys want to come in?" He backed away from the door and held it open for me. I walked through the doorway, and for one, brief, nightmare-Sumo moment our bellies rubbed against each other. I blushed, and I think Spike might have too, but it was hard to tell, given the sickly orange hue of his skin.

The room was a small, white-painted box with pale grey indoor-outdoor carpeting and furniture straight out of the Ikea sale aisle. Al and I sat down on a pressed wood and canvas couch that was probably named something like the "Fjärk." Spike settled into a "Snügens" sling-chair and leaned back with a groan.

"Sorry. Up late last night," he said.

"Improv practice?"

"I wish. Catering gig. Premiere at Fox."

"Good movie?"

"Hell if I know. They don't let the help into the screening room. We're supposed to pass the hors d'oeuvres, pour the champagne, and disappear into the woodwork." His tone was matter-of-fact; almost entirely devoid of bitterness.

I nodded sympathetically and said, "You're the director of the Left Coast Players?"

"I am."

"Have you been doing it long?"

He groaned. "Long enough. Twenty-two years."

I stifled my own groan. How could he stand it? How could any of them? Struggling along on the fringes of Hollywood, waiting tables, acting in comedy troupes and television commercials and desperately hoping for a break. It was enough to make a person crazy, or suicidal. Was it enough to drive someone to murder?

Al said, "What can you tell us about Bingie McPurge?"

"Julia Brennan's character? From *New York Live?*" He asked, disingenuously.

"Our understanding is that Alicia Felix created the character," I said.

He sighed.

"Did she?"

"I've gotta have some coffee," he said, leaping to his feet. "You guys want some?"

"Sure."

Twenty minutes later we were sitting at a table in the Starbucks on the corner of his block. Spike had tried to make us coffee, but had been out of filters, milk, and sugar. And coffee.

"Bingie McPurge," I said, once he'd taken his first sip of the coffee he so clearly needed. "Was she Alicia's creation? Did Julia steal her?"

He smacked his lips and moaned ostentatiously, "Ah, the royal bean. Nectar of the gods."

"Spike," Al said sharply.

"Oh, all right. Don't get your panties in a twist. Yes, Alicia had a similar character as one of her Left Coast characters."

"One of them?" I said.

"Okay, her only character. But as I see it, Julia has improved significantly on the idea. Really developed it."

"But it was Alicia's to begin with?"

He nodded. "Alicia inspired the character. Birthed her, if you will. But Julia has made Bingie her own."

I took a gulp of coffee and inhaled with relief as the

caffeine rushed to my head and chased my headache away. "Alicia didn't give Julia permission to 'make Bingie her own,' though, did she?"

He waved his hand. "Permission? Since when does an artist need permission? Art is about taking risks, about gobbling up life. The artist is a selfish being, in thrall to his own creative muse. Who can say from where inspiration will spring?"

I was surprised that Al managed to keep the coffee from spraying out of his nose; his snort of derision was that loud.

Poor Alicia. How frustrating, how miserable, it must have been to create something, only to have someone steal it away; and not only that, but to become so successful with it.

"Alicia was planning on suing Julia, wasn't she?"

Spike sighed heavily. "Poor Alicia. She just didn't have a good understanding of the creative muse. She made herself quite unpleasant around this issue."

"What do you mean?"

"Julia told me that Alicia tried to contact her a number of times. Called her. Wrote her letters. I finally had to step in."

"You?"

He nodded. "Julia asked me to. To, you know, see if I could calm Alicia down. Explain how things were. Let her know the steps Julia would have to take should she continue with her harassment."

"Harassment? Alicia was harassing Julia?" Al said.

He winced. "No, that's the wrong word. Forgive me. Julia just asked me to try to calm Alicia down."

"And did you?" I asked.

He nodded. "Yes, I think I did. Look, Alicia was never going to be happy about the whole Bingie McPurge thing. But even she came to recognize that there was nothing she could do about it."

"She gave up her idea of suing Julia?"

He smiled with a certain self-satisfaction. "She seemed, after our conversation, to understand that it would be a bad idea."

"I take it you and Julia are still close. It sounds like she relies on you."

He nodded. "Of course. We're all friends at the Left Coast Players. In fact," he said modestly, "I'll probably be joining Julia in New York soon. I just have to set things up here. You know, find someone who is willing to take over the troupe."

"Oh really? Is Julia helping you get an audition at *New York Live?*"

He shook his head. "She's a doll, and I'm sure she'll put a word in, but this has been in the works for quite some time."

Sure. Sure it had. There was something in Spike's eyes that let me know that he recognized my doubt full well, and, in fact, possessed plenty of his own. Still, I wasn't likely to convince this man to say anything negative about the woman upon whom his future might or might not lie. I was going to have to do the legwork on my own.

"Do you happen to have a video tape of the Left Coast Players? One with Alicia on it?" Al asked.

Spike wrinkled his brow. "I don't, but a few of the players did an appearance on *Talking Pictures* a few years ago. You might try them. They might keep tapes of old shows."

"*Talking Pictures?*" I said.

"It's a public access TV show out of the Valley. Hosted by Candy Gerard. You probably remember her, she used to have a series on CBS back in the mid-seventies, *Mary Jane and Rodolpho in Space?*"

I nodded my head. I vaguely remembered the series from my childhood. It had something to do with a love affair between a girl from the Bronx and an Italian space robot.

"Anyway, Alicia and some of the other players went on the show."

"Was Julia Brennan there?"

"God no. Public Access? Julia was never that desperate. Neither was I, for that matter. Alicia did the show with a couple of the guys. You should call Candy. She might have a tape."

I jotted the name of the show in my notebook, and then asked Spike, "Did Alicia's death come as a surprise to you?"

He wrinkled his brow. "What do you mean?"

"I mean, were you shocked? Or weren't you?"

He closed his eyes for a moment. "Frankly, I wasn't surprised. Don't get me wrong, it never occurred to me that someone would kill her. But Alicia didn't seem like someone who would live to a ripe old age."

"How so?"

He sighed. "Did you ever meet her?"

I flashed on the image of Alicia's brutalized body lying in her bathtub. "No," I said. My voice came out a hollow croak, and I cleared my throat. Al glanced at me, and I smiled reassuringly.

He shook his head. "Well, let's just say that a character with an eating disorder wasn't too great a stretch for Alicia Felix. In all the years I knew the woman, I don't think I ever saw her eat more than a single leaf of lettuce. She was so thin. I mean, they're all thin, all the baby actresses, but she seemed thinner than most. Sometimes she looked positively cadaverous."

I couldn't help but remember, as clearly as if I was holding before me a coroner's photograph, Alicia's sharp ribs, concave belly, and the hollow cup of her pelvis. "She was anorexic," I said.

He nodded. "Of course. I mean, she never said anything, but she had to be."

Here finally was someone who was willing to say what everybody else surely knew. It struck me, without knowing him too well, that Spike was that kind of guy. For all his Hollywood shtick, he seemed like someone who called things like he saw them. Even his self-aggrandizing puffery had just a trace of self-mockery to it. It was as if he was wordlessly letting me know that he was fully aware how ridiculous it was for a man of his age still to be engaged in the miserable rat race that was the quest for stardom. I liked him, orange skin, bloated belly, and all.

"If you told me that Alicia had starved to death, I probably wouldn't have keeled over in shock," Spike said. He took a large gulp of coffee, and looked about to launch into another homily to the speedy brew.

I spoke before he could. "But were you surprised that she was murdered?"

He licked away the pale brown mustache the coffee had left on his upper lip. "That's something else. I mean, who expects anybody to be murdered?"

Al interrupted. "Did she have any enemies?"

He laughed. "Enemies? Honey, this is LA. Everyone has enemies. Hell, your drycleaner has enemies."

I leaned back in my chair and put a hand to the small of my back where it had suddenly begun to ache. I wondered if other interrogators had to deal with these same indignities— back ache, swollen ankles, stretch marks. I shifted in my seat and asked my follow-up question. "Do you know who some of her enemies might be? Would Julia Brennan be one of Alicia's enemies?"

He rolled his eyes at me as if he'd never heard anything

so stupid. "Hardly. Now, if you were investigating *Julia's* murder, that would be a different story. Then it might have made sense to wonder about Alicia's feelings toward her. But I promise you, Julia Brennan didn't consider Alicia an enemy. In fact, I doubt she thought much about her at all."

"And was there anyone else?"

Spike narrowed his eyes, and it was brought home to me, once again, that this was a man far more insightful and intelligent than he allowed himself to seem. "You want to know if I know anyone who would like to see Alicia dead?"

"Yes."

He leaned back in his chair, tented his fingers over his belly, and said, "Alicia was not a particularly nice woman. Don't get me wrong. She could be very charming and friendly, when it suited her purpose. And she did have friends; Moira Sarsfield, for one. But Alicia was ambitious. She was more ambitious than she was talented, I think, but then that's true of most of us. She wanted success, she wanted adoration, she wanted the kind of things stardom brings you. Again, we all want that to a certain degree, but Alicia's desire was more . . . what? Palpable, I guess, than, say, mine. So did she make enemies? Sure. I'm sure she did. But I couldn't tell you who, and it's something of a mystery to me why someone would want to kill her."

"Why? If she was so ambitious, doesn't it stand to reason that she might have trampled on the wrong person?"

He leaned forward again, grabbing his cup of coffee and shaking his head at what he clearly considered my dense lack of understanding. "Alicia never attained any success to speak of. She couldn't have inspired any real envy. That can't be the reason for her murder. You'll have to find the motive somewhere else, my dear."

There was more than a kernel of truth to the man's word. Alicia may have done more than her share of professional trampling, but it surely hadn't resulted in much.

I couldn't resist asking one final question. "Spike's not your real name, is it?"

He pushed his coffee cup away and waggled a finger at me. "Trade secret, my girl."

"No, really."

He winked. "Oh, what the hell. Larry Finkelman, at your service." He extended his hand to me, and I shook it.

"Thanks for your help, Larry."

"Don't mention it," he said. "And call me Spike."

Twelve

CANDY Gerard's talk show was filmed in a long, grey building in a strip mall out in Studio City. There was an Arab grocery store flying a large American flag and advertising Jordanian olives and Israeli newspapers on one side of the studio, and a Vietnamese nail salon on the other. I imagined for a minute soaking my feet in hot paraffin, having my nails painted vermillion, rather than looking for tapes of Alicia Felix. The indulgence of a pedicure was far more attractive, but I doubted that Harvey Brodsky would hire Al and me based on the loveliness of my toes. I had to figure out who killed Alicia Felix, and while I wasn't sure I was going to get any closer to the solution to the crime by watching her appearances on public access TV, it wasn't like I was exactly inundated with better ideas.

I dragged open the heavy metal door of the unmarked studio and walked in. Maybe it was the hyper-sensitivity of my pregnant nose, but the place stank to high heaven. It smelled like old socks and onions, with a whiff of cheap perfume. It smelled like a tenement just after the hookers and the smack-addicts had been rousted out, and just before the place was demolished. And it didn't look any better. The walls were cement blocks, and exposed pipes trailing filthy streamers of shredded duct-tape sagged from the ceiling. Two young women in short skirts and high heels were lounging on a faded purple couch pushed up against the wall. One of the girls leaned against a broken armrest, her long legs draped across the other's lap. The second girl was holding a tiny mirror and studiously popping the pimples on her forehead.

"Is this where they shoot *Talking Pictures?*" I asked.

The long-legged girl, who had dyed black hair and severely cut bangs, pointed in the direction of a closed door marked "Do Not Enter When Light Is On." There was a large red signal light above the door. She snapped her gum loudly, and the other girl, who had finished ravaging her forehead and was now carefully painting her collagen-enhanced lips a noxious shade of plum that contrasted strangely with her platinum-blond hair, giggled.

"Are you two on the show?"

This reduced both of them to heaps of intense laughter. The black-haired girl actually had to press one long-fingernailed hand to her inflated chest to quell her hysterics.

"We work over there," she said, finally, pointing to the far end of the hall. A large poster decorated with a silhouette of a naked woman and the words "Man-Eater Productions" marked a set of double doors. Another red signal light glowed over the top of the doors.

"Are you actresses?"

The blond smiled. "Actresses? Sure, that's what we are. Right, Toni?"

"You'd better believe it," her friend said, emphatically. "I'm acting every minute of every working day."

"We're fluffers," the blond said, and winked.

Before I had a change to inquire just what a fluffer might be, or even to decide if I really wanted to know, the light over the Man-Eater door went out, and a heavyset man wearing a beret and a Sundance Film Festival T-shirt stuck his head out. "Girls, time to get busy," he said.

The two leapt to their feet, dragging their tiny skirts down over their rear ends, and tottered through the door on their impossibly high heels.

"Bye!" the blond called over her shoulder.

"Bye," I replied, and watched them go through the door as I sat down on the couch to wait. I caught a glimpse of a sound stage, decorated with a large, round bed covered in a wrinkled, red velvet spread. There was a naked man kneeling in the middle of the bed, his back to me. Suddenly I had a pretty good idea what a fluffer was. When Toni and her friend had come out to Hollywood from Nebraska, or Alabama, or Anaheim, or whichever small town or city that regularly launched its naïve young women across the country to be chewed up and swallowed by the Hollywood machine, had they imagined that fantasies of stardom would result in jobs keeping male porn stars prepped and ready? Somehow, I doubted it. Like every other wanna-be starlet, like Alicia for that matter, those two girls had probably spent their years in high school playing Emily in *Our Town* or tap dancing through *Bye Bye Birdie,* dewey-skinned and starry-eyed Kim McAfees. They'd honed their Oscar acceptance speeches on the bus to LA, and spent their last two hundred dollars on the perfect set of head shots, designed to make them look like leading ladies, ingénues, comic geniuses. And perhaps it wasn't yet all over for them. Perhaps they weren't permanently doomed to be nothing more than fluffers. Perhaps one or the other of them would become the serious actress she had surely imagined herself to be. But I doubted it. If these girls saw their dreams of stardom realized, it would most likely be in the seedy and depressing part of the industry that already employed them.

When the *Talking Pictures* light blinked and went out, I heaved myself to my feet, using my hands to lift my belly. It was getting harder and harder to get myself out of a chair. Pretty soon I was going to need a hoist and a forklift.

I opened the door and looked inside. The studio was larger than I expected, and painted entirely black. Half was taken up with a darkened set that looked much like the one across the hall at Man-Eater Productions—not much more than a bed. Clearly another porn set. At the far end of the long room, lit with two heavy banks of lights, was a set with two easy chairs. A thin woman with a frozen helmet of orange hair, false eyelashes so long they were obvious even where I was standing a good thirty feet away, and a mouth painted in a shade that almost, but not quite, matched her hair, perched on the edge of her seat. Somewhere under the makeup and taut, surgically altered cheeks and eyes was the ghost of Mary Jane, the girl from the Bronx who'd fallen in love with a robot from Naples.

A young man, no older than twenty, huddled in the other chair. His hair was artfully mussed, and his lime-green polyester shirt was buttoned high on his skinny neck.

"You gotta make sure you put the graphic up, dude," the young man was saying as I walked into the room. "They gotta see the graphic."

"They'll see it," a voice muttered from behind the huge camera hunkered down in front of the set.

"Of course they'll see it," Candy said. Her voice was

roughened and harsh, as if she'd spent a lifetime smoking unfiltered cigarettes.

"All I'm saying is they gotta see that graphic. Plug the movie. That's why I'm here."

Candy rose to her feet. She unsnapped a small micro-phone from the ruffles of her low-cut blouse, and said to the young man, "Thank you so much for your time. It was a ter-rific interview. Just terrific, don't you think?"

She stomped off toward me before he could answer her, and I swore I heard her mutter something that sounded sus-piciously like, "Goddamn film school brats." Then she no-ticed me. "Can I help you?" she snapped.

"I'm so sorry if I'm intruding," I said.

She put her hands on her hips. "Can I help you?" she re-peated. "This is a closed set."

"I'm Juliet Applebaum. I called a little while ago? I think I talked to your producer. I'm looking for a tape of one of your shows."

She called over her shoulder. "Spencer! Did you speak to someone about a tape?"

The man behind the camera raised his head. I immedi-ately recognized the thick Cockney accent that had an-swered my call when I'd telephoned after leaving Spike at the café. "Yeah. She's looking for that comedy group. The one we had on a few years ago, remember?"

Candy turned back to me and gave me the once-over with a suspicious eye. "Are you in the industry?"

I shook my head. "I'm not."

She shook her head and began to walk away from me. "My husband's a screenwriter," I said hurriedly. She turned back around, one eyebrow raised. "I'm an investigator," I continued, and then began to explain about Alicia Felix. Candy held up her hand.

"Any credits?"

"Excuse me?"

"Your husband. Do I know his work?"

Maybe. "He wrote the *Flesh Eater* series. The most recent one is called *The Cannibal's Vacation*. He's working on *Beach Blanket Bloodbath* now."

Her whole demeanor suddenly changed. "How fabulous!" she cooed. "I'm a huge fan. Huge. Come on over to my office. We *must* talk!"

Her office was down the hall from Man-Eater Productions and consisted of a room about the size of a storage closet. One wall was entirely taken up with shelves full of plastic videotape boxes marked with dates and names in thick black marker. Candy perched on the edge of a card table and motioned for me to take the single seat, a rickety metal folding chair that I was sure would not be able to carry my weight. I sat down carefully, wincing at the creak of the seat under my behind.

"So, your husband writes those wonderful films," she said. "They're so unusual. So exceptional for the genre. I really consider them to be almost like art films, don't you?"

I blinked. I wasn't quite sure what the technical definition of art cinema was, but I had a feeling it couldn't encompass both Truffaut's *The 400 Blows* and Peter's homage to the undead.

"I'd love to have him on the show!" Candy said. "Give him the exposure he so clearly deserves."

I smiled politely, imaging what my husband would say if I told him he had to drive out to the Valley to appear on public access television with a washed-up 70s sitcom queen. "I'd be happy to pass that along to him."

"Just have his agent give me a call." She reached across the table and rifled through a pile of papers. She pulled a crumpled business card out of the stack and handed it to me. "We're, uh, in between bookers right now, so he should just talk to Spencer, or to me."

"Great," I said, pocketing the card. "So, I'm really hoping to get a copy of the Left Coast Players' appearance on your show."

Candy smiled and waved at the wall of videocassettes. "We've got a complete archive, as you can see. They were on, what, two, three years ago?"

"I think so," I said.

Within no more than two minutes, Candy had pulled out a videocassette in a plastic box marked L.C. Players. "Here it is," she announced. She tried to blow the thick layer of dust off the case, and when that didn't work she rubbed it against her skin-tight black leather pants. The case left a grey smear of dust along her thigh.

"Thanks so much," I said. "Do you think I can get a copy?"

She smiled. "Do you think you're husband will do the show?"

I paused, and she blinked her long eyelashes benignly.

"I'm sure he will," I said.

She smiled again. "Excellent. Come with me."

She led me out the door of her office and to the Man-Eater studio. The light over the door was off, and she pushed the door open, motioning me to follow her.

"Fred!" she called out as we walked into the studio. The man in the beret was sitting in a director's chair, talking to two other burly men. They were the only fully dressed people in the room. A few women wrapped in bathrobes were standing around a long table full of picked-over boxes of donuts and half-empty bottles of diet soda. I looked over at the bed, and froze. Toni was there, hunched over a naked man, probably the same guy I saw from the back. This time it was *her* back I saw, and the realization of what she was doing crept over me slowly. I felt the heat of my blush burning my cheeks, and I was all the more self-conscious because I was the only person who seemed at all shocked by what was going on. I turned my back on the scene, and gulped nervously.

"Can you dub this for me, hon?" Candy said to the beret-wearing man. She handed him the video.

"Sure, Candy," he said.

She turned to me. "Juliet? You don't mind if he does it on a high speed, do you? He can do higher resolution, but it'll take longer."

"That's fine," I said, looking down at my shoes. For some reason I just wasn't capable of looking anyone in the face. Not with Toni and the unidentified man over on the bed.

Candy seemed to notice my embarrassment for the first time, and she laughed. "Never been on an adult film set?"

I shook my head.

Candy nodded in the direction of Toni's busily bobbing head. "The fluffer's got to keep the guys in working order."

"Right," I said, trying unsuccessfully to appear nonchalant. "Of course."

"You know, there's some cutting-edge work going on in the adult-film arena. A lot of studio directors are finding inspiration in adult film director's creative risk taking. Aren't they Fred?"

"Give me ten, fifteen minutes, and I'll have this dubbed," Fred said, ignoring her question. He tossed the tape to one of the other men.

"Thanks, hon," Candy said. "Juliet, would you prefer to wait in my office?"

"God, yes," I said. They all burst out laughing, and she led me back out the door.

Thirteen

"You know what I love about you the most?" I asked Peter as we were driving to Spago.

"My rock-hard buns and washboard stomach?"

"Those, too. But I was really thinking of how supportive you are. How eager you are to help me succeed in this wild new path my career has taken."

He glanced over at me and narrowed his eyes.

"Juliet?"

"What, darling?" I smiled innocently.

"What did you get me into, now?"

"Nothing. I'm just talking about this dinner."

He turned back to the road, just in time to avoid hitting a bright yellow Humvee that had shot out of a blind driveway directly into our path. He swore under his breath.

"Wow! Great job avoiding that monster truck! You are such a *terrific* driver, sweetie."

"Okay, that's it!" he shouted, and screeched the car

over, right in the middle of Little Santa Monica Boulevard.

"Peter! What are you doing?"

"What? *What?* You tell *me* what. What is going on?"

I leaned over and patted his arm. "Nothing. Really. Let's just get to the restaurant."

He pulled back out into traffic. Within a few moments he was handing the car over to the valet parker with his usual elaborate instructions. The young valet parker just nodded, clearly not understanding a word my husband was saying. Peter has never made peace with that fact that vintage orange BMW 2002s with wood trim, velour seats, delayed wash wipe, and the rarest of Alpina Butterfly throttle injection systems just aren't the valued commodity in the rest of the world that they are around the Applebaum/Wyeth house-hold. The valet took off with a squeal of wheels, and Peter swore again. I wrapped my arm around his waist and leaned my head against his upper arm, the closest to his shoulder that I could reach while we were standing up. He hugged me back, and we walked into the restaurant.

As we were heading over to the table where Hoynes and his guest were already waiting for us, I said, "Oh, Peter. I forgot to tell you. You're booked onto this talk show. *Talking Pictures?* You're shooting next week. Wednesday."

He turned to me, his mouth open, but we'd arrived at the table.

"Hi!" I said brightly. "I'm Juliet Applebaum. And you know my husband, Peter Wyeth, of course."

It was a thing of beauty—by the time the hand shaking was completed, my husband's stunned expression had been replaced by one of resignation.

Alicia Felix's boyfriend, Charlie Hoynes, was a fat man. Not obese, necessarily, but bloated somehow, with an immense abdomen that appeared to begin right under his neck, and continued down, to the tops of his thighs. His thinning hair was cut short, almost buzzed, and a single gold hoop dangled from one bulbous earlobe. His nose was squashed flat, and redder than the rest of his face. It looked like it had been palpated, squeezed, and pressed deep into the flesh between his cheeks. His grip was firm, and somehow sticky, and it was all I could do to resist wiping my palm on my leg when he finally released my hand.

It was impossible to imagine him in any kind of intimate situation with his date, a rail-thin blond with oversized breasts, improbably named Dakota Swain. How could her delicate frame survive contact with his bulk? Dakota had sharp, mouse-like features, and narrow lips outlined heavily in bright red lipstick. She looked incredibly familiar to me, and for the first few minutes of dinner I was distracted by trying to place her. This always happens to me in Los Angeles. During our first few years in the city, I would constantly greet people, sure I'd met them before. I even asked, on more than one occasion, if the possessor of that familiar face was someone who had gone to college with me. I was invariably shut down with a glare, and the comment that the person had just had a guest spot on *Seinfeld.*

But I did know Dakota. I was sure of it. Finally, I just asked her. "Dakota, do we know each other? I swear I know you."

She smiled. "I'm an actress. You've probably seen my work."

I smiled back, doubtfully. "What have you been in?"

"Oh God, what haven't I been in! Sitcoms, commercials. You name it."

Charlie patted her talon-like hand with his broad, damp

one. "And now Dakota is going to be in the latest Hoynes Production, *The Vampire Evenings*. We're shooting the pilot and eight episodes over the next few months."

That's when I figured out why I felt like I knew Dakota Swain. I hadn't caught any one of her various TV or movie appearances, at least not that I could remember. She looked familiar because she looked like Alicia Felix. Like Alicia, Dakota was a skinny blond with fake breasts, approaching forty, and desperately trying to look a dozen years younger. Hoynes clearly had a type.

I smiled noncommittally, and then complimented Dakota on the black spandex midriff-baring top she was wearing. There were two tears in the fabric, carefully placed just barely to avoid exposing her nipples. "Booty Rags?" I asked.

She nodded. "I bought it at Fred Segal. They have the best selection in the city."

I nodded, wondering if she really thought that information would be useful to a woman at the end of her pregnancy.

Through the appetizers, Hoynes grilled Peter on his career, what films he'd written, what projects he'd been up for but hadn't got, what he'd turned down. At one point, his chin glistening with melted butter, and his mouth full of Clams Casino, the producer pointed a finger at my long-suffering husband and bellowed, "So what's your quote, kid? What are you getting now? Two, three hundred K a picture? More? Less?"

Peter smiled sickly and pinched me under the table: I hadn't been paying much attention to what Hoynes was saying; I found myself unable to keep my eyes off Dakota. She was carefully slicing and dicing every item on her plate. She had reduced her smoked salmon to tiny pink shreds, and her blini to a pile of mashed dough. So far I hadn't seen her raise her fork to her lips even once. I dragged my eyes away from her plate and interrupted Hoynes's flow of words.

"So, Charlie, what can you tell me about Alicia Felix?" Awkward, I know, but that's what we were there for, and the guy had been torturing my husband long enough.

He banged his hand down on the table. "Call me Tracker!" he announced in a voice uncomfortably close to a bellow. Diners at neighboring tables looked over at us, and one fastidious-looking man in a black suit jacket and muted grey tie winced.

"Tracker?" Peter said. "Since when are you known as Tracker?"

"Since last year. I had it legally changed."

Peter and I exchanged a look. "Er, Tracker," I said. "What can you tell me about Alicia?"

"What do you want to know?" he asked. At that moment a busboy swooped down on our table and cleared our plates. Dakota pushed her plate away with one hand, and putting the other over her chest, filled her cheeks to indicate how full she was. Of air, I assume, since she hadn't actually consumed a single morsel of her first course.

"Were you two . . . er . . ." I looked over at his date.

He laughed again. "An item? We were; we were indeed. Dakota here knows all about Alicia. I don't keep secrets from my girls, do I, babe? It's all out in the open with the Tracker-Man. You see what you get, and you get what you see!" He reached his fork over to the butter dish, speared a ball of butter, and popped it into his mouth. He smiled at my astonished expression and said, "Atkins diet, babe."

I discreetly refrained from mentioning the breadcrumbs that had been baked onto his appetizer. Dakota looked nauseated at the sight of him eating butter, or maybe by the very idea of butter itself. Or perhaps it was simply old Tracker who made her ill. I was willing to bet that was it. I thought I was detecting a resurgence of my own morning sickness.

"So how long were you seeing Alicia?" I asked.

He wrinkled his brow. "Let's see. Six, nine months maybe? Dakota, you'd know. I met you both at the vampire auditions. When was that?"

"Closer to nine months ago."

I felt decidedly awkward asking him these questions in front of her. How desperate was Alicia, how desperate was Dakota, that the two of them had forced themselves to be intimate with this grotesque man? Because desperation could be the only reason for their choices. Nothing else made sense. As little as I wanted to, I needed to know more. I decided to take Tracker at his word that he was a man who brooked no secrets. "Were you and Alicia serious?"

"Serious? I don't know. I liked her, sure. Just like I like Dakota here." He reached one hefty arm around his girl-friend and squished her close, placing a kiss on her cheek with a loud smack. She furtively wiped the grease left from his lips with a napkin.

"How often did you see each other?"

"Two, maybe three times a week. She was a good kid. She helped me out with my daughter. Dakota's not a big one for kids, are you babe?"

Dakota curled her lip and shook her head.

"Alicia always stayed over on Halley's night with me. I've got the kid every, what is it . . .?" He looked at his girl-friend.

"Tuesday," she murmured.

"Right. Halley's at my house on Tuesdays. So Alicia al-ways came over that night. I'll tell you, I miss her one hell of a lot." He paused, wiping carefully at his dry eyes with his napkin. "Especially on Tuesdays." He sighed at the wearying thought Tuesdays. "Halley loved Alicia. She really did. And that girl doesn't take to just anyone. For instance," he dropped his napkin and chuckled. "She sure as hell can't stand Dakota, can she?"

"The feeling's mutual," Dakota said, taking a gulp of wine.

Two waiters arrived at our table and lay our laden plates down with a flourish. I was momentarily distracted by the pile of fluffy mashed potatoes sitting next to my lamb chop. I always order according to the side dish. Steak, stew, fish, I like them all. But what really catches my attention is a nice butter-laden gratin, or a mound of pureed squash. I gobbled up a few bites, blissing out at the creamy texture, the buttery flavor. Food always tastes so good to me when I'm pregnant. I looked up just in time to catch Dakota's disgusted expression. I imagined that to a woman who took finicky eating to such an extreme that it nearly qualified as performance art, Hoynes and I were one and the same—overweight, greasy-cheeked gluttons. I felt a spark of sympathy for Tracker. Sure, he'd made his own bed, but how could he stand to share it with such a judgmental twig?

I swallowed the food in my mouth and continued with my questioning.

"Had you cast Alicia in your vampire series?"

He spread his hands wide. "Hey, nothing's final until the show's on the air, you know? Sure, I was considering using her. I probably would have, you know? But I hadn't made any final decision. I still haven't."

Dakota's head snapped upward. She'd been staring at her plate, busily performing an autopsy on her halibut filet. "What the hell does that mean, Charlie?" She seemed suddenly to have forgotten his new name.

He patted her hand and chuckled. "It means what it

always means. Nothing's final until it's in the can." He turned back to me. "I got lots of parts for girls in this series. We'll suck 'em dry every week, if you get my meaning." He bellowed with laughter, making the diners at the neighboring table jump in their seats. "Alicia wanted the part of Empress of the Night. Just like Dakota does."

"Did Alicia think she would get that part?"

"She might have. But she knew it was still up in the air. That's just how I work, isn't it Dakota?"

"Tracker, you promised *me* that role. Months ago." Dakota's face was pale, and the hand she had wrapped around her wine glass was trembling, making the liquid slosh in the glass. "You did!"

He sighed and looked at me. "A producer's life—it ain't easy, let me tell you."

"Goddamn you, Charlie Hoynes. Goddamn you!" Dakota shouted. She leapt to her feet and rushed out of the restaurant. Peter and I stared after her. I turned back to Hoynes. It took me a moment to realize that he was not in the least upset. His shoulders were shaking only because he was laughing.

"That is one feisty girl, let me tell you. She'll make a damn fine Empress."

"Don't you want to go after her?" I asked.

He shook his head and placed a huge bite of steak in his mouth. Then, with his mouth still full of food, he said, "She'll find her way back to my house. Or not. Don't worry about it. Dakota's a big girl. She can take care of herself."

I didn't want to spend another minute at the table with that vulgar, greasy-mouthed pig. But I had no choice. Whatever *she* had meant to *him*, Alicia had considered Charlie Hoynes her boyfriend, and as depressing and sad at that was, I needed information from him. I also wondered just how much a role in a soft-core porn TV series meant to Dakota Swain. Enough to run out of Spago and make her own way home, sure. But how about enough to commit murder?

"I take it Dakota and Alicia didn't get along," I said.

He laughed, and I could see a clot of pink meat on his tongue. "I'm honest with my girls. It's all out in the open with me."

"Did they spend much time together?"

"I doubt it. They didn't have much in common, those two. Oil and water."

That certainly rang false. They seemed to have absolutely everything in common, except an affection for Hoynes's daughter.

"Your daughter, Halley, how old is she?"

He took a large swallow of wine and wrinkled his brow. "Let's see . . . sixteen? No, wait a minute. She was born in 1986. That'll make her seventeen. Or was it '87? No, '86, I'm sure of it."

By now my husband had pinched me under the table so many times that I was sure I had a bruise the size of a grapefruit on my thigh.

"And she and Alicia were friends?"

Hoynes nodded, his mouth once again full of food. "Alicia helped her out. Halley's a little bit anorexic. Won't eat. It's just a teenage phase, but Alicia'd been through that when she was a kid, so she knew what was going on with Halley. She got where the kid was coming from, which is more than I can say for Halley's hag of a mother."

Could that really be true? Had Alicia confided in Hoynes that she had been anorexic, when she hadn't even admitted it to her best friend, Moira?

"She told you she used to have anorexia?"

He shook his head. "She didn't tell me anything. She told

Halley. And Halley told her mother. And her goddamn mother called up my lawyer screaming her head off, lunatic that she is."

"I don't understand. Why would that upset your wife?" I said.

"Hell if I know. My lawyer is always getting hysterical phone calls from my ex. Seems the kid went home and told her mother that she hated her—and who can blame her?—and that she wanted to move in with me and Alicia." He laughed, genuinely tickled by the idea. "Like that would have happened. Anyway, Halley said only Alicia understood her, because she knew first-hand what it was like to have this crazy anorexia thing. Barbara freaked out—so what else is new. And when Ms. Barbara Hoynes freaks, she calls her lawyers."

Hoynes scraped his fork against his empty plate, gathering up the last of the juices. "You'd think she would have been glad Halley had found someone to talk to about her problem, wouldn't you? I mean, the goddamn girl didn't talk to *anybody,* not even the shrinks they've got me paying through the nose for. But Barbara's a jealous woman. She just couldn't stand to see Halley close to anyone but her. And especially not one of my girls."

I could sort of understand that. But one might imagine that Halley's wellbeing would override her mother's vindictiveness or sense of competition. For that matter, one might have imagined that the ex–Mrs. Hoynes would consider herself well rid of her vile ex-husband.

"Did Alicia keep seeing Halley after that?"

"Sure she did. You think I'm going to let Barbara say who I can and can't have in my house? She threatened to take me back to court, but I'd like to have seen her try. Lunatic."

"What would her grounds have been to take you to court?"

"Grounds? You think that woman needs *grounds?* Who knows. She wanted Alicia away from the kid. She thought she was a bad influence, and she told me she'd go to court to keep her out of Halley's life." He belched softly, covering his mouth with a curled fist. "She didn't need to in the end, though, did she?"

"What do you mean?"

"Well, someone took care of that for her, didn't they?"

"Do you think your ex-wife could have had something to do with the murder?"

"Nah, I mean, she's a nut-case, but not a murderer. Anyway, she's got all she can handle with Halley. Girl's back in the hospital."

"She's in the hospital?"

Hoynes sat back, letting out a sigh of contentment and patting himself on the stomach. "Halley's in and out every few months. Whenever her weight drops below eighty pounds, her mother checks her back in. Thank God I've got health insurance through the Guild, that's all I can say. Hey, you know what I just thought of? I should sell my own damn story. Beloved girlfriend brutally murdered. Killers at large. Disease-of-the-week daughter. Make a great TV movie, don't you think?"

I blinked.

Hoynes laughed and said, "Hell, maybe I should option it myself! How about that? Give myself a hundred grand for the rights."

Fourteen

"YOU owe me big time," Peter said. We were lying in bed, doing our best to recover from our evening with the charming Tracker Hoynes. The man had actually imagined that we'd go out "clubbing" with him after dinner. Was he out of his mind? Had he not noticed that I was the size and shape of a dirigible? Even if I hadn't been pregnant, I would never have gone out dancing with him. First of all, I hadn't been out to a bar since I met Peter and was finally relieved of the obligation to spend my weekends searching for a man. More importantly, however, I knew that if I spent another minute in Hoynes's presence I would end up grabbing a chair and whacking him over the head with it.

"How should I pay you back for tonight?" I asked.

"Find us somewhere to live."

I groaned. "Anything I can do in the interim?" Despite the advanced stage of my pregnancy, I did the best I could to compensate my husband both for our terrible evening and for my lack of real estate progress. Afterward, I put the videotape of Alicia's appearance on *Talking Pictures* on the VCR in our bedroom. The production values were every bit as dreadful as I had expected, given the company with whom the show shared studio space. The tinny music started up, and the camera swooped in on Candy's face. She was harshly lit, the glare coming from above her head and casting the lower half of her face in shadow. She presented a decidedly cadaverous appearance to the camera.

"Hallo, I'm Candy Gerard. Welcome to *Talking Pictures,*" she said, staring steamily into the camera. I'm sure it was my imagination, but I could swear she was doing a Marlene Dietrich imitation.

Peter turned to me. *"Talking Pictures?"* he said.

I smiled wanly.

"This is the show *I'm* booked on?"

"Um. Yeah."

"Who booked me on it?"

"Um, I did."

"You do realize you'll have to pay me back for that, too."

"Tonight?"

"No. I'll take a raincheck."

"Sure, honey. Now be quiet, here's Alicia."

The Left Coast Players troupe consisted of two men dressed as high school nerds and Alicia wearing a miniskirt, a tube-top, and a ponytail high on her head. One of the men went off screen and returned dressed as a dozen Krispy Kreme donuts, complete with huge, pink cardboard box and sprinkles. Alicia and the donuts engaged in a dance that looked more like simulated sex than Balanchine, and then she started miming eating the donuts. Once she'd faked consuming what appeared to be at least a dozen, she began to stick her fingers down her throat. At that moment, she tripped over the dancing donuts and got her hands stuck in the box. The shtick proceeded for another few minutes, with Alicia trying to get her fingers down her throat to make herself throw up, and something interfering at the last second. The bulimic who couldn't purge. Ha ha ha. Ho ho ho.

"Is it me, or is this really not funny?" I said.

"It's not you."

Finally, the sketch was over, and Candy interviewed the players. Alicia didn't say much, other than to drop the name and contact number of her agent. The discussion was dominated by the donut box, who spoke at great length about the historical and cultural antecedents of urban comedy. Peter was nearly asleep when the half hour was up.

"I can't wait to be on that show," he said when I poked him awake. "Really."

"I'm sorry."

"You should be." He leaned over and kissed me on the lips. "You're lucky you're so damn cute, otherwise I'd be really upset. And honey?"

"Yes?"

"The San Diego Comic Con is next weekend. And I am *so* going."

"Okay."

"Juliet?"

"Yeah, sweetie?"

"Does Felix know you're only representing him to get a hold of his house?"

I sat up. "That's not the only reason I'm investigating this case!"

"But it's the main reason. Don't get me wrong. I want to move as badly as you do. I haven't gotten a minute's work done since that damn construction project started. But it just seems . . . I don't know."

"What?"

"Unethical."

"It isn't. Really. Farzad and I even talked about how much I want the house." I felt a little knot in my stomach. What had been unethical was implying to Harvey Brodsky that Felix was my client even before he'd hired me. But all that was okay now. I'd been hired. And I'd find the killer. And Brodsky would hire us, and Al and I wouldn't have to shut down the agency. I hoped.

I snuggled closer to Peter. "I wish I could see Julia Brennan's Bingie McPurge. I wonder if she's any funnier than Alicia was."

"Wait a sec," Peter said, and took the remote out of my hand. He clicked over to his new toy, TIVO. Within minutes he had an episode of *New York Live* playing on the television set.

"You recorded this?" I said.

He shook his head. "No, but the software thinks I like it, so it keeps recording it for me, I think because I have it catching *Monty Python*. I haven't bothered to correct it yet, so you're in luck."

Julia Brennan didn't dance with a box of donuts, and *New York Live* had a slicker set and better costumes to lend that much-needed air of verisimilitude. Bingie McPurge's attempts at emesis were thwarted by elaborate casts on her arms, by catching her thumbs in a pair of mouse-traps, by a toilet seat that was stuck shut, by a pair of Chinese finger cuffs. But it was the same gimmick exactly. The bulimic binges, and then cannot purge. And it was just as humorless in its more professional incarnation.

"Well, that's pretty clear," Peter said when the skit was over and Julia had gagged her way off screen.

"She stole the character from Alicia."

He nodded. "Definitely. Although it does raise one really important question."

"What's that?"

He pounded on his pillow with his fist and lay back down in the bed, drawing the down comforter up to his chin. "Why in God's name did she bother?"

I laughed. "It's just unbelievably awful, isn't it?"

"Yup."

"Wanna hear something really horrible?" I turned off the light and curled up around him.

"What?" he murmured, already half asleep.

"They're making it into a movie."

"What?" He sat bolt upright.

"You heard me."

"Oh my God!" He collapsed back onto the pillow. "Sometimes I really hate this business."

Fifteen

THE next morning, right as I was walking out the door to drive the kids to school, my phone rang. It was Farzad.

"There is a detective from the LA police department here. He wants to talk to Felix."

"Damn," I muttered, looking at my watch. Peter was sound asleep, and the kids needed to be at school in ten minutes. "Where is he?"

"Waiting in the living room."

"And where's Felix?"

"In the shower."

"Okay, here's what I want you to do. Give the detective a cup of coffee, and tell Felix to take his time getting dressed. I'll be there in half an hour."

"Good," he said.

"Oh, and Farzad?"

"Yes?"

"Don't say anything to the cop, okay?"

He grimaced. "What do you take me for, Juliet? I'm not some stupid American who confesses everything to the secret police."

"Good," I said, and hung up the phone, wondering if I should have pointed out to him that while the LAPD was far from perfect, their powers did not yet include hauling people from their homes in the middle of the night and making them disappear. At least, I didn't think they did. I called Al and told him to meet me there, luckily catching him on his cell phone in the Ikea parking lot. He was only too happy to leave Jeanelle to shop on her own. It wasn't until I was speeding down Beverly Boulevard to dump the kids and get to Felix's house that it occurred to me to wonder what exactly it was that Farzad wasn't dumb enough to confess to the police.

I managed to dump each of my children off in front of their respective schools. I gave Ruby to a mother with whom I'd once shared field trip carpool duties, and Isaac to the nanny of his best friend. I crossed my fingers that both women would sign the kids in correctly and make sure their lunches made it into their cubbies, and tore over to Felix's house. For once, I actually made it in significantly less time than I'd promised.

Farzad answered the door and nodded his head in the direction of the living room.

"Where's Felix?" I asked in a low voice.

He pointed up the stairs.

"Come with me," I said.

We found Felix in his bedroom, sitting on the edge of the bed, his forearms resting on his knees, and his head bent low.

"Hey," I said.

He raised his head at the sound of my voice, and I could see the tracks of tears down his cheeks.

"Thanks for coming over," he said.

"Hey, that's what you pay me for," I replied. "Felix, do you have an attorney?"

He nodded. "Of course. I mean, the business does."

A corporate lawyer adept at contract negotiations and employee disputes was not going to do Felix much good under these particular circumstances.

I sat down next to him and gave him the speech I gave every client about to be questioned by the authorities. Most of the people I'd represented had faced examination by the FBI or DEA, both agencies that tended to employ agents significantly more professional and educated than the average LAPD cop. I hadn't often supervised an interview with a regular police officer, but I was confident in my ability to do so. While federal agents tend at least to simulate a respect for the strictures of the Constitution, they are also generally wilier and more skilled in the art of interrogation. The most important thing he was to remember, I told Felix, was to pause after hearing each question and before replying, both to make sure he understood the question and knew the answer, and to give me time to indicate to him not to reply if I felt that doing so would not be in his best interest.

"Why don't I just tell the cops I won't talk to them?" he said.

"You can do that. It's up to you."

"Will that make them think I had something to do with Alicia's death?"

"It might. But then, they might think that already. It's not what they're suspicious of that matters. It's what they can prove."

He groaned. "I had nothing to do with it, you know that, don't you?"

"Absolutely," I said, although of course I knew nothing of the kind.

"I want to help them find her killer. I really do."

I waited.

"I'll talk to him," he said, finally.

"Are you sure?"

He nodded.

"Okay then, let's go. Don't worry, I'll stop the questioning if I think it's going somewhere it shouldn't."

Before we were halfway down the stairs, the doorbell rang. I introduced Al to our clients, *sotto voce,* and together we went into the living room, where we discovered the detective peering at the photographs on the walls.

"Mapplethorpe," he said, smiling.

Felix nodded.

"He's one of my favorites."

Felix and Farzad looked at each other quickly, and then back at the detective. I joined them in their appraisal, and agreed silently with what I knew was their conclusion. I looked over at Al, who was rocking back and forth on his heels, his eyes nearly bugging out of his head at the photographs. My partner is, like many aggressively masculine men, not particularly comfortable with gay people. To his credit, though, his political commitment to the libertarian cause makes him a live-and-let-live kind of guy.

"Detective Antoine Goodenough," the cop said, extending a large hand with tapered fingers.

Felix's hand disappeared into Detective Goodenough's proffered mitt, and he very nearly smiled a greeting.

I stepped forward and introduced myself. "I'm Juliet Applebaum, and this is Al Hockey."

The detective raised one, arched eyebrow.

"I'm an attorney, and a friend of Felix and Farzad's. I hope you don't mind if we sit in on the conversation."

He paused, and looked for a moment like he was going

to object. Then he smiled pleasantly. "Where were you on the job?" he asked Al.

"Hollywood," Al said. "Been retired nearly ten years now."

The detective nodded. Then he turned to me and said, "You're the woman who found the body, correct?"

He'd recognized my name from the report. "Yes," I said.

Detective Goodenough was a tall man, with broad shoulders and a slim waist. His skin was the color of cinnamon, and a glint of russet was just visible in his shorn brown hair. His lips were thin, and he wore a narrow line of moustache as if to enhance, or deflect, attention from them. His eyes were almond-shaped, lending his face a faintly Asian cast. He looked like a Tartar, I decided. A very handsome, African-American Genghis Khan.

He reached a hand into his pocket and removed a silver card case. Unlike the one floating around in the bottom of my purse, his was untarnished, and had no lint-furred sucking candies stuck to its surface. He flipped it open with an elegant finger, removed four business cards, and handed one to each of us.

"I'm new to your sister's case," he said to Felix. "I wanted to come by to tell you how very sorry I am for your loss."

Felix bent his head. "Thank you," he murmured.

"I've read the reports prepared by the detectives who first arrived on the scene, as well as the crime scene and forensic files."

"Detective Goodenough," I interjected. "Is the case now yours?" Had the LAPD reassigned the case because they were either biased enough or savvy enough to assume that Detective Goodenough would be more adept at eliciting information from Alicia's brother than a heterosexual officer?

"Please, sit down," he said, welcoming Felix and Farzad

to their own living room. We followed his bidding. "This crime is a very high priority for my department. I want you to know that we're devoting as much of our resources to it as possible. I'm now the lead detective on the case, but the entire department is working hard to find Alicia's murderer."

For what felt like hours, Detective Goodenough asked question after question about Alicia's life, her childhood, her career. Al took his usual careful notes, and I listened closely.

"Did Alicia have any problems growing up? Was she, say, involved with drugs?" Goodenough asked.

Felix shook his head. "No, not at all."

"Not at all," Goodenough said, with a smile.

Felix smiled back. "Well, no more than was normal. You know, she smoked pot a little. Maybe even did some cocaine. Hell . . . we . . ."

I interrupted him quickly. "Felix," I said.

He turned to me. "What?"

"I think the detective just wants to know if Alicia had any kind of a drug problem." I stressed his sister's name.

He nodded, and turned back to the detective. "She didn't have a drug problem. At all."

"Did she have any other problems?"

Felix nodded. "She had an eating disorder when she was a teenager."

Goodenough made a note, and asked, "Any other issues?"

Felix shook his head.

I wanted to know more, however. "She was anorexic as a child, wasn't she?" I asked.

Felix nodded.

"Severely?"

He nodded again. "Enough to be hospitalized a couple of times. She made it through, though. She went to this inpatient facility back home in Florida for the whole summer before her senior year of high school. That cured her."

But had it? I thought of her emaciated corpse with the pang of horror complicated by pity that struck me every time that image entered my mind. "Are you sure the problem hadn't recurred?" I asked.

Felix shook his head. "Look, I'm a fashion designer. I can tell you—all women have an eating disorder. Alicia was no worse in the end than any one of the women who model my clothes."

I thought this wasn't saying very much.

"Was she ever *dangerously* thin? I mean, after that time she had to go to inpatient treatment?" I asked.

Felix shook his head, but Farzad said, "She was always too thin. Always."

"Farzad!" Felix snapped.

"You spend too much of your time with models," Farzad said. "Alicia *never* ate enough, and she was *always* too skinny."

Felix shook his head and turned to the detective. "You'll have to excuse my partner. He's Iranian, and he's gay. He has no idea what a normal-sized woman looks like."

Al shifted uncomfortably in his seat. Thank goodness none of the other three men seemed to notice.

"That is ridiculous!" Farzad said. "Iranian women are *beautiful,* and stylish. And for your information they are not fat! They are very thin. Too thin, in fact, like your models. A woman should look like a woman! Not like a little boy. A woman should look like her!" He pointed to me, and all of them turned and fixed appraising gazes on my body. I could tell that Felix thought I was anything but normal-sized, and I blushed furiously.

"Except not so pregnant," Farzad said.

"My sister was thin, but not abnormally so," Felix said.

Detective Goodenough seemed to decide that we'd covered this topic in far more detail than necessary, and he reassumed control of the interview. He was, in the end, more thorough than I would have expected, and I was both impressed and made a bit anxious by his attention to detail. He jotted down a long list of every one of Alicia's friends, family, members of her comedy troupe, people she came in contact with through her work as Felix's assistant. He asked about boyfriends, and Farzad told him about Charlie Hoynes. I was glad not to have had to provide that information myself. It was surely something he needed to know, but I have a very hard time, both because of my training and because of my temperment, cooperating with the police, even when I know I should. A useless, even counter-productive holdover from my public defender days.

When the detective asked about people with whom Alicia had had conflicts, Farzad brought up Julia Brennan.

"Oh, don't be so melodramatic," Felix said at his boyfriend's characterization of Alicia's feelings toward the successful actress. "Alicia didn't hate Julia. She was just a little jealous. Who wouldn't be?"

Farzad pursed his lips. "She was planning on suing the woman. And what about the letter?" he said.

"Farzad!" Felix nearly shouted.

"What letter?" the detective asked.

"Julia Brennan had her lawyers send Alicia a letter."

"A threatening letter?" Al asked.

Farzad glanced over at Felix. "I would say so," the Iranian man said. "The lawyers told Alicia that if she continued to claim the character was hers, they would sue *her*."

"But the character *was* hers!" I said.

"Since when does that make any difference?" Farzad replied.

"What was Alicia's response?" I said.

Felix spoke. "She didn't have time to respond. At least, I don't think she did. She got the letter just a little while before . . . before . . ." his voice trailed away.

Detective Goodenough turned to Farzad, "Do you think this woman, Julia, felt the same way toward Alicia as Alicia felt toward her?"

Farzad waggled his head in his half-nod, half-shake. "I have no idea. All I know is that Alicia hated Julia Brennan. It's hard enough to make a name for yourself in this business without someone stealing your ideas. Frankly, I wouldn't have been surprised if *Alicia* had killed *Julia!*"

"Farzad!" Felix said sharply. "Alicia would never have hurt anybody. She was not that kind of person, and you know that."

Farzad waved a hand in the air. "Whatever."

It was time for me to step in. Nothing they were saying was exactly against their interests, but at the same time I wasn't eager to expose my clients bickering to the curious eye of this very intelligent police officer.

"Detective, are there any other questions you have for Felix and Farzad?"

He nodded, fully aware of what I was doing, and then spent a few minutes going over the two men's alibis for the night of Alicia's murder. He took down the names of the maid and cook who kept the Palm Springs house in running order.

Felix sighed, and his eyes welled up with tears. "I just thought to myself, 'I'll have to get Alicia to call him with the phone numbers.'"

"She took care of that kind of thing for you?" the detective asked.

Felix nodded. "I've never had much of a head for details. And I'm so busy with my business. I have an assistant at work, of course, but he never had to deal with any personal stuff. I guess he'll have to, now."

"What kind of personal stuff?" Goodenough said.

"Oh, you know. She would take the clothes to the laundry. Make sure the cars got serviced. Deal with the house-cleaner and the gardener. Plan our dinner parties."

"Buy our toiletries," Farzad said. "You wouldn't believe the different unguents Felix uses. Every part of his body has its own lotion, and God only knows where Alicia would get them all. If you think *I'm* going to be able to do that for you, sweetheart, you've got another thing coming."

Felix seemed about to rebuke the younger man, but I shot him a warning glance. Instead, he said, "Alicia did all those errands that it's hard for a busy person to get to. You know."

I did know. I'd run out of deodorant over a week before, and I had no idea when I'd make it to the drug store. I was counting on it becoming apparent if things got out of control. For now I resisted the urge to sniff under my arm.

Goodenough tapped his pen on his notebook. "Alicia was your older sister, yes?"

Felix nodded.

"She didn't mind running these kinds of errands for you?"

"No. Alicia had always taken care of me. Even when we were kids. This wasn't any different. Anyway, she needed the money, and I needed the help."

I could see that the detective didn't buy that any more than I had. He was probably a younger sibling. Perhaps the

relationship between Alicia and Felix was every bit as un-
complicated as Felix claimed. Perhaps not. It was hard to
imagine an older sister who wouldn't resent buying her little brother's toilet paper and toothpaste, or even his two-
hundred dollar bottles of algae and placenta wrinkle cream.
And a history of having been forced to babysit a younger
sibling was, I thought, more likely to instill antipathy,
rather than a willingness to continue a lifetime of selfless
devotion. Still, Felix seemed entirely unaware there might
be anything unusual or unbelievable about the way he characterized his relationship with his sister. Theirs had either
been a very special bond indeed, or he was a singularly insensitive man.

Detective Goodenough finally wrapped up his questions
and left.

After the door closed behind the handsome detective,
Farzad whistled through his teeth. "Mmm," he said.

"Oh, please!" Felix replied.

I looked over at Al, who was blushing. It was, I thought,
the first time I'd seen him turn that shade of crimson.

I interrupted Felix and Farzad's banter to reassure myself
that neither man was worried about the interview. They
were more interested in discussing the relative attractive-
ness of their interrogator than going over his questions, so
there wasn't anything more for Al and me to do.

We found Goodenough leaning against the hood of my
car. He stood up when he saw me, shot his cuffs, and
stepped forward.

"Ms. Applebaum, Mr. Hockey," he said mildly. "I wonder if I might have a word."

"Of course."

"Ms. Applebaum, you said that you're an attorney?"

"I am."

"How long have you known Mr. Felix?"

"Not very long."

"How long?"

"I met him after the death of his sister, if that's what you're asking."

He looked surprised.

"Felix has retained us to assist him during the course of the investigation of his sister's murder," I said.

"How do you mean? Are you acting as his defense counsel?"

"No, of course not. He doesn't need a defense attorney. My partner and I are merely assisting Felix and Farzad to navigate these very unfamiliar waters."

He narrowed his eyes at me. "Do you have a ticket?"

"Excuse me?"

Al interrupted. "I do. Juliet works with me."

Goodenough turned to Al. "You're a licensed private investigator?"

Al nodded.

"But she's not," the detective said.

I was, in fact, in the process of getting licensed. The exams weren't a problem; after all, I'd successfully taken and passed both the New York and California Bar Exams. The private investigator's exam was nothing compared to those horrors. However, while Al was certainly qualified to supervise me, my hours weren't exactly regular, what with taking care of Ruby and Isaac, and spending much of my first trimester vomiting instead of working. I was still nearly one hundred hours short of what was required for me to get licensed.

"Our goal isn't to get in your way, Detective Goodenough," I said.

The tall man smoothed the fabric of his expensive suit and picked an invisible piece of lint off the sleeve. Where did an LAPD cop get the money for those clothes? "Of course not," he said.

"Is your working theory of the case that it was a home invasion by a stranger? Using the lockbox on the door?" I asked.

He waggled his head in something between a nod and a shake. "That's one possibility."

"Have there been other, similar, cases in the city?"

"If you're asking whether we've had a rash of Charles Manson–like murders, then the answer is no. But of course there have been other home invasions."

Now it was my turn to raise my eyebrows.

"Two young men in Watts were killed when rival gang members broke into their homes last week," he said. "And a mother of three was strangled in her bed while her children slept in the next room."

"Domestic violence?" I asked.

He nodded. "We've arrested the children's father."

"But nothing like this?"

He shook his head. "No. No other rich, single women have been stabbed to death in their bathtubs."

I had a feeling there was another adjective he might have substituted in that description. It took a very generous definition of the word to describe Alicia as rich, but she was most certainly white.

"Was there evidence of sexual assault?" I asked.

He pursed his lips and gazed at me, appraisingly. Finally he said, "I suppose it doesn't hurt to tell you. She had had sexual intercourse within the previous twenty-four hours, but there was no evidence of assault."

"How did you rule out rape?"

"No sign of bruising or tearing, and the presence of Nonoxynol 9."

Well that seemed pretty clear. It's a rare rapist who is both gentle and solicitous enough to use a condom. Alicia had most likely had consensual sex a day or so before she was killed.

"Did her body turn up any other evidence?" I asked. "Fingernail scrapings? Hairs?"

The detective shook his head. "As I'm sure your partner will explain to you, Ms. Applebaum, our information sharing cannot be the two-way street you would like it to be. I'm trusting you to turn over to me anything you discover. I will not be able to do the same. I'm sure you understand why not."

I sighed. Of course I did. And I was used to being on the short end of the informational stick. As a public defender, what I knew was always limited to what my client was willing to tell me, and what I was able to pry out of the prosecutor, sometimes with the help of a judicial order. I didn't expect Detective Goodenough to come entirely clean. Nonetheless, he'd already told me enough to convince me of one thing. I just didn't believe Alicia was the victim of a random act of violence. Sure there were killers who didn't rape their victims, but more often than not, this kind of stranger-attack was a sex crime. Perhaps the very fact that Alicia had been naked and in the shower was in and of itself sufficient to satisfy her killer's sexual perversion. But I doubted it. The lack of any kind of physical violation seemed to preclude a stranger attack. Furthermore, Alicia had been murdered by someone who knew how to get the key out of the lock box, or someone who had keys to the house. Now, again, it was possible that there was a serial-killer/real estate agent on the loose in the greater Los Angeles area, but I didn't believe that, and I was certain Detective Goodenough shared my doubts. No. Alicia Felix had been murdered by someone who knew her well enough to gain access to her home. I hoped to God it wasn't her brother, because I had every intention of figuring out who had killed her. And I seriously doubted Felix would sell me his house if I ended up putting him in jail.

ON my way home I stopped at the supermarket. We were entirely out of breakfast cereal, and I didn't relish trying to force something else down my finicky children's throats in the morning. It was hard enough getting them to eat a small bowl of organic chocolate crispies. Anything else was beyond them, and me.

Once inside the store I surprised myself by remembering deodorant, and a new tube of bubblegum-flavored toothpaste for the kids. I was so pleased with this feat of deep-pregnancy recall that I decided to reward myself with a donut. I still hadn't gotten that life-size box of Krispie Kremes out of my mind. The pastry counter offered my honey glazed favorites in boxes of four, just enough, I told myself, for my perfectly sized little family. I ate my donut as I waited in line behind an elderly woman with a hand tremor who was insisting on paying by check. The confection went down altogether too fast. While the ancient woman consulted her calendar for the date, and laboriously filled in and then crossed out the number "19" in the spot for the year, I decided that not only wouldn't Peter really expect me to bring him a donut, but that since I was eating for two, I really deserved another one myself. As long as I still had two left for Ruby and Isaac, I was fine.

Once I was in the car, I recollected what the kids' dentist had said about sugary snacks late in the day, and the need for better toothbrushing. Well, I'd been trying, but I couldn't get the kids to brush with anything resembling the commitment the dentist demanded. I was going to have to limit the amount of sweets they were allowed. Therefore, it was my duty as their mother to eat the other two donuts.

I'd like to say I felt sick, or regretted my gluttony. I didn't. In fact, I felt like I could easily put away another four-pack. But turning the car around and heading back to the pastry counter was beyond even me, wasn't it? I checked my watch. Alas, I didn't have time. I had to pick up the kids from school.

I started feeling bad while I was waiting out in front of Ruby's school in the pick-up line. I don't mean physically bad. Physically, I was just fine. No, what got to me wasn't abdominal discomfort, but rather a bit of good old fashioned self-hatred. A group of moms had gotten out of their cars and were chatting amiably as they waited for the doors to open and the children to pour out. I joined them, and was confronted with the ugly truth. I was, by far, the fattest woman there. Now granted, I was pregnant, and moreover I wasn't really *fat* by any stretch of the imagination. At least not fat like any normal person would consider fat. After all, when not under the influence of a developing fetus I fit more or less comfortably into a size 10, and could even manage an 8 if I was willing to forgo respiration. The problem was that these were all *Los Angeles* mothers. Not all were actresses, or even in the industry at all. In fact, these particular women were mostly stay-at-home mothers. But nonetheless they looked, to a one, like they had just walked off a movie set. They weren't dressed particularly glamorously—a pair of tight yoga pants and a stretchy T-shirt was the style of the moment. But they were all thin. They were aerobicized and stepped and Zone-dieted down to a svelteness that only a town that idolized the broomstick likes of Calista Flockheart and Lara Flynn Boyle could have considered normal. Alongside them, I felt hugely, lumberingly, hideously fat. I'm fully aware that it is simply unreasonable for a woman who has given birth even to just one child to have an abdomen that looks good in hip-hugger pants and a belly button ring. Still, it bothered me that my belly button, after three pregnancies, was going to look more like a deflated party balloon than a body part that deserved its own jewelry, and that even if I had a pupik-plasty or whatever that surgery was called, I still would never have the courage to bare my midriff.

I made as much small talk as I could stomach and then made my way back to my car, pulling my shirt over the behind that suddenly seemed bigger than anything that could easily fit into my station wagon. I thought of the donuts, each of them in turn, oily and coated with its gray scum of sugar. For the first time in my life I felt, or at least understood, the compulsion of women like Alicia. I wanted to run to the nearest ladies room, stick my finger down my throat, and get rid of the pounds of carbohydrate and fat that would soon be taking up permanent residence on my thighs.

Then the image of Alicia's emaciated, vandalized body sprang before my eyes. Was that really what I wanted to be? I looked out the window at the woman gathered together in front of the school. How many of them maintained their slimness by denying themselves basic sustenance? How many of them vomited up any item not on the paltry list of foods they considered acceptable? I was willing to bet that it was more than a few. Not many of us ended up like Alicia, institutionalized and force-fed, but we were all completely crazy when it came to food. Felix was right. We all had eating disorders. It was only a question of degree.

Just then, the door to the school burst open, and the children began to pour out. I caught sight of Ruby's gleaming red curls immediately. When she saw my car she smiled widely, revealing the gap where her front tooth had just begun to grow in. I smiled back and waved. I was damned if I was going to let my little girl grow up feeling the way I did about my body. Ruby was going to be proud of how she looked, and take pleasure in every morsel that passed her lips, if I had to tie down every Tab-drinking mother in the city of Los Angeles and force feed them Ding-Dongs from now until doomsday.

Sixteen

I didn't notice the Mercedes parked in front of my house. If I had, I might have hustled the kids off to the park, or to the movies, or anywhere at all to avoid the scene that greeted me when I walked into my apartment. Kat was huddled in an armchair, her face mottled with a humiliated blush, and her hands knotted in her lap. She was staring out the window, doing her best not to look at her mother-in-law and my husband, who were sitting side by side on the couch, their heads bent together in an altogether disturbing tête-à-tête. While I stood in the doorway, Nahid's tinkling laugh filled the room, and she reached out one manicured hand, pushing at my husband's sweatshirt-clad chest, as if he had said something so witty, so daring, that she needed to swat him for it. He laughed in reply, and leaned ever so slightly into her.

I coughed, loudly, and released my hold on Ruby's and Isaac's hands. They flung themselves into the room and onto their father's lap, reminding him, I hope, that he was married, and that flirting with middle-aged, artfully sculpted real estate agents was a singularly inappropriate activity.

Nahid looked at me, and her smile turned acid. Kat shot me a worried glance and turned back to the window. For a moment, I felt a tightening in my stomach. I shook it off, firmly reminding myself that Nahid Lahidji was not *my* mother-in-law. She couldn't scare me. Could she?

"Hello Kat, Mrs. Lahidji. What's up?" I said in a sprightly voice.

Peter set the children on the floor and said, "Guys, go play in Ruby's room for a minute, we've got grown-up things to talk about."

"But we just got home!" Ruby whined.

"And you said we'd play *Bionicles* today!" Isaac said, matching her tone.

"Give us a few minutes, kids," I said, shooing them out of the room. "Daddy will be in to play with you soon."

As soon as they were gone, I said, "Can I get you something to drink? Coffee? Tea?"

Kat raised a grateful face, and nodded, but Nahid said, "No, no. We're fine. Your *darling* husband has already made us very comfortable." I could swear she batted her eyelashes at him.

"Well, what can I do for you?" I asked, settling myself on the ottoman that passed for a second chair in our living room.

"Juliet," Peter said, "Mrs. Lahidji is worried about the whole house thing." There was just the tiniest hint of 'I told you so' in his voice, and I scowled at him.

"Juliet, dear," Nahid said. "I'm sure you had only the best intentions. After all, I know just how desperate you must be to move from here before the baby is born." She waved a condescending hand around my living room, as if to say that of course no one could imagine bringing a child into such desperate and meager surroundings. "But I'm afraid I must ask you to refrain from disturbing poor Felix and Farzad. They've gone through so much."

"Disturbing them?" I sputtered.

"Katayoun has told me of your *plan.*"

"Kat!" I said to my friend. She winced, and shrugged as though to ask me what I had expected from her. Clearly I should not have imagined that she would withstand the force of nature that was her husband's mother.

Nahid said, "She has told me everything. That you have befriended the poor grieving man. That you have worked your way into his confidences. All to convince him to sell you the house. Sell it *below marker value!*" The outrage, the horror in her voice filled the room.

"Listen, Mrs. Lahidji, you're being ridiculous. Yes, of course I'm interested in the house, and maybe my motives weren't entirely altruistic at first. But I'm not trying to cheat Felix out of anything. Anyway, Felix has hired me to investigate his sister's murder. He's my client."

She shook her head furiously. "How long do you think you'll be working for him if I tell him you're just after his home?"

"First of all, he knows I'm interested in his house. That's the reason Kat and I were there in the first place. Second of all, how long do you think you'll be his real estate agent if I tell him you care more about the price of his house then you do about finding out who killed Alicia?"

She sputtered for a moment, and then seemed to deflate just the tiniest bit. "Look my dear," she said. "We are both on the same side here. We both want this situation with Alicia resolved as quickly as possible so that the house will be free to be sold. Let's not argue."

I turned to my husband. "Sweetie, give me your seat," I said.

"Huh?"

"Your seat. My back is killing me."

He leapt to his feet and gave me a hand up off the ottoman. "Maybe I should see how the kids are doing," he said.

"Good idea."

I sat down on the couch next to Nahid. "Mrs. Lahidji, I promise I won't go behind your back, okay? If Felix ever decides to sell me the house, I promise you'll not only be the first to know, but I'll make sure you're involved in the sale, okay? You'll be able to advise him on a fair price."

She pursed her lips together, and then stretched her mouth into a smile. "Very good, my dear. That is all I was asking."

"On one condition."

Her smile died. "What is that?"

I reached over for my purse and pulled out my little notebook. "Let's talk a little bit about Alicia. Did you know her?"

"We should not discuss this unpleasantness."

"How else will we achieve our mutual goal of resolving the issue quickly?"

Nahid narrowed her eyes. "I'd met her. But only once, when Farzad first had me over to look at the house. She was there, cleaning up after a dinner party. Or, rather, she was ordering the maid to clean up." Her tone of voice made it clear that she had not liked Alicia.

"Did you talk to her?"

"No, my business was not with her. I was there to appraise the value of the house. Whether she liked it or not."

"What do you mean?"

"Well, the girl obviously didn't want her brother to sell

the house and move permanently to Palm Springs. She would have had to get a *job*. Find someplace to live. God knows how she would manage that. She was supposed to have been an actress, but Farzad said she hadn't gotten a part in years. She was nothing but her little brother's nanny!"

I looked up from my notebook, surprised. "Farzad told you that? He told you that she didn't want Felix to move?"

Nahid waved a dismissive hand at me. Her diamond ring caught the light, and we were both momentarily distracted by its brilliance. "Lovely, isn't it?" she purred. "I will tell your husband where my husband bought it. His cousin, Momo, is in the diamond business. He'll give you a special deal."

It looked like the glass shade on the Czechoslovakian floor lamp in my Bubbe's old apartment. Only larger.

"That's okay," I said. "You were telling me about what Farzad told you?"

"Farzad didn't need to tell me anything. The girl threw a tantrum as soon as she realized what I was doing. She began screaming at Farzad, telling him she would tell her brother he was trying to throw her in the street. She was like a wild person. Tears, howls. Awful. So tacky. So low class."

"What did Farzad do?"

Nahid smiled. "He yelled right back at her! Farzad is like his mother, Lida. No one has ever won a fight with my cousin Lida Bahari. She is the most formidable woman I know."

Kat and I sat in stunned silence for a few moments, contemplating just what a woman scarier than Nahid would be like.

"What did Farzad say to Alicia?" I asked, finally.

Nahid laughed. "He told her he'd throw her out right then if she didn't close her mouth, and then he chased her out to the guest house where she lived. Such a scene. The two of them, screaming like a couple of fishwives. Farzad is just like his mother. Only prettier." She laughed again.

Suddenly, Kat leaned forward. "Nahidjoon, maybe we should go. Juliet probably has things to do."

I scowled at her. She had been too afraid to speak a word the entire time, and now she mustered up the courage to cut our conversation off just when things where getting interesting?

Nahid nodded. "I must get back to the office. And you," she said to Kat. "You need to get to work on those rental units. I need a full inventory of tenants and rents by the end of the day."

Kat sighed, following in her mother-in-law's wake out the door.

Once the two women had gone, I sat for a moment in my quiet living room, pondering what Nahid had told me. There was no love lost between Alicia and Farzad. If he had had his way, and it appeared like he had been about to, she would have been out on the street. I was supposed to be finding out who might have had a motive to kill Alicia, and instead I kept coming up with people whom *she* would have liked to see dead.

Seventeen

THE next morning I dropped by Felix's house. I found Farzad in the dining room conferring with two very young women over a pile of fabrics printed with black and white photographs.

"Hello, Juliet," he said, when the housekeeper had shown me in. "Come, tell us what you think of these. Gorgeous, aren't they?"

I fingered a corner of the soft gossamer fabric, and then held it up. "Are these crime scene photographs?" I asked, trying not to sound as horrified as I felt.

"Yes, aren't they fabulous?" one of the young women said. "So edgy."

"And so bloody," I said. The length of silk I was holding had the image of a woman sprawled on a bed. Her head hung over the side, dripping a pool of black blood onto the floor. "What are these for?"

"Felix's new line," Farzad said. "Mostly formal-wear. He's having problems with the final designs."

"Gee, I wonder why?" I said.

Farzad smiled thinly. "I know what you're saying, but Aimee and Bethany have been working on these for months. Long before Alicia died. It was Felix's idea to use the Weegee photographs, and it cost a fortune to get the rights. We can't exactly just toss the entire line because he's having a personal crisis."

I didn't reply. What good would it have done to point out to my client's partner that he was an insensitive ghoul?

"Felix is resting," Farzad said. "Is there something important? Should I wake him?"

"No, don't. Actually, I've come to talk to you." I shot the girls a glance.

He gathered the fabric swathes into a pile and dumped them into the arms of one of the girls. "These are fine. Call the factory and tell them we'll have final designs by the end of next week."

"Are you sure?" the girl said. "I mean, if they get set to go, and we don't have the drawings for them, they're going to freak."

"That's Felix's problem, darling, not yours."

"Okay," she said, doubtfully, and headed out of the room. The other girl scooped up their two identical Burberry totes and followed.

Farzad sighed and collapsed onto a leather Morris chair. He kicked off his embroidered slippers and tucked his feet up under him.

"I spoke to Nahid Lahidji yesterday," I said, sitting down on the couch.

"Ah, Auntie Nahid, the dragon lady. I must call her."

"She's pretty anxious to get your house on the market."

"No more anxious than I am. But we're both going to have to wait. Felix won't even talk about it."

"He just needs some time to deal with everything that's happened. I'm sure once Alicia's murder has been resolved, and—he's further along in his grieving process, he'll be ready to contemplate leaving Los Angeles."

"You may be right." He glanced at me. "Or it could be wishful thinking, couldn't it?"

I didn't answer. I felt a twist of guilt. Farzad and I both knew that I was hoping that his poor lover would grieve quickly enough to sell me his house before I was forced to buy something else.

I eyed the leather ottoman tucked in next to the couch I was sitting on, wondering if it would be indelicate to heave my aching feet up on it.

"Please, relax," Farzad said. "You must be exhausted."

I nodded gratefully, and put my feet up. "I understand from Nahid that Alicia was very upset at your plans to sell the house."

He wrapped his arms around his knees. There was something feline about Farzad—graceful, elegant and utterly consumed with his own comfort. "Of course she was. She was furious. She was going to have to pay for her own apartment."

"Did she try to convince you and Felix to stay in LA?"

"Look, we all knew that this was really for the best. Alicia had always been much too dependent on Felix. It was time to cut the cord. Even she knew that."

"But did she try to convince you to stay?"

He ran a careful hand through his thick hair. "Alicia was an actress."

"Meaning?"

"She threw a fabulous tantrum. But Felix and I had our minds made up."

"And did she realize that? Did she come to terms with it?"

He laughed. "Alicia never came to terms with anything in her life. She managed to convince Felix to keep her on salary, to do whatever he needed done in the city, God knows what that would have been. She was working on him to keep the house as a sort of *pied á terre*. And who knows, she might have succeeded."

I sat forward a bit and fixed my eyes on him. "It's ironic, don't you think?"

"What is?"

"Well, here Alicia was trying so hard to convince Felix not to sell the house, and now she's dead, and he can't bring himself to sell."

"I don't know if it's ironic, but it's definitely typical of Alicia."

"How so?"

He laughed again, without the slightest hint of humor. "She was the most stubborn woman in the world, and you've met my auntie Nahid, so you know I know what I'm talking about. Alicia would never rest until she had her way. I'm not at all surprised that she's manipulating her brother, even from the grave."

I wasn't sure how to respond to this, and decided that it was best to let the bitterness of his words go unacknowledged. "Farzad," I said. "Why are you so eager to leave Los Angeles?"

"This place is toxic, darling. Truly toxic."

"How do you mean?"

"I've been here since I was a teenager, ever since I left Iran. For ten years I've been trying to become an actor. You know how many parts I've gotten?"

I shook my head.

"Eleven. Eleven roles in movies and television. What do you think of that?"

"That actually sounds pretty good to me."

He stretched a leg out, and then tucked it back under him. "You know how many times I played a terrorist, of those eleven?"

I was afraid to guess.

"Seven! Seven terrorists, two taxi drivers, one shooting victim, and a Mexican gardener. And I'm not a man without connections. Felix knows many people—famous people, directors, producers, actors. Still, with all his help, I am never more than a terrorist or a cabbie."

"That must be incredibly frustrating."

"Worse. Worse than frustrating. It eats you up inside. Makes you feel small and useless. Ugly. I can't stand it anymore. But acting is like a disease. It infects you. I can't be in the city and not be an actor. So I must get away."

"And what do you plan to do in Palm Springs?"

"I will take care of Felix, take care of the business. We'll be a family. Who knows, maybe we'll even adopt a baby."

I blinked, and then reminded myself that a lot of people who seem far too self-absorbed to be parents end up rising to the occasion.

"And Felix? Is he as eager to leave Los Angeles as you are?"

"LA is bad for Felix, too. It's full of people who want something from him. The pretty boys want to model in his shows, the actresses want free dresses. Everybody pretends to be his friend, and everybody wants something. Felix knows this. Sure, he's seduced by the honey of their words, but he sees right through them. As I do."

That all too familiar feeling of guilt stabbed me in the stomach. What was I but yet another person who wanted something from them? Here I was, manipulating myself into their lives, pretending to be interested in helping, but really only wanting a chance to tape my children's drawings up on that Sub-Zero. Farzad obviously could tell what I was feeling, because, after gazing at me for a moment, he winked.

I said, "But will moving to Palm Springs really get Felix away from it? He's still going to have to deal with the models and actresses, and the demands of his job."

Farzad plucked a loose thread from the sleeve of his creamy white shirt. He wore his French cuffs unbuttoned and hanging over his narrow wrists and hands.

"Perhaps," he said. "But the farther we are away from it all, the less it will influence him. The less it will damage us."

"Damage you? As a couple?"

He looked away, as if regretting his words.

"What do you mean by damage?" I said, insistently.

He shook his head. "Oh, nothing. We're fine. Rock solid. It's just that LA is a toxic city. We are much happier in Palm Springs."

Perhaps it was as simple as he claimed—perhaps he wanted to leave Los Angeles because of the extent of the demands on Felix's time. I couldn't help but wonder, however, if there were some more particular reason. Was their relationship in jeopardy? Had something else precipitated Farzad's insistence on a move?

Try as I did, I couldn't get any more out of him on that topic. Instead, I turned to another line of questioning. "Was the fact that you were both actors something that made you and Alicia closer, do you think?"

He waggled his head in something that might have been either a nod or a shake. "It gave us something in common, certainly. We could complain to one another about our agents, about auditions, that kind of thing."

"Something to bond over?"

"Yes, well, until it got to be too much for me."

"What do you mean?"

"You know how Alicia's career had been going. After a while I didn't like to talk to her about things too much. She was . . ." He paused and looked up at the ceiling. "She was kind of a black hole. You know. An abyss. Too much failure in one place."

I blinked.

"It wasn't like she was depressed or anything. She wasn't that kind of person. She was always moving, always hustling. It's just that . . . well, that kind of bad luck can be contagious," he said.

I nodded slightly, not enough to indicate that I agreed, but enough, I hoped, to keep him talking.

"But things had gotten better recently," he said, as if to reassure me.

"Between the two of you?"

"Better for Alicia. There was that series with the man she was sleeping with, Hoynes. It really seemed like that was going to work out for her."

I thought for a moment about Dakota Swain. How sure a thing had the vampire series been, really?

"Alicia and I used to go to the gym together sometimes," Farzad said suddenly. "We both work out at Corps Sain on Sunset. I mean, she used to. I'd better make sure they've canceled her membership. They're probably still charging her credit card.

"Did Alicia work out a lot?"

He laughed. "Alicia? What do you think? The woman was obsessed with her weight. She was a compulsive exerciser. She was there every day for at least two hours."

"Do you think she was really cured of her anorexia? When I . . . er . . . saw her, she didn't look . . ." I searched for the word. "Normal, I guess. She was so terribly thin."

"Normal? What's normal? Like Felix told that detective, Alicia was no thinner than plenty of other Hollywood actresses. But yes, she was much too thin. She obsessed about what she looked like. Her weight wasn't the only thing. She worried about her clothes, about her face, everything. Worry is too weak a word."

"But do you think she still had an eating disorder?"

He waved the question away. "Of course she did. Who doesn't? Half the people I know are getting their meals delivered by that high-protein diet guru. Alicia was crazy, sure, but she was no crazier than a lot of other girls."

I thought about my adventures in the land of Krispy Kreme. "Did she do any bingeing?"

"Bingeing?"

"You know, eating huge quantities and then forcing herself to vomit."

"Oh, you mean like Mia, her comedy character. That was fiction, only. Alicia would never have done that. She had tremendous control. She never ate anything she didn't want to eat. It was amazing." A note of admiration crept into his voice.

"What about plastic surgery?" I asked. If Alicia's best friend Moira had had a facelift, then Alicia probably had one as well.

Farzad laughed. "My dear, you think we all look this good by accident?"

I gazed into his face. He winked at me. "A little nip here, a tuck there. Bigger breasts, a cleaner jawline. Everyone does it."

I surreptitiously patted the loose flesh that made up my double and triple chins. Maybe my squeamishness about carving up my face and body was silly. After all, everyone was doing it. A little nip. A little tuck. Was it really so bad?

I thought of Moira's scars, and the tight, shiny faces of the women Peter and I met at industry parties. In a world like this, did *normal* have any meaning?

"Did you two use the same doctor?"

"We two?"

"I'm sorry. I thought you meant that you'd had something . . . er . . . done," I mumbled hastily.

He laughed at me. "Alicia's doctor was Bruce Calma. In Westwood, at UCLA. He's the best. Everyone uses him."

I noted the name, even though I could see no way that Alicia's plastic surgeon had anything to do with her death. Still, the picture of her was becoming clearer and clearer to me. She was an ambitious woman, verging on the desperate, engaged in a battle with time that, despite diets, exercise, and surgery, she was doomed to lose. Could it possibly have been this ambition, this battle, that got her killed?

Eighteen

"How about this one?" Peter said, holding up a brown checked shirt.

I shook my head. After I had left Farzad, I had swung by my house and picked up my husband for a quick trip to Fred Segal. My ostensible excuse was that I wanted to check out the Booty Rags line in the stores—see what it looked like, how it was displayed, even ask the salespeople how well it was selling. The truth was, however, that hanging around a fashion designer had inspired in me a need to shop. Worse, it made me realize just how woefully lacking my husband's wardrobe was. For all the contrived tatters of Felix's clothing line, he and Farzad were always dressed to the nines. Now, I wasn't fool enough to want my husband draped in a pair of butt-baring cargo pants, but there wasn't any reason he couldn't buy some new clothes. I had to satisfy my shopping jones somehow, and I certainly I wasn't willing to spend any more money on my own ballooning self.

Fred Segal was the perfect spot. It was achingly trendy, and chock full of celebrities and the random LA wealthy. Despite that, I knew they'd have enough classic men's clothes—read jeans and T-shirts—to satisfy my fashion-phobic husband.

Peter presented me with another flannel shirt, this one in a blue check.

"Honey, the whole point of this exercise is to buy you something *other* than flannel shirts and khakis."

"Should we really be spending the money? I mean, aren't we supposed to be saving for a down-payment on that house you were going to find for us?"

Since when had my husband become so adept at passive-aggression?

Peter poked listlessly at the artfully displayed clothing, and I dug through a pile of shirts until I found one I liked. I brought it over and held it up under Peter's chin. "This one's cool," I said.

He grimaced, fingering the pink rayon. "It's got little teapots all over it."

"They're cute!"

"Juliet, I can't wear *teapots*. I just can't. Toasters, maybe. But not teapots."

"Fabulous shirt," a smooth voice said. I turned to find a young man with spiky black hair, wearing hip hugger jeans and a mint green T-shirt. He nodded approvingly. "Leo bought one of those the other day. And I think Justin's got it in blue."

I didn't bother asking who Leo and Justin were. I just put the shirt back on the rack.

"Can I pull some things for you?" the young man asked.

"Sure," I said, at the same time as Peter said, "No thanks."

"Can you find some more . . . *traditional* stuff?" I asked.

The young man heaved a sigh and nodded. He pulled a blue wool jersey off the rack and handed it to me. "Like this?"

It felt like it was woven from spider webs, soft and delicate, yet resilient.

"Perfect," I said, handing it to my husband.

"Wow, this feels great," Peter said, sounding surprised.

"Why don't you take it to the fitting room," the salesclerk said. "I'll bring you some other things. Pants, too?"

"Definitely," I said.

I left the two of them, purposefully ignoring my husband's desperate glare, and wandered off to the shoe department. I was modeling a pair of bright red, doeskin ankle boots for the mirror when I saw Charlie Hoynes's girlfriend, Dakota, across the floor, holding up a stiletto-heeled alligator pump. "Can I see this in an eight and half?" she called to the clerk who had helped me cram my swollen feet into the boots.

"I'll be with you in a moment, Madam," he said.

"Go on, it's okay," I said to him, then I smiled at Dakota. "Hi, it's me. Juliet Applebaum? From the other night?"

She looked me up and down, as if trying to decide whether to recognize me or not. "Of course. Spago."

"Right."

She put the shoe back on the display and fingered the leather thong of a pair of sandals. Finally, she said, "I suppose I owe you an apology."

"No, of course not." I limped over in my too-tight, too-high boots.

"I love those boots."

"Aren't they great?" I held one foot out, lost my balance, and then, just like that, fell onto my behind.

"Oh my god!" Dakota said, running over to me. She grabbed my arm and tried to heave me up. My bulk was just too much for her, and she toppled over, almost in slow motion. By the time she was next to me on the floor we were both laughing so hard the tears were streaming down our faces. I rolled over on one side and, using a chair for support, yanked myself to my feet. I held out my hand to her and hoisted her up. She was so light I nearly pulled her all the way over on to me. That set us off even more, and soon I had to sit down in a chair. "Stop!" I cried, holding my belly. "I can't laugh anymore or I'll pee in my pants."

"Are you okay?" she asked. She was almost hyperventilating.

"I'm fine." I wiped the tears from my eyes. "God, that was insane."

"No kidding."

"I'm really not this big. I mean, normally."

"You're pregnant."

"Right. And huge. Especially my butt."

"Well . . ."

"My son once said to me, 'You know, Mama, other ladies get pregnant only from the front!'"

We giggled again for a moment, but when the salesclerk showed up with Dakota's shoes, we calmed down.

"Gorgeous," I said.

She slipped them on and strutted around the room. "Yeah, but can I afford them?"

I pulled the box over to me, looked at the price, and whistled. "Wow. Twelve hundred bucks."

"I know," she said, sighing. She sat back down and took them off her feet. "I should just buy them. The series is going to go, I'm sure of it."

"Buy them!" I sure couldn't shell out the four hundred bucks the red boots cost, and I wanted *someone* to make an inadvisable, even insane, purchase, otherwise what was the point of the whole shopping trip?

"I shouldn't," she said. "I'm still paying off these." She grabbed a breast in each hand and squeezed.

"Really?" I said. "They look so real!"

"They'd better look real. I paid Bruce Calma four thousand bucks for them."

"Huh," I said. "Same doc who did Alicia."

"I'm not surprised. Everyone knows he's the best. Not many doctors are as good as he is on both boobs *and* faces. I wouldn't use anyone else."

"Did you know she'd gone to him as well?"

Dakota shook her head. "Alicia and I didn't talk much. For obvious reasons."

"That can't have been easy," I said sympathetically.

Dakota frowned—or at least I think she frowned. Her brow remained entirely unwrinkled, her eyebrows stayed in the same position, but her mouth turned down at the edges. "Tracker Hoynes is a pig."

I caught myself in time to keep from nodding in agreement.

"Anyway, as soon as the pilot shoots, I plan never to see the cretin again." She held the shoes up. "I'm going to buy them."

"You should."

Suddenly, she scowled at me. "I suppose you think I had a good reason to kill Alicia Felix."

I had been, in fact, thinking exactly that. Two desperate women competing for the same last-chance role. What better motive for murder was there in Hollywood?

"I can't say I was particularly upset when she got killed," Dakota continued. "You probably think that makes me a terrible person."

I didn't reply.

"I didn't kill her."

Again I remained silent.

"I didn't."

"You should buy the shoes," I said. With a last, longing look at the buttery crimson boots that were slowly cutting off the circulation to my feet, I tugged them off and put them back in the box.

"I'm going to," she said.

"I haven't laughed like that in a long time."

She smiled. "Me either."

By the time I returned to my men's department, Peter was out of the dressing room and waiting for his purchases to be wrapped by the now-sycophantic salesclerk.

"When you see this bill you are going to be so sorry," my husband said.

"Don't worry about it. I just saved us four hundred dollars."

Nineteen

I decided to visit Charlie Hoynes's ex-wife not because I thought that anyone in her right mind would feel sufficiently rivalrous over ol' Tracker's affections to kill his current girlfriend—especially not when there seemed to be a virtual harem of skinny blond women at the man's disposal—but because Hoynes had been so adamant about his ex-wife's loathing of Alicia. I didn't imagine that jealousy over your daughter's affections provided quite the same motive as that over your lover's or husband's, but interviewing her seemed the only sensible thing to do.

A few minutes on the web was enough to give me Barbara Hoynes's home telephone number and address. She lived in Brentwood, plenty close enough to my house to warrant a quick trip while Peter was getting the kids to bed after dinner. It was too dark to see what ersatz architectural style Hoyne's ex-wife had chosen for her house. Unlike most of her neighbors, Barbara hadn't lit the front of her home with floodlights and tracking beams—or perhaps she simply hadn't turned hers on. I could see enough to know that the place was large. She'd clearly come out well in the divorce, or had money of her own.

The woman who answered the door looked nothing at all like the two other women with whom Hoynes had chosen to spend his time; neither did it seem like she'd ever looked like them, even when she was young. She was shorter, first of all, and a brunette. She hadn't had the assistance of a plastic surgeon—on the contrary, Barbara Hoynes looked her age, and then some. She looked like a middle-aged woman who had spent many sleepless nights worrying about her daughter in the hospital.

"Can I help you?" she asked, in the wary tone of a woman not looking forward to dealing with the demands of a late-night solicitor.

Since I knew this was a woman who despised her ex-husband, I figured the easiest way to get her to talk to me was to align myself with her. "Ms. Hoynes, I'm so sorry to bother you in the evening. My name is Juliet Applebaum, and I'm investigating the circumstances of Alicia Felix's death, particularly her relationship with Charlie Hoynes. I was hoping you would be willing to answer a few questions. Just as background really."

She gave a dry bark of laughter. "Is Charlie a suspect?"

"It's too early to rule anyone out, of course," I said, letting rest the implication that I had any legitimate business drawing up lists of suspects.

She leaned against the doorjamb, crossing her arms over her chest. "What do you want to know?"

I put my hands to my back, which wasn't aching more than usual, and winced. "Do you mind if I sit down?" I asked, looking vaguely around me. I was standing on the long flat porch, but there were no benches or chairs in evidence. I winced at the imaginary pain.

Barbara was obviously fighting an internal battle. She didn't want to ask me in, but neither did she want to force a pregnant woman to stand, sway-backed and uncomfortable, outside her door. Finally, she said, "Why don't we just sit on the steps." She checked the latch with one finger and then let the door slam shut behind her. Frustrated, I followed her down a step or two and settled myself next to her. Without the light from inside the house, I could only just barely see her face.

"Did you know Alicia Felix?" I asked.

"I never met her, no."

"Had your daughter?"

"Yes."

I did my best to make out her expression in the dim light from the streetlamps. The moon was far too thin and too high in the sky to be of much use. "Were they friendly?" I asked, pretending I'd heard nothing from Hoynes himself.

Barbara didn't answer, and I could swear I could see the knot of her jaw working, as if she were gritting her teeth. Finally, she said, "My ex-husband takes a sick pride in parading his girlfriends in front of his teenage daughter. Alicia Felix was just one of them. I doubt Halley thought much about her at all."

I considered this, and decided to confront her with at least part of what Hoynes had told me. "I was under the impression that Halley was a bit closer to Alicia. That they had some things in common."

This time, Barbara's voice came suddenly, and harshly. "In common? No. No, they had nothing in common. That woman did her best to worm herself into my daughter's affections, but they had nothing in common."

"Your ex-husband made a statement that Alicia was helping Halley in her battle with anorexia." Well, it was a statement. Not sworn, true, but a statement nonetheless.

Barbara leapt to her feet. "Helping her? Helping her? Is that what that miserable son of a bitch said? Exactly how was that wretched woman helping my child? By traipsing around in front of her like some kind of human skeleton? By giving her lessons in how to starve herself to death? What kind of help is that? What does he think, that Alicia was some kind of role model for Halley? Is he out of his mind?"

I opened my mouth, but before I could say anything, she wrenched the front door open.

"I don't need to talk to you anymore. None of this has anything to do with me, or my daughter. Charlie Hoynes is a sick cretin, and I'd bet every dime I have that he's the one who murdered that horrible woman." She slammed the door, leaving me sitting on the steps in the dark.

Twenty

THE next morning, for lack of anything better to do, I called Dr. Calma's office. It would have been only marginally more difficult for this particular chubby, pregnant Jewish girl from New Jersey to get an audience with the pope than with the plastic surgeon to the stars. It took an entire morning to get beyond the receptionist's assistant or perhaps it was the receptionist's assistant's receptionist—anyway, when I did finally reach the woman, I was told that Dr. Calma had no time to speak to *anyone,* especially not someone investigating a murder, and that he had, in fact, just turned away an interviewer from *Redbook* magazine. Dr. Calma was being profiled in *Vanity Fair,* and even other periodicals were simply too prosaic and pedestrian for the great man to waste his time with, so who exactly did I think *I* was?

Out of desperation, I called back, and, hiding my voice by reinvigorating the New Jersey accent I'd long ago lost, tried make an appointment. That inspired a bout of pitying mirth. Wasn't I aware, the receptionist asked, that without a personal referral the wait to see His Gloriousness was nearly *six months?* And that even *with* a letter from a previous patient I'd be lucky to get in before the *summer?* My obvious frustration inspired a brief but inspiring lecture on the desirability of Dr. Calma's talents.

Finally, just as I was about to fling the phone to the floor in frustration, the woman said, "Please hold."

I nearly hung up. I'm not sure what kept me on the line, but within a few moments the woman came back. "My goodness, this is your lucky day."

"What do you mean?"

"That was Dr. Calma's nine thirty-five. She has a callback this morning for a Spielberg film. She canceled, even though I told her that Dr. Calma wouldn't see her again if she did. So if you can be here in twenty-two minutes, the appointment is yours."

I managed to get dressed, drop the kids off at school, and make it to Beverly Hills in just under half an hour. Thank God the good doctor had valet parking, because if I'd had to troll the streets looking for a space I would have been even later. As it was, the scowl on the receptionist's face when I walked in at nine forty-three made me feel like a misbehaving schoolgirl.

She pursed her lips and gazed ostentatiously at the clock.

"I'm sorry I'm late."

"Lucky for you the doctor is a bit behind schedule, otherwise you would have forfeited your appointment."

She handed me a clipboard, and I took it to a long, white couch. There were at least fifteen women waiting to see the doctor, and there was only one seat left in the crowded room. They were mostly of a certain age, although a few were quite young. I figured the younger women for breast enhancement or liposuction. Most of the older women looked as though they had already had those procedures. They were surely in for facelifts, although it was difficult to imagine why they thought they needed them. Surprisingly, I wasn't the only pregnant woman in the room, although I was certainly the largest. The other two were the olive-on-a-toothpicks one sees in Los Angeles gyms, stairmastering away any semblance of a pregnant body.

I glanced down at the clipboard in my hand. It was the usual patient information sheet. I debated handing it back to the receptionist and letting her know that I was just interested in talking to the doctor, but frankly the woman scared me. I laboriously recorded my history of caesarian sections, my father's heart disease, my mother's high blood pressure. By the time I was done I had acquired a whole host of psychosomatic ailments. Headaches, backaches, nausea. I was trying to decide whether I saw spots—I sort of thought I did—when the receptionist cleared her throat.

"Have you finished with that?" she said.

I leapt to my feet, assuming that she wanted the form back because I was about to be seen by the doctor. Wishful thinking, that. An hour later, I was still cooling my heels in the waiting room, entertaining myself by looking through photo albums full of before and after pictures. It didn't seem quite fair; the before photos of the facial surgery were all harshly lit and featured women with hair hauled back from their foreheads, their faces stripped of makeup. The after shots, on the other hand, had clearly benefited from the ministrations of makeup artists and soft-focus camera lenses. Still, the difference post-surgery was pretty dramatic. Dr. Calma appeared to be carving away years.

The liposuction pictures were even more remarkable.

It was all I could do to keep from pinching my expanding thighs as I leafed through the pages. However, my favorites were the breast enlargement photographs. Neither Dr. Calma nor his patients seemed interested in moderation. I suppose it's like buying a pair of shoes. The small ones aren't any cheaper.

After I'd been waiting for nearly an hour an a half, the nurse in the lavender scrubs who had periodically been peeping her head into the room and announcing everyone else's name, called mine. I followed her down a long hallway, past half a dozen closed doors, to a small exam room furnished in tasteful purples and pinks. The nurse and the wallpaper matched perfectly.

"Please take everything off and put on this gown," the nurse said, handing me the most beautiful hospital gown I'd ever seen. It too was lavender, like the nurse's scrubs, and had pale pink lace on the collar and hems.

"Um, I'm really just here to talk to the doctor," I said, backing away from the proffered gown.

The nurse shook her head. "Everything off, dear. It opens in the front."

She left me alone, and I stood fingering the gown. Finally, I stripped off my clothes, leaving the white socks with red jalapeños that I'd grabbed from my sock drawer. They clashed terribly with the elegant hospital gown. The gown was made for a woman who was rather less vast than I. It might have been *designed* to close in the front, but it gaped around my protruding belly. I did my best to hold it closed and sat on the edge of the pink exam chair. The seat was tilted upward like a birthing chair, and it was upholstered in a slippery vinyl. I kept sliding off the edge, and I wished for a set of stirrups on which to prop my legs to keep me from falling right off.

I sat there for much longer than any woman should have to in a too-small hospital gown. By the time Dr. Calma burst into the room, followed by his lavender nurse, I was feeling about as dejected as I ever had in my life. What exactly was I doing there, half naked, waiting for an examination for which I had absolutely no need?

The doctor was much younger than I expected, or perhaps he was just a satisfied consumer of his own products and procedures. He was handsome, in a kind of Ken-doll way. His face was tanned an unnaturally even brown, and his hair was impeccably waved. One lock hung over his eye in a facsimile of rakishness that probably enchanted his patients. I was too irritated by my long wait to feel even remotely captivated.

"Okay, so what have we here?" he said, standing a few feet back from me and staring at me critically.

How far was I planning on going with this charade. "Dr. Calma," I began.

"A little mother!" he interrupted. "When are you due?"

"In a couple of months, but—"

"Hmm, I hope I'll be able to fit you in. Most of my little mamas come here a bit earlier to arrange for their tummy tucks. Let the nurse know when the c-section is scheduled for, and she'll check on my availability. If I'm booked we'll have to do it after the birth. Two months of recovery is usually enough. You don't want to look like this longer than you have to." He shocked me by reaching out a hand and gripping the hammock of fat that was slung below my pregnant belly. I jumped.

"Yup, we'll get rid of all this jelly for you! You'll be sleek and trim in no time. Stand up."

"Dr. Calma, I have a few—"

"Up you go!" he said, hoisting me to my feet. "We should do some lipo here," he said, pushing aside the gown and tracing a warm hand down my hips and outer thighs. "And in here as well." I was gratified that he refrained from actually touching my inner thigh; he just pointed at it. "*Upper arms*—that goes without saying."

Upper arms? What was wrong with my upper arms?

"Turn around, please."

Despite myself, I turned my back to him.

He raised the hem of my gown and clucked his tongue. "We can certainly solve this problem," he said.

Problem? Was my rear end really a *problem?* I mean, I knew it was, well, sizeable, but wasn't that a good thing? And anyway, I was *pregnant!* I glanced back over my shoulder and nearly groaned aloud. He was right. I was looking at one huge, gelatinous problem.

"Now, let's get to your face. You can have a seat."

I collapsed onto the chair, too horrified by the state of my belly, hips, thighs, upper arms, and above all my butt, to continue arguing.

He leaned in and peered at me closely, so close, in fact, that I could smell the warm cinnamon of his breath.

"Not too bad, considering how old you are," he said. "We'll just need to botox the forehead and lip, maybe tug back the jowls." He traced a finger along the edge of my jaw. "We'll erase these fine lines by the sides of your eyes, and get rid of this mole, and that'll be all. Practically nothing!"

"What mole?" I said, and then I blushed. I hadn't intended to shout.

"This one," he said, pointing at a freckle on the side of my lip.

"That's a beauty mark!"

"Hmm. Well, it's up to you. I'd take it off, but it's certainly your decision. Some people are rather inordinately attached to their moles."

"It's not a mole!" The doctor's attack on the freckle of which I was, in fact, very fond, finally roused me from the stupor of self-loathing his criticism had inspired. Unfortunately, it also prevented me from continuing with my plan of delicately and carefully bringing up Alicia Felix. "I'm not actually here to schedule *any* surgery. I just wanted to ask you a few questions about one of your patients, Alicia Felix. She was murdered last week, and I'm representing her family in the investigation of the crime."

Dr. Calma stepped back, looking horrified. "You're not here for a pre-surgical consultation?"

"No."

He snapped the medical chart closed. "I'm sure you understand how very busy I am."

"Yes, and I'm sorry. I know it was ridiculous for me to come here like this, but there was simply no other way for me to get in to speak to you."

He shook his head, clearly furious. "Haven't you ever heard of the doctor/patient privilege? I'm not going to tell you anything about one of my patients!"

"But Alicia is dead, Dr. Calma. And, anyway, I'm just trying to find out anything about her that might shed light on who *murdered* her, and why."

He spun on his heel. When he reached the door, he turned back to his nurse. "You can submit your questions in writing to my attorneys. Florence, have the front desk give her the information." He turned back to me. "You know, you really could use some work. I'd be happy to talk to you about that. Anything else is quite simply out of the question." And with that blistering comment about my appearance, he left the room, closing the door behind him with a firm click.

"Tsk tsk tsk," the nurse clucked.

"Sorry," I said.

"Don't worry, hon." She patted my hand. "Someday you'll probably be grateful for Dr. Calma's discretion. He's a wonderful plastic surgeon. The best."

"I'm sure he is." I gathered the robe around me and clambering down from the exam chair."

"Here, hon, let me help you." She took my arm and hoisted me down.

"Thanks. I'm not getting around real well lately."

She laughed. "Of course you're not. My goodness, you should have seen me with my twins. I was as big as a house. I had to get my poor husband to help me roll over in bed!"

I smiled. "I know the feeling."

"Now, hon, what did you say that poor girl's name was?"

"The murder victim? Alicia Felix."

She nodded. "Wait right here. I'll be right back."

I dressed quickly and sat down on the doctor's stool to wait for her. I wasn't about to risk the exam chair again.

Within a couple of minutes she returned with two of the large photo albums that I'd looked through out in the waiting room.

"There's no harm in showing you these," the nurse said. "After all, Alicia posed for the photographs." She began turning pages until she found what she was looking for. "Here's your friend."

The page she handed me was one that I recognized from my earlier perusal. It showed two photographs of a woman's torso. Her face was turned away from the camera, leaving visible only a sheaf of long, blond hair. In the first photograph, her breasts looked almost prepubescent; they were nothing more than small, flat discs on which perched pale nipples. Her ribs stuck out farther than they did. The bones of her clavicle were sharp, and the hollow of her sternum looked deep enough to sink a finger in up to the second knuckle. The "after" picture could not have looked more different. Alicia had been as uninterested in the concept of less-is-more as the rest of Dr. Calma's patients. Or perhaps it was the doctor himself who preferred melons to oranges. Alicia's new boobs were certainly lovely. They were round, and gravity defying, with nearly invisible scars. However, they looked somewhat bizarre, I thought, set on top of that bony torso.

"Pretty, aren't they?" the nurse asked.

"Oh yeah," I said, trying to sound enthusiastic. "Really nice ones."

"Now, she had a double procedure. Lots of girls do. You'd probably want to consider the same thing. Here, let me show you." She picked up the other album and flipped through it until she found the page she was looking for. I hadn't spent enough time with the face book while waiting for my appointment—I'd been too eager to move on to boobs and hips. Alicia's photographs were toward the back.

I took the book from the nurse and stared intently at the pictures. Alicia had had her face pulled and tugged to remove all wrinkles. She'd also had her nose narrowed slightly, and, if I wasn't mistaken, she'd had some kind of implant put into her chin.

"Isn't she lovely?" the nurse breathed.

"Oh yes," I said. And she was, in a kind of ethereal, hollow-cheeked way.

"Dr. Calma works wonders. He really does. You should make another appointment. He could turn you into a princess!"

"I'm sure he could."

Here again was more evidence of Alicia's desperate attempts to make herself ever more beautiful, ever young.

There was something so achingly sad about the lengths she went to in what was doomed, finally, to be a failed endeavor. Alicia, and all the women in that waiting room, were engaged in a hopeless battle against an enemy that there is, ultimately, no way to fight. We all grow old, no matter how much we carve away at our bodies, no matter how much silicone and botox we inject. We can suck out the extra pounds middle age deposits on our hips, but the years will pass with an inexorable certainty. I glanced at myself in the full-length mirror on the wall of the exam room. There was no getting around it; everything the doctor said about my body was probably true. I was only in my mid-thirties, but I was heavy, and getting older every day. But was the answer really to hack and chop and diet and starve? Or was there some other approach to this inevitable collapse?

Twenty-one

"HAVE you lost your mind?"

I sighed deeply into the cell phone. "Probably, yes."

"Exactly how are we going to bill the client for that? I'm pretty sure our automatic billing program has no entry for 'plastic surgery consult,'" Al said.

"Very funny."

By the time Stacey blew into the restaurant with her hands extended before her like a blind woman, I'd had to endure a good ten minutes of that kind of abuse.

"Read me the specials," she said as she sat down.

"Why? What's wrong with your eyes?"

"What are you talking about? Nothing's wrong with my eyes. I just had my nails done, and I don't want to touch the menu."

I looked at her gleaming burgundy fingernails. "And you give me grief about *my* work ethic? Getting your nails done before lunch!"

She tossed her hair over her shoulder. "My girl comes to the office. I did an entire morning's worth of telephone calls while she was doing my hands and feet."

I leaned back in my chair and gaped at her. "You have manicures and pedicures in the office?"

"Of course. Like I've got time to go to a salon every week? I don't *think* so."

What would I do without Stacy and her excesses to remind me what's wrong with Hollywood?

"What's next? Getting a bikini wax at your desk?"

She laughed. "Could you imagine? Crouching naked on my hands and knees on top of my credenza?"

"On your hands and knees?"

"You know. For when they do the—"

"Too much information, Stace!"

"Oh, please. Don't tell me you've suddenly become a prude. Like you've never had a Brazilian bikini wax."

"Uh, no." I couldn't even remember the last time I got near a *bathing suit,* let alone required the services of a sadist armed with pink wax and a bunch of cloth strips.

"Well, that's just disgusting," she said. "What's the salad of the day?"

I looked down at my menu. "No-carb Cobb."

"Perfect." When the waitress came, however, it was clear that the choice was far from perfect. By the time Stacy had finished substituting goat cheese for the blue, sliced turkey for the bacon, and adding two extra hard-boiled eggs, she'd made it into something different all together. But that's my friend in a nutshell. She's a woman who knows what she wants. Exactly, precisely, completely what she wants.

"I'll just have the regular Cobb salad," I said to the waitress, smiling to let her know that I knew just what a relief it was to have a pleasant, easy-going person like myself to wait on.

The girl shook her head. "That blue isn't pasteurized."

I wrinkled my brow. "Excuse me?"

"Blue cheese? Listeria?"

I sighed. The pregnancy police were everywhere. "Okay, I'll have the goat cheese, instead."

"Ma'am!" she said, outraged. "That's even worse! How about some Kraft slices?"

I closed my menu and stretched my irritated frown into a smile. "Why don't you just hold the cheese altogether."

"Of course. And I'll give you a plain vinaigrette." She raised her eyes from her pad and appraised me critically. "Unless you'd like the nonfat?"

"Vinaigrette is fine," I said sharply.

She turned away, looking miffed.

Stacy spread her hands on the table and blew on them. "Harvey Brodsky called me this morning."

I winced. "I'm such an ingrate. I haven't even thanked you yet for that referral." I'd gotten a message to Lilly that Brodsky might be calling her, but I'd never called Stacy to express my gratitude, and I felt bad. It should have been the first thing I'd done.

"You haven't gotten the job yet," she said.

"I know."

She waggled her fingers in the air. "He seems pretty excited about this murder you're investigating. My sense was that if this came out well, he'd be interested in putting you and your crazy partner on contract."

"That's basically what he said. And that's why I called and asked you to lunch."

Stacy interrupted me, suddenly calling out to the waitress.

"We'll need two black napkins here!" She turned to me. "I don't want white fluff all over my suit. And that black top of yours doesn't need any more lint than it already has."

I glanced down at my maternity smock and sighed. It wasn't particularly linty, but there was a swath of pale green toothpaste where Isaac had wiped his mouth across my belly. When the waitress returned, I dipped a corner of my newly acquired black napkin in my water glass and dabbed at the stain. Something about the general sloppiness of my appearance reminded me of my adventures in personal improvement. "I went to see a plastic surgeon yesterday," I said, and recounted the horror of my visit. "Can you believe he actually wanted to do all that stuff to me?"

"Ridiculous." Then she paused. "What did he want to do to your face?"

I tugged back on the skin at my jaw.

"Hmm," she said.

"Hmm what?"

"Nothing. I mean, it's absurd, of course. Only . . ." her voice trailed off.

"Only what?" I scowled at her.

"No, no. I don't mean for you. I'm just thinking about myself. I mean, about my own jaw line." She patted at her jaw with the pads of her impeccably painted fingers. "Don't you think I'd look better like this?" She pulled the skin back toward her ears.

"No," I said, without looking.

"No, really. I mean, lately it's just getting kind of, I don't know, heavy. Droopy."

"Stacy, what's up with you?"

She dropped her hands to the table. "Nothing. You know. Just the usual. Andy."

"Oh no, not again!" I said. Stacy's husband has a notoriously roving eye. The two of them have been separated and reconciled more times than I can count.

"No, no. He's not seeing anyone. I mean, I don't *think* he is." Stacy shook her head. I looked closely at her. Was that the glint of a tear in her eye?

"What's going on, sweetie?" I said, softly, reaching out and patting her hand, well above her still-drying nails.

"Nothing. Nothing. It's just, you know. It's just so much easier for men. Andy's still so young. I mean, we're the same age, but for him that's young. Thirty-five for a man is nothing. But for us . . ."

"For us, what?"

She looked down at her hands, shaking her bright blond hair down over her cheek. "It's older. A thirty-five-year-old woman is just older than a man of the same age. If he wanted to, Andy could be dating women ten, even fifteen years younger than he is. How many twenty-year-old guys would be interested in me?"

I leaned back in my chair. "First of all, hundreds. Thousands even. You're gorgeous. You're successful. You're rich. If you weren't married you'd be beating them away with a stick. But second of all, why would you ever *want* to go out with a twenty-year-old? Remember what the guys at college were like?" I shivered. "Is that really what you want? Some self-obsessed, over-grown child with no staying power?"

She laughed bitterly. "Isn't that exactly what I've got?"

"Oh honey." I tried to lean over the table to give her a hug, but my belly got in the way. At that moment the waitress arrived with our salads, and we disentangled ourselves and dug in.

"Well?" Stacy said, taking a delicate sip of her iced tea.

"What gives? Why the urgent lunch? How can I help you seal the deal with Harvey Brodsky?"

"Julia Brennan."

"The comedienne? What about her?"

"Can I?" I reached a fork toward Stacy's plate.

She pushed it toward me, wordlessly, and I scooped up some of her cheese. With a glance over my shoulder to make sure the waitress wasn't watching, I sprinkled a bit over my salad. Stacy laughed.

"What?"

"You know what I love about you?"

"What?"

"You're perfectly willing to stare down a murderer with a loaded gun, but you're afraid of some self-righteous dingbat of a waitress."

I sighed. "You should see me with my hairdresser."

She laughed again.

"Anyway, Julia Brennan," I said. "Is she a client of ICA?"

"She is."

"Would you be willing to get me an introduction?"

Stacy lifted a heavily laden lettuce leaf to her lips and chewed contemplatively. "Why?"

Briefly, I told her about the Alicia Felix connection.

Stacy stabbed her lettuce leaves angrily and took a huge mouthful of food. "I can't believe you," she muttered.

"What?"

"Juliet, you really expect me to introduce you to one of my agency's clients so you can accuse her of stealing her character from someone? You take the cake. You really do."

Of course she was right. Had I really asked my friend to go out on that kind of limb? "I promise I'll be delicate."

She set her fork down, clattering it in her plate.

I said, "I just want to talk to her a little about the conflict she had with Alicia. I want to make sure Alicia really had dropped her claim against Julia, like the director of Left Coast said she had."

"Are you planning on accusing Julia of murder?"

"No!" I did my best to manufacture a tone of outrage, but that was, of course, exactly what I was doing. Not necessarily accusing the woman, but investigating her. I wanted to find out exactly what was going on between those two women. What was the extent of the conflict? How far had it gone? Had Spike really succeeded in getting Alicia to drop her plans for a lawsuit?

Stacy was glaring at me, balefully, and I finally said, "You're right. Of course you're right. You can't introduce me to her. I'll figure out something else."

Stacy looked thoughtful. "Did she really steal that character?"

"Absolutely. I mean, I have a videotape of Alicia doing it on some incredibly lame public access TV show out of the Valley years ago."

"Maybe she stole it from Julia!"

"That's not what the director of Left Coast says."

"Left Coast?"

"Left Coast Players. The comedy troupe."

"I think I've heard of it. Hmm."

"Hmm, what?"

"Just, hmm. Do you mind if I tell this to my partners?"

Oy. Of course I should have anticipated this. The last thing I wanted was to precipitate the ruin of someone's career. Particularly not someone who I was hoping would talk to me. "Maybe you shouldn't."

"Why not?"

"I don't know. Let me figure out what's going on, first. Okay? Give me some time to get a handle on what happened to Alicia. When I do, then we'll talk about it again."

"*When* you do?"

"*If* I do."

Stacy smiled. "I was just teasing. I'm sure you'll figure out what happened to her. You always do. You can do anything you set your mind to."

I shook my head. "I wish that were true."

"It is," Stacy said firmly. And that, in a nutshell, is why our friendship has survived so many years, and our two such divergent lives. Stacy and I, for all the entirely different things we value, are each absolutely convinced that the other is not only the smartest woman out there, but is capable of absolutely anything. We're one another's greatest fans. Everyone needs a friend like that.

Twenty-two

I left the restaurant with plenty of time to pick Ruby up at school. I'd arranged for Isaac to go to a friend's house for a playdate, but I hadn't been able to unload Ruby on anyone— perhaps due to her recently acquired habit of gagging and holding her nose whenever offered a snack that didn't fit precisely into her guidelines of acceptable foodstuffs—so I was going to have to take her with me. Hers was not an entirely inconvenient presence, however. I was fixating too much on Alicia and her various body-image problems and career anxieties. I wasn't blind to the possibility that my concentration on those issues was more a reflection of my own neuroses than a realistic assessment of what might have caused Alicia's murder. I had to explore other avenues, and the one I decided to devote the afternoon to was Kat's mother-in-law, the formidable Nahid Lahidji. I was betting that Nahid would be less likely to rip my head off if I showed up at her office with a delightfully cute child in tow.

Ruby greeted me with a hug and her usual prattle about the day's events. Her brother invariably answers the question, "How was school?" with a scowl, and the comment "a *little* good." Ruby, on the other hand, always has a long list of items that require discussion. Our trip in the direction of the Lahidji real estate office was taken up with a monologue on her new social studies unit, the American Indian tribes of Southern California. Ruby's teacher, a young woman fresh out of the education program at Harvard, was a devoted and energetic soul, but if she had a failing it was her desperation to single-handedly right the wrongs of centuries of American racism and xenophobia. The six-year-olds studied slavery, the trail of tears, the Japanese internment in World War II, the expulsion of the Mormons, current English-only initiatives, and the problems faced by illegal immigrants. Whatever one thought the general depressing nature of the material, Ruby was reading well, could add a mean column of numbers, and was more adept at navigating a computer than I. So who was I to complain?

"You guys still talking about that epidemic of obesity?" I asked.

Ruby shook her head and in a voice dripping with disgust said, "We're on another *unit,* Mama. That was the *last* unit."

"Oh. Okay. And what about Madison? Is she still on a diet?"

No response from the back seat.

"Rubes? What's going on with Madison and the other girls? Are they still on diets?"

"Madison doesn't play with me anymore."

I looked in the rear view mirror. Ruby had her knee propped up under her chin. She was dabbing her tongue on the fabric of her jeans, making a large, round wet spot. "Why not, sweetie?"

She shrugged.

"Ruby? Honey? What happened?"

Her eyes were dry, but her lip trembled. "I said I wasn't going to be a diet girl anymore. And Madison said only diet girls can play with her."

I felt a sinking in my chest, and an overwhelming urge to tear off Madison's perfect little head. "She's a stinky girl, Ruby. She really is."

"I know."

"Are the other girls still diet girls?"

"Some of them."

"Well, don't play with them. Play with the ones who aren't. Those are the smarter girls."

"I know."

"I'll tell you what, honey. I'll call Madison's mom. And your teacher. I'll tell them—" Ruby's wails interrupted me. "What? What, honey?"

"Don't call! Don't call! They'll call me a tattletale. Pinky swear you won't call!"

"Okay, okay, honey. I won't. I won't call." I pulled over into a strip mall. "Want some ice cream?" I said.

"Okay. And can we go to the library, afterwards?"

"Sure! What a great idea!" I'm ashamed to say that I pretended to my daughter that my sole reason for agreeing to the library stop was for her edification and pleasure. She was fooled, but only as long as it took for me to settle down in front of one of the computer terminals. Then she scowled at me and stomped off in the direction of the children's department, warning me over her shoulder that she intended to read "lots of *inappropriate* books!"

I put Nahid's name into Google and got over five hundred hits. Most looked to be property listings, but there were a number of write ups in local real estate magazines, and even the real estate section of the *Los Angeles Times*. The reporter for the *Times* had clearly found Nahid to be a more interesting subject than the run-of-the-mill realtor profiled by his section. Nahid was the daughter of an Iranian general and close confederate of the Shah's who had been executed during the Iranian revolution. Her husband, a military man who served under her father, had also been killed. She had escaped to the United States with her mother and son, and had, with only the portion of the family fortune that had been invested abroad and was thus safe from the greedy fingers of the new regime, begun a lucrative real estate business. She received her real estate license in 1983, a mere two years after arriving in the United States. Nahid's hardness, her aggressiveness, suddenly made sense to me. Here was a woman who had been torn from her luxurious lifestyle, seen her father and husband murdered, and who had single-handedly supported her mother and son and, I would bet, countless cousins and friends, ensuring that their transition to life in America would be easier than her own. Reading about Nahid didn't make me like her any more, but now I admired and respected her.

Over the course of the past twenty-five years, Nahid had become one of the wealthiest and most powerful realtors in Los Angeles. She still sold primarily residential properties ranging from Brentwood mansions to smaller homes in better neighborhoods, but she also owned both commercial buildings and residential multi-unit dwellings all over the city. Nahid Lahidji was a very wealthy woman. I shifted over to the Lexis-Nexis real property listing and looked up her various holdings. While most of them were mortgaged, there were no liens, second mortgages, or tax violations on any of them. Her finances seemed entirely secure. So much for my notion that Alicia's objections to the sale of her brother's house would cause Nahid some kind of financial hardship. On the contrary. The house in Larchmont was a bargain by Nahid's standards, and the commission on it was small change to her. So why was she bothering at all? Probably as a favor to Farzad and his mother. As for why she had gotten so angry with me for my interference, I imagined that Nahid was simply a woman who did not like her plans to be disrupted in any way.

I jotted down a few URLs for the more helpful sites and then went to find Ruby. She had, in fact, found herself something entirely inappropriate to read. I discovered her stretched out on a bench in the children's section, chewing on the sleeve of her shirt, and reading *Seventeen* magazine.

"Hey!" I said. "You are way too young to be reading that junk."

She continued leafing through the pages, teeth busily gnawing holes in the sequined turtleneck she'd made me order off a website called "Gurlsdreemz" after swearing to me that she couldn't live without it.

"Ruby! Stop chewing on your clothes. You're ruining that shirt."

She spat the fabric out and rolled over on her back. "Can I have a prescription to this magazine for my birthday?"

"Sure," I said.

"Really?" she asked, obviously shocked.

"Your seventeenth birthday."

"Mom," she said.

"C'mon kiddo. We need to get going."

"Wait a sec. I want to show you something." She paged through the magazine until she came to a photograph of a skinny model wearing a pair of jeans that hung on her narrow hip-bones like clothes on a hook. She wore no shirt, and had her arms wrapped around her virtually nonexistent breasts.

"See?" Ruby said.

"See what?"

"See her belly-button ring? Isn't it pretty?"

I grabbed my daughter around her waist and hoisted her to her feet, groaning at her unaccustomed weight. It had been a while since I'd tried to pick this big girl up. "You're not getting your pupik pierced, my love. Let's go."

"No."

"Come on, honey. We have to pick Isaac up in an hour, and I have something I need to do before then."

I wish I could say I sounded as patient the fifth and sixth times I told Ruby we had to leave. It would be truly wonderful if I could report that we walked out of the library hand-in-hand, an accommodating child and a devoted parent. Alas, it's more likely that we resembled a screaming banshee and the banshee's ill-tempered herder. Thankfully, Ruby's sobs had abated by the time we reached Nahid's office.

The boss herself wasn't there, but Kat was. I was shown back to her tiny office by a lovely young receptionist with dark, waist-length hair, and gold fingernails with tiny jewels imbedded in the polish. I found my friend hunched over her computer, a stricken look on her face.

"Hey, Kat," I said. "What's up? What are you doing?"

"Evicting someone," she replied morosely. She tugged out the pencil that had been holding her hair up on the top of her head and combed it through the locks that tumbled down over her shoulder. "What's going on? Has something happened with Farzad and Felix?"

I shook my head. "Not that I know of. I was hoping to have a little chat with your mother-in-law. You know, just background stuff."

"She's not going to talk to you. I mean, she might talk *at* you, but she's not going to let you interview her." Suddenly

Kat seemed to notice Ruby's presence. "Hi honey," she said.
"How are you? How's school?"

Ruby plopped herself down in the corner of the office
where Kat had a small pile of toys. Ruby picked up a toy by
the edge, her face wrinkled in a pout of utter disgust, as
though she were handling a dead rodent, rather than a
Matchbox car.

"These are *boys'* toys," she said.

"That's because they belong to Ashkon," I told her.

She sighed heavily and began to drive the car over the
carpet with an ostentatious listlessness. No matter how hard
I try, no matter how many gender-neutral toys I buy, my
children still persist in acting out the roles assigned to them
by contemporary culture. Why is it that that continues to
surprise me?

I turned back to Kat. "Have you heard anything new?"

She glanced down at Ruby and then at her open office
door. I pushed the door closed with my toe.

"What's going on?"

"I was going to call you today. You know the lock box?"
she said.

"On the door of the house? What about it?"

"Well, the boxes have a little chip inside them."

"A memory chip?"

"Exactly. And someone was messing with the lock box on
Felix's house."

I leaned forward excitedly. "What do you mean?"

Kat reached into her desk drawer and pulled out a lock
box. It was grey, with a black hasp that fit through the door
handle, and a little metal trap door in the bottom. Then she
reached into her purse and pulled out a little keypad.

"This looks just like the one on Felix's door. You see this
keypad?"

I nodded.

"It's called a programmer. Every agent has his or her own programmer, with a four-digit code. You snap your programmer into the box, input your code, and the box opens and you pull out the key." She punched in four numbers, and the metal trap door opened. She yanked out a little drawer. I nodded again; I knew all this. I'd seen her use the lock-box on Felix's door.

"The chip in the lock box remembers the previous ten numbers."

"It does!"

"Yeah. You know that detective on the case? The really nice-looking black guy with the weird name?"

"Detective Goodenough?"

She nodded. "He came by and asked Nahid to show him how the box worked. She accessed the codes for him. I know all this because she called me into her office to make sure that the most recent number on Felix's lock box was mine; which it was, of course. There shouldn't have been anybody else's number in there, except maybe Nahid's or her assistant's, if one of them had tried the lockbox after it was put on. Because, remember, the house wasn't really on the market."

"But there were more numbers in the box's memory?"

"In a way. There was mine, like I said, and before that someone had input the same number nine times."

"What was the code? Do you know who it belonged to?" I asked, holding my breath.

She nodded. "Detective Goodenough traced the number. He called to ask Nahid if the woman worked with us or if she had another reason to have gone to the house."

"And?"

"The code belonged to an agent at Crowden Century 21,

in Bel Air, named Marilyn Farley. Nahid asked me if I knew her, or had told her about the house, but I hadn't. Anyway, it couldn't have been her."

"Why not?"

"Because Marilyn's on bed rest—she's pregnant with twins. She hasn't been allowed up except to pee for nearly two weeks. Nahid had me call her. The detective had already been to see her, but she was so desperate for distraction that she talked to me for almost an hour."

"Has she been home on her own, or is there anybody who can testify that she's really been home like she's supposed to be?"

Kat smiled. "I asked her that. She said her husband is afraid to leave her alone, so whenever he's not with her, he has his mother or her mother stay there."

I nodded. "Good job," I said. "Tell me if you get sick of this real estate business. You might have a future as an investigator."

"I wish," she said wistfully. "Wouldn't that be cool? But Nahid would never let me go. She likes having me right here, where she can watch me."

"Did you ask Marilyn if she has ever lent anyone her number, or if anyone else knew it?' Could someone have taken it and used it?"

"You can't just lend the number. You have to have the programmer."

"Could someone have reprogrammed *their* programmer with *her* code number?"

Kat shook her head. "No. Only the Board of Realtors can change the code on a programmer."

"So who ever it was has to have used her programmer, right?"

"Yup."

"Or had some access to the Board of Realtors."

"Right."

"Where's her programmer now?"

"Here's the really interesting part," Kat said. "It's lost."

"What do you mean?"

"She told me that the detective asked to see her programmer, and she went to give it to him. Except it wasn't in her purse. The day she went on bed rest, she did an open house. She told me that she knows she had her programmer that morning, because she used it at the house, but she hasn't seen it since. She didn't notice it was gone, because she hasn't had to use it since she's been in bed."

"So maybe someone at the open house got hold of her programmer."

"That's what I was thinking."

"Does she know who was there?"

"She said it was a zoo. I mean, you know what the market's like. If it's a halfway decent house you can get a couple of hundred people at an open house."

"What about the sign-in sheet? Isn't there always a sign-in sheet?"

Kat nodded. "Marilyn told me that Detective Goodenough got the sheet from her office. But sometimes people don't bother signing in."

Then I thought of something. "But even if someone stole the programmer, he still couldn't *use* it, right? Unless he knew her code number."

Kat winced. "Marilyn swore me to secrecy."

"Kat!"

"You promise you won't tell? She'll definitely get fired if you tell."

"Of course I promise. I mean, I won't tell unless I absolutely have to."

She sighed and leaned closer to me. "She said she'd been having a horrible time remembering anything since she got pregnant. She kept forgetting her code number, and even had to go back to the Board once to have them input a new number."

"Please don't tell me she wrote the number on her programmer."

Kat nodded. "On a sticker."

"So whoever it was who took her programmer also got the code number."

"Right."

"Does Detective Goodenough know that?"

"I don't know. She must have told him, don't you think? I mean, it's a murder investigation."

For far too many people, self-interest trumps civic responsibility. "When was that open house?"

"Right before she went on bed rest. Just about two weeks ago."

"Before Alicia was killed."

Kat nodded.

I wrinkled my brow. "So someone went to the open house, stole the programmer, and then used it to break into the house and kill Alicia."

"Yup," Kat said.

"But Alicia was in the guest house. Would they really have needed the programmer to get in there?"

"The courtyard is entirely fenced in. There's no access either to the garage or to the side yard from the guesthouse. The only way out is through the main house."

"Still, it seems like pretty convoluted coincidence, don't you think? You just happen to find the programmer, it just happens to have the code written on it, and there just happens to be a lock box on the door of the person you want to kill."

"Maybe the person stole the programmer first, and that's what gave him the idea of using it to get into the house and kill her."

"Maybe. Or maybe he went to an open house hoping to steal a programmer, and just lucked into the number. However it happened, why did he bother inputting the number so many times? Why didn't he just use the stolen programmer once, to get in?"

Kat paused, thinking.

"What do you get out of inputting the number?" I murmured more to myself than her.

"What do you mean?"

"What happens when you input the number again and again? You erase the previously recorded code numbers, right?"

Kat nodded. "Right!"

I leaned back in my chair and winced. My sciatica was killing me. "Someone was trying to hide the codes that had been previously used. They were making sure no one would know who had been there before them."

At that moment, Ruby jumped to her feet. "Mama!"

I looked over at her.

"Mama! It's almost five o'clock!"

I looked up at the clock hanging on Kat's wall. "That's right honey. Good job reading the time."

She scowled at me. "*Mama!* We're late picking Isaac up from his playdate!"

We most certainly were.

Twenty-three

WHEN we arrived back home, I dumped the children with their father and called Detective Goodenough. Unlike every other cop I'd ever tried to reach on the telephone, he actually answered his own extension. His voice was deep and resonant, and he projected a stern authority, even over the fiber-optic lines.

The detective reassured me that he was following up on the open house attendees, and greeted my tentative request for a copy of the open house register with a bark of laughter. He was steps ahead of me on the Board of Realtors, as well, and was already in possession of the names and addresses of everyone on the Board, as well as of the various employees. It wasn't surprising that he refused to share that information, either, but that at least I could acquire for myself quite easily over the Internet.

Goodenough was polite, but he neither needed nor wanted my input on his investigation. And who could blame him, really? As far as he was concerned, I was at best an overly aggressive defense attorney, and at worst a busybody pregnant lady.

I hung up the phone feeling frustrated, and called Al, who volunteered to find out who was on the Board of Realtors. We'd sit down together and figure out if any of the members had a connection to Alicia. I took on the rather hopeless task of tracking down the list of people who had attended the open house. I knew Goodenough wouldn't share the sign-up sheet with us, and I doubted that Kat's friend, the pregnant, bedridden real estate agent with the bad memory, would be able to recreate it for me.

Feeling a bit better about my lack of progress, I wandered into Peter's office where the rest of my family was crouched on the floor, building the Bottle City of Kandor out of Legos.

"So, I've got some bad news," Peter said.

I groaned. "What?"

"I've got to fly to New York for a meeting."

I lowered myself to the carpet and leaned against him. I nestled my head against the smooth warmth of his ancient flannel shirt and felt the soft give of the layer of flesh that had lately overtaken his once-thin chest and belly. I toyed with the broken button on his shirt cuff. "Bummer," I said. "When?"

"Tomorrow."

I groaned again, and Peter kissed the top of my head.

Ruby, always on the lookout for any physical contact between her parents that didn't specifically include her, picked her head up from the pile of bricks she was snapping into the shape of Krypto the Superdog. "We should go with you, Daddy."

He ruffled her curls with his hand. "I wish you could, sweetie pie."

"It's been a very long time since I've seen my Bubbe and Zayde," she said.

"Not that long," I reminded her. "Bubbe was just here when Mama and Daddy went to Mexico."

"That was months and months ago," she said.

Suddenly, I thought of Julia Brennan, and *New York Live.* I might not be able to investigate the people who'd shown up at Marilyn Farley's open house, but Goodenough couldn't keep me away from Julia Brennan. I pushed against Peter's chest, leveraging myself into a sitting position. "Honey, you know, that might not be such a bad idea," I said.

"What?" Peter said.

"We should go with you to New York! We'll see my folks, and I can do a little follow up on this case."

"Tomorrow? You want to go to New York with me tomorrow?"

"Sure! It's a great idea. Ruby and Isaac will stay with my parents, and the two of us will have a romantic couple of days in the city."

"Are you allowed to fly? I mean, aren't you too pregnant?"

"The airlines let you on up to thirty-six weeks, and I know Dr. Kline won't care."

"But I'm going to be *working*. And, anyway, do you know how much a ticket will cost at the last minute?"

"Nothing, if we use frequent flyer miles. I'm going to get on the phone and see what I can do." Suddenly I narrowed my eyes at him. "Unless you don't *want* us to go with you."

He smiled a sickly smile. "No, no. I can't think of anything more fun than flying cross-country with the kids for a two-day visit with your parents."

Lucky for us, the flight the studio had booked Peter on

still had two seats available for frequent flyers. I gulped, and paid full fare for the third seat, reassuring myself that at least it was tax deductible. I was, after all, working on a case. Maybe I'd even be able to bill some part of the fare to Felix's account—if it didn't turn out to be a total waste of time, that is.

What I didn't remember until we actually arrived at the airport the next morning is that the Screenwriters Guild requires that all its members be flown *first class*. Not Business Class, and most certainly not, God forbid, coach. Peter boarded the plane at his leisure and began snacking on warm nuts and champagne, while I did my best to browbeat two people into swapping seats so that Ruby and Isaac would be sitting next to me. My entreaties fell on deaf ears. No one was willing to swap their aisle and window for any one of our three middle seats. Finally, I walked up to the florid man in the New York Jets sweatshirt sitting in the aisle seat next to Isaac and handed him an airsickness bag.

"His name is Isaac, and he usually stops vomiting twenty minutes or so after take-off. I find it helpful to have a second bag at the ready, just in case he fills the first."

The man's face turned even redder, and he leapt to his feet and stumbled over himself on his way to the seat that had been assigned to me.

The flight attendant came over at this point, her perfectly made-up face twisted into a grim smile. "You're going to have to take your seat, Ma'am."

"Okay, I just need another minute," I said.

"We can't push back until you sit down, Ma'am," she said firmly.

"I know, and I'm so sorry. I'll be just a second." I craned my neck to find where Ruby's seat was, and knelt down to point it out to her.

"*Now,* Ma'am."

I stifled my irritation—you can never win an argument with a flight attendant. I once represented a woman who had an altercation with a stewardess over whether her stroller could fit in the overhead compartment. My client ended up getting charged with assault, all because she had tapped the stewardess's name badge and told her she was going to report her to the airline. My poor client, a harried mother of three, was taken off the airplane in handcuffs.

Now, the flight attendant seemed to notice my belly for the first time. Her face tightened into an expression that looked suspiciously victorious. "Ma'am, we don't allow women in advanced stages pregnancy to fly." She smiled at me maliciously. "You'll have to come with me."

I looked her dead in the eye and said, in a voice so shocked and horrified that I nearly frightened *myself,* "What are you talking about? I'm not *pregnant!*" I lifted a trembling hand to my chest. "I've never been so offended in my life."

Ruby opened her mouth as if to protest, but I squeezed her shoulder.

The flight attendant blushed a deep red, and stammered, "Oh. Oh no. I'm so sorry. I didn't mean . . . I'm so. . . . Oh, *no.*" She stumbled away from me back up the aisle. I turned my attention to the young woman in the window seat. She stared back at me over her copy of *The Joy Luck Club,* and then smiled.

"All right," she said. "You win." She got up, and I pushed Ruby into the seat she vacated.

"It's 23B," I said. "And thank you."

"No problem. When are you due?"

I winked at her, snapping my seat belt closed.

Here's the irony of that particular flight. The truth was, Isaac never vomits on airplanes. He's a *terrific* flyer. In fact, unlike his sister, who heaves her food at the drop of a hat, he almost never gets sick. However, I'd forgotten about his recent bout of stomach flu. Worse yet, the red-faced man hadn't given me back the airsickness bag I'd handed him. Isaac did indeed fill more than one bag, but the second didn't have the airline's logo printed on it. With remarkable quick thinking for a six-year old, Ruby grabbed my purse, dumped the contents into her lap, and handed it to me while I held Isaac's head in my hands. Peter and I were going to need to make a stop at the Kate Spade boutique.

At the end of the five-hour flight, my ankles had swollen to the size of basketballs, and Ruby, Isaac, and I were covered in a combination of orange juice, chicken gravy, and other things too disgusting to contemplate. Ruby's hair resembled a pile of brightly colored autumn leaves, so that gave me some idea about what was probably going on with my own. We tumbled out of our seats and found Peter waiting for us at the door to the plane. His smile slowly faded as we approached.

"Have a nice nap?" I asked him.

He shook his head. "I didn't sleep for more than an hour or two. I watched that new Sylvester Stallone movie."

If there were any justice in the world, the heat of my scowl would have burned a hole right through his chest. I handed him our flight bags and waddled after the children who had scampered out ahead of us.

"I forgot my Lactaid!" he called after me. "So I got a really bad stomach ache from the ice cream sundae. And you know how much I hate caviar. The gravlax was covered in it."

It was all I could do to keep from flinging myself at his throat.

Twenty-four

IT was over lunch the next day at the Union Square Café that I finally forgave my husband. His meeting was in the morning, and he'd begged off a business lunch in order to meet me. The kids were at my parents' house in New Jersey, being stuffed with New York bagels, Stella D'oro cookies, and other delicacies unavailable in the wilds of California. Peter and I had had a lovely night on our own at the St. Regis hotel, one of those indulgences you are permitted only when traveling on the tab of someone far richer and more spoiled than yourself. The movie studio for which Peter had agreed to rewrite a Victorian Frankenstein romp qualified nicely.

While Peter had been stuck in meetings, I'd spent the morning replacing the purse I'd sacrificed on the altar of Isaac's roiling stomach, and was feeling pretty darn content. I'd even managed to find a maternity store in Soho that had, hidden on a crooked rack at the rear of the store, a few items in my size. At five feet tall, I'd never before considered myself an XXL, but the tunic with Chinese writing all over it was too cute to pass up purely because of size-related shame. I was a little worried that the letters might actually spell out something like "Ugly, fat, white woman," or "Many years of bad luck to wearer," but I suppressed that concern as soon as I realized how good the top looked with my new faded, flare jeans.

"Hey! You look adorable," Peter said as soon as I walked in the door of the restaurant.

I smiled brightly and showed off my purse. "What do you think?"

He blinked. "Is that new, too?"

"No, I spent the morning hosing the vomit out of the old one. Of course it's new!"

"Isn't it the same bag?"

"Not at all. This one has a thin red stripe in the fabric. See?" I held the bag out to him and he nodded suspiciously. "And the other one had blue piping, not black."

"Nice," he said.

We sat down at a table by the window, and I spent a delightful few minutes perusing the menu, specifically avoiding anything that could be considered even remotely kid-friendly. I was seriously considering an entire meal of shellfish and carpacio when I remembered that Ruby and Isaac's absence didn't liberate me in any real way, after all. I was carrying around my very own diet regulator. I would have to make due with grilled flank steak sandwich and fries, but I satisfied my urge to misbehave by ordering a glass of red wine. The New York waitress didn't bat an eye, merely brought me my drink with a practiced flourish, and I tossed off half the glass with equal aplomb.

As we waited for our food and made short work of the breadbasket, Peter said, "We've got an appointment to go to the set of *New York Live* after lunch." I'd sent Peter to his meeting with instructions to ask if anyone there had a connection to *New York Live* that might result in an introduction to Julia Brennan. "One of the producers of my film used to write for the show. She made a call for me."

"That's fabulous!" I exclaimed, nearly toppling my chair as I leaned to kiss my husband on his rough, stubbly cheek. Peter is the kind of guy who shaves only when not to would result in his being taken for an Orthodox Jew, or an Amish farmer.

The *New York Live* set was an old theater, the Stanley, on 43rd street at Broadway. Rehearsals took place on the stage, and the red velvet and gilt of the hanging curtains and proscenium, combined with the hilarious antics of the actors, lent the proceeding something of the hysterical air of late 19th century vaudeville. We walked in on a lesson in pratfalling. A man with a bulbous forehead and a red, fleshy proboscis was flinging himself from a ladder onto the stage while a hovering crowd laughed and leapt out of the way. I recognized some of the actors from the show, including Julia Brennan.

After a particularly dramatic tumble from the top of the ladder, the man limped off the stage and a young woman with a clipboard and an officious air called a break. We told her that we'd come to see Julia, and she called up to the stage, catching the comedienne right before she went off with the others. Julia came up to the row in front of ours and, leaning back over a chair, extended her hand in a friendly greeting. She was about twenty-five or -six years old and tall, taller than she seemed on television, with large hands and sharp, bony features. She looked somehow androgynous, manly even, like a transsexual who has given up the struggle for persuasive femininity and must content himself with a casual ambiguity.

"Randy, the assistant stage-manager, tells me you write those cannibal movies," she said to Peter.

"Yup."

"Love them. They're fun." Then she looked at me. "What can I do for you?"

"Ms. Brennan," I began.

"Julia."

The ancient seat springs groaned as I shifted my weight. Even had she not been so tall, Julia, standing there, would have loomed above me; but as it was, I felt like one of the Munchkins talking to the Great and Powerful Oz. She seemed to notice my discomfort and sat down, still in the row ahead, her long legs crossed and her arms resting on the seat back.

"I'm an investigator. I work for Felix. Do you know who he is?"

"The fashion designer? Sure! Tariq Jones, one of our younger comedians, does a bit spoofing his line."

I smiled, wondering what name Tariq could come up with that would seem more farcical than "Booty Rags." "I think you knew his sister, Alicia Felix."

Julia narrowed her eyes at me for a moment and then assumed an expression of heartfelt sympathy. "Yeah, it's really awful. I heard all about it from Spike Stevens."

"Felix has hired me to look into the circumstances of the murder."

"And that's why you want to talk to me?"

"I'm trying to get a sense of what kind of person Alicia was. What might have been going on in her life."

"Uh huh."

"I understand that in recent years you two had some . . . difficulties."

Julia raised an eyebrow. "Difficulties? What do you mean?"

"The character you do on the show, Bingie McPurge. It's based on Alicia's Mia bit, isn't it?"

"Based on? Hardly."

"Well, Alicia was doing Mia long before you were doing Bingie McPurge, wasn't she?"

Julia stood up suddenly. "I don't think I should be talking to you. My lawyers are dealing with this."

I lifted a mollifying hand. "I'm just doing the best I can to find out about Alicia. Her disappointment over her career seems to have been one of the defining things about her, and your success with a very similar comedy schtick was clearly a source of frustration for her."

Julia folded her arms in front of her, but she didn't walk away. "And? So what? I certainly hope you're not trying to say that I had anything to do with her death."

Now it was my turn to pause. I hadn't made any such implication, had I? "No. But you can't deny the similarity of the characters."

"Let's just say that Mia inspired me."

"Did Alicia ever speak to you personally about Bingie McPurge? Or were all your contacts through your lawyers?"

Julia unfolded her arms and seemed to relax. "She certainly tried to."

"What do you mean?"

"Look, I won't lie to you. You know Alicia was upset. She called my agent a few times, pretty hysterical. We even had to ask Spike to try to mellow her out. Anyway, there wasn't much she could do, was there?

"Wasn't there? Weren't you afraid she would, say, sue you?"

Julia shook her head. "She might have threatened that, but she didn't have any grounds, and she knew it. Sure, she had a character that was a bulimic. But I didn't steal any of her jokes—honestly, why would I have? Alicia was no writer. Her routine basically consisted of gagging noises. Even if she had tried to sue, my agents, lawyers, the studio people, everyone said that she didn't have a leg to stand on. Anyway, Alicia was, like, forty years old." Julia looked at me, as if assessing whether or not I was close to that witching age. "She couldn't play the part anymore. It was ridiculous."

Then Julia leaned over and lowered her voice. "I'll tell you something; you should be looking at a whole different part of Alicia Felix's life if you want to really get to know what she was like."

"What do you mean?"

Julia smiled. "She was a freak. I mean, really. My lawyers found out all sorts of stuff about her."

I deliberately forced my face to remain blandly neutral.

"What kind of stuff?"

"That woman was insane. I mean, really nuts. You want to know why she died, you should look at her website."

"Her website?"

At that moment, a voice called out. "Actors, places. Let's go!"

Julia turned her back on me and loped in the direction of the stage, her long legs carrying her like an elegant stick insect. Right before she reached the end of the row she turned back. "Hey," she called. "Don't you want to know where I was the night Alicia was killed?"

Her jocular tone struck me as so inappropriate I didn't even reply.

"I was here, in the city. I have been for weeks. We've got rehearsal every day but Sunday, and the show is live on Saturdays."

"Okay," I said. It wouldn't take too much to follow up on her alibi. And even if it stuck, there was always the possibility that she had arranged for someone else to do the murder. Although the truth is, it's a lot more difficult to find a hit man than you might think.

Julia said, "I hope you find out who killed her. I really do. Whatever Alicia and I thought of each other, nobody deserves to die like that."

The woman sounded absolutely sincere, and genuinely unconcerned. Her callousness might have been a product of her success, or simply of her youth. Whatever its source, she didn't sound like someone who would have felt compelled to murder in order to protect her career. I wasn't ready to dismiss the possibility of her guilt absolutely—after all, she might have been a better actress than the few minutes of the show Peter and I watched indicated—but something told me that my short list was down another suspect.

Back at the hotel, I logged on to the Web and found Alicia's website. I spent a good hour going through every page, but I could find nothing on the site that made Alicia seem any more bizarre than any other wannabe in Hollywood. For that matter, I could find nothing that would have inspired the letters from the young girls that I'd seen tacked up on the bulletin board in the guest house. The site consisted of no more and no less than a series of photographs of Alicia in various theatrical incarnations, and her at once lengthy and spotty filmography. The closest I got to "freaky" was a series of photographs of Alicia in which she was naked, although her arms were wrapped tightly around her body, hiding everything from the lens. She looked lovely, almost ethereally beautiful, but also frightening. Alicia was just so thin. Like a half-starved Ophelia. Was this what Julia was referring to? Was it Alicia's anorexia that made her, in the eyes of Bingie McPurge, a freak?

Twenty-five

ON the way home to Los Angeles, Peter gave me the first class seat. All the way onto the plane, I was the happiest woman on earth. So happy, in fact, that I was wishing for thick fog over LAX so we would have to circle the airport for a couple of extra hours. I was the first one on the plane, and I settled myself excitedly in my over-stuffed seat, two fashion magazines and a mystery novel tucked into the back pocket of the seat in front of me, my shoes kicked off, my hand ready to receive my orange juice and cup of warmed nuts. Then my seatmate joined me. My very, very large seatmate. My very, very large seatmate, with a sinus condition. The man snorted and snuffed his way through an entire box of tissues before we had even taken off. I refused to allow myself to be troubled. I put my headphones on, turned the volume up loud, and pushed back against the massive elbow that had worked its way across the armrest and into my seat.

The headphones were no match, however, for the twins

sitting in the seat in front of me. When their frazzled young
mother made it onto the plane, seconds before the door
closed, dragging two car seats with her, I nearly burst into
tears. *My* babies were in coach! Far away from me. I was lib-
erated from them, free to enjoy an adult-only universe. And
here, in first class, was a mother traveling with a set of in-
fant twins. A set of twins who, apparently, had outgrown
their naps. They could not have been more than eighteen
months old, and neither of them shut up for the entire
flight. They screamed, they cried, they wailed, and no matter how loud I turned up the volume on my headset, I heard
them. Worst of all, I had to pretend I didn't care. I had to
pretend that, unlike the other sour-faced denizens of first
class, I, as a mother, had sympathy for the young woman. I
knew her pain. And I did. I really did. Yet I still wanted to
throttle her and her wretchedly behaved children.

By the time the flight attendant dumped my hot fudge
sundae in my lap, I had grown somewhat fatalistic about the
possibility of enjoying my flight. Her cheerily apologetic
"Oopsie!" didn't even bother me. Neither did the snicker of
the fat man with the runny nose. Or the resounding wails of
the twins as their mother put them down for a moment to
pass me a handful of baby wipes so I could swab ineffectu-
ally at the sticky, wet stain on my slacks.

Peter, on the other hand, reported that the children had
been so tired from their two days with my parents that
they'd both fallen asleep as soon as the plane took off. He'd
spent the flight happily rereading a copy of *Dune* he'd found
in the seatback pocket. Once again I had to restrain myself
from beating him about the head and shoulders.

The studio had arranged for a car to pick Peter up and
take him home, and the look on the driver's face when he realized that three sticky urchins, one of them pregnant, were

going to be joining his client in the impeccably maintained Lincoln Continental was a cross between horror and despair. He was even less pleased when it became obvious that our luggage could barely fit on a single cart. The poor man had to lug both booster seats himself. I did dump out the cookie crumbs, sand, and gobs of melted gummy bears before handing him the seats. There was nothing I could do about the crusted-on yogurt, short of throwing the seats away and starting fresh.

My cell phone rang almost as soon as we got settled in the car. It was Al.

"Where are you?" he shouted into the phone.

I held the receiver a few inches from my ear. "On the ten heading for home.

"So?" Al asked. "What did you find out?"

"One dead end after another." I told him about my conversation with Julia. "How did you do on the Board of Realtors list?"

"Got it," he said. When I first met Al, he had been something of a Luddite, suspicious of the Internet, certain it was a tool of the government for spying on innocent and unwary citizens. While he's still convinced that the FBI and NSA are amassing piles of information on individual tax payers, a suspicion that has lately begun to sound less and less crazy to me, he has grown adept at using the Internet for his own purposes, both professional and otherwise. While once he had to rely on buddies on the force to whisper in his ear, he can now find almost anything out with a few clicks of the mouse. He also uses the Internet to keep in close touch with his militia and anti-tax cronies.

"Read me the list of names," I said.

He did, but unfortunately I didn't recognize any of them.

"I'll email it to you," he promised.

One of the joys of flying from east to west, is that that time difference allows you much of your day once you're home. Peter took pity on me after my hellish flight and volunteered to stay home with the kids. I called Kat and browbeat her into arranging a visit with Marilyn Farley, who was still stuck in bed, trying to stave off the delivery of her twins. I told Peter, albeit half-heartedly, that I would take Ruby and Isaac with me, but they were busy getting back in touch with their stuffed animals and action figures and were unwilling to leave the house.

Kat met me in front of Marilyn's bungalow in the neighborhood known to real estate agents, and to real estate agents alone, as Beverly Hills Adjacent. The rest of us call it Los Angeles. Kat was leaning against the door of her car, and she looked just terrible.

"Hey," I said, walking up to her.

She smiled wanly.

"What's wrong?"

"Wrong? Nothing's wrong."

But she was clearly lying. Her face was drawn and thin, and her pregnant belly looked like it was hanging from her shoulder blades like a basketball on a hanger. Her skin was pallid, and almost green.

I opened the door of her car and got in, motioning for her to do the same. She followed me and leaned her head against the steering wheel.

"What is it, sweetie?" I said, patting her shoulder. "Is it this investigation? Is Nahid giving you a hard time?"

She shook her head. "No, no. Nothing like that. I'm just under pressure. You know, with the baby coming. Nothing's ready. I haven't moved Ashkon out of the nursery. I haven't set up his big boy bed. There's just so much to do."

I sighed sympathetically. I hadn't made any preparations

for my baby, either. But by the third, you just sort of assume
everything will fall into place.

"It'll work out, Kat. It's just a matter of one intense
weekend's worth of work. If you want, I can give you a
hand. We'll go shopping for all the stuff you need, including Ashkon's new furniture."

She sat up and shook her head. "That's sweet of you, but
it's not just that."

I waited.

She seemed to muster up her courage. "Sometimes, when
I'm feeling stressed out . . . I . . . well . . ."

"What?" I asked softly.

She sighed. "God, this is so embarrassing. It's just that I
thought I was over all this. I mean, I *was* over it all. And
then last week I just started doing it again."

"Doing what?"

She rubbed her hand across her mouth, swallowed, and
then said, "I used to be bulimic. I mean, I guess I still
am."

For a moment, I was surprised. And then I wasn't at all.
Kat's confession made all too much sense. Her thinness
always seemed somehow unnatural to her. Here she was, this
beautiful, voluptuous, middle-eastern woman, who somehow managed to be rail-thin even while pregnant. While
virtually every Persian woman I've ever met has been fash-
ionably thin, Kat always looked like someone on a drastic
diet. It was as though her flesh seemed empty—missing its
accustomed fullness and heft. Her sharp cheekbones cried
out for a layer of padding, her neck sank oddly into a bosom
too round and soft for her bony chest and torso.

"You've been making yourself throw up?" I asked, doing
my best not to sound judgmental.

She nodded. "I know it's awful. For the baby, especially."

"The baby will probably take the nutrients it needs from your body. I'm more worried about you."

"I should go back to my meetings."

"Like AA?"

"Yeah, but for bulimics. I stopped going a few years ago. I didn't need it. But now I guess I do."

"Do you have a therapist?" I asked.

"I did."

"Maybe you should see her again, too."

"I don't have time! I mean, I told you, I've got like nine million things to do, and Nahid is running me ragged at work."

"And here I am, making things even harder for you. Please, Kat. Make time. Call the therapist. You can't keep doing this to yourself. You'll make yourself sick. And at some point the baby will start to suffer, too."

She closed her eyes, as if to keep her tears from falling, and then said, "We'd better go in. Marilyn is expecting us." She opened her door and walked out, leaving me to follow behind.

This eating disorder thing was so tenacious, so impossibly ubiquitous. Was there a woman in the city of Los Angeles who was not somehow stuck in its claws? What was most remarkable to me was how it could rear its ugly head years after Kat had assumed she was cured, after she had moved beyond that kind of mindset and behavior. Just like, for that matter, Alicia Felix.

MARILYN Farley was lying in bed, on her left side, looking about as bored as any woman has ever looked. We were shown to her room by an older woman who could only have been her mother-in-law, given the combination of politeness and impatience with which Marilyn treated her.

"It's great to meet you!" Marilyn said, a bit hysterically. "God, I'm so pathetic. You just can't have any idea how horrible this is. I've been stuck in this bed forever. I'm not even allowed to roll over! I'm just supposed to lie here on my left side and hope I don't have to pee more than a few times a day. I can't even read, because the medication they have me on gives me blurry vision. So all I do all day is watch crappy movies on cable. There was the one really horrible one about a cannibal wedding that gave me nightmares for days."

I blushed. "Yeah, That's not the greatest movie. I'm so sorry about the bedrest." I could never have managed it. Who would drive carpool? Who would go the grocery store? Who would run out to the shoe store to buy the pair of pink ballet slippers without which the recital could not proceed? Then I gave it a moment's reflection. Would it really be so bad? Trapped in bed watching movies? Even Peter's movies? With no other responsibilities? I wondered if there was something I could do to induce a little preterm labor of my own.

Marilyn, despite her understandable embarrassment at having lost her programmer, was willing to try to list for us the individuals who had come to her open house. She confessed to me that she was afraid that her irresponsibility had somehow led to Alicia's death. I got the feeling that Detective Goodenough had not done a particularly good job of convincing her otherwise. I reassured her that even if her programmer had been used, it had, at worst, made the murderer's job a little easier.

"If someone really wants to kill someone else," I told her, "he'll find a way. It would have been just as easy to break a window."

"But then the alarm would have gone off," Kat said.

I shook my head. "The alarm can't have been on, otherwise it would have gone off when the murderer opened the front door, even if he had used a key." I jotted down a note to ask Felix if Alicia normally turned the alarm on when she was home alone. If she did, then why had she left it off this time? Was she expecting someone?

As Marilyn did her best to remember the various realtors who had come to her open house, and whether or not they had brought clients with them, I took careful notes. None of the names sounded familiar, and while Kat knew some of the agents, she couldn't link them to Alicia in any way. Marilyn told me that there were a few people who had wandered in off the street, and that while she couldn't, of course, remember their names, she was fairly certain they'd signed in. So those individuals, at least, would be on the list Detective Goodenough had taken from her. That is, if they'd given their real names.

Once we'd exhausted the conversation about the open house, I spent a frustrating half hour trying delicately to figure out whether Marilyn was hiding anything. None of my gently put questions resulted in any kind of lead. Marilyn seemed genuinely never to have met Alicia Felix, not to know her, not to have had anything to do with the case in any way. Except that it was her programmer than had allowed the murderer access to the house.

Twenty-six

AL and I spent the next few days working on other cases, doing routine skip traces. I refused to set foot in the office until Julio was absolutely finished finding rat corpses, and Al had reluctantly admitted that the place was still plagued by the odor of dead vermin.

"I don't know where the hell they could be," he said. "In the walls, maybe? Anyway, Julio's going to poke some holes in the sheet rock and then repaint the whole damn garage."

"Good," I said. "He needs the work, and your garage could do with a renovation."

We were operating out of my kitchen, and his car. We didn't normally bother with skip traces—while they were once the bread and butter of private investigative services, nowadays most companies are aware of online tracing services and don't bother paying investigative fees to find the welshers and absconders that plague their businesses. We were doing these as a favor for a friend of Al's who had set up a semi-shady limited partnership scheme, only to find that the bulk of his investors had disappeared as soon as the economy had turned the least bit ugly. I tried to tell Al that the guy was probably paying us to avoid getting his own legs shot off by the people we were trying to find, but my partner ignored me. At any rate, none of the dozen disbarred lawyers and unlicensed physicians we tracked down seemed particularly dangerous. Just scrambling for cash, and not particularly honest.

The weekend found me absolutely gleeful at the *prospect* of time with the children, and out of Al's Suburban. That is, until Ruby began her by-now tedious refrain.

"I don't understand, why do I have to wait until I'm twelve to get my ears pierced?" she said.

"Because you have to be old enough to take care of the holes yourself. And that will be when you're twelve."

"But I'm old enough now! Both Isabel and Sophie got their ears pierced! All they had to do was clean the holes with special stuff and keep twirling their earrings. I can do that. I'm not a baby."

How could I explain to my child that the thought of a needle being jammed through her little white lobes, those pads of sweet flesh as precious to me as every other tiny, innocent part of her adorable little body, just made my heart rush to my mouth? We own our children's bodies when they're small. We created those little pearl toes, those dimpled elbows, those rounded cheeks. Our children belong to us as much—no *more*—than they belong to themselves. I reached around Ruby's waist and dragged her onto what lap I had left. She wriggled out of my arms, unintentionally jabbing me in the belly.

"Ouch!" I said.

"I don't feel like sitting on your lap."

"Okay," I said, my feelings hurt. Then, I looked at her. She was standing in a way that was unfamiliar to me. Her hip jutted out at an angle, and she had the toe of one sneaker balanced on the other foot. Her arms were crossed in front of her chest and she looked almost comically furious. She wanted to grow up, and I wasn't letting her. Then I thought of horrible little Madison and the other diet girls, and how scary that had all come to seem to me, in the wake of the tide of anorexia and bulimia that seemed to be washing over everything in my life. I was so afraid for Ruby, and so desperate for her to stay close to me so that I could protect her from all that.

"You know what, Ruby?" I said. "Let's go get your ears pierced."

Her shrieks of joy were so loud they made her little sister in my belly kick me in the ribs. Hard.

OUR first stop was the mall. None of the jewelry stores did ear-piercing, but we found a gift shop that advertised the service in the window. We waited at the register while the sales girl talked into her cell phone.

"He is like such a complete pig, and I like totally told him so. I instant messaged him, and I'm like, if you think I'm gonna just sit here while you boff her—"

"Excuse me!" I said loudly.

The salesgirl looked up at me from under her stiff, blond bangs. "What?"

"We need some help," I said.

"Mama?" Ruby said. "What does 'boff' mean?"

The girl laughed and said into her phone, "O'migod, I gotta go. I'll call you back in like a minute."

"Mama!" Ruby insisted.

"Nothing, honey. It's teenager talk." Then I turned to the girl. "We're interested in having her ears pierced."

"Cool!" she said, ducking under the counter and coming out to stand by us. "I just learned how to do that the other day. C'mon."

She led us to the front of the store where a little stool was set up in the window. She pointed at a row of stud earrings and told Ruby to pick out a pair.

"I've just got to remember how to do this," she said, picking up a white piercing gun. "Oops!" she shrieked, howling with laughter as a gold stud flew out of the gun and landed on the floor. "I guess someone loaded it already."

Ruby pointed out a pair of blue glass earrings, and the sales girl bit her lipsticked lip, leaving teeth marks in the heavy gloss. "Um, when's your birthday, because those are for December," she said.

"It doesn't matter," I told her.

"Well, like it totally does. I mean, she can't have like someone else's birthstone."

Ruby's lip began to tremble, giving lie to the notion that she was old enough to be doing this in the first place.

"Just give her the blue ones," I said.

"Okay, whatever," the sales girl said, and then, as if entirely unaware of our presence, reached a talon-nail up to her forehead and picked at a shiny pimple. I watched horrified as the zit popped under her finger. She glanced at the smear of puss on her nail and then wiped it casually on her jeans.

"You know what?" I said. "I've changed my mind. Come on, Ruby." I grabbed my daughter by the arm and dragged her out of the store. By the time we hit the parking lot, she was hysterical.

"Stop crying!" I said, opening the car door and lifting her

inside. "Stop crying, Ruby. We'll get your ears pierced. I promise. Just not there. That place was disgusting"

"Well then, where?" she snuffled.

"I don't know."

She looked as if she was about to being sobbing again.

"Ruby!" I warned. "Enough."

She sniffed dramatically, and we pulled out of the parking lot. We drove down Beverly Boulevard in silence, and then suddenly Ruby said, "How about there?"

She was pointing at a store-front brightly painted with geometric designs that looked vaguely tribal. A huge, green neon signed flashed the words "Body Piercing." Two young men were leaning up against the wall of the building, their skateboards tipped up against their legs, their dreadlocks blowing in the gentle breeze.

I was about to say no, when a thought occurred to me. Who better to entrust with my baby's precious lobes than someone whose business encompassed body parts far more sensitive and susceptible to infection?

I was probably not the first mother of two to hop out of her Volvo station wagon and into the waiting area of Tribal Memory Tat and Hole Works, but I doubt that they'd seen much of my kind of woman. The gaping mouths on the long line of bepierced and betatted young people waiting patiently on the paint-spattered vinyl couch and stools made that abundantly clear. Ruby and I crossed the cement floor with trepidation, both because we were nervous, and because the floor was decorated with a painting of the huge portrait of a Maori warrior in full face-paint, and it felt kind of weird to be stomping across his protruding tongue.

"Can I help you?" the young man behind the counter asked politely. He was young and part Asian, with long black hair caught up in a bun on top of his head. His ears were pierced with large, round, steel plugs that measured at least one inch in diameter, causing his lobes to hang low and distended against his cheeks. Each of his eyebrows sported a dozen rings of various sizes. I couldn't see under his clothes, but I was willing to bet that getting through a metal detector would have involved some nearly pornographic maneuvering.

"Exactly how sanitary are your facilities?" I said, ignoring the fact that I sounded like my Bubbe, who used to travel everywhere with a purse-sized bottle of Formula 409 with which she freely sprayed down park benches, bus seats, and even the chairs in restaurants.

"Good question," he said, and then he proceeded to outline for me the various cleansing tools he used. He showed me the prepackaged needles, each individually wrapped and sealed. He described the technique he used to sterilize the earrings, and then promised that he wore gloves throughout the procedure.

His professional thoroughness won my heart. Ruby's belonged to him the moment he showed her the gold hoops with the little mother-of-pearl beads he planned to use in her ears.

"Doesn't she have to have studs at first?" I asked.

"Nope," he said. "We find these work much better."

The procedure wasn't painless, but Squeak (that was what he told Ruby to call him) was true to his word. He washed his hands thoroughly, he changed gloves every time he touched something that hadn't been sterilized, and he took a good five minutes meticulously evening out the dots he drew on Ruby's ears. He assured me that if she ever wanted any more piercings in her ears, or if she ever planned on getting plugs like his own, there would be plenty of room in her lobes. I somehow managed to refrain from shouting, "Over my dead body!" The actual piercing was done with a long, black needle, and Ruby managed it with nary a tear, although her arms, wrapped tightly around my neck, seemed to be shaking. It's possible, though, that the trembling was my own.

The line of young men and women we had jumped (Squeak had asked them if they minded, and they had all assured us that they didn't) burst into applause when we walked out of the curtained piercing room. Ruby blushed and showed off her little hoops.

"Ooh!" a tall, blond girl of about eighteen exclaimed. "Mother-of-pearl! That's just what I want in my nipple!"

Twenty-seven

THAT Monday I took the list of Board of Realtor members, as well as the names Marilyn had remembered, over to Felix's house. Detective Goodenough arrived moments after I did.

"Ms. Applebaum," he said, not sounding at all surprised to see me. I was waiting in the living room for Farzad to get Felix, and the maid had let the detective in.

"How is the investigation proceeding?" I asked him. "Finding out about the tampering with the programmer will certainly help, I imagine."

He narrowed his eyes at me, and then nodded. "You're friends with the younger Mrs. Lahidji."

"Yes, I am."

We waited in silence until Felix and Farzad walked into the room. The men were obviously surprised to see the detective. They had been expecting only me. Goodenough pulled a long list of names out of his briefcase. In addition to the names of the members of the Board of Realtors that I had also brought, he had others that must have been from the sign-up sheet. After a quick glance at me, to which I replied with a nod, Felix and Farzad agreed to look over the names. The four of us passed over them, one at time, using Felix's Palm Pilot to see if anything hit. Nothing did. And neither did any of the names strike either man as familiar. I wasn't surprised. After we were done, the detective piled his papers together and slipped them back into his case.

"Do you think I could get a copy of the list?" I asked.

He smiled thinly and shook his head. "How's that certification coming, Ms. Applebaum?" he asked, instead of replying to my request.

I opened my mouth but could think of no searing reply.

He stood up. "I'll see myself out. If you think of anything new, you'll call me," he stated, rather than asked.

After he'd gone, Felix excused himself.

"I've got a lunch meeting at Barney's. I haven't met with the buyers there in ages, and I want to give them a sneak peek at the new line."

"So you're working again?"

He passed his hand over the stubble on his head. "I guess so. I mean, I have to get back sometime, don't I? Too many people depend on me." He didn't look at Farzad, but I did. The younger man had his lips pursed in a tiny frown.

After he left the room, I turned to Farzad. "It's good he's working, don't you think?"

"It's about time," the slight man said, kicking off his slippers and tucking his feet up under him. "So, you haven't found out anything, have you?"

"Not much, I'm afraid."

"So much for your house."

I winced and examined his face, hoping to see reflected

there at least some humor. He still wore his almost petulant moue. I felt a sinking in my stomach. There was just no way he would allow me to buy Felix's house unless this case came to some kind of satisfactory conclusion.

"You're still billing us, too, aren't you?" Farzad said.

"If you aren't satisfied, or if you think the bill is too high, you won't have to pay it." Now, that wasn't generally Al's and my policy, but neither did we usually force our services on people whose homes we hoped to buy.

Farzad acknowledged my statement as if it were no more than his due.

"So, who do *you* think killed Alicia?" I asked him.

"That detective thinks it was just a random sex-crime," he said.

"Did he tell you that?"

The little man shook his head. "No, but that's what he thinks. I'm sure of it."

"And what do *you* think?" I asked again.

He leaned his chin in his hands and cocked his head co-quettishly. "What does it matter what I think? Aren't you the private eye? Maybe you think I did it?"

"Did you?" I asked in a pleasant tone of voice.

He raised his eyebrows in mock surprise. Then he said, "No, no of course not. Don't get me wrong, sometimes I felt like killing the woman. I mean, not really. But you know how it is. She was exasperating. She wasn't an easy person to share Felix with."

"Was that what it felt like? Sharing your boyfriend?"

"She lived with us, didn't she? And she worked for Felix. Alicia was always around, and she was a presence, if you know what I mean. She wasn't someone you could ignore."

I nodded. "That must have made moving to Palm Springs pretty attractive."

He smiled. "Absolutely. Of course that wasn't the only reason, and we still want to go. But getting away from her was definitely part of it. For me, at least."

I shifted tacks. "Farzad, why wasn't the alarm on the night Alicia was killed?"

He wrinkled his brow. "Well, it wouldn't have been, would it? We never used it when we were home, only when we went out. And even then Alicia was pretty bad about turning it on. Anyway, if there's nothing else . . ." He rose to his feet both suddenly and languidly, like a cat. "Let me see you out."

I was about to object, but there really wasn't anything more I could ask Farzad. Perhaps he had killed her. He certainly had motive. But he, like Felix, had been in Palm Springs. They would have to have conspired to kill her together, and to provide one another with an alibi, and that just didn't make any sense.

As I drove cross-town to my prenatal appointment, I ran through the list of suspects in my mind. There was Charlie Hoynes, and Dakota. And his ex-wife. There was Felix and Farzad. Nahid Lahidji, Julia Brennan. None of them seemed any more or less likely than the others. So who had killed Alicia, and why? Was it just some crazed psychopath, after all?

Just then, my cell phone rang. It was Kat. "You're not going to believe this," she said.

"What?"

"Marilyn found her programmer."

"She what?"

"She found her programmer. It was in the glove compartment of her car the whole time. She only thought it was in her purse. She hadn't driven the car, so she didn't see it."

"How did she suddenly find it?"

"She went into labor yesterday, and her husband was on the other side of town at a meeting. Her mother-in-law drove her to the hospital in Marilyn's car. Marilyn opened the glove compartment to look for some tapes to take into the delivery room with her."

What did this mean? If Marilyn's programmer hadn't been stolen, how had her number been used? Someone must have programmed her number into a different programmer. But who? And why?

"Did she tell all this to the detective?"

"I'm sure," Kat said. "Her babies are fine, by the way. Still in the NICU, but she says they'll be out in a few days."

"That's wonderful. Um, Kat?"

"Yes?"

"How are you feeling?"

There was silence on the other end of the line. "Okay, I guess."

That morning, before I'd gone out, I'd done a little Web surfing. I hadn't been sure whether I was going to talk to Kat about what I'd found out, but now that I had her on the phone, I couldn't bear not to. "Sweetie," I said. "I hope you don't think this is presumptuous of me, but I got a few names for you."

"Names?" she said warily.

"Of therapists. People who specialize in bulimia among women our age."

"I had a therapist."

"Did you like her?"

She didn't reply.

"Do you want me to give you the names?"

After a few seconds of silence, she said, "Okay."

"I'll email them to you."

"Okay."

"I hope you don't think I'm butting in to something that's none of my business."

"No. No," she said listlessly.

"Kat, you know you can call me. Anytime. Day or night. If you feel like doing something, or if you just want to talk."

"I know."

"Have you gone back to a meeting?"

"I was thinking about it."

"Maybe you should go to one. Is there one tonight?"

"There's one on Saturday, at Cedars."

"How about you bring Ashkon to my house, he can hang out with Isaac and Ruby, have a sleepover, even. And you can go to the meeting. You won't even have to tell Reza if you don't want to."

I wasn't sure whether or not she'd accept my offer, and I was tremendously relieved when she did.

I walked into the doctor's office, mulling over what Kat had told me about Marilyn's programmer, and nearly fell over with surprise. Peter was sitting, waiting for me, reading a copy of *Baby* magazine.

"Hey!" I said. My eyes nearly filled with tears at the unexpected sight.

"Hey, yourself."

I sat down next to him and grabbed his hand in my own. I squeezed, tightly. "What are you doing here?"

"Finding out all sorts of interesting things. Did you know that you're not supposed to be eating tunafish sandwiches while you're pregnant?"

"Really? Why not?"

"Mercury poisoning. Tuna is full of mercury. Which causes birth defects and learning disabilities."

When the nurse came to get me, she found Peter on his

knees between my legs, doing his best to administer a Stanford/Binet to my belly button.

Of all the appointments for Peter to join me for, he had to be there when my doctor read me the riot act about my weight.

"Twenty-five to thirty-five pounds," she said. "That's what we recommend."

I smiled a sickly smile.

"Juliet, you've already put on close to fifty pounds. And you're nowhere near done."

I nodded. "I know. Scary, isn't it?"

She shook her head. "Your blood sugar is perfect, so that's a good thing. Are we scheduling a c-section, given that you've had two? Recent studies do indicate a heightened risk of uterine rupture in post-caesarian trials of labor, particular multiple caesarians."

It took me all of a second to decide. "Yes, let's schedule it."

"Good choice. Given that, the size of the baby isn't as important as if you were planning on a natural birth. But still. You are gaining weight faster than we would like."

I looked over the doctor's shoulder in time to catch Peter snickering into his hand. I freed a foot from the stirrup and aimed a kick at his groin. He jumped out of reach.

"I want you to watch what you eat," the doctor said, helping me sit up.

And watch, I did. I watched the milkshake and the French fries all the way from my plate to my lips. In my defense, I will say that it was Peter's idea that we go to Swingers for lunch after the appointment. I couldn't be expected to satisfy myself with some limp salad while he downed a burger, could I?

I had just turned down, with considerable ceremony, a

refill on my milkshake when Peter's cell phone rang. He answered it and murmured into the receiver for a minute. When he hung up, his face was pale.

"You're not going to believe this," he said.

"What?"

"That was Jake."

"Jake your agent?"

"Yeah."

"And?"

"Charlie Hoynes's daughter is dead."

"His daughter? You mean Halley?"

"Jake was on his way to the funeral, and he remembered that Hoynes and I had just got together. He called to make sure we knew about it."

I thought of Hoynes's wife, and her obvious desperation on the day we'd spoken. "Oh, No. That's awful. Did she die in the hospital? Was it the anorexia?"

Peter nodded. "I guess she starved herself to death."

The French fries and ice cream roiled in my stomach, and I put a hand over my mouth and ran to the ladies room.

Twenty-eight

PETER did not want to go to the funeral. He was right; we barely knew Hoynes, had never met his poor daughter, and my motivation for insisting we attend was entirely suspect. Nonetheless, within half an hour we'd gone home, changed our clothes, and were on our way out to the cemetery. I called the kids' schools from the car and arranged for Ruby and Isaac to stay late in their after-school programs.

The service had already started when we arrived at the chapel on the cemetery grounds, but it had clearly not been going on long. A thin woman with limp brown hair hanging shapelessly over her ears led the assembled congregation in a hymn that I'd never heard before. Something about sheep and water and Isaiah. She wore traditional priestly vestments, but draped with a shawl made out of some kind of African Kinte cloth. I'm not particularly good at distinguishing among the various Christian clergy, but the formality of her robes, combined with the consciously inclusive nature of her language and clothing, led me to infer that it might be an Episcopal service.

The hymn singing went on long enough for me to peruse the crowd. There was something familiar about it—something that seemed less than funereal, and it took me a while to put my finger on it. Finally, it hit me. But for the somberness of the tone, the room had the feel of a bat mitzvah. People were dressed in regulation black, but that had long since become the color of choice at every life-ceremony, from weddings to brises to bar mitzvahs. There were a few people weeping, most noticeably Charlie Hoynes's ex-wife. What gave the proceedings their adolescent, nearly celebratory feel, however, were the rows of teenagers, strictly segregated by sex—the boys in bright, barely-worn suits, the girls in dresses either too childlike for their size, or too skimpy and revealing for the event. The children seemed genuinely upset; all of the girls, and even one or two of the boys, were crying. I couldn't help but notice, however, that most of the children kept one eye on their compatriots to make sure their tears were carefully modulated to that of every other girl, no more nor less dramatic, their grief neither more nor less apparent.

After the service, I made Peter join the procession of cars out to the gravesite. I refrained, however, from forcing him to take one of the white roses handed out by the black-gloved attendants. We stood at the rear of the crowd, while the Episcopal priest murmured a few additional prayers. Halley Hoynes's mother was seated on a white wooden chair at the edge of the grave, and as the line of people began to pass by her, dropping their rose on top of the polished, golden wooden casket as it was lowered slowly into the black, loamy earth, she began to wail. Her cries were soft at first, high pitched and impossible to understand. Soon, though, her voice grew louder and clearer. She was keening the words 'my baby' over and over again. Hoynes sat a few feet away from her, Dakota at his side. He stared grimly into the rectangular hole, his face flushed, his lips clamped shut. Dakota wore a pair of oversized, black sunglasses and lipstick that shone dark and almost purple against her pallid cheeks. She too stared straight ahead, ignoring the cries that had now grown to shrieks. The procession passed, flower by flower, in front of Halley's wailing mother.

Finally, just when I felt that I, who knew the poor woman not at all, might be forced to approach her to offer some kind of a comfort, another woman, small, round, dressed in a grey coat, crouched next to the grieving mother and pressed her damp face to her own doughy cheeks. The little woman cried, too, but silently, and something about her noiseless grief seemed to still her friend's howling. They rocked together at the edge of the grave, until the last flower was tossed on the casket, and the priest had come to offer her arm.

As we made our way back down the narrow paths to our cars, the priest announced that the family would like us to join them at Barbara Hoynes's home in Brentwood. I pulled out my pad and jotted down the address. Peter glared at me.

"We're not going," he said.

"Yeah, we are."

"Why?"

I pulled open my car door and motioned for him to get in. I didn't want anyone else to hear this argument. "I don't know. Because Alicia Felix was murdered just a few weeks ago, and now Halley Hoynes is dead, and I just have a feeling about it all."

Peter slammed the car into reverse and began to back slowly down the hill. "How can you possibly have a feeling? That's ridiculous. Shameless. Charlie's daughter died of anorexia. What could that possibly have to do with Alicia's murder?"

"Alicia was anorexic, too!"

He shook his head at me. "And so is half of Los Angeles. So what?"

I sighed and, slipping off my shoes, lifted my swollen feet onto the dashboard, making sure to tuck my skirt under me so as not to flash any of the other mourners. "You know what Al always says about coincidences."

Peter shook his head impatiently. "Juliet, we don't know the woman. We never met her daughter. How can we just show up at her house? It's absurd. Anyway, aren't you afraid she'll recognize you?"

"There were at least a hundred people at this service. Do you honestly think anyone will notice us there?"

"You're not exactly small enough to fade into the wood-work, honey. And with my luck, Hoynes will trap me in some corner, and I'll end up committing to writing his wretched movie, just because I feel sorry for him!"

"Don't be absurd. His daughter is dead. The last thing Hoynes is going to want to do is talk business."

But of course that's exactly what Hoynes did want. As soon as we walked into the living room of the ostentatious plantation-style McMansion off Mulholland Drive, Hoynes grabbed Peter and dragged him off to talk business. Thank God Jake caught sight of the two of them and insinuated himself into their tête-à-tête, otherwise Peter's career would surely have foundered on the rocky shoals of a vampire abor-tion comedy.

Once I realized that my husband was safe in the hands of

his agent, I felt free to wander the edges of the crowd, eaves-dropping. It was essentially a typical Hollywood scene, al-though there were more overdeveloped young women in tight funeral wear than I'd seen before at the kind of parties Peter and I attended. I supposed that these were Charlie's actresses, all there to prove their allegiance and hope it would be remembered when it came time to cast the next television show or movie.

Barbara Hoynes's friends looked like they had wandered in off the set of an entirely different picture. They were much older, in their late forties or early fifties, as was she. Many of them were typically thin and elegant, but the woman who had comforted her at the graveside was not the only one who looked like a regular person. There were one or two other women who, like Barbara herself, looked their ages. Barbara sat in an armchair in front of the empty fireplace, her face by now more or less composed. It was obvious even sitting down that she was a tall woman, and one who had once been shapely but had now grown more stately and imposing. She had a broad shelf of a bosom and a wide, flat face interlaced with a fine webbing of wrinkles around her mouth and eyes. Unlike her husband's current girlfriends, she had clearly avoided the plastic surgeon's knife, although perhaps the size of her breasts indicated a long-ago familiarity with the shape-altering for-mula so prevalent among the younger women in the room.

I was doing my best not to look like I was staring at Hal-ley's mother, when I felt a hand on my arm.

"Hi," Dakota said. She was still wearing her sunglasses.

"Hi."

"This is a nightmare."

"It's very sad."

Dakota ran a trembling hand through her hair. "I just can't believe it. That stupid girl."

I glanced at her, surprised. Most of us try not to express those kinds of sentiments, even if we do feel them.

Dakota took a huge gulp of the drink she held in her hands, grimaced, and sucked in air. "I just can't believe it," she said again.

"I'm sure it's a terrible shock."

"Halley was just so *stupid*. I mean, to end up killing herself?" She took another swallow, sucking the last bit of alcohol out of the plastic tumbler. She crunched an ice cube between her teeth and then swayed, grabbing my arm with her hand. It was only then that I realized how drunk she was. "If that bitch finds out about the pills, I am going to be so screwed," she mumbled.

I held my breath, willing her to continue.

"That's all I need, is for Tracker's lunatic wife to figure out that I gave that crazy girl some of my pills." She put a hand over her eyes. "Get me another drink, okay?"

I propped her against the wall and crossed quickly to the bar, sniffing the glass she'd put in my hand. Gin. I motioned to the bartender to refill the drink. "Gin. Straight up," I said.

He glanced at my belly, but followed my instructions.

Dakota was still waiting for me, and I pressed the glass into her hands. She lifted to her lips and drained it in a single, huge gulp.

"Dakota," I said softly. "What kind of pills did you give Halley?"

She wiped her mouth on the back of her hand, leaving a smear of red lipstick like a bloodstain. "Just normal pills. Speed, you know. But, like, natural."

"Ephedrine?" I asked.

"Natural ephedrine. It works great." Then, without another word, she stumbled off.

I heard a disgusted snort and turned to find the small,

heavy-set woman who had comforted Barbara when she had broken down at the graveside.

"Horrible woman," she said.

I nodded and extended my hand. "I'm Juliet Applebaum."

"Susan Kromm. Poor Barbara, to have to deal with that woman."

I nodded.

A man who was clearly her husband stepped up next to her. His head was a dome of mottled pink skin. He hadn't, thank goodness, attempted the dreaded comb-over, but the bedraggled length of the few strands of baby-fine hair remaining on his head led me to believe that he might be considering it. He put his hand on the small of his wife's back and she leaned into him.

"This is so hard," she whispered.

"I know, dear," he said, reaching a trembling finger to wipe a tear from her plump cheek.

The moment was so intimate that it made me feel uncomfortable to be part of it. Just then, though, my attention was distracted by a stifled giggle. Crowded around a grand piano, not too far from Barbara, was gathered a group of teenage girls. Three of them sat thigh by thigh on the piano bench, and the others leaned against the heavy black sides of the instrument. The girls were whispering to one another, and every once in a while one of them giggled, and was immediately hushed by her peers. What was remarkable about the girls, or perhaps what was unremarkable about them, was their size. There were all, to a one, tiny. Tall or short, their waists could easily have been spanned by my hands. They had long legs, revealed by miniskirts, on which their knees bulged round and bony, separating fleshless thigh from sticklike calf. Individually, they might have seemed skinny, perhaps a bit unusually so, but together, in a group, they looked like nothing so much as a well-dressed, carefully made-up group of concentration camp survivors.

I was not the only one whose attention was riveted on the girls. Barbara Hoynes's eyes kept returning to them as though drawn by an irresistible force. One by one her guests approached her, murmuring their condolences. Each time she shook the proffered hand, nodded her thanks, and then looked back at the collection of bony limbs huddled around her piano. At last, her attention seemed diverted once and for all. Charlie, who had finally released Peter from his grip, crossed the room toward his ex-wife. He held Dakota's hand in his, and she swayed against him. He came to a stop in front of Barbara's chair and cleared his throat ostentatiously.

"My dear—" he began, but Barbara cut him off.

"Not now. Just shut up, Charlie."

The room grew absolutely silent. It was so quiet that one could almost hear the ticking of a hundred watches on a hundred wrists.

"Just shut up, Charlie. Please." Her voice was thick with pain and suppressed rage.

"Our poor little girl," Hoynes said, his face growing red, his eyes filling with tears. His grief seemed tried-on, like an ill-fitting outfit from the back of a studio's costume warehouse. And yet it was most likely real, wasn't it? He had lost his daughter. His only child.

Barbara's composure broke, and she began to scream. "You pig. You son of a bitch. You killed her. You and your gaunt and wasted girlfriends. She knew what you liked. She knew what you wanted, and she starved herself to try to be that for you. Look at that . . . that *stick* you're with! Look at her! That's what killed your daughter. You're what killed my Halley!"

She stabbed her finger at Dakota, and lunged at her. The younger woman leapt back, tripping over her feet, Hoynes's hand the only thing that kept her from tumbling to the floor in a pile of twig limbs and falsely inflated breasts.

The crowd of people had stopped even pretending to look away or be busy with their own conversations. Even Susan Kromm seemed frozen by shock and horror. Suddenly, the grieving mother turned toward the group of girls who had claimed her attention before her ex-husband's approach.

"And you!" she shouted. "What is wrong with all of you? You watch your friends die, one after the other, and it makes no impression on you at all. Are you trying to kill yourselves? Is that it? Will you only be happy when every last one of you is dead?"

The girls at first seemed to shrink into themselves, then one of the three on the piano bench rose on shaky legs and ran from the room. Within seconds, the others followed. Barbara collapsed back in her chair and began to weep. The sound of her tears seemed to liberate the frozen crowd. Susan Kromm rushed up to her, along with a few other women. They crowded around her chair, stroking her hair and back. The others in the room began at first to whisper to one another, but quickly their voices rose to a low hum, and the tinkling of glasses and silverware resumed.

Peter caught my eye from across the room, his eyebrows wiggling frantically. My husband wanted out of there. I shook my head at him and held up a finger. I needed just another minute or two.

I walked out of the living room, through the front hall, searching for the girls. I found them outside, sitting on the wide low steps leading up the front porch. I opened the door and let myself out. As soon as they saw me, their voices hushed.

"Hi," I said.

There were five of them, gawky, skinny girls with identical long, straight hair and pale skin. None of them responded to my greeting.

"That was pretty awful, wasn't it?" I said.

A girl with brown hair and a mouth full of teal blue braces nodded, shivering dramatically and hugging herself with wrapped arms. "God," she said.

"She acts like it's our fault," another girl whispered. This one was the prettiest of the group, although her perfect features were marred by a rash of angry pimples across her chin and forehead.

The other girls nodded. A tiny girl with close-set eyes, wearing a pale-pink childlike jumper over a Peter Pan blouse said, "She's got it so backwards. I like almost told her, Halley was the one who taught *me* how to do a fifty calorie fast. She was like my mentor!"

"Really?" I said, sitting down next to them on the step.

The girl immediately seemed to regret her words.

One of her friends rolled her eyes, and then said, in a cloying, rehearsed voice, "Halley had a terrible problem."

"Did she?" I asked. Then, watching the girls out of the corner of my eye, I said in a soft voice, "Well, I wish I had that problem."

They grew still, staring at me.

"I mean," I continued. "Look at me. I'm so fat."

"Aren't you, like, pregnant?" the girl with the braces asked.

"Yeah," I said. "But I'm so *huge*. I'll never get back to the way I'm *supposed* to look. Not by normal means. I wish I could figure out what to do about it."

The pretty girl leaned toward me, her blond hair falling

over her pale grey eyes. "It's just a question of control," she said.

"What do you mean?"

"I mean, the only reason you look like that is because you aren't *controlling* yourself. I totally understand. I mean, look at me." She poked one boney thigh. "I'm a total gross pig, but this is nothing compared to what I looked like six months ago. You've just got to assert some control."

The girl in the pink jumper nodded her head vigorously. "You know, support really helps. I mean, the world is full of people who just want you to be as fat and disgusting as they are. You have to try to find other people to help you. To inspire you."

"Like you guys found each other?" I said.

They nodded.

"Where did you all meet?"

They glanced at one another, an unspoken debate going on. I smiled encouragingly, and finally the girl with the braces said, "We met online. In a Pro-Ana chat room."

Twenty-nine

THE story the girls told me sounded like some kind of sick joke, an urban legend passed along in whispers from one hysterical parent to another. They were, however, in dead earnest. These girls were, the five of them, Anas. Actually, the girl in pink was an Ana and a Mia, but the others seemed to look down on her indecisiveness. She would occasionally allow food to pass her lips, so long as she promptly forced herself to purge. Theirs was a purer devotion; like the girl they had gathered to mourn, they preferred never to eat at all.

Anas, they told me, viewed their anorexia not as a disease that must be cured, but rather as something to nurture and celebrate.

"Look," the girl with the braces told me. "We're not stupid. I mean, I think every single one of us is on the honor roll." They others all nodded. "We know anorexia is a mental illness," she said. "It's just that we prefer to suffer from it than to look . . ." Here she paused, and it was quite clear what she meant. Than to look like me.

One of the girls, a tall, stoop-shouldered creature with a sharp nose and a small mouth crowded with teeth, piped up, "We don't try to, what's the word? Make other people join us, or anything."

"Proselytize," I said.

She nodded. "Right. We don't do that. In fact, there isn't a single Ana website that doesn't say right off that it's not a place to come to try to learn how to be anorexic, it's just there to help and support people who already are."

"But not support like 'help cure,'" the pretty blond with the bad skin interjected. "There's always some idiot coming on the sites to flame us and tell us we're crazy and we need therapy and all that. We shut them down pretty quick."

The girl with the braces nodded. "I mean, *hello.* We're *all* in therapy. We're in like more therapy than anyone in the free world!"

The girls giggled.

"Why are you in therapy?" I asked. "Why bother, if you don't want to stop being anorexic?"

The girl in pink waved one tiny hand at the door behind us. "Why do you think?" she said. "Our parents. They make us go."

I nodded. "Halley was in the hospital, wasn't she? When she died?"

At the mention of what was clearly a dreaded place, a palpable shudder ran through the group. I turned to the last girl, the only one who hadn't spoken yet. She looked like a slightly mousier version of her blond friend. Her hair was dirty blond, and she wasn't as pretty, although her skin was clearer. It was brilliantly clear, in fact. So pale and white that I could see the blue of her veins pulsing in the hollows of her forehead. "Have you ever been the hospital?"

"Yes," she said in a small voice. "I was there with Halley. That's why I look like this." She wrapped her arms around herself, trying to shrink her already miniscule body into something even smaller and more invisible.

"Like what?" I asked gently.

"You know. Fat."

The girl with the braces leaned across and hugged her friend. "It's okay Tawna. It's not your fault."

I did, I thought, a good job of wiping the astonishment from my face. Was this child serious? She looked like she weighed no more than Ruby, even though she was a few inches taller than I. Did she really think she was *fat?* And did the others *agree* with her?

"They don't let you out until you reach a certain weight," the girl in pink explained to me. "It's awful. They watch you at every meal; they even force-feed you. You get weighed every day, and they won't discharge you until you reach whatever weight they decide is enough."

"What was their goal weight for you, Tawna?" I asked.

She shook her head silently, as if the number were too depressing even to express aloud.

I let the question hang in the air for a moment, and then I asked the others, "So what happened to Halley, do you know? How did she die?"

Tawna shook her head, a queer glow lighting her luminous skin. "She was amazing," she whispered.

"What do you mean?"

The other girls all leaned in to hear. I wasn't sure if this story was being told for the first time, or if it was simply one so compelling that they were eager to hear it again and again.

"Halley was regal. Like a queen. No, better than a queen. Like a goddess. The doctors would come with their weight charts, and she would stare them down. She'd sit at meals and not even touch her food. Not even move it around on her plate. She just sat there with her hands in her lap, staring at the nurses, daring them to try to force-feed her."

"Wow," breathed the girl with the braces.

"The night she died, it was like a presence went through the ward. I could feel her passing through us, saying goodbye. You know, giving us some of her power. I know it sounds crazy, but I think she just willed her own heart to stop, I really do."

"If anybody could do that, it was Halley," the blond said.

They all nodded, sighing in appreciation of their friend's supreme control.

"Halley always said that was how Dina died. That she killed herself without killing herself, you know? She just willed herself dead," Tawna said.

"Dina?" I asked.

"Dina Kromm. She's another girl from the website," Tawna said. "She died a few months ago."

No wonder Susan Kromm had been so distraught. Halley's funeral must have reminded her of her own daughter's.

"Dina was a Mia *and* an Ana, like me," the girl in pink said, with pride.

"Not really," the girl with braces scowled. "She was a Mia like a hundred years ago. In junior high. By the time she died she was pure Ana." She said this with pride.

"Do you know lots of girls who end up killing themselves?" I asked.

"Not really," Tawna said. "I mean, you meet them in the hospital; it's kind of unavoidable because that's where they end up. And sometimes people from the websites just kind of disappear, and you aren't sure why. But we knew Dina and Halley, because we're all from LA."

"Do you get together often, in person?"

"No, not really," Tawna said. "We talk every day, but online. We instant message, or post to the boards. It's too hard to get to each other's houses. I mean, Rachel lives in the valley, in like Calabasas, right?"

The girl in pink, Rachel, nodded. "I think Dina and Halley used to see more of each other, because they were both from Brentwood. But they didn't go to school together or anything. They met on the websites, just like we all did."

Our conversation was interrupted by the tinkling of a cell phone. "That's my ring," the girl with the braces said. She pulled out her phone and glanced at the caller ID screen. She answered the phone, saying, "What?" in a long-suffering tone. She looked at the blond girl. "It's my mom. Twyla, you ready to go?"

Twyla nodded. As if on cue, the other girls pulled out their phones and dialed their parents to come pick them up. I was dismissed. As I watched them drive away, I wondered if Alicia had introduced Halley to her Pro-Ana life. What had the supposedly recovered anorexic said to her boyfriend's daughter about this terrifying cyber-world? Had Halley spoken to Dakota about it, perhaps? Their relationship had been terrible, by all accounts, but Dakota had admitted giving Halley diet pills. Maybe they had shared the online world, as well.

Thirty

"GODDAMN it, Ruby!" I shouted. "Finish your food!"

She clamped her lips together and pushed the plate of noodles away.

"Ruby!"

"I hate it," she said through gritted teeth. "I hate it."

"You do *not!* It's beef and macaroni, just like Grandma Wyeth makes. Eat it!"

"I hate it when the noodles and the meat are touching! It's gross!"

"They have to touch; that's the whole point. It is not gross. You like this. You're the reason Daddy made it, because you like it so much at Grandma's house. Now eat it!"

"No!" she bellowed, throwing herself to her feet.

I grabbed her as she was running out the kitchen door and dragged her kicking and screaming back to the table.

"Juliet!" Peter said loudly.

I looked up at him.

"Honey," he said gently. "It's okay. She doesn't have to eat it. Leave her alone."

Suddenly, I saw myself through his eyes, my hair hanging in my eyes, my forehead sweaty, my face red with the effort of holding my squirming daughter.

"Oh God," I whispered, dropping Ruby. She collapsed into her chair, crying. "I'm sorry, Ruby," I said, and then I burst into tears myself. I ran out of the room and threw myself onto my bed.

I buried my face in my pillow and cradled my belly in my hands. Here was another girl, another chance for me to screw up, to create a person who so loathed herself and her body that she would rather die than look like a normal woman. Than look like me.

The bed shifted and I felt a warm hand stroking my hair. I leaned into Peter's leg, pressing my face against the slick softness of his ancient jeans. I squeezed my eyes shut. He kissed me on the back of the neck.

"Shades of Margie Applebaum, huh?" he said.

I opened my eyes. "My mother used to make me sit at the table all night until I cleaned my plate."

"Did that work?"

I nodded. "Usually. By the time the TV went on I'd gag whatever it was down. I didn't want to miss *Three's Company*."

He laughed.

I sat up and leaned against his chest. "Once, I remember she made this disgusting carrot thing. Like some kind of vegetable stew. Tsimmes, I guess. I must have sat in front of it for hours. I tried to eat it, I really did, but every time it got close to my lips, I would feel like I had to throw up. I couldn't do it."

"So what happened?" He pulled me close to him and kissed my neck again.

"My dad tiptoed into the kitchen and gobbled it up for me. He didn't say anything; he just stood over my plate and ate it as fast as he could. I don't think my mom ever knew what happened."

"Why didn't he just throw it out?"

"Because she would have found it in the trash and killed us both."

Peter laughed. I began to, as well, but then my eyes filled with tears.

"It's okay, sweetie. It really is. Ruby will get over it. And you apologized."

I nodded, wiping the tears from my eyes. I reached over him and, taking a tissue, blew my nose loudly. "What's she doing?"

"Eating a peanut butter sandwich in front of the TV."

"And Isaac?"

"Him, too."

"But he doesn't even like peanut butter!"

Peter smiled. "You know how it is; if Ruby's allowed to have a peanut butter sandwich in front of the television, then Isaac's going to want one, too, even if he has to choke it down."

I sighed. "Food. I just can't bear it. Why is it so *fraught?* Why don't we just eat what we want, until we're full, and that's it? Why is it such a *thing?*"

He squeezed me tighter. "I don't know, baby. But it's not as bad as you think it is. You're just freaking out because you spent too much time talking to those crazy girls today. Most people aren't like them. They're not normal."

"I know," I said.

He gave me a last kiss on the cheek and said, "I'm going to go clean up the kitchen. Why don't you relax. Read a book. Do your email. I'll put the kids to bed tonight."

I nodded and rolled over on to my side. I was debating a hot bath when the phone rang. It was Al.

"So, did you find out anything at the funeral?" he asked.

I groaned. The last thing I felt like doing was describing my conversation with the skeletal girls. "His ex-wife hated Alicia, that's for sure. I mean, not just her, specifically. She blamed her daughter's death on her husband's obsession with skinny women."

"Hmm. She's a pretty obvious suspect. I imagine Good-enough has questioned her already."

"I suppose so," I said. I told him about Dakota. "Maybe Alicia found out about the pills, and Dakota killed her to keep her from talking about it."

"But don't you think that would have been a pretty drastic reaction? I mean, maybe now it's a motive for murder, what with Halley dead. But Halley was still alive when Alicia was killed."

"You're right." I sighed.

"What's wrong with you?"

"What do you mean?"

"You sound strange. Is it the baby?"

"No, no. I'm fine. Just tired."

"Tell you what," he said. "I've got nothing going on tomorrow. You take the day off and relax, and I'll spend the day checking on all the possibles. Not the grieving parents, but the others. That friend of Alicia's. The waitress? Dakota the pill pusher. The Board of Realtors folks. I'll feel around one last time, and if I don't find anything, we'll call it a day on this case, okay?"

"You think we should give up?"

His voice softened. "I think this is one of those crimes better left to the professionals, kiddo. It was probably a B&E gone wrong. We're not going to find anything out, and

I'm betting Detective Goodenough won't, either. Someday the creep will do it again, and maybe he'll get cocky and leave more of a trail."

I knew he was right. I had allowed myself to get distracted with the Hollywood types, the anorexic girls. But I knew as well as he did that this was just one of those random, horrible crimes that never get solved. Didn't I? Then I remembered Brodsky.

"But if we don't solve this crime, we're not going to get hired by Brodsky, and our entire business is going to go under!" I groaned.

"There's nothing we can do about that."

I felt the prick of tears in my eyes, and swallowed, hard. Damn those pregnancy hormones. "I won't get my house, either. No house, and no business. Great."

"Look, Juliet. That's what this business is like. Sometimes we catch the guy, sometimes we don't."

I sighed. "I know."

"There's just nothing we can do about it."

"I know that, too."

"Get some rest," he said, and then he hung up.

I lay in bed for a while, listening to Peter do the dishes, and then the sounds of the children splashing in the bathtub. Ruby was instructing Isaac on what his role would be in the mermaid game they were about to play. That's always the way it is with them. They spend hours planning their games, deciding who will do what, who will say what, but they rarely get around to the actual game. It's the set up, the preparation, that's the fun, apparently.

After a little while, Peter called to me.

"Marcel wants his mother!" he said.

Like a modern-day, Batman-loving version of Proust, Isaac couldn't go to sleep without a kiss and what he called a "lie with me." As I lay cuddling my boy, who never seemed as small and baby-like as when dressed in his footy-pajamas, lying in his too-large expanse of bed, his face flushed from the bath and his fine hair still wet, I wondered what adult experience would trigger memories of these times with me. What would be his *madeleine?* The scent of Mr. Bubble? The taste of chocolate chip Teddy Bear grahams? The sensation of nestling his face against a woman's breast?

Lying next to Isaac made me feel infinitely calmer and less hopeless. When his breathing had grown deep and soft, I carefully heaved myself out of his bed and wandered down the hall to kiss his sister good night. She was in her own bed, surrounded by stuffed animals. I kissed her lightly on the forehead, turned off her light, and went to find her father.

Peter was stretched out on the sofa, a comic book catalogue in his hand.

"Feeling better?" he asked.

I nodded and sat down next to him. "Nothing like a few Isaac and Ruby hugs to improve my mood. Especially when someone else has gotten them cleaned up and into bed." I took his laptop off the coffee table. "Mind if I use this?"

I hadn't really meant to do it. Truthfully, I was feeling done with the case, sick of Alicia, sick of her problems, sick of the skinny girls. Yet, for some reason I found myself launching a search engine and inputting the words "Pro-Ana." The sites were every bit as horrifying as I had imagined they would be. They were all maintained by the girls themselves. Some were pretty basic, weblogs with a diary entries about progress losing weight, poems about their alienation from the world, complaints about their parents.

Others were remarkably sophisticated. These often had entire archives of "trigger" photographs—pictures of particularly skinny Hollywood actresses and models, and occasionally pictures of the girls themselves.

At one point Peter looked over my shoulder. "Oh, *gross,*" he groaned. Peter, a man whose imagination includes cannibals with strips of flesh hanging from their teeth, couldn't bear to look at the photographs.

I followed a link to a message board. In page after page, girls wrote each other begging for advice on how to lose weight, asking for support in dealing with their parents, complaining about how awful they looked and felt—not because they were so thin, but because at eighty or ninety pounds, they were 'pigs.' I found a series of postings of girls joining forces to support each other through fasts. Every once in a while there would be a desperate message from a girl who felt herself succumbing to the urge to break the fast. The others would email frantically, encouraging her to be strong, sending her trigger photographs, sometimes even giving her their home phone numbers to call for more immediate support. These group fasts lasted a week, or ten days.

Most girls had a signature line that it took me a few minutes to figure out. Finally, I got it. They would sign their names, or their online nicknames, and then the initials "CW," "HWE," "LWE," "GW," followed by numbers. Each girl was letting the others know the most salient facts about her—her current weight, her highest weight ever, her lowest weight ever, and her goal weight. It was the last number that I found most disturbing. Not a single girl quoted a number over 100, and many listed seventy or eighty pounds as their goal. Some even hoped one day to break sixty-five. A few of the girls had the most chilling notation of all. At the

end of their lists of weights they wrote the initials "UG,"
ultimate goal. And then the single word 'death.'

Finally, sickened and ultimately bored with the sameness
of the pathology on exhibit, I clicked back over to the search
engine and input Halley Hoynes's name. She didn't have a
site of her own, but she had been a very active poster on a
number of the bigger Pro-Ana sites. The last message I
found from her was a desperate rant about how she was being forced to go into the hospital. She begged the girls to
think of her and send her strength. There was a flurry of
supportive postings, including a promise to pray for God to
help her "keep the sick fat away."

I clicked to a page maintained by a girl who called herself
Thin-Lizzie. On her links page, I scrolled through page after
page of weblogs and chatroom sites. More of the same. At the
bottom of the last page was a link marked "pics." I clicked on
it and found the image that would lead me, finally, to Alicia
Felix's murderer.

In the middle of the page of photographs was one of a
woman with long blond hair, facing away from the camera.
Her emaciated torso glowed white against the black background. I had seen that photograph before, in the album Dr.
Calma's nurse had shown me. It was Alicia.

I clicked on the photograph and was led to Alicia Felix's
Pro-Ana website. Her name was not, of course, anywhere on
the site. Her photographs, however, were everywhere. In addition to the one from Dr. Calma's album, there were dozens
of others, each showing off her gaunt body from a different
perspective, and carefully hiding her face. The website was
not merely a photo essay, however. Alicia provided more of
the same kind of information and sick support that the
other girls did on their pages, but there was something special about hers. The banner across the top of the page read

"Successfully and Beautifully Ana for Twenty Years!" Her message was quite simple. She had done it, and they could, too.

Alicia called herself Ana-Belle, and described herself as a television and film actress "whom you all would recognize immediately." One long essay called "The Perils of Plump," detailed her difficulties finding roles when her body size exceeded her goal weight. She did not list her credits, but she did make repeated references to actors, directors, and producers who had cast her because of her "perfect Ana body." One of the names she mentioned was Charlie Hoynes.

Alicia's, like the other sites, had links pages, inspirational photographs, diet tips, and 100 calorie a day foodplans. She also provided information for Mias, whom she described as "our bingeing sisters." She encouraged them to end a binge with milk or ice cream, because those dairy products came up easily. She cautioned them to brush their teeth frequently, lest they lose the enamel on their teeth and their teeth themselves begin to loosen in the bone. She also warned against "busy-body dentists" who might recognize the warning signs of bulimia. She suggested that Mias try to find older dentists because they wouldn't be as clued into the contemporary issues like eating disorders.

The most chilling section was a stark white page with a quotation at the top—"Scorn the Flesh and Love the Bone." It was a step-by-step instruction manual for surviving a hospital stay without gaining weight. Alicia told the girls what to say to make the physicians believe they were making progress in therapy. She told them to resist at first, but slowly to pretend to be coming around. Alicia told the girls to thank the therapists and nurses, to cry frequently in group therapy sessions, to warn other girls against the dangers of starvation. "The idea," Alicia wrote, "is to snow them with your words and your tears, so they don't even notice that you haven't eaten anything."

Alicia also gave specific information on how to plump up for weigh-ins. She suggested the girls drink large amounts of water, not so much as to make the nurses suspect they were bingeing on water, but enough to add pounds for the scale. She told the girls that in some cases their water consumption would be strictly monitored, and that some hospitals even turned off the sinks in bathrooms to prevent the girls from drinking to hide their weight loss. She suggested the toilet tanks. "That water is clean—it's not from the toilet itself—and there's enough water in your average tank to get you up to weight. Remember, even a few ounces will put the doctors on your side."

Alicia provided specific fat-burning exercises the girls could do in their beds in the middle of the night. Finally, she exhorted them to help one another. "Send a hospitalized friend some laxatives," she wrote. Unfortunately, she said, doctors had grown wise to the trick of sewing pills into the bodies of stuffed animals, but stick deodorant containers were a good place to smuggle pills.

There was more, much more, but by now I was too appalled to read on.

Alicia Felix was, quite clearly, the doyenne of the Pro-Ana universe. She was a role-model—a source of information and inspiration to these pathetic girls. She was, I could not help but feel, a monster, preying on their worst insecurities. Why had she done it? I wondered. What had it given her? Power? A sense of control? Or was she some kind of twisted altruist, wanting to share the skills she had acquired over a lifetime of anorexia?

I thought of Barbara Hoynes's rage earlier in the day, at

her daughter's funeral. How much angrier would she have been had she known exactly what Alicia was up to? Or perhaps she *had* known. Perhaps that was why she screamed at her ex-husband, blaming him and his girlfriends for their daughter's death. Perhaps that's what she had meant when she told me of Alicia's pernicious influence on her daughter.

Thirty-one

THE next morning, when I opened the door to pick up the newspaper, I found a terrifying man on our front stoop. He was huge, well over six feet tall, with a shaved head, a smashed, prize-fighter's nose, and a tattoo of a death's head climbing up from his neck over his left cheek. I gasped, as did he. He looked as scared to see me as I was to see him. He was clutching a letter in his hand, and had obviously been about to drop it in the mail-slot in the door when I opened the door.

"Who are you?" I said.

He pushed the letter toward me, but I backed away from his hand.

"Take it," he said, seeming to regain his composure. "Take it!"

"No," I said, grabbing the door behind me. I tried to slam it, but he wrenched the door out of my hands. That's when I screamed. Within seconds, Peter was tearing down the steps behind me.

"Take the letter!" the man said, just as Peter skidded to a stop next to me.

"Larry?" Peter said.

"Oh my God!" the scary guy said, staring at my husband. "Mr. Wyeth?"

"Call me Peter, please. What's up Larry? What are you doing here?"

"You know this guy?" I said.

"Sure I do," Peter said. "Larry played a corpse on the last Cannibal movie. Didn't you, Larry?"

The man was smiling now. "I sure did. A one-legged corpse. I'm hoping to get a shot at a speaking part in the sequel."

I raised my hands. "What's going on here?"

"Oh man," Larry groaned. "Look, I had no idea who you were. I mean, that you were Mr. Wyeth's wife and all. I was just doing a favor for a friend. I wasn't going to hurt you or anything. I was just supposed to drop this off." He turned to Peter. "Swear to God, man. I wasn't going to hurt your wife."

I snatched the letter out of his hand and tore open the envelope. In magic marker, on a sheet of plain white paper, it said, "Keep quiet about Dakota Swain, or else." I raised my eyes to those of the massive man standing in front of my door. "You have got to be kidding," I said.

He blushed. "I'm sorry, man. Dakota just asked me to deliver it. I don't even know what it said."

"Okay, well. Consider it delivered."

"You're not mad?" he said to Peter.

My husband looked at me, and I shook my head.

"Don't worry about it," Peter replied.

"Cool," Larry said. "Well, bye."

"Bye."

He took off down the steps and jumped into the cab of a pick-up truck that had been pulled up onto our front lawn, crushing the grass. He leaned his head out the window. "Dakota's cool!" he called. "She's just all freaked out because that kid died and all."

I slammed the door shut and leaned against it.

"What the hell?" Peter asked.

I shook my head.

"Are you going to call the cops?"

"I don't know."

"Because Larry's a real sweetheart."

"Right."

"He just looks scary." Peter took my hand and began leading me up the steps. "Do you think it's a real threat?"

"I doubt it," I said. "She's just terrified I'll tell Hoynes about the pills, and then he won't give her the part."

"Maybe you should call the cops. I mean, you can't be sure she's not dangerous," Peter said. Once burned, twice shy, but that's another story.

"I'll figure it out later. There's something I need to do first, this morning."

When Jews are mourning, we sit *shiva*. We sit in our homes, welcome guests, share food, and simply experience our grief for a period of seven days. I knew that Episcopalians had no similar formal ritual, but I was hoping that Barbara Hoynes would be home—I couldn't imagine that a mother would go anywhere on the day after burying her daughter. Still, I didn't expect to find Barbara Hoynes as I did, alone in her lavish home, wearing a bathrobe over her pajamas, rubbing sleep from her eyes.

"I'm so sorry." I said when she answered the door. "I woke you."

She leaned against the doorjamb. "Can I help you?" she mumbled in a voice thickened by sleep, or grief, or a combination of both.

I reminded her who I was.

She stared at me, wordlessly. Her hair was matted down on one side, caught in a single barrette that swung free as she shook her head.

"I'm so sorry to bother you, Ms. Hoynes, especially so soon after your daughter's death. I know how you felt about Alicia. I know it's asking a lot, but I hope you might consider talking to me, just for a few minutes."

"What time is it?" the woman asked.

I looked at my watch. "11:15," I said.

She shook her head. "I've been asleep for thirteen hours."

My eyes widened, but I merely said, "Well, that's to be expected, given everything."

She sighed. "It's to be expected given the three *Ambien* I took last night."

I nodded sympathetically. "I would have done the same. The nights must be unbearable."

She nodded. "They never end." She leaned back in the doorway. "Come in," she said, to my surprise.

She led me through the darkened rooms to the kitchen. She motioned to a chair, and then stood in the middle of the room, looking vaguely around her.

"Here," I said. "You sit down. Can I make you a cup of coffee, or tea?"

She collapsed into the chair and nodded. "Coffee. Over there." She pointed at a complicated piece of equipment that looked more like a flight simulator than an espresso machine. I did my best, trying to imitate the baristas from whom I bought coffee every day. I didn't do too badly, until it came time to steam the milk.

"Don't bother," Barbara said, holding out her hand for the cup. I splashed some cold milk in mine and sat down next to her.

"When we spoke last time, you told me that Alicia was a bad influence on your daughter. Did Alicia Felix actively encourage Halley to become anorexic? Was that how she got the disease?"

Barbara took a careful sip of her coffee and then set the cup down on the table with a trembling hand. "I wish I could blame that on Alicia, but Halley has had an eating disorder for years. Since she was a little girl. Alicia didn't make Halley anorexic. I did that all by myself."

"No," I murmured. "You can't blame yourself."

"Can't I?" Barbara said, staring at her hands. "Halley was always a chubby little girl. The first time I had her on a diet was when she was two. I sent her to summer camps for over-weight children from the time she was seven until she was twelve. Suddenly, she didn't need them any more. She was thin. It took a couple of years before I realized that she wasn't just healthy and slim; she was actually too thin. It took even longer for me to figure out that she was sick. So you see, as much as I wish I could, I can't blame Alicia. I can only blame myself."

I didn't know what to say. Instead, I just patted her hand.

Finally, I said, "Halley spent a lot of time on those Pro-Ana websites, didn't she?"

Barbara nodded, and then suddenly sobbed. She rubbed roughly at her eyes. "They all do. All those girls. *That* I blame on Alicia Felix. That I can lay squarely at her feet. She's the one who got Halley started on those." She beat her hands against the tabletop, and I jumped. "I was so stupid and naïve. At first I believed Halley when she told me that her father's girlfriend was helping her, that she'd got her involved in an online support group. I even got a DSL line so Halley could get online more quickly. I actually thought it was like some kind of group therapy. I was such an idiot."

"How did you find out what the sites really were? Did you track Halley's Internet usage?"

She shook her head. "I wish I had. But I was too trusting. It never occurred to me that anything like that whole Pro-Ana thing could even exist. I didn't find out about it until it was too late, until Halley was so far into it that I couldn't save her." She was crying freely now, wiping at her nose and mouth with the back of her fist. I looked around the room and, not finding any tissues, reached for a dishtowel that was hanging from the handle of the oven I gave it to her, and she wiped away the mucus that was dripping from her nose.

"How did you find out what was really going on?" I asked.

"Alicia's best friend, Dina Kromm. Her mother told me."

"Dina? The girl who died?"

Barbara nodded. "After her death, Susan and Duane went through Dina's computer. She'd bookmarked the Pro-Ana sites. They came to me and told me about them. They even showed them to me. That's how we found out about Alicia."

"They showed you her website?"

She blew her nose again. "They wanted me to join them on a campaign to get the sites shut down, or at least barred from the larger search engines. We were going through the sites, reading them. Alicia's is anonymous, but there were the pictures. She hid her face, but I could tell from her body that she was one of Charlie's girls. They all look the same. Massive breasts, blond hair. Skinny. And Alicia mentions Charlie's noxious TV show on the site. I knew right away it had to be Alicia. Halley said that Alicia had led her to the online support groups, and here was a site mentioning Charlie. It was too much of a coincidence. It had to be her."

"Did you confront your husband with what you'd found out?"

"I tried to, but he refused to take my calls. He never would, that despicable creep. He always made me go through his lawyer when I wanted to talk to him."

"Did you confront Halley about it?"

She nodded. "Right then, in front of Duane and Susan. I thought that given what happened to Dina, Halley would tell us the truth. And she did, in a way."

"In a way?"

"I called her downstairs and showed her the site. I remember I was screaming. I asked her if *this* was what she meant by support groups. I asked her if this was her father's girlfriend."

"What did she say?"

Barbara knotted her hands together, her knuckles white against her chapped, red fingers. "She screamed right back at me. She gave me this ridiculous nonsense about anorexia being a life-choice not a disease. She said Alicia was her idol, that she was beautiful. That all the girls worshipped her. That . . . that . . ." her voice broke. She continued in a whisper. "She said she wished Alicia was her mother."

I leaned across the table and put my arm around her. Her body shook with sobs.

We sat like that for a moment, and then she said, "I told Halley she couldn't see Alicia anymore. I called Charlie's lawyer; I called his office. But he wouldn't speak to me. I was going to take him to court. I was going to get a restraining order against Alicia, and maybe even try to stop Halley's un-supervised visitation with him. At least get rid of those overnights. Then Alicia was killed. And you know what? I was happy. I really was. Because she could never hurt Halley again. It never occurred to me that it was already too late."

Barbara sat up in her chair, shaking away my arm. I leaned back and looked at her. She took a shaky breath. "You probably want to know if I killed her, don't you?"

I did, but I doubted she'd tell me if she had.

"The day she died was Halley's first day in the hospital. I spent the whole day there with her. They let me sleep with her for the first night until they moved her to the ward. I almost wish it had been me who killed Alicia Felix, but it wasn't."

Thirty-two

I got the address of the Kromms and then left Barbara alone in her house. I didn't want to. The idea of a mother grieving in a place empty but for memories of her child was nearly more than I could bear. Barbara was there, forced to stare at the beautifully framed photographs of her child, compelled to walk by the room with its pastel sheets and poster of Buffy The Vampire Slayer, the stacks of CDs by Fiona Apple and Alanis Morissette, the outgrown stuffed animals and American Girl dolls gathering dust on the shelves, the iMac covered in stickers with its Grrl Power mouse pad. Halley's room might have looked nothing like I imagined. The silence in the house, however, I knew would be exactly like that of my worst fears. The silence of a disappeared child is like no other.

I picked Ruby up from school, leaving Isaac for his father. I needed some time with my girl, and I figured Peter and Isaac could amuse themselves with Legos and superheroes for a little while. Ruby and I had tea in her favorite café in Santa Monica, then we went on a drive through the Canyon. It was while we were winding through the narrow streets, counting Jacaranda trees, that I realized we were only a few blocks from where Halley's friend Dina had lived. I rechecked the address and telephone number that Barbara Hoynes had given me, and then turned to Ruby.

"Hey, chickadee. Do you mind if we make a stop?"

She was chewing on the neck of her T-shirt. She spat out the fabric. "A work stop?"

"Don't chew your clothes. Yes, a work stop. But a short one."

She flicked out her tongue, catching the stretched out, damp bit of shirt in her mouth. "Okay," she said.

"Don't chew your clothes."

"It's all chewed up, already."

The blue cotton was crumpled and wadded, full of tiny holes made by her teeth. There was no point in trying to save it.

Dina's parents, Duane and Susan Kromm, lived in a stucco house set back from the road and nestled in a flower garden. It didn't look any larger than my apartment, but given the neighborhood, probably cost well over two million dollars.

Susan Kromm answered the door. "Can I help you?" she said in a soft, sweet voice.

She glanced down at Ruby. "Hello," she said.

"Hi," Ruby said.

"I'm Juliet Applebaum," I said. "We met at Halley's funeral?"

She smiled uncertainly.

"I hope you don't mind us dropping by like this. I know this is a painful time for you. But Barbara Hoynes gave me your name and address. I'm investigating what happened to Alicia Felix."

Susan Kromm's face paled, and she bit her lip. "Why are you here? I mean, we didn't know the woman. We never met her."

"I understand. I was hoping to talk to you a bit about the Pro-Ana websites. Barbara told me that you and your husband were involved in a campaign to have them shut down."

Susan nodded.

"Do you mind if we come in?" I asked.

She looked at Ruby.

"Ruby will amuse herself," I reassured the woman. "I have some paper and a pen in my purse."

Still looking unwilling, and suspicious, Susan motioned us inside. "Does she watch television?" she asked.

"Yes, I do!" Ruby replied.

Ruby and I followed Susan into her kitchen. There was a small sitting area on one end of the room. She snapped on the TV, changed the channel, and handed Ruby the remote. "It's on Cartoon Disney, honey. Don't change it without asking your mom, okay?"

"Okay," Ruby said.

"Would you like a cookie? I have Girl Scout cookies." She turned to me. "They got delivered a few days ago. Dina must have ordered them from one of the neighbor girls." The older woman's cheeks twitched as she tried to hold back tears. "She ordered my favorite, Thin Mints, and her dad's, Tagalongs. She never would have eaten them herself, but she liked to see us eat. I used to think she just liked to see us enjoying our food. Now I think it had more to do with feeling better than us, because she could resist a cookie, and neither Duane nor I could."

I laid a comforting hang on her arm. "I'm fine," she said, swallowing hard. She bustled around her kitchen, laying a small pile of cookies on a plate for Ruby, and pouring a glass of milk to go with them.

"What do you say?" I said, when Ruby had accepted the proffered plate and glass.

"Thank you," my daughter mumbled, her face already smeared with chocolate. "Is this nonfat milk?"

"Ruby!"

"What?"

"Yes, honey. It's nonfat. Is that okay?" Susan said.

Ruby nodded. "Good. Nonfat is the best."

I resisted the urge to spank her. It wouldn't have done any good. I satisfied myself with watching her gobble the cookies. Milk or no, she was getting plenty of good old fashioned fat into her body.

"I'm so sorry about that," I said, as Susan and I sat down at the kitchen table on the far side of the room.

"Oh, no. Please don't apologize. It's fine," Susan said. She put another plate of cookies in front of me, and I popped a Thin Mint into my mouth before considering how I was going to question the woman with my mouth full of food.

"She was a terrible person, that Alicia," Susan said.

I nodded.

"Those hospital 'tips?' Did you see those?"

"Yes," I said.

"That's what killed Dina. And Halley, too."

Tears had begun to spill down her cheeks.

"What happened to Dina?" I asked gently.

She wiped her eyes with a pale pink tissue she pulled from a box with a crocheted cover. "She drank the water in the toilet tank in her hospital room. Trying to fake weight gain. She was so weak from starvation that her kidneys couldn't handle the strain. They shut down, and then her heart just stopped." Susan's voice was so quiet it was almost inaudible.

"And you think she learned how to do that from Alicia's website?"

"I know she did. And it wasn't just the site. That woman would instant message her. Email her. Encourage her. She killed my little girl. Alicia Felix killed my daughter. You can't know what that feels like. You just can't."

At the same moment, we looked over at Ruby who was trying to see how many cookies she could cram, unchewed, into her mouth. Susan reached out a trembling hand and gripped mine, tightly. "Hold on to her. As tight as you can," she whispered.

"I will. I will."

We sat there for what felt like hours, but was probably not more than a moment or two. We were silent, until we heard the front door open, and a voice called out, "Susan? Sue?"

"In here, Duane," she called back.

Duane Kromm came back into the room, stopping when he saw Ruby. "Hello there," he said.

"Hi," she replied. Then, for no reason that I can think of, as my daughter is not known for her willingness to share anything, especially not cookies, Ruby held the plate out toward Dina's father. "Want one?"

"Don't mind if I do," he said, taking a Tagalong.

"They're best if you just pop them in," Ruby said. "Don't chew until it's all in your mouth."

Duane followed her instructions carefully. He swallowed, and then smiled at Ruby, his teeth covered in chocolate. "You're absolutely right. That's the way to eat them."

She nodded seriously, and then she turned her attention back to the television.

He crossed the room and extended his hand. "Duane Kromm," he said.

Susan said, "This is Juliet . . . er . . ."

"Applebaum," I said. "We met at Halley's funeral."

"She's investigating the murder of Alicia Felix," Susan said.

The smile faded from Duane's face, and he sat down heavily in the chair next to his wife.

"I was hoping you could tell me a little bit about your campaign to shut down the Pro-Ana sites," I said.

Duane and Susan looked at each other. Finally, she said, "We . . . we haven't really gotten very far."

"No?" I said, surprised.

"We've been busy, with work and all."

"Work?"

She nodded. Her face was flushed.

"What do you do?"

"We work in real estate. I mean, Duane's a realtor. I don't sell much anymore. I sit on the Board of Realtors."

I stared at her, comprehension hitting me suddenly. I opened my mouth, but no words came out. Finally, I said, "Why did you choose Marilyn Farley's programmer, Susan?"

Duane stared at me. His lips were bright pink, and a bead of saliva sat in the center of the lower one.

At that moment, Ruby giggled, and I realized what I had done. I had brought my little girl into the home of a murderer. I stood up slowly. "Ruby, come here," I said.

Her head snapped up. She could hear the fear in my voice.

Duane also stood.

"No!" Susan moaned.

I began to back up in Ruby's direction. I held my hand out to her.

Duane took a step toward me, and I flinched.

"Stop," Susan said. "Duane, stop."

He looked back at her, his entire face, even his head, flushed bright red. "She knows," he said.

"The little girl. Look at her little girl." Susan's voice was shrill, and tears had begun to course down her cheeks.

Her husband looked at Ruby who had stood up, her face smeared in chocolate, her lower lip trembling.

"Mommy," she whispered. I crossed the room and scooped her up into my arms.

"He won't hurt you," Susan said. "He won't."

I looked at her husband. He collapsed into a chair and put his head in his hands.

"It doesn't matter. It doesn't matter anymore," he said.

His wife rushed to his side and wrapped her arms around him. Suddenly, he looked up at me. "Susan wasn't involved. She only changed the programmer to protect me," he said. "I used her programmer to get in the door of the house. When I told her what I'd done, she took the programmer down to the Board office right away, in the middle of the night, and used the computer to reprogram it. She just picked the number randomly. We were lucky Alicia was alone in the house. We made it back in plenty of time to put the programmer back in and erase the other numbers."

"Hush, Duane. Hush," Susan whispered, reaching her hand to her husband's lips.

He shook free of her. "There's no point. She knows I killed that woman." He turned to me. "I stabbed her, and I'm not sorry. She killed our little girl."

Susan, her voice ragged with weeping, said, "What are you going to do? Call the police?"

My breath was caught in my chest, and I squeezed Ruby close to me. How was I going to get my little girl out of this house, safely away from him?

He shook his head, very slightly. "I'm not going to hurt you," he said. "Or your beautiful little girl."

"What are you going to do?" I asked, willing my voice not to tremble.

"It would be better for me if I turned myself in, wouldn't it?"

"Yes," I said.

He sighed. "Okay then."

Thirty-three

I called Felix and Farzad as soon as I knew for sure that Duane Kromm was under arrest. I had, in fact, watched from my car, Ruby strapped into the booster seat she was fast outgrowing, as Detective Goodenough pulled up to the Kromm's house, accompanied by a police cruiser with two uniformed officers. I had called the detective directly, not really expecting that he would carry out the arrest himself. He had, though. It had been his hand on Duane's shoulder, steering the older man out the door and into the back seat of the cruiser. The handcuffs had seemed unnecessary to me, although of course I knew that they were standard procedure.

My conversation with Farzad, who had answered the telephone, had been brief. I outlined quickly what had happened, and I promised to come by the next day to give him more details.

When I arrived the next morning at their house, I found

Detective Goodenough there before me. He was out of mufti, dressed in a pair of jeans and a thin silk T-shirt rather than his usual suit and tie. The maid led me into the living room, where the three men sat drinking small cups of Farzad's excellent coffee. I felt, for a moment, like I was interrupting something.

"Detective Goodenough was . . . uh . . . good enough to come by on his day off to tell us about the arrest," Felix said, smiling at his pun.

I waited to see what the detective would say. Would he acknowledge my role in the arrest, or would he assume credit himself?

The tall man raised a cinnamon-colored eyebrow at me and said, "I was just recounting the tale of your excellent detective work, Ms. Applebaum. You'll be a force to reckon with if you ever get yourself certified."

I lowered myself into the remaining empty armchair. "Thank you," I said.

"I still don't really understand it," Felix said, leaning forward in his chair. "I mean, I can't believe the man would blame poor Alicia for his daughter's death, just because of those websites. It seems so crazy."

I slid my eyes over to Farzad. He sipped delicately at his coffee. I got the feeling that he understood full well why Duane had felt a murderous rage toward Alicia Felix. I certainly did. Detective Goodenough didn't respond to Felix, and it seemed to me that he, too, comprehended the motive for the murder. Felix's inability to do so probably stemmed from the fact that he loved his sister too much to imagine her as a kind of Pied Piper of anorexia, playing the girls to their grim deaths.

"Will there be a trial, do you think?" Farzad asked.

I looked over at Goodenough, who seemed inclined to let

me answer for him. "I don't know," I said. "Probably not, given that he turned himself in. I think the prosecution will likely offer a deal to avoid a trial. A jury is likely to feel . . ." and here I paused.

We were all silent for a moment, and then Felix said, "Sympathy. That's what you were going to say, isn't it? The jury will have sympathy for that man."

I leaned forward and placed what I hoped was a comforting hand on his knee. "Perhaps. Not because of anything about Alicia, but rather because Duane was a grieving father." But of course it was because of the kind of woman Alicia was. Any defense lawyer worth his or her salt would make sure the jury knew exactly what she had done, the damage she had wrought.

Felix sighed heavily. "So if there's no trial, then what? How long will he go to jail?"

I let the detective handle that.

"We'll be pushing for murder 2," he said. "The defense will probably ask for voluntary manslaughter. We'll see how it pans out. I promise you, Felix, I'll be calling the DA, putting pressure on for the maximum."

Felix nodded at the other man. I glanced over at Farzad who was chewing on his lower lip. Perhaps he felt, as I did, that there was not much to be gained, in the larger scheme of things, by putting Duane Kromm in jail for decades. I knew, however, that neither of us would ever say as much to Felix.

"Do you think you'll be moving to Palm Springs, now?" I asked.

Farzad smiled and cast a sly eye in my direction. "Juliet wants to know if we'll keep up our side of the bargain."

"What bargain?" Felix asked.

I looked down at my hands resting on my belly. At that

moment, the baby kicked me, hard, right in the ribs, and I grunted. "Sorry," I said. "Baby's kicking."

"What bargain?" Felix asked again.

"You know Juliet wants to buy the house. That's why she was here in the first place. I told her that if she found out who killed Alicia, we'd give her first shot at making an offer."

"You did not!" Felix said.

"I did indeed," he said.

Felix glared at me. "And is that why you helped us?"

Shame kept me from looking into his eyes. "I helped you because I wanted to find out what happened to your sister. And because you hired me. And, well, yes it's true, because I wanted the house. But of course you're under no obligation. Obviously."

Goodenough interrupted us. "Without Ms. Applebaum's assistance, we may never have found the killer. It certainly would have taken us significantly longer. And who knows if we would have been able to obtain a full confession."

I looked at him, gratefully.

Felix jerked to his feet. "I'm sorry. I'm just . . . this is all so hard to deal with . . ." He stumbled out of the room. I leaned my head in my hands, embarrassed at the hash I'd made of the conversation.

"Juliet," Farzad said gently. I raised my eyes to his. "Give him time. He's angry now, but not at you."

"I know. I'm sorry," I said.

"I'll call Nahid."

"No, really. I mean, let's just leave that alone for now, okay?"

He nodded. "And your bill?"

I smiled thinly. "That I have," I said reaching into my bag.

Thirty-four

"You have got to get rid of this wallpaper," Stacy said, her head cocked to one side, and her hands on her hips.

It really was awful. Flocked gold roses on a background of red velvet. It wasn't however, as disturbing as the mirrored ceiling in the master bedroom. "We can't. It's original. Ramon Navarro apparently designed it himself. Or at least that's what Nahid said. Still, even with the wallpaper, it's a pretty great house, don't you think?"

At that moment, Kat walked through the French doors into the living room. "I don't know what that inspector was talking about. That's no fifty thousand dollars in dry rot damage."

"Thank God!" I exclaimed. What with covering over the fish pond in the kitchen and repairing the railings in all the various balconies overlooking the first floor from the second, there wasn't going to be much money left for structural repairs.

"That's going to cost you at least one hundred and fifty thousand dollars. Definitely. They've eaten through the foundation, for heaven's sake! I've never seen that before." Kat continued.

I groaned.

"Is Peter really going to use the dungeon as his office?" Stacy asked. "It's so gloomy and depressing down there."

"Uh, Stacy? Peter? Gloomy and depressing?"

"Right. Right. It's perfect for him. Is it true that it has iron handcuff holders pounded into the walls?"

"That's nothing," Kat said. "There's an old wooden saw-horse down there. I can't even imagine what Ramon was getting up to on that."

"If he really did own the house," I said.

"Oh, he owned it," Kat said. "Not even Nahid would lie about that. I'm just not sure he ever lived here. He might have rented it to some other weird silent movie star friend of his."

"Or else kept it for one of his mistresses," Stacy said.

I looked down to the crook of my arm where Sadie rested, quiet for once. Moving with a newborn is not something I recommend to anyone. Between nursing and napping, I wasn't spending much time unpacking. The bulk of the work was falling to Peter and the kids. That meant that we were still living out of boxes two weeks after moving in, and probably would be for the next couple of months. Every time one of the children needed a clean pair of jeans or wanted to locate a missing toy they would upend a box and leave the contents scattered on the floor. So far I still wasn't able to bend over and pick anything up, but I was hoping to feel better any day.

Felix hadn't, in the end, sold us his house. Nahid Lahidji had put it on the open market and had started a bidding war the likes of which the LA real estate market hadn't seen in months. Apparently, I wasn't the only person not put off by the home's grisly history. Truth be told, by the time Duane Kromm was arrested for Alicia Felix's murder, I wasn't entirely sure I wanted any more to do with that beautiful house. There were a few images I knew I'd never get out of my mind. One was Alicia in the bath tub, her skeletal body torn and stiff. The other was one I hadn't seen but only imagined—that same woman, hunched over a computer, weaving her malignant web to ensnare those wretched girls.

Felix had done me a more important favor, however. He had called Harvey Brodsky. I'm not sure what he told him, but it was enough to convince the man to offer us a contract. From now on, Al and I would be providing investigative services to Brodsky's high-profile clients. The man had advanced us enough money to hire an exterminator, put Julio on salary as a part-time receptionist (with strict instructions to stay away from the computers . . . at least until we could convince his probation officer otherwise), and even, wonder of wonders, pay ourselves a little.

Kat had also come through in the end. The house she found for us was nowhere near as impeccably done as Felix's house; in fact it was pretty much a crumbling pile, but it was certainly fabulous. It hadn't been touched since 1926, when Ramon Navarro had it built, which meant it had its original tile bathrooms, moldings and built-ins, and Maxwell Parish–style murals sprinkled throughout the house. It also had its original electricity, plumbing, and roof, but someday we'd have the money to fix all that. The fixtures were all a kind of Hollywood Gothic wrought iron and ornate, with the occasional ghoul's head popping out of nowhere on a chandelier or sconce.

Peter had fallen in love with the house at first sight. The

dungeon was definitely his favorite room, but the ballroom on the first floor was a close second. He was already full of plans to redo the cracked black and white parquet floor himself. I wasn't planning on holding my breath. The room was vast enough for the kids to ride their bikes in on rainy days. The whole house was huge, in fact. There were bedrooms galore, although many of them were oddly shaped and tucked under the eaves, or accessible only through a bathroom, or a closet. It was a strange house, which, as Ruby pointed out, was entirely appropriate, given that her family was pretty strange, as least when compared to those of the other kids in school. I took issue with that, vociferously. Peter's an odd bird, sure, but I consider myself absolutely and completely normal. More or less.

I could tell that the house was going to suck up every spare cent we ever earned, but somehow that didn't bother me much. Perhaps because I had no time to be worried. Miss Sadie had made her surprise appearance a good two weeks before my scheduled c-section date. We'd planned on being moved in in plenty of time to welcome her home. Instead, the movers had loaded dozens of newborn diapers into their boxes, and I'd limped my way up the jacaranda- and jasmine-flanked front path with the baby in my arms. It didn't really matter that I didn't have the nursery set up for her; Sadie refused to sleep in her brother's old crib. The only place she'd close her eyes was our bed. That wasn't that unusual; both the other kids had spent a few weeks sleeping with us. The problem was that Ruby and Isaac had decided that what was good enough for the baby was good enough for them, and we had yet to spend a night without three extra sets of toes digging into our sides, and pushing us to the far ends of the bed. I was grateful that Mr. Navarro's old bedstead was still in the master bedroom. I wasn't sure where I was going so find a new mattress to replace the musty, sagging one—they don't make them in that size anymore, if they ever did. He'd probably had to special order the king and a half we were currently inhabiting with varying levels of comfort from a special company that catered especially to silent movie Lotharios. I hoped they were still in business.

"How are you feeling?" Stacy asked Kat.

Kat smiled. "Okay. Ready to give birth."

"When are you due?"

"In a couple of weeks. Although I don't think I can last that long. It's going to be castor oil for me in a few days."

I smiled at Kat. For all her desperation to be done with the pregnancy, she looked better than she had in weeks. She had started seeing a new therapist, and was working on coming to peace with the various elements in her life that had conspired to reinvigorate her bulimia. She had decided not to go back to work for Nahid after her maternity leave, but to spend at least a few years home with her kids. Reza, to my surprise, had not only supported her decision, but had defended it to his mother. Kat had finally come clean with him about her problem, and they were working on it together. I wasn't naïve enough to think all was solved for Kat, and that now she would be fine forever. Alicia Felix's case had taught me just how tenacious and persistent a foe an eating disorder is. But Kat had a good chance of being all right, especially if we all made sure to be there for her. And I wasn't going anywhere.

The baby woke in my arms and began to cry. I sat down on a wooden crate that contained the pieces of the Appalachian rocking chair Lilly had sent to me as a baby present. Peter had sworn he would assemble the thing before the baby was weaned, but in the meantime the box made for an adequate nursing chair. I lifted my shirt, and Sadie flung herself at my breast, grunting and snuffling like a miniature water buffalo. I sighed as I felt the tingling of my milk letting down and stroked her velvet cheek with my finger. I knew that one day this little girl, like her sister, would start to think about how she looked and what she ate. Right now, though, I was filling up her body, plumping up her flesh, building her bones and brain. Life is a meager business, sometimes. There are lean times, shortages, tough winters, barren patches. It was my job, my duty and pleasure, to see that she started out suitably, and blessed to be, fat.